A collection of short stories and novellas tying up some...

KRISTEN ASHLEY

New York Times Bestselling Author

Loose Ends
Kristen Ashley
Published by Kristen Ashley

This book is a work of fiction. Names, characters, places, and incidents are the product of the author's imagination or are used fictitiously. Any resemblance to actual events, locales, or persons, living or dead, is coincidental.

Interior Design & Formatting by:
Christine Borgford, Type A Formatting
www.typeAformatting.com

Cover Art by:
PixelMischief Design

ISBN-13: 978-1726140256
ISBN-10: 1726140253

Introduction

I ALWAYS THOUGHT I COULDN'T do short.

That is, write short books. Never mind short stories.

Forget about it.

Then along came *1,001 Dark Nights*.

Liz Berry and MJ Rose asked me to be a part of their imprint and write a novella in one of my current series for their awesome project.

A writer needs challenges, so I took it (with, I will admit, some trepidation as I was diving into two characters who were beloved by me who I thought would *never* have their story told, Daisy and Marcus of the *Rock Chicks*—a story that would become *1,001 Dark Nights Rock Chick Reawakening*).

I not only fell in love with the process, an entire new avenue opened not only for me as a writer, but more importantly for my characters.

That's right.

I didn't have to say goodbye.

And that means my readers don't have to either.

I can go back to my babies, just for a spell, spend some time, see how they're doing, how they're raising their families, how their happily ever after stays happy.

But there was a big bonus for me.

Huge.

Colossal.

Most romance novels are anywhere in the range of 60,000 to 110,000 words.

Not mine.

My novels tend to be anywhere upwards of 160,000 words. In my books, I get into the meat of a variety of matters.

And I was struggling with some dangling characters from concluded books and series who *needed* their HEA. However, if I attempted to write a full-blown book, there would be a lot of filler, or forced conflict I wasn't getting from my characters.

I simply can't write like that.

So these beloved characters were left hanging.

My "loose ends."

Not anymore.

With this new concept of a personal anthology, I was able to go back to The 'Burg. I got to visit Glacier Lily Cottages.

And after the personal loss of my dear friend Rick Chew, who Tod of the *Rock Chick* series was based on, I had the bittersweet experience of spending some time with him again as my Tod with his Stevie.

But I also was able to tell Hap and Luci's story (from *Heaven and Hell*) as it was *meant* to be told.

Not to mention I could immediately deal with the demons plaguing Diesel from the ménage I introduced in *The Greatest Risk*, rather than leaving him stuck in an emotional pit of darkness. Which meant I got to give goodness not only to him, but to his Maddox and Molly.

Without delay.

If this concept works . . . that is, if you—my reader—enjoys it, I'll do these as often as I can because I *adored* being back with Joe, Vi, Deacon and his Cassidy, Tod and Stevie (and the crew), Kia and Sam, Sixx and Stellan, and of course Hap, Luci, Diesel, Maddox and Molly.

The possibilities are endless. The happy endings of my characters never really have to end, and my *Loose Ends* can get tied up all nice and tidy.

In other words, I hope you enjoy.

I really, *really* do.

Because these stories took me other places as well . . . and new ideas were born. And I want to unleash them (does anyone feel Henry from

The Will needs to find love? I do!).

So read on.

And as always . . .

Rock on!

One final note, if you haven't taken the dive into my series, *The Honey*, because erotica just isn't your gig, I'll caution you about reading *More Than Everything* in this anthology. It is a very erotic M/M/F ménage. I think it's beautiful and the message of love and acceptance is crucial.

But the last thing I wish to do is shock any of my readers. I hope you try it, but I understand everything is not for everybody.

And as Diesel, Maddox and Molly would all agree, you do *you*.

All my love,

~Kristen Ashley

No Clue

A short story from The 'Burg Series
featuring Joe and Vi of At Peace

JOE CALLAHAN WALKED THROUGH THE side door of the house, which brought him into his family's kitchen.

And total pandemonium.

He tossed his keys on the counter and moved from the kitchen to the living room where he saw, rolling around on the floor, a tangle of arms, legs, heads, hair and bodies.

There were grunts of effort.

There was also shouting.

"Mom's totally mad and says she washes her hands of the both of them."

These words came from Cal's left.

He turned that way and saw his girl, Angie, lounging on the couch in front of their TV, which had onscreen the show where women tried on wedding dresses.

No wonder his boys were fighting.

Better to do that than watch that fucking show.

She was his oldest blood child.

She was twirling her hair.

She was also the most beautiful thing he'd ever seen.

Outside her mother.

And her older sisters.

And her two brothers, who were right then wrestling on the floor.

He turned his attention to that.

"*Yo!*" he bellowed.

Instantly, the wrestling stopped, both his sons disconnected, scooted from each other and took their feet.

Sam, his oldest boy and the one who learned fast-talking somewhere along the line, and learned it well, opened his mouth to speak.

Cal got there before him.

"I don't care."

"But . . . *Dad!*" Ben yelled.

Cal turned his eyes to his youngest.

If it was up to him, they'd have had two, maybe three more.

Vi drew the line at Ben.

Well, not really. They got pregnant one more time, purely by accident since she'd drawn the line at Ben, they just fucked a lot (still, thankfully) and apparently, birth control pills really were not a hundred percent.

She'd lost it in month two.

She'd been devastated because she thought he would be devastated.

He took it as a sign from God to stop knocking up his wife and God knew what He was doing, so Cal was all good.

When she found out he was all good, Violet was all good (mostly).

"What'd I say about fighting?" Cal asked his boys.

"But he—" Sam began.

"No," Cal cut in. "What. Did. I. Say. About. Fighting?"

Sam glared at Ben. Ben looked to his feet.

"Sorry? Did I lose my hearing?" Cal prompted when neither said a word.

"Don't do it," they muttered in unison.

"And what did I come home to?" Cal pushed.

"Us fightin'," Ben mumbled.

"A fight," Sam bit out at the same time.

"How happy do you think I am right now?" Cal asked.

"Not very," Ben said.

"How happy is your mother right now?" Cal went on.

Both boys moved away from their father, Sam leaning back, Ben actually taking a step back.

They knew what this line of questioning bought them.

He didn't let up.

"You disrespect me by doing something I told you not to do, I can swallow that. Boys push shit. I was you once. I get that. Your mother hates you fightin'. So you also disrespect your mother when you fight. Now, when's it okay to disrespect your mother?"

"Never," both mumbled to their feet.

"Look at me and say that again," he growled and got his sons' eyes.

"Never," they pushed out, louder, stronger.

They loved their mom.

They felt like assholes.

Good.

"Clean rooms. Homework done. Trash out," he ordered. "Later I'll think of other shit you can do to make me less pissed at you. And when I talk your mother into acknowledging you exist again, you're both apologizing. Am I heard?"

"Yeah, Dad," Ben said.

"You're heard," Sam said.

"Thank God I'm perfect," Angie called from the couch.

"Barf," Sam muttered, but Cal tossed a smile and a wink at his girl because she was teasing.

But she spoke truth.

She was sheer perfection.

After his boys took off, Cal went to his girl to bend and give her a kiss on the top of her head, earning her sunny smile that he could swear to fuck made the earth go around, before he walked through the living room then the den to the master.

He opened the door and found his wife flat on her back on the bed, calves over the side like she'd turned her back to it and plopped down.

And yeah.

He instantly wanted to fuck her.

He'd never been with a woman as long as he had with Vi. He didn't think about it, but if he had, he would have figured, naturally, shit would settle and it would be about grocery runs and oil changes and occasional bickering with some fights thrown in and a lot of TV watching.

It was about that. With a lot of bickering and some huge-ass, knock-down, drag-out fights, and not the ones his boys had.

It was also about a lot of laughter, quiet golden moments, silken moments of utter pride, and a shit ton of sex.

In other words, he was living the life.

He kinda knew he'd get that the minute he laid eyes on her.

He fought it, but he still knew.

Thank God he quit fighting.

"Did they kill each other?" she asked the ceiling.

"No," he answered the underside of her chin, making his way to her.

"Then why did you stop them?"

He chuckled, put a knee in the bed by her thigh, climbed in and straddled her body on hands and knees, dipping down so they were face to face.

Christ, she was beautiful.

"I heard you. You made them stop by shouting, 'yo'," she pointed out.

"They're nine and eleven, but they're already fluent in speaking man," he explained.

Her face cracked but she didn't let the laughter loose.

"I had girls down," she declared. "Kate and Keira are treasures. Angie came, and she's aptly named. She's an angel. I was certain I'd perfected the art of creating exceptional children. And then along came Sam and Ben."

"They're aptly named too. Your brother and my cousin were not choirboys."

"We should have named them Michael and Gabriel."

"I figure we got better than if we'd named them Diablo and Beelzebub."

Another lip quirk from his wife before she observed, "They haven't hit puberty and they already have too much testosterone."

He was not gonna field that one, so he just hummed, "Mm."

Vi was Vi. She didn't let him get away with shit.

"I blame you," she declared.

"Babe, if you think for a second I'm not super fuckin' happy my boys are all boy, think again."

"So you'd have a problem if one of them was gay?" she asked.

"Are you sayin' bein' gay isn't bein' a boy? Because as far as I know, a gay guy is still a guy," he returned. "Back in the day, I seen a lot of shit as a bouncer, and I saw a drag queen lay one motherfucker *out*. In drag. It was fuckin' spectacular."

That got her.

She started giggling.

So he kissed her.

Best taste in the world, Vi laughing.

He didn't want to break the kiss, but a house full of kids who were awake was not conducive to what would happen next if he didn't, especially when his wife stopped laughing into his mouth and slid her fingers into his hair.

He lifted his head and looked into eyes that held a little laughter and a little daze from the kiss.

And again, he wanted to fuck her.

"Can we put the kids to bed at six o'clock?" she asked.

He grinned down at her.

But unfortunately he had to answer, "Probably not."

"Gluh."

He kept grinning.

"I suppose it's time to start thinking about dinner," she noted.

"Dinner is me tossin' chops on the grill and rallying Angie to make a salad," he replied.

She frowned up at him and asked, "You've met your boys, yes?"

He nodded his head and kept smiling at her.

She continued, "How do you think chops and salad are gonna go over with them?"

"I'll grill 'em two chops each. Maybe three."

Her eyes slid away as she muttered, "A dinner of meat. That might work."

One could say, their boys were big eaters.

"I'll fire up the grill," he muttered but stopped making his move to exit the bed when her fingers fisted in his hair.

He caught her gaze and was about to do something about her hand and the look in her eye when Angie shouted, "Mom! Dad! Mr. Ryker is here!"

"Oh shit," Vi whispered.

"Fuck," Cal bit off.

They had reason for their curses.

Ryker showing without warning could be anything. He'd pissed off an entire biker gang and needed a safe house (or more likely, fire power since Ryker was not a man to hide). He was in a fight with his woman and wanted a man at his side while he slammed bourbon and bitched. Or he could have a hankering to make a chocolate pie and needed a recipe.

The last was not probable, but with Ryker, anything was possible.

"Coming!" Vi yelled as she scooted out from under him.

He came up with her and they walked out of their room together. It was only once they moved through the door that he caught her with an arm around her shoulders, she slid hers along his waist, and they walked side by side into the living room.

There, Ryker had Angie in a headlock that held her to his massive chest. This was a hold that might send a father who didn't know him to finding his gun. But since Cal knew him, he just shook his head and took in his girl, who was grinning like a fool.

Neither he or Vi got a word out before both boys came gunning in, shouting, "Mr. Ryker!"

Angie got strung up so Ryker could kiss the crown of her head before he let her go, set her aside and went into battle stance, in a squat, hands up, like he was about to do some MMA shit to Cal's boys in the living room.

They tackled him as one, and within seconds Ben was held upside down to Ryker's side and Sam was in a different kind of headlock, both of them laughing and shouting, "Let go!" and, "No fair!"

"Yo," Ryker called to Cal and Vi like he didn't have hold on two pre-pubescent boys.

"Hey, Ryker," Vi called back.

Cal just lifted his chin.

Ryker shook his sons and they kept laughing and shouting.

It was not a surprise the guy could lock them down so easy. He was a tall, built, bald-headed, ugly-as-fuck monster who looked like he drank blood for breakfast.

Vi and Cal stopped a few feet away and that was when Cal spoke.

"You wanna let my son go before so much blood rushes to his head, he passes out when you put him down?"

Ryker shot Cal a nasty grin that was his normal grin, just nasty on his mug naturally, released Sam and put Ben on his feet.

"We're gonna get you next time," Ben warned.

"Boy, I'll be in a wheelchair before you get me," Ryker scoffed.

"Huh!" Ben shouted through a smile.

"Rooms. Trash. Homework," Cal reminded them. "And Angie, baby, throw together a salad, will you? I'm cookin' chops."

"Okay, Daddy," Angie agreed.

"Chops, killer! And tots?" Sam asked.

"You need more plant-based foods in your system," Vi said to their son.

He grinned at his mom. "Potatoes are plants."

"You need more plant-based foods that aren't immersed in boiling fat before they're consumed," she amended.

Sam kept grinning then got serious. "Me and Ben are jerks."

That was his oldest boy. Right in front of Ryker.

He could be a pain in the ass.

But he was a straight up good kid who had guts and integrity and loved his mom.

"No you aren't," Vi replied quietly. "You're a boy. But boys become men and we gotta cut out the jerk tendencies before they take root."

His grin came back.

But it grew unsure when he turned it to his dad.

Cal dipped his chin at his boy.

The uncertainty vanished and Sam's smile again grew bright.

That was all it took. Sam was in no doubt he had his father's love because Cal made sure that was the case. And he loved his old man. They'd had times like these, they'd have more.

But in the end it would always be all good.

"Rooms. Trash. Homework," Cal said again, and Sam took off.

Ben went to his mother and gave her a squeeze around her middle. Shooting up fast, the kid might be taller than Cal when it was all said and done.

The hug was his apology. Ben wasn't a fast talker or a smooth one. He was an actions-speak-louder-than-words kid.

Like his dad.

Vi in turn gave her son a hug like all the hugs she gave her children.

For moments through it, it wasn't a given she'd ever let go.

Then she did.

And when she did, Ben switched to his dad.

Cal suspected he gave his kids the same kind of hugs his wife did.

After he did that and Ben took off, Cal reclaimed Vi as she looked to Ryker. "You want a drink?"

"Nope. Need to chat. On the deck," Ryker answered.

Then, not being asked, he stalked through the room, the den and out the back door to the deck.

Cal looked down at his wife. Vi looked up at him.

Then he turned them around and they followed Ryker, still connected.

They stayed connected as Cal slid the door shut behind them and they faced their friend.

"What's up?" Cal asked.

But Ryker was looking at Vi.

"What color roses say, 'I'm shy but I wanna fuck you, but not just fuck you, I think I like you'?"

Cal stared at Ryker.

He knew when she didn't answer that Violet was doing the same thing.

"Well?" Ryker pushed. "Purple?" he said, like he hoped that was the answer.

Ryker and roses and the color purple did not compute.

What the fuck was going on?

"Ryker—" Cal started.

Ryker spoke over him, still to Vi. "You know flowers and shit, lay it on me."

She did know flowers "and shit." When Ben went into kindergarten, they got serious about her landscaping business. Now she designed and installed yards in the 'Burg, Danville, Plainfield, Zionsville, Avon. She even had some clients in Indy.

"I'm not sure there's a color that says all that, Ryker," Vi answered.

Ryker's face got hard, which didn't mean he was pissed, just disappointed.

Vi read it. "But orange, peach or coral usually mean desire or fascination."

"Not purple?" he asked.

"Sorry, no."

Cal pressed his lips together when he heard through his wife's words she was also suppressing laughter.

At this point, Cal cut into the conversation. "What's this about?"

Ryker looked to him. "I'll get to you in a minute."

The man looked back to Violet, and Cal didn't take offense to the brush off. If you took offense to Ryker's ways, you'd either be in prison for murdering him or not have him in your life in another way, as in, cutting him out for being a jackass most of the time.

The man was a prickly character, but he was good people.

Ryker started with, "So, you know, not to be insensitive and shit, but time has passed, you got your happy ending, so I figure you're all good."

This made Cal tense but Vi giving his waist a squeeze made him cool it as Ryker went on.

"What did it for you with Cal? Was it him rescuing himself from his own kidnapping? Saving you from yours? Or killing a guy for you?"

"What's this about?" Cal repeated on a growl, no squeeze from Vi making him cool with this line of questioning.

"It's okay, Joe," Vi said softly.

"It fuckin' is not," Cal returned, his attention not leaving Ryker.

Ryker looked to Cal and he did it appearing impatient, like Cal butting in was wasting time he did not have.

"I know this dude, yeah?" he stated. "Good guy. Fuckin' *skilled* at pool. I bought Lissa some fancy-ass blender *and* food processor with a killing we made on a game against a couple of tools. He's solid. And the bro is good-lookin'. I mean, he's so good-lookin', I can say that shit without feelin' my dick shrink. You feel me?"

Cal did not confirm he felt him.

He urged, "Keep going."

Ryker kept going.

"But the fucker is shy. I don't get it, but he just is. He likes this girl. Good girl. Pretty. Nice. But he's like, *terrified* of her or something. I could tell she was interested at first but he didn't make a move, so Lissa says this chick reckons he's not into her so she moved on. He's bummed."

Ryker stopped speaking.

Cal still didn't know what the fuck he was talking about.

"And?" Cal prompted.

"And, so, you know, shit has calmed down. No one has been kidnapped or got involved with the mob or anything for a while but it's not like you don't remember shit like that. So, I was thinkin' how he could get this girl's attention and I thought, fake kidnap her, he could save her, she'd be happy he did, like *real* happy, if you know what I mean, and then he could give her some roses to seal the deal."

Cal and Vi were both totally silent.

"Just gotta make sure he doesn't have to do anything extreme, like shoot the motherfucker, since the motherfucker will be me, you know, wearin' a ski mask so she doesn't know it's me," Ryker finished.

Cal and Vi remained silent.

Ryker focused on Vi. "So, gotta know, would it have been all good if Cal just rescued you or does this shit have to be whole hog, 'cause I'm gonna have to come up with another scenario seein' as I like this dude, but I'm not feelin' bein' shot so he can get laid."

"You're going to kidnap a woman so some guy can get her attention?" Cal asked, and Ryker looked to him.

"Yeah," he answered, like he'd done that yesterday, and the day before, and was totally down with doing it tomorrow.

"And you can say that shit with a straight face, not realizing you sound like a lunatic," Cal noted.

Vi swallowed a giggle.

Ryker's face got hard in a different way and he jerked his head toward Violet. "Seemed to work for you, motherfucker."

"We were living together before we both got kidnapped, Ryker," Cal pointed out.

"You were?" Ryker asked.

"Yeah," Cal answered.

"Shit, I wasn't around for your gig," Ryker muttered.

"You do know that's not the lunatic part of your plan, right?" Cal queried.

Ryker threw up both his big mitts, which creaked the leather of the biker jacket that he was wearing even though it was late April, they were having a warm spell, and it was seventy degrees.

This was not a bad thing considering for Ryker it was biker jacket or wife beater (what he was currently wearing under the jacket) and Ryker appearing in nothing but jeans, New Rock boots (something he was also right then wearing) and a wife beater usually cleared entire rooms of people who didn't know him.

"What am I supposed to do?" he demanded.

Vi spoke up. "Go to this girl, tell him your boy is shy, but he likes her, and see if she'll make the first move. Then be his wingman so he doesn't mess it up."

"Are you blind?" Ryker asked Vi.

"No," Vi answered calmly.

Ryker threw a hand up his front. "She's not exactly gonna smile and pull up a chair for me if I make an approach for my bro."

He had a point.

She might actually run screaming.

"I see this as a problem," Vi murmured. Then she offered, "Joe can go talk to her."

Cal looked down at his wife. "Say what?"

She looked up at him. "You can go talk to her."

"Uh, no," Ryker cut in, and they both turned to him. "Have you looked at your man recently?"

"Uh . . ." Vi trailed off, clearly not feeling like stating the obvious.

"He ain't young anymore, like my boy, but he can take the panties off a woman with a look, especially a woman who don't know why he's approaching," Ryker explained.

"He's wearing a ring," Vi reminded him.

Ryker shook his head. "She won't give a fuck. Serious. And my bro don't need competition, having some broad thinkin' of Cal doing the deed with her when he finally gets in there."

"Jesus Christ," Cal muttered.

Vi giggled.

"You don't want no girl thinkin' of you either," Ryker aimed this at Cal. "You're taken."

"I don't give a shit about what anyone thinks but my wife," Cal returned. "Now round up Lissa, take her to the bar, have her sit down with this girl and explain things, arrange a meet, hang close so your man doesn't fuck shit up and done."

"I don't take my woman to this bar, man," Ryker declared, visibly appalled by the thought. "It's rough. She's sweet. She don't go to joints like that."

Cal sighed.

Vi giggled again.

"It's gotta be a kidnapping," Ryker decreed.

"It does not gotta be a kidnapping," Cal returned.

Ryker looked to the back yard and muttered, "I shoulda asked Jasper. He's up for anything."

"You are not going to ask my daughter's husband to help you kidnap some woman," Cal clipped, and Ryker returned his attention to Cal, lifting his hands again, but this time to press them down.

"All right. All right, hoss. Calm down."

"Find another way," Cal ordered.

"I could—" Vi started.

Christ, she'd be all in and probably corral Feb, Rocky, Dusty, Jessie, Mimi and Cher on the act, calling Frankie to come down from Chicago, more strength in numbers, if he didn't nip that in the bud immediately.

So Cal tightened his hold on her, saying, "You're not gonna do dick."

"Okay," she mumbled, giving big eyes to Ryker.

Jesus.

"Well, the only good thing about this waste of time is that I probably don't gotta get shot," Ryker shared.

He'd said "probably."

Not a good sign.

Fuck.

"Do you want to stay for dinner?" Vi suggested, and Cal shifted his eyes to the sky.

That was his woman. Ryker suggests a fake kidnapping, she asks him to dinner.

"Thanks, beautiful, but no go. Lissa's cookin'. I should get my ass home. Maybe brainstorm with her alternate scenarios," Ryker replied. He looked to Cal, lifted a hand, clapped him on the shoulder so hard Cal had to brace so he didn't send Vi flying. "Later, bro." His attention went to Vi. "Later, babe. You don't have to walk me to the door."

And then he walked to the door, through it, the house, and calling shit to the kids to say goodbye, out the front door.

What he did not do was close the sliding door to the deck, so Cal reached out to do that.

When he straightened from that effort, Vi curled around to his front so she was pressed there, holding him with both arms.

He wrapped his free one around her to return the favor and looked down at her face.

"He's totally gonna kidnap this woman," she noted.

"Yup. Totally," Cal replied.

They could just say that things had settled down with their crew since the last of them—that would be Cher and Merry—had sorted out their shit.

But things had not settled down for Ryker.

He was not a magnet for trouble.

He was the instigator of it.

And a fake kidnapping was not the most ludicrous thing he'd come up with.

"You totally gotta follow him so he doesn't kidnap this woman," she went on.

He clenched his teeth, felt his cheek pulse, then unclenched them to say, "I'll grill, eat, round up Colt or Layne, or Mike or Merry and sort him out."

She smiled. "It's totally cute. Ryker as matchmaker."

He gave her a squeeze. "There's nothing cute about Ryker."

"This is."

He shook his head.

She rolled up on her toes.

And Cal had long ago vowed to himself that not ever, not even during a fight when he was pissed as shit at her, was he going to ignore an invitation like that.

So he never did.

And he didn't right then.

He dipped in and took her mouth.

The sliding door opened, they broke their kiss and turned their heads to see Ben sticking his out.

"Mom, how firm are you on no tots tonight?" he asked.

It was Cal who answered.

"It was less than twenty minutes ago so your mother and me have not forgotten your disrespect earlier."

Ben tucked his lips in and ducked out of the door, closing it behind him.

"I'm gonna go get out the fryer," Vi decreed.

"Babe," Cal held tight when she started to pull away. "You're a push-over for that kid."

And she was.

Ben. And Sam.

And Angie, Keira and Kate.

She shook her head. "Nope. I'm a mom. He apologized. It's done for me. I carry a grudge, he learns to carry grudges. You can be the bad guy and take care of the follow through to make sure they learn their lesson from this." She shot him a huge smile. "I'm gonna be the awesome mom who fries up tots."

She was an awesome mom not frying up tots.

"Deal?" she pushed.

"Deal, baby," he murmured.

Her smile got even bigger.

He kissed that too.

Then he let her go.

She went inside to the kitchen, her daughter and the fryer.

He went to turn on the grill and then back to the door where he stopped, looking in.

Sam was sitting on a barstool, leaned into the bar toward the kitchen, his mouth moving.

Ben was helping his mom out (and getting something out of it) by pulling out the fryer.

Angie was chopping something Cal couldn't see.

Violet was leaned into the counter opposite her blabbing son, her attention on him, her lips curved into a smile.

She had two girls from her first marriage, a good marriage to a man she loved who'd been killed.

She gave those girls to Cal.

He had a son from his first marriage, a shit marriage where his junkie wife committed negligent homicide, letting their baby drown in a bath, something that caused Cal's sick father to have the heart attack that ended his days.

Cal thought nothing could pull him out of the pit that threw him in. He'd been drained so dry by that, it felt like his insides had split and cracked.

And there . . .

Right there . . .

All his wife had given him.

She said he balanced their scale of give and take.

She had no clue.

No clue.

No clue any time he was with Kate and Keira, any time he looked at Angie or Sam or Ben, any time he woke up to hear her breathing at his side in the middle of the night . . .

He knew he was the luckiest man on earth.

She thought she was the luckiest woman.

He stared at Violet Callahan smiling at the boy they made.

Yeah.

She had no clue.

On that thought, Cal walked into his house, through the den, into the kitchen, to his family.

The End

The Stars Aligned

A novella tying up a Loose End from the book Heaven and Hell *featuring Hap and Luci*

ONE

Second Best to a Dead Man

Luci

LUCIANA GORDON SAT IN A chair on the eighth floor of Saks Fifth Avenue, the one *on* Fifth Avenue, staring unseeing at the boxes of shoes all around her.

She'd taken the express elevator.

She shouldn't have bothered.

After she'd had a salad, alone in the restaurant, she'd wandered the enormous floor filled with shoes, sprinkled with handbags for decoration, and asked Elena, her salesperson, to bring her thirteen pairs of shoes.

She'd tried on one shoe of one pair.

And then she remembered like she often remembered, all the time, suddenly, with no warning.

She remembered Hap's face after she'd pulled away from the kiss she'd given him. She remembered how hard her heart had been beating. She remembered how her skin felt heated and cold at the same time.

Desire.

And terror.

She then remembered how it felt to be swept up in his arms as he carried her from her deck to her couch.

That feel had been just desire.

She blinked her thoughts away and saw she had on a blue Aquazurra pump with a triple layer of fringe as an ankle strap.

It was fabulous.

It was also ridiculous.

She'd never wear that shoe in North Carolina, even in her shop, where she wore all her fabulous shoes.

She'd found a zone she never thought she'd enter.

Putting on a shoe that was *too fabulous*.

No. It wasn't too fabulous. She could do fabulous anywhere, any way she pleased, even wearing shoe fringe at her boutique in Kingston.

It was that Hap would be in fits of laughter if he saw her in that shoe and there would be no end to the teasing.

This would be . . . back then. Back before she kissed him. Back before she pulled away from that kiss and saw that look on his face that was gentle and fiery and greedy and hesitant, and something more. Something *so much more*, something that held promise, something that held riches beyond imagining, all of this at the same time.

Back before he carried her to the couch.

Back before he stopped all the wonderful things they were doing on the couch, left her and ended any possibility of *them*.

Back when she actually saw him, which now she did not. Not anymore. Not for months.

Because he was avoiding her to make his point that all of that had been a mistake.

"Luci?"

Her head came up and for a second, she was so deep in her thoughts she did not recognize the petite, slightly stooped woman hovering beside her.

"Hon, are you all right?" the woman asked.

Oh Dio, she thought.

Pearl.

Pearl Bazer, wearing a purple velvet jumpsuit, a chunky purple, red, yellow, gold, black and green necklace, a clack of thick gold and black bangles on her wrist that had two indomitable, instantly recognizable interweaving Cs, gold rings on every finger, and the biggest, roundest pair of glasses ever made over her eyes. Glasses molded of Kelly green, embedded with rhinestones.

Oh yes.

And her signature ruby-red lipstick.

Her face was lined to profusion.

Her hair was short, spiky and white with just a hint of lilac.

And she was as she always was, without fail.

Unique.

Individual.

Dancing to the beat of her own drummer.

In other words, she was the most fashionable person on the planet.

"Pearl," Luci murmured.

Pearl bent closer, peering harder at Luci's face through lenses that made her eyes look enormous.

"Now that you've succeeded in remembering who I am, even though I met you at a Massimo show what feels like a lifetime ago, came to your wedding, had lunch with you not too long ago at your villa in Lake Como and spent time with you on countless occasions in between, would you kindly answer my question?"

Luci was confused. "Your question?"

Pearl fluttered a thin, veined, spotted hand with perfectly rounded nails varnished in cobalt blue between them.

"Are you all right?"

Vaguely, Luci looked to her feet, using that gesture to pull herself together before she looked back to Pearl, pinning a smile on her face.

That smile (among other things) had won her contracts for exorbitant fees in order for her to twist her body into insane positions in such places as under a red-hot sun, looking gorgeous and happy doing so (if the photographer called for that, which in fashion didn't happen often—girls were expected to look bored, or expressionless, the better to divert attention to the clothes or make said clothes look superior).

"I'm shopping for shoes so obviously I'm fabulous," she lied.

A bony finger with a blue nail wagged in Luci's face.

"*Yekirati*, don't kid a kidder."

Luci blinked up at her.

"We're going to Cipriani," Pearl declared out of the blue, leaning back in a gesture that stated clearly, that was that.

Oh no.

She was not going to Cipriani with Pearl Bazer, one of the most eclectic, singular, extraordinary individuals Luci had met (and Luci had met a lot of people).

She was also one of the most opinionated.

And outspoken.

Maybe *the* most opinionated.

And outspoken.

"I . . . just had a salad," Luci tried to demur.

"Not *now*," Pearl stated, aghast. "You go to Cipriani for dinner. You order something with white truffles in it. I'm assured they're kosher. But if they're not, just don't tell my rabbi. I'll meet you there. Eight sharp."

Luci started to stand as it appeared Pearl was going to leave it at that and totter off.

But Pearl stopped all movement and turned sharp eyes in her eighty-something-year-old face to Luci.

"If you're not there, there's nothing I can do. Except worry. Worry greatly. And you will be responsible for making an old lady worry. Worry and not enjoy her meal at Cipriani. And if you have that in you, Luciana Gordon, I will be sad that I ever met you."

And with that, she tottered off, not very fast, and definitely not spry, in her green Doc Martens boots.

Luci settled in her chair, her head bowed, her eyes again not seeing the thirteen boxes of shoes around her.

She was not the kind of woman who would wish to make anyone worry, old lady or not.

She'd done enough of that recently, making people she cared about worry.

Too much.

Though she didn't mean to.

She sighed as she realized she was meeting Pearl at Cipriani at eight sharp.

"Can I help you try on?"

Luci again looked up, and there she saw Elena, ready to assist.

"I'll just slip on the Dolce and Gabbana slides," Luci replied. Slides, even D&G ones, far more appropriate for her home on the beach in North Carolina.

"You're not taking the Aquazurras?" Elena asked, deflated. "They look beautiful on you."

Luci looked down.

They did.

They looked beautiful on her.

They were the kind of shoes that would look beautiful on anyone.

But she was a former model. She'd even been called a supermodel in her day (now she was a *former* supermodel). So even if she was vain—and she was, slightly, the appropriate amount, considering she was gorgeous, knew it, and it would be disingenuous to pretend she didn't—she had to admit to even more vanity about her feet.

She had beautiful feet.

And even better ankles.

Kia would love those shoes. And Kia helped out at the shop on occasion. Kia was her best friend in Kingston. In fact, Kia was becoming her best friend *ever* (and she had a lot of friends, but Kia was special).

She could let her try them on. Even wear them, if Sam took Kia somewhere lovely.

She lifted her head yet again. "Yes, I'll take them."

Elena beamed.

Luci felt a profound sadness inside because it was highly unlikely Hap would ever see her in those shoes.

She was putting the other one on—just in case—when her fingers stilled on the zip in the back.

She hadn't thought of what Travis would think.

She always thought of what Travis would think, even if her beloved husband was very dead.

He'd love them. He'd *make* love to her as she wore them.

Hap would find them amusing, but Luci did not know if he was the kind of man who would tease his woman, doing this partially to hide how he admired her when she took care of herself, looking pretty and dressing up, and then he would show how he appreciated them in another manner.

She'd never know that.

And that was what made her the saddest of all.

Hap

"YOU'RE A SCREAMIN' IDIOT."

Hap had his crab sandwich up to his face, his eyes on Sam and Kia sitting at the picnic table in front of him, but he slid his gaze to the side and up to see Skip standing there, looking pissed (not an unusual look), glaring at Hap.

It also wasn't unusual for Skip to be at the crab shack seeing as it was called Skippy's Crab Shack.

Hap just wasn't in the mood to put up with Skip's mood.

He started to lower his sandwich at the same time open his mouth to speak, but Skip (also as usual, especially with his mouth) was faster.

"So Luci's in New York City, drownin' her sorrows in stupidly expensive shoes she's got no business ownin' when she lives on a beach, and half the time she's barefoot. So you're down here," he swung his arm out in front of him, "havin' a visit when you're nowhere *near* here when Luci's around."

Hap had once been banned from Skippy's Crab Shack after an ill-advised discussion (read: fight that he thought was funny, but Skip had not) about the Army v. Navy game (Army had won, Hap was a first sergeant, stationed at Bragg, Skip was retired Navy).

It hadn't been very long ago he'd been granted permission to return to the Shack.

He liked Skip's sandwiches. And if pressed, say through water torture, he would admit to liking Skip.

He didn't want to be banned again.

That wasn't why he kept his mouth shut.

"Lay off, Skip," Sam warned.

Good, Sam had his back.

Not a surprise.

Skip turned his attention to Sam. "I can tell you're gearin' up to back his play. I can also tell you it's disappointing, when you're one of the few males I know who primarily thinks with his *first* brain, those times you think with your *second*."

Sam's face got hard.

Kia giggled, and if Hap's glance at Skip hadn't happened the precise instant it did, he'd have missed the softness come into its craggy depths when he heard Kia's laugh.

That was Skip. No woman on earth would think he had a soft spot for them, but as far as Hap could tell, he had a soft spot for *all* of them.

He was the crankiest, most foul-mouthed asshole of a ladies' man in history.

"I'm sorry?" Sam said low.

Hmm.

Not good.

"Only a man thinkin' with his johnson would be okay with another man pissin' his life away and hurtin' a woman he cares about," Skip retorted.

Sam's back got straight. "It's called brotherhood, Skip."

Skip jabbed a finger Sam's way. "That. That right there. Thinkin' with your johnson."

Hap entered the fray.

"Maybe you can let us eat our sandwiches?"

Skip squinted at him.

Then he leaned into his fists at the table.

"If I thought it was worth my time, instead of a waste of it, to tell you a story that would get your head out of your ass, I'd do it. Since it'll be a waste of it, I won't. But you're a damn fool, George Cunningham. Never thought I'd say that, even you . . . a grunt. But you're a *damn fool*."

Hap felt his jaw get hard, but Skip just pushed up and stomped away.

"Let it go," Sam advised quietly.

Hap stopped watching Skip storm away and turned his head to study his sandwich.

"Eat your sandwich. We'll take off, get some beers, hang out on the deck, and you can relax and let that shit go," Sam suggested.

"Skip's right," Kia chimed in, also quietly.

"Baby," Sam murmured.

Hap looked at Kia. "I don't need this."

Kia looked right back at Hap. "Yes, you do."

At that, Hap felt his lips thin.

"Let it go, honey," Sam urged his wife.

Kia gave her husband a stubborn look then she picked up her basket of food, twisted on her seat and swung her legs around, muttering, "I'm eating in the kitchen with Skip, the only man of my acquaintance here who's using his *first* brain."

Sam made a noise in his throat that was part humor, part annoyance, and Kia took off.

Hap watched her go and wondered when she'd start showing. She was only four months pregnant, so he figured it'd happen soon.

Hap bent his neck, lifted his sandwich and took a huge bite.

"Skip's not gonna let this go," Sam noted.

Hap kept his eyes on his sandwich as he chewed, swallowed, then grunted, "He'll let it go."

"Man, you gotta swing things back around with Luci."

Hap lifted his gaze to his friend. His brother in arms. Just his brother, not by blood, but that was where they were at.

Like Gordo was there with them.

Always and forever, even after Gordo and Sam left the Army.

Travis "Gordo" Gordon.

Their brother.

Luciana's dead husband.

"She finds someone else, I'll get there."

Fuck, it was a miracle he could get that out.

He pushed the miracle.

"And she'll find someone else, Sam. She's ready. She's got herself past the hard part. It won't take her long."

Yeah, that was harder.

A fuckuva lot harder.

The thought of Luci with another man made him want to hurl.

He took another bite of his sandwich to get the sick taste out of his mouth.

It didn't help. Not surprisingly, it made it worse.

"You shouldn't have gone there with her." There was an edge of pissed in Sam's voice that made Hap look at him again while he swallowed.

"We were drunk," he replied.

"That's no fuckin' excuse and you know it."

He did.

"Shit just got outta hand," Hap muttered.

"With Gordo's wife?" Sam asked irately.

"No, with *Luci*," Hap bit back, shocking the shit out of himself not only at the bite, but at his words.

She wasn't Luci.

She was Gordo's. Gordo's wife. Gordo's everything.

He was a brother.

Which meant she should only ever be a sister.

But he couldn't for the life of him put her there.

She'd kissed him, tasted so damn good, *looked* so damn good, and when she'd pulled away, the anxiousness and heat and want and beauty in her face, her eyes . . .

She was just Luci.

"It was turned around, you'd rise from the dead for the sole purpose of breakin' his neck," Sam retorted.

"If it was turned around, I'd rise from the dead for the sole purpose of having one more minute with my wife."

Sam shut his trap.

Yeah, he felt that.

He felt that with watching Luci lose what she lost. Watching his younger brother, his *blood* brother's girlfriend lose what she lost when his brother died in the line of duty. And now having a wife who he loved more than his own life.

So yeah.

He felt that.

Hap stared at him and let that sink in.

Only when he thought he'd given it enough time did he speak.

"It got outta hand, Sam," Hap clipped. "She'll find some dude and we'll make our way back to each other. Just peace out on this shit. I don't need to lose Luci, have Kia and Skip ticked at me, and take your shit too."

"Just tell her it was a mistake and you're not going to go there and do it now so we can have the family back together again," Sam encouraged.

Oh, he'd told her it was a mistake. He'd told her that afternoon, at the barbeque Sam and Kia had for Sam's high school football team.

She'd looked at him like he'd sunk a knife in her gut.

Then she'd taken off.

He'd gone after her for the purpose of having it out and putting it behind them, once and for all.

Then, chickenshit and fucked in the head, he'd gotten in his truck and driven home.

That was where they were at. He hadn't seen her since. Nearly three months.

He missed her.

Like *fuck*.

Shit.

"Hap, are you hearin' me?" Sam pushed.

"I told her that. It hurt her, bro." He shut his eyes quick and hard at the memory then opened them with a shake of his head. "It hurt her. Just leave it lie."

Sam was now staring at him and Hap knew him well, could read him, so it was not hard to see he didn't like the idea of Luci hurting.

"She'll move on," Hap assured. "She was just . . . feelin' shit out. Doin' it with someone she thought was safe. She had a bumpy road when we lost Gordo. She was just pullin' out onto the straightaway, checkin' her groove. When she realizes that, and that I don't give a shit she used me to do it, it'll be all good. But she's stubborn, so she probably won't realize that shit until she has another guy."

Sam looked sick at that, neither of them wanting Luci to move on, which would mean she left Gordo behind (though, Hap had shit messing with his head that made him dislike that idea a fuckuva lot more).

It was healthy.

It was right.

They should want that for her.

They both *did* want that for her.

It still sucked.

For Hap, it sucked *hard*.

And that had nothing to do with Travis "Gordo" Gordon.

Which made it suck harder.

"Got a kid comin', want all my family around me, around my baby, all good, copacetic, nothing messin' with it," Sam replied.

"We'll get there, man."

"Maybe she gets back from New York, you try to find some time to get her there faster."

Hap wanted to get up, lean across the table, and shout, *"Lay the fuck off!"*

He did not do that.

A younger George Cunningham would.

No hesitation.

He'd learned control since he was a perpetual, immature jackass.

Or control when a beautiful woman he'd loved from afar from the minute he'd clapped eyes on her did not lay a sweet, wet kiss on him.

Fuck.

"We'll see."

Sam hesitated before he sighed.

Hap took another bite of sandwich, trying not to think of Luci in New York.

He was not a city guy.

But she probably knew that place like the back of her hand. She'd know the good restaurants and bars and places to take a walk in Central Park. She'd stroll in somewhere and folks would probably know her, call to her, greet her, kiss her fuckin' cheek like those lame-assed city folk did. Maybe even kiss *both* her cheeks, like those lame-assed European folk did.

He'd grown up on a farm in Iowa. What the city folk called a "flyover" state. What they did on the rare occasion they had to get to LA or San Francisco so they could do what they had to do in LA or San Francisco, but do it looking down on LA or San Fran, dying to get back to the "city."

So he had no problem looking down his nose right back at those city folk and he had no problem sharing it.

He'd teased Luci about that shit for years, Gordo backing him up, both of them busting her chops.

But he knew one thing and he knew it for certain.

He would take pride in his place if he walked into some ritzy, up-its-own-ass restaurant in New York City and someone called out to her and came to kiss her cheek and she was on his arm.

She was on his arm.

Damn.

It was not about having seen the look on Gordo's face the million times he watched his brother proudly introduce his stunning wife to someone who hadn't met her. And it was not about knowing what he knew with no doubt, the fact that shit had nothing to do with how drop-dead gorgeous she was. That she was an ex-supermodel.

But instead it was about the fact she was Luci, who drank beer and ate three hotdogs in one sitting because she liked them so much she could tell you her favorite (Hebrew National, bun length).

For Hap, it would be about having her long, elegant fingers curled around his elbow, having her close, smelling her hair, her exotic perfume, the turn of her head to get those exquisitely formed eyes looking right into his, and having her.

Having her.

Knowing later he'd tease her about her ridiculous shoes that cost more than most made in a month and put her just as tall as him (right, maybe an inch taller). And she'd pretend to be pissed, but she'd love it, like she always pretended to be pissed when he gave her shit, but he could tell by the way her lips curved up she loved it. And he'd know what kind of beer she drank and how her hair looked windswept after a walk on the beach and how she took her coffee and how she looked naked and spread out . . .

Hap bit off another huge hunk of his sandwich, stopping his train of thought, reminding himself he'd never have Luciana Gordon on his arm.

Not only because he should not ever go there because she was his brother's woman.

Though that was part of it.

But because he knew where she was at.

She was feeling things out.

She was trying to find her new groove.

But once she found it, with someone else, that man—no matter how decent he was, how rich, how good-looking, how smart or funny . . . no matter what he was.

He would always come second best to a dead man.

TWO

The Code

Luci

LUCI WALKED INTO CIPRIANI AND the place was its usual crush.

She'd always loved it there. The gold glow of the room. The warm wood. The scribble of the bartender shaking a cocktail shaker with glasses in front of him—the Cipriani symbol, subtle and chic and everywhere, even etched into the cutlery.

The tables were close together, scores of servers rushing about as best they could, squeezing through the non-existent space.

But even with that, she saw Pearl right away, and this was mostly because she was in what Luci suspected was head-to-toe gold lamé. And Luci suspected this was head to toe even though she couldn't see her lower half, but she was wearing a gold lamé turban.

Pearl was also not alone.

Henry Gagnon was with her.

This did not alarm Luci. She knew Henry well. He was one of the best photographers working in fashion, or anywhere. She'd done dozens of shoots with him over the years and immensely enjoyed working with him.

He didn't only do fashion and celebrity layouts, or portraits of Nobel prize winners and Secretaries of State, but also the results of drought-stricken nations, starving children, or war-torn urban landscapes.

He was not only talented, he was wealthy, in demand, outrageously handsome, charming, intelligent and witty.

Further, he was "officially" single, but even so, everyone in the life knew he was head over heels in love with Josephine, his personal assistant, who returned that affection with quiet dignity. Although none of their set fully understood why those two, together for years, didn't make it official. However, it might have something to do with the fact that they both were known to stray (Henry especially).

Even so, they always came back home.

As Pearl gestured to her with a lavishly adorned hand to join them, Henry twisted in his seat to smile his impeccable smile at her.

Luci felt her face get soft.

She also felt relief.

With Henry there, perhaps (and that was a big perhaps), Pearl would not do whatever she was going to do to set Luci straight, something Luci was certain she intended to try to do.

She made her way to their table and bent to Pearl to touch each cheek in turn and give her greeting before she turned to Henry, who'd stood and was now smiling down at her from close proximity.

And looking into his handsome face, she not only wished he wasn't in love with Josephine, she wished that she was one of those women who liked the kind of men who made up their part of that circle of her life.

That would be so much easier.

But no.

She liked them no-nonsense. Even rough. Frank to the point of blunt. Honest. Also assertive, almost aggressive.

Alpha.

And if they could talk about a good beer like other men talked about good wine, wore baseball hats—forward or backward, she didn't care—and loved their trucks more than anything (outside their women), all the better.

Like Travis.

Like Hap.

Henry put a hand to her waist and bent to her.

She put both her hands to his biceps, tipped her head back, and he kissed her cheek before he murmured into her ear, "Luci. Always a masterpiece."

She pulled away to catch his gaze, but didn't drop her hands when she replied, "Henry, always a charmer."

His eyes twinkled and he gave her waist a squeeze. She took that cue and moved away. He held her chair out for her (she wondered if Hap was the kind of man who would do that, and then she forced herself to stop wondering). She sat, he helped her toward the table and only then resumed his seat.

Luci had barely gotten her napkin on her lap before Pearl announced, "You two make a gorgeous couple. Normally I don't like a man and a woman together who have the same color hair. But you two are *delicious* together."

Luci turned big eyes to Pearl at the same time she heard Henry sigh.

Everyone knew about Josephine. *Everyone.* And if they were on a break, or whatever it was that meant they turned to others (Luci could not understand it, if you loved someone, the operative part of that word was *one*), Henry or Josephine made their selections. No one *set them up*.

Pearl ignored Luci's big eyes and carried on.

"Then again, I learned the hard way that everyone's hair turns the same shade in the end," she flipped out both hands, "so it's no big whoop."

Luci shot her a look then turned to Henry and asked pointedly, "How's Josephine? I haven't seen her in ages."

Henry reached to his lowball glass, and if her memory was correct, in it was an old fashioned.

He did this speaking.

And what he said shocked her.

It also made the relief she'd felt earlier march right out the door.

"I presume she's perfectly fine, even happy, as she's married to a former boxer and living in the tiny Maine town where she grew up."

Now Luci was blinking at Henry.

Josephine lived in a tiny Maine town and was not as she always was: wherever Henry was.

She was married to someone else.

Henry was now officially, and in all other ways, *single*?

"I'm . . . *sorry*?" she queried.

Henry took a sip and turned his eyes toward her as he replaced his glass on the table. "Josephine married a man named Jake Spear, quit her job with me, and they live in the house her grandmother left her in Maine. I believe she also officially adopted his youngest son."

Josephine had *quit* Henry.

How could that be?

He was the talent, the eye behind the lens.

But she was the woman behind the man, and as far as Luci knew, it had been that way for *decades*.

She was also his muse. Everyone knew that as well. If he wasn't taking pictures of a model or an orphan, his lens was trained on her.

And now she was married to a . . . a . . .

Boxer?

That was so *not* Josephine.

"Oh Henry," she whispered, "I had no idea. I—"

He shook his head and interrupted her. "I do believe, sweetheart, that you know even better than me that you don't waste life, you absolutely don't waste love, but most of all, you don't waste time. I did all of that with Josephine. And now she's happy, married to another man, and raising a son."

Oh yes.

Very much yes.

She'd learned all of that.

Luci reached out a hand to capture and squeeze his just as Pearl ordered, "She'll have a Bellini and she'll be selecting her food soon so don't waste time coming back."

Luci turned her head to watch a waiter scurry away then watch Pearl wave toward the menu sitting on her plate to urge her to peruse.

"Speaking of not wasting time," she continued, "I have a lot less of it than you do and although I'd rather not sleep it away, my body has other ideas. So if I'm not in bed by ten, I'll be no good to anyone and Henry is shooting me tomorrow for . . ." She looked to Henry. "What's it for?"

Henry opened his mouth to answer but Pearl kept talking.

"Whatever it's for, so the train has left the station on anything resembling beauty sleep for me. I still don't want to be dragging my behind around all day tomorrow when I need to be even more fabulous than my normal fabulous and *emote* that for a camera. So, let's order. Then we can focus on catching up."

Dutifully, Luci picked up her menu, not surprised Pearl had a photo shoot with Henry on her schedule.

Long ago, Pearl's husband, Nicolas, had been an up-and-coming fashion designer, gaining popularity and clients due to his extraordinary work in some small but notable, due to their costume design, films in Hollywood.

Then there would come the day when he was doing an advertising shoot and someone on his team hired a young, flamboyant, opinionated woman who had, at the time, wanted to be a photographer, but who was, at the time, hired to be a set assistant.

Nicolas Bazer had been a genius, but he'd also been shy. He detested the limelight and most social functions unless they were private functions given for close friends at his home.

The woman who he would fall in love with was the exact opposite.

She came to be the face and spokesperson of his label. She would also learn that her talents lay in set design and production, not photography, and she not only became her husband's Creative Director, but also collaborated with giant names in the industry, as well as getting involved in a number of films over decades that had been shot in the city.

Last, the Bazers were renown for throwing lavish parties after his shows, or just whenever the spirit moved them, be it in their home or in some fabulous location somewhere in New York City, with Nicolas the quiet, enchanting host and Pearl the outrageous, and outrageously dressed, hostess.

With her style, her manner, and it was not to be missed, her heart, and most assuredly her talent, Pearl had earned respect and then fame in her own right, to the point she'd become an icon.

Nicolas had died three years ago.

And it was not once, but many times after Travis had died that Luci had thought about Pearl's loss and tried to find the source in her own heart and mind that Pearl had somehow found in order to carry on after being with her husband for over sixty years.

Perhaps you should listen to what the woman has to say, she thought.

This would be wise. Her father, if he was there, would likely tell her the same, but of course, he'd say it in Italian, not just the language, but Italian in spirit with the forcefulness behind it.

But doing this would be dangerous.

Then again, honesty and wisdom often held danger.

It was only those who risked listening to the wise who learned to be the same.

She scanned the menu, made her selection and set it aside just as the Bellini was set in front of her.

"Fabulous! Let's order," Pearl announced.

Luci sipped and ordered something with white truffles, not because Pearl would disapprove if she didn't, but because, well . . . *white truffles*.

No other words needed.

The waiter scurried off and Pearl instantly leaned into the table, looking at Luci but addressing Henry, "No offense, hon, but we've already had our chat so you know my feelings about how you royally screwed things up with Josephine."

Luci bit back a gasp as Henry sighed, "Yes, Pearl, we've had our chat," in a manner that explicitly shared that chat had not been enjoyable.

"Now," she wagged a finger at Luci, ignoring Henry's manner, and Henry on the whole, "you're on the hot seat."

Suddenly, Luci wasn't in the mood to learn to be wise and definitely not in the mood for honesty.

She reached for her drink, murmuring, "I'd prefer simply to catch up and not be on any hot seat."

"I'm sure you would, though you knew that wasn't going to happen before you arrived, so just sit back and experience the moment, sister," Pearl retorted, sitting back herself (or more aptly, settling in).

After taking a sip, she trained her eyes on Pearl. "You know, you shouldn't be so dismissive of Henry's situation. He and Josephine were together for ages. I can imagine that he's—"

"Google Jake Spear," Pearl commanded. "I did. There were a number of celebrities at the wedding, pictures all over social media. But also pictures when he was a professional athlete. When you see him, you'll get it."

Henry sighed again.

But Luci was curious.

She didn't share that.

"I still think—" she began.

"He never made his move," Pearl announced, and Luci felt her eyes get big again.

Unable to stop them, slowly, they moved to Henry.

"I thought you were lovers," she noted.

"I do believe I've made my point about wasting time," Henry drawled.

Mio Dio, she thought.

"Oh Henry, *caro*, I'm now *very* sorry for you," she said softly.

He simply tipped the drink he was holding her way.

Then he put it to his lips and drained it.

"So you," Pearl butted in, and Luci looked her way again. "I'll warn you, my girl, I'm going to be blunt. And I'll start that by saying, we all loved Travis. *You know I know* how difficult it is to lose the man who was put on this earth for you. My heart was in tatters when I heard you lost him. So young. It defies belief and gives new meaning to the concept of unfair. But *yekirati*, for you, the show is going on and *you must go on with it*."

"I've come to terms with Travis's death, Pearl," Luci told her.

Pearl didn't believe a word she said and didn't only express that with her face, but with words.

"So why, precisely, were you a million miles away when you had a beautiful shoe on your foot and a dozen boxes of the same surrounding you?" Pearl demanded.

"Because I've met someone else."

Pearl's chin lifted slightly, and she murmured, "I see."

"But he won't have me," Luci went on.

Henry made a choking noise.

Pearl's already magnified eyes behind her glasses took up her face.

"I beg your pardon?" she asked.

"He won't have me," Luci repeated.

Pearl leaned forward. "For goodness sakes, *why*?"

"He's one of Travis's dearest friends."

Henry made a low noise of male understanding while Pearl's wrinkles rearranged themselves into supreme annoyance.

She aimed her glare at Henry.

"So you approve of this nonsense?" she queried.

"Approve? No. Understand? Yes," Henry answered.

"Then please," Pearl threw out both hands, palms up, and spread them wide to indicate the table, "educate us."

"That would be impossible for me to do without offending you both greatly," Henry replied.

"Because we're too dim to understand?" Pearl asked.

"Because it's a piss around your property issue that a woman simply cannot comprehend, mostly because it's ridiculously stupid," Henry returned.

Pearl was mollified by this and shared it by reaching toward her Bellini and taking only a half-still-annoyed sip.

But Luci turned her attention to Henry.

"You think it's ridiculously stupid?"

He nodded. "As a philosophy, yes. Logically, it makes no sense. Emotionally, if, to try to find a like comparison, I had not foolishly thrown away any chance I had to win the only woman I've ever loved, and we had wed and built a life together, and we found ourselves at that time where we discussed the tragic and hopefully very unlikely event that one of us should pass before the other, in the prime of our lives, or whenever, I would find it very difficult to say with any authenticity that I would be fine with the idea of another man with Josephine."

"That's preposterous," Pearl snapped. "Not to mention selfish."

"I said with any authenticity, Pearl," Henry stated soothingly. "Of course I would want her to move on. I would want her to find happiness again. Of course. Logically. Because I love her and I would not want her ever to be unhappy. But would it make me happy in the slightest to think of her with another man? Not a chance. A nightmare, I'll remind you, I'm living right now in another way, but I'm still living it. Make that man a friend? I'd be infuriated and feel betrayed just by the thought."

"That's preposterous and selfish too," Pearl retorted.

"Nevertheless," Henry said, catching the eyes of the waiter and lifting his chin before he tipped his head to his empty glass then flicked his hand to indicate he wanted the table to have another round, "it's true." He returned his attention to Pearl. "And I'm here because you like me. You like annoying me. You like beguiling me. You enjoy making me laugh and entertaining me. But you didn't call two hours ago to invite me to dinner for any of that. Nor did you do it to set me up with Luciana. You did it so I could state the facts for my gender."

"I also like looking at you," Pearl huffed, and Henry grinned.

So did Luci.

She also took another sip of her drink.

It was very Henry to be certain they all had their drinks refreshed, he was a gentleman like that in all ways. And later, even if he'd been invited, he would argue with Luci and Pearl (and then when Luci bowed out due to politeness, just with Pearl) about who would pay the check.

But Luci was also glad he did it because she had a feeling she was going to need another drink before this was all over.

"Well then, onward," Pearl declared as Luci put her glass back to the table. "If this man is fool enough not to accept your affection, Luci, then find another."

"I don't want another."

She had not intended to say that.

However, she did, and she felt both their focus after she did.

"So, you're emotionally involved with him?" Henry asked quietly.

She looked to him. "I've known him years. We were all very close. Of course, when I had Travis, he never occurred to me *in that way*. Until he did. We kissed and . . . other things . . ."

Henry gave her a small smile to encourage her to carry on after she'd trailed off.

"So I know he cares for me and is at least attracted to me."

"Of course he's attracted to you," Pearl said.

"I'm not every man's type," Luci told her.

"Yes, those who swing toward their own," Pearl somewhat agreed. "You're not *their* type. Other than that . . ." It was she who trailed off then, lifting her brows.

"You'd be very annoying if you weren't so lovable," Luci returned.

"I've been hearing that since I was two," Pearl remarked before she drank more Bellini.

Luci shook her head at her and took her own sip.

"Getting back to what Pearl said earlier," Henry called her attention back to him, "I encourage you to forget this man and move on."

"And *I* encourage you to find this schmuck and make clear to him how absurd he's being and *then* move on," Pearl offered her opinion.

"He's a friend," Luci reminded her.

"Then he shouldn't have kissed you," Pearl returned.

This was true.

Why did he do that?

If it was such a big *mistake* when it happened, why wasn't he gentle and sweet and pull away and share they couldn't take their relationship to that place? She would have been mortified, but she also would have found her way beyond that and they would be again what they always were.

Why did he show her the entry back into heaven?

And then walk away?

And furthermore, what had been behind that *look*? That look of promise and longing in his eyes.

"You're right," she said softly. "I don't . . . I don't understand that part."

Pearl gave *Explain!* eyes to Henry.

"I really wish I'd said no to this dinner," Henry muttered, shifting so the waiter could serve their drinks.

"Well you didn't, and you're here, so hit us," Pearl ordered.

Henry looked right at Luci. "It's Travis, sweetheart. This man, I don't know him, but you're you, all of you, the beauty within and without, it could be he's harbored an attraction to you for years, and due to the code knew he could do nothing about it. Therefore, he slotted you in as friend and that was what it was. Travis gone, things shifted, and he lost sight of what you shared, and perhaps had a momentary lapse of control and kissed you, only to regret it, *not*," he stressed, "because of you, but because of Travis."

"I think at this juncture I should make it clear that I kissed him," Luci shared.

Henry took a drink and murmured, "That explains it."

"It surely does," Pearl agreed.

"It does?" Luci asked.

Henry leaned slightly her way. "Darling, if you kissed me, you're my friend, a colleague, I like you, I respect you, I would not want to lose any of a relationship that means something to me, but I would kiss you back even knowing doing it could put at risk what we have." He straightened in his seat, his mouth quirking. "Pure male instinct."

"For certain," Pearl again agreed.

Luci pressed against her seat so her food could be set in front of her, doing it asking, "Now what do I do?"

"Have you spoken to him since?" Pearl asked.

"Yes, he said we can't *go there* and that it was a *mistake* and we need to get beyond it and back to the way we were," she answered the white truffle risotto in front of her.

"Fine, he feels that way, go back to what you had with him and move on," Pearl advised.

"I can't," Luci replied.

"Why?" Pearl inquired.

Luci looked into Pearl's eyes. "Because I think . . . no, it's got nothing to do with thinking, I *know* I've fallen in love with him."

"Fuck," Henry muttered.

"I'm not a big fan of foul language, but what he said," Pearl added.

"I can't seem to think about anything but him. That kiss. What happened after. When he told me it was a mistake." Her gaze swung to Pearl. "What he'd think of those shoes I tried on today and how I know he'd tease me about them. But what I don't know is if he'd like them secretly and how he would show me that." She turned her focus to Henry. "If he's the kind of man who would pull my chair out for me if we went to a restaurant together." She shook her head. "He's always on my mind. When I go to sleep. When I wake. He's just always . . . *there*."

"And it's not just an obsession, hon?" Pearl asked gently. "You know, fixating on him after Travis?"

Luci shook her head again. "I wish it was. I could see it with someone else. Not Hap. Not someone who's a member of the family. It's just *him*. He's handsome and funny and I love the way he teases me, and how I started to catch him looking at me and what I saw on his face when I did. He was *there* when Travis died. Not as much as Sam . . . you both know Sam, yes?"

When she got two nods, she went on.

"But he was there. Sam treated me like I was fragile, the finest crystal. But Hap spoke openly of Travis. In his way, guiding my way to carry on, understanding that wound would never heal, but doing it anyway. He was just *firmer* about it. Not pushy or unkind, but making it clear Travis lived, and was loved, and now he is no longer living, if he is no less loved, but the rest of us *are* living so we must keep going."

"I think I might like this guy," Pearl mumbled.

"He's likable. You especially, Pearl, would love him. He'd go tit for tat with you, shock you silly with his language and pretty much everything he says. He's affable, but so impertinent, but it doesn't hide the sweet or the sincerity. You couldn't help but adore him."

Pearl had kind eyes on her when she was done. "I'm beginning to understand your dilemma."

Even if Luci was no longer hungry, she picked up her fork.

"And he was also firm he thought this was a mistake?" Henry asked carefully.

Luci shoved her fork into the rice. "Yes." She didn't lift the bite, just her head to look at Henry. "It's this *code* you mentioned. It's like they held a ceremony and vowed, should something like this happen, the others would take care of the wife left behind, but hands off. And those men take vows like the most devout of priests. There is no shaking it."

"I'm sorry, sweetheart," Henry murmured.

That meant she was right.

Which meant her insides deflated and this was not a good feeling.

Luci looked back to her risotto. "I am too."

"Escape to New York was a good plan to hatch," Pearl put in. "But I fear you're just going to have to find more strength, *yekirati*, once you get home so you can ride this out. And ride it out you will, my girl."

That was what Luci feared too.

Except Hap was taking himself away, not only from Luci, but Sam and Kia, who adored him.

They were like a family, their own mismatched family, but there was still love.

So much love.

This meant Pearl was right.

She just had to find more strength.

But it had taken everything out of her to find her way back to life when it felt like she lost hers as sure as Travis's had leaked out of him.

She had, and she realized she was ready for life again, *and* love, watching Sam and Kia find all they had and knowing she wanted that for herself again one day.

Even so, she didn't know if she could dig into a well that felt so very empty to find more.

The problem was, she had no choice.

"You'll get there, hon," Pearl murmured reassuringly, reaching out to pat Luci's thigh.

"I will," Luci replied, but the way the words came out, she didn't even believe herself.

"Darling," Henry called.

Luci looked to him.

"You will," he whispered. "It doesn't feel like it, but you will."

Luci tipped her head to the side, and curiously, not callously, asked, "Do you think you'll get over Josephine?"

"In this very moment, even if some time has already passed, no." He smiled a soft smile at her. "But I still will. The right woman. The right place. The right time. The stars will align and I'll find someone to make me happy. And you will too, Luciana. You'll again be very, very happy. Perhaps not with this man. Hell, perhaps not with *any* man. But you have too much light in you for it to stay dimmed for too long. So *something* will come along to make you happy. And if it's something or if it's someone, or if it's both, then that will make me happy."

"It goes without saying, me too," Pearl chimed in.

"You both are such loves, *amori della mia vita*," Luci murmured, feeling her throat get itchy and thick.

"Yes, as are you. We're also done with this conversation and we're further done with depressing things," Pearl decreed. "Now, I have a photo shoot tomorrow but fortunately it's with the most talented photographer on the planet. It's your job, *motek*, to make me fabulous," Pearl said to Henry. "And I'm sorry, but I'm going to challenge you seeing as tonight we're living it up, getting very drunk, staying out very late, and making memories that will last a lifetime."

"I'm in for that," Henry agreed.

"Luci?" Pearl prompted.

Luci stared at the white truffle risotto she had not taken a bite of but knew it would be amazing. It was also frighteningly expensive (even for her).

Travis wouldn't blink at paying the bill after she'd ordered it, she'd feed him some from her fork and he'd love it.

Hap would give her no end of grief for ordering it, probably turn his nose up at it, but she suspected he'd try it anyway . . .

And also, probably, he wouldn't blink at paying the bill after she'd ordered it.

But neither of them was there right now.

She was there.

Pearl was there.

Henry was there.

They were living. Breathing.

And it was time she started living and not just breathing.

She finally lifted her fork and suggested, "Monkey Bar after this."

Henry smiled.

Pearl hooted.

Luci took her bite.

And it was amazing.

THREE

Sterling Idea

Hap

HAP SAT IN HIS TRUCK with his phone in his hand, but his eyes were trained to the back door of Skippy's Crab Shack.

If I thought it was worth my time, instead of a waste of it, to tell you a story that would get your head out of your ass, I'd do it. Since it'll be a waste of it, I won't. But you're a damn fool, George Cunningham.

Hap wanted to know Skip's story. This was why he was sitting like a thief casing the joint in a lane down the road from the parking lot at the front of Skip's place, a lane only used for deliveries and by Skip's employees.

He looked at his phone and saw it had gone dark since the last time he'd looked at it a minute ago.

He engaged it and what he'd left there came right up.

She's home. Take some time. Go to her. Make things good again.

The text was from Sam.

Luciana was home.

Hap drew in a breath through his nose and looked back at Skip's place.

But you're a damn fool, George Cunningham.

He had been, returning Luci's kiss like that.

Now he was again, avoiding her and making his fuckup even worse.

He tossed his phone to the seat beside him, turned on his truck and reversed out of the lane, onto the road.

He put it in drive, and for the first time since it had all gone down, he headed straight to Luci's.

It was Saturday. The sun was shining. There was a chill in the air. It was November. It was only going to get worse, then it was going to get better again.

Hap was the kind of guy who would retire in Florida or Phoenix in an effort to avoid even a chill. Probably Phoenix. He figured he could deal with the dust and temps that could fry an egg on the sidewalk not to have to put up with humidity.

But that time was not close, so he had the time to make the decision.

On the turn to the beachfront road, instead of going left, toward Sam and Kia's, he went right, toward Luci's.

He felt his chest tighten as her house came into view.

She'd lived on this road, just a ways farther down it, when Gordo had been alive and awhile after. It was only a few months ago when she'd sold the bigger house, a house they were going to fill with children after they had their alone time together.

But they'd waited too long.

This one was a lot smaller and a lot more Luci. Clean lines. Modern. Sleek.

The bottom was a two-car garage with two types of storage—one general, one that had a door to the outside for towels and beach chairs and that kind of shit. There was a shower off to the side to rinse off the sand when you got back from the beach. The lower level space was rounded out with a small guest suite that had a private entry, bedroom, bathroom and its own porch that had a view of dunes and the sound of the sea.

Above that, a massive great room, all open plan, seating areas, dining, half bath tucked behind a pantry, big modern kitchen with white cabinets and countertops, stainless steel appliances, with three kickass pendants over the island that looked like they were made of shards of mirror.

Finishing that was a wall of windows that all folded open to provide access to a massive deck that ran the width of the house, jutting out over the dunes.

Floor above that, Luci's master suite. Something he had not seen and did not think about.

And the floor above that, kind of an observation deck that could function as a guest room with its own full bath. But mostly it was like a studio/vanity room with tons of framed shots on the walls of Luci at work in fashion spreads or on catwalks, or pictures of Gordo in uniform, from fatigues to mess dress, or with his buds in the field.

And then there were those of both of them together living her high life globally or living his normal life locally.

There were even pictures with Hap in them up there.

He had no idea what she did up there.

He actually had no idea what she did at all when he wasn't with her, outside jetting around, going back to Italy to see her family or commune with friends at her house in Lake Como, hanging with Kia, Sam and Kia, Hap and Sam and Kia (when he wasn't avoiding her) or working in her shop in town.

He really didn't know her at all, outside her being Gordo's wife.

That's a damn lie and you know it, he thought as he pulled into her drive that widened so the essentially two-bedroom house could have parking enough for a moderately sized shindig.

He stopped the truck, put her in park and switched off the ignition.

"Fuck," he said as he stared at the steps that led up to the door on the second level.

He hoped she'd heard his truck pull in. He hoped she looked out to see him there so she had warning.

But even if she didn't, he had to do this, for Sam and Kia, Skip, her and him.

And also for Gordo.

He should phone and tell her he was there. Give her the opportunity not to let him in. Give her the opportunity to tell him to go away. Or just give her the opportunity to prepare for the talk she knew they had to have.

Hap did not phone her.

He opened his door, shoved his body out and slammed the door behind him.

He adjusted the baseball cap on his head as he walked up the stairs.

He wouldn't use words like "mistake" or "regret" this time.

He wouldn't mention Gordo.

He'd talk about how much he cared about her, how important she was in his life, and he'd share how he didn't want that to change and he really didn't want to do anything to harm it.

Yeah.

That was the way to go.

He stood at the pristine white door surrounded by the light gray of the house and looked in the narrow rectangular window that ran down half of one side.

He only saw himself. It was smoked out his way, but Luci would be able to see him.

He hit the doorbell, feeling his mouth get dry.

Christ.

Why had he kissed her back?

You know why, asshole.

He did.

She was beautiful. She was funny. She ate hotdogs and didn't talk about how they were unhealthy or how many calories they had. She had great legs, phenomenal hair and an unbelievable ass. She dressed fantastic. She showed love and affection without a hint of hesitation. She could make a stranger feel like a lifelong friend in five minutes flat.

She was Luci.

And he was in love with her.

So he kissed her back.

Shit.

The door opened and his focus snapped into place as every muscle in his body snapped taut.

And then he nearly busted out laughing.

She was wearing a light-blue, what looked like man's shirt, tied at the tails at her waist, the tail at the back hanging down.

But on her bottom, she was wearing a pair of wide-leg pants made entirely of sequins. At the top the sequins were the color of the shirt, but they got darker and darker as the color intensified to the hems, which were covering her feet.

He just barely hit six foot.

Since she was five-ten, and now barefoot, he had two inches on her.

She put on pretty much any shoe she owned, she was taller than him.

If she was his, he would not give that first crap.

"Hey," he said softly.

Her focus was on his cap, but at his greeting it came to his face.

"Hap," she replied, eyes guarded, body visibly as taut as his.

She had not heard his truck pull in.

Hurricane glass. Necessary, but usually soundproof.

"Going to a disco?"

It came out as habit. The tease. He was that guy and he loved it that she was the kind of woman who not only could take it but enjoyed it and shoveled it back.

It was the wrong call. She went from guarded to wounded.

Shit.

"Luce—"

She opened the door wider, effectively inviting him in while cutting him off, and did it verbally as well. "I suppose we should talk."

She didn't seem to be fired up about the possibility.

He was there with her.

But at her invitation, since this had to get done, he walked in.

She shut the door behind him, and it wasn't the first time he found it funny that she'd decorated the common areas pretty much in all white. The thing was, even as clean-lined and stark the place was, it was also gorgeous, and her sofa had super wide seats so it was incredibly comfortable.

And incredibly advantageous when you were making out hot and heavy on it.

He avoided teasing her about her couch again, and he definitely avoided thinking about the last time he'd been on that couch, making out hot and heavy with her, as he walked to the edge of said couch and turned to her.

The sequins at the hems of her pants swished the tiled floor as she moved to him in her graceful way.

She stopped, not close.

"I wish you'd given me some warning," she said.

Her words made Hap feel like someone dropped a hundred-pound weight on his chest.

Not because he'd been rude.

It didn't appear she had makeup on, but she didn't need it.

But she did have a great outfit on, which meant she might be going out.

Maybe on a date.

It was not two in the afternoon, but maybe it was a late lunch date.

Or someone was coming over and this was Luci's way of being casual and at home, but amazing.

Fuck.

"You got plans?" he asked, his voice unsurprisingly tight.

"No."

Thank you, God.

"So, what's with the outfit?"

"I had the trousers altered while I was in New York. They arrived today. I was trying them on for fit."

That was a relief.

"Do you want to start or shall I?" she prompted.

She wanted this to get done.

The last time they spoke, he unintentionally gutted her, so he was not surprised.

Not to mention, he wanted to get this done too.

"Luce—"

She interrupted him again.

"I need more time." She lifted both hands then dropped them like she wished she hadn't made the gesture. "I know we must move on and I'm making more out of what happened than I should, but I still need more time, Hap."

Making more out of what happened than I should.

Why did he not like that?

He needed her to think that.

So why the hell did he not like it?

He started carefully. "What I failed to mention the last time we spoke was that it was a great kiss. But—"

"It was," she agreed on a sharp movement of her head. "It was a great kiss. It was a great *everything*. And I don't just mean your mouth and hands on me on my couch." She flung her hand out to indicate the couch behind him. "Before that, when we were with Sam and Kia, having fun. And after that, when they left, when it was just you and me doing shots and being stupid and having fun. I like spending time with you. You make me laugh. You treat me like a normal person, not some untouchable goddess or some breakable piece of glass. I have never felt more 'Just Luci' than I've felt that with you."

Him and Gordo.

"Babe—" he began.

"And I'll have that back, we'll get that back how you want it to be . . . just later."

"Kia's pregnant and—"

He ceased speaking when her face twisted in a way he hadn't seen, not ever.

Not even after they lost Gordo.

"I know," she stated flatly.

He took a step toward her, stopped, and whispered, "Babe. I know you didn't get there with Gordo, but—"

She lifted a hand up, palm out his way, and this time kept it up. "Pease, don't talk about Travis. That isn't about Travis. It isn't about what I lost with him."

She glanced to the side, drew in breath at the same time she pulled her fingers through her hair at the front, snatching it back, before she looked again to him.

The hair thing was a magnificent show.

Hap tried to ignore it.

"I'm over the moon for Sam and Kia. So happy for them. They'll make marvelous parents. They'll create beautiful babies. But it is not lost on me that I'm not getting any younger and I want children. That takes nothing away from Sam and Kia. It's just that a friend of mine assured me that one day, I will again be happy. This could be in the form of finding someone to love and making a family. Or it could be something quite different and I just find a way to happiness alone. However, I do not fancy finding happiness alone. This is not the statement of weakness many of womankind might judge it to be. I don't need a man in my life. I *want* one. And not just one so I can have children. I can do that without a man. I simply want a man to share my life with."

It stuck in his throat so he had to push out, "You'll find him."

"I thought I did."

Hap went still.

"But I did not," Luci kept at him.

"Luce, honey," he whispered.

"And now I have to . . . I have to . . ." she looked side to side, suddenly appearing like she had no idea where the fuck she was. "I have to . . ."

Her eyes again came to him and the lost expression on her face unraveled him completely.

"I don't know what I have to do, Hap," she said softly.

He couldn't have controlled his feet, though he didn't try.

He just moved. Got toe to toe with her, dipped his face to hers and framed it with both his hands.

"You'll figure it out, baby," he promised her.

She lifted her hands to his wrists, not to push him away, but to wrap her long, slender fingers around his wrists.

"I'm sorry I kissed you," she told him, her eyes turbulent, her words rough.

"I'm not, Luce, it was a good kiss."

"I messed us up."

"We're not messed up."

"I've changed us."

"We're not changed."

Her fingers tightened on him and her gaze grew laser focused. "I can't lose you."

"I'm right here."

"You are but you want to be anywhere but here."

He almost laughed.

There was nowhere on earth he'd rather be, in a way he knew it would last a lifetime, than standing right in Luciana Gordon's space with his hands on her, hers on him, and her face all he could see.

His chin dipped closer and he whispered, "I'll always want to spend time with you, honey."

Her attention dropped to his mouth and the look in her eyes changed again.

Shit.

Shit.

"Baby," he called.

Her gaze lifted.

"You should probably stop touching me," she warned.

But she did not step away. She did not take her fingers from his wrists.

She stayed right there, looking in his eyes, hers openly telling him what she wanted but thought she could not have.

And serious as shit, he wanted her to have everything she wanted.

So his chin dipped closer, he cocked his head so he wouldn't hit her with the bill of his cap, and he kissed her.

Shit.

Fuck.

Christ, she tasted good.

He broke the kiss and moved to pull away, his mouth still tasting her, his mind all about her, his dick reminding him of its presence, his will trying to find a way in there to get his shit tight and not fuck this up . . . again.

But she caught him with a hand cupping the back of his head and he froze, looking into her eyes, feeling her breath whisper across his lips, her fingers still at his wrist, holding tight like she simply refused to let go.

"You want me," she whispered.

He did.

Fuck him, he did.

So damned bad.

"Luce—"

"You want this."

"Luciana."

Her hand at his head slid down to curl tight around the back of his neck and she pushed closer, her eyes changing yet again.

Determined.

"Fuck your code, George Cunningham," she said in a voice that was part purr, part growl.

Then she was kissing him.

God dammit.

He tried to fight it. He did. He tried to latch onto anything that would give him the strength to pull away.

It was just that his tongue found its way into her mouth and the world dissolved and it was only her, their kiss, and suddenly he was totally all right with that.

He let go of her face to pull her into his arms so he could feel that long body pressed to his.

And he felt it because Luci pressed herself tight, burrowing in, like she wanted to meld with him, and through it, she kissed him back.

The kiss didn't end, even if they took short breaths, it went on forever, and Hap didn't know when the groping began, or who started it. He just knew eventually his hand was cupping her breast when her hand cupped his junk.

He growled into her mouth, nipped her lower lip and ended the kiss staring into her eyes and breathing hard.

She held his rigid cock through his jeans and her expression held a dare.

"Luci—"

She squeezed lightly then dragged the heel of her palm down his length.

He closed his eyes so he could experience that awesomeness, and only that awesomeness, when she gave him even more awesomeness because her tongue was in his mouth and she was rubbing determined at his dick.

Hap grasped her hair at the back and pulled her away, warning, "Only so much a man can take."

"I hope you're right," she returned, her voice now just a purr.

Yeah.

And a dare.

He scrubbed his thumb across her nipple over her shirt.

It was already hard, but it budded harder at his touch.

Fuck.

Nice.

She sighed, her lids lowered, and she bit her lip.

Holy Christ.

Goddamn beautiful.

Okay.

Fuck it.

He yanked his hips from her and her eyes shot wide.

"Hap—"

He caught her hand that had been at his cock, ordered, "No talking," then commenced dragging her across her great room toward the stairs like he was a brooding hero in a gothic novel.

Even when that entered his head, it didn't stop him.

He also didn't stop when he pulled her into her bedroom.

Jesus, more white.

But the room was the shit.

Best part, the bed sat on a squat, freestanding platform about four feet from and facing the floor to ceiling windows in a way that it would feel like you were hovering right over the ocean.

He did not figure they'd be paying any attention.

He stopped at the side of the bed and tugged her toward him.

Looking down at her as he slid his arms around her, he muttered, "We're gonna regret this."

He barely got out the word "this" when her finger was to his lips.

"Like you said, *caro*, no talking."

And then she kissed him again.

He took over the kiss, turned her so her back was to the bed, and leaned into her so they fell in, him on top.

Christ, he could be all about her mouth for years, fucking *decades*.

And then he got her shirt open and the cup of her bra tugged down (both sides) and he discovered he could be all about pulling her nipple into his mouth for centuries, listening to those noises she made while he did and trying hard not to grind his cock into her thigh.

And then he was pulling those ridiculous, and ridiculously sexy pants down her legs. The material slithered off the side, over the edge of the platform, and made a soft, expensive sound, like a sigh, when it hit the floor.

But Hap was too busy seeing Luci spread on her bed, her long, dark hair everywhere, her sweet little tits pushed up over her bra, a tiny pair of panties covering her sex.

He drank her in.

It was a mistake to give himself that. His inattention to where she was at meant he found himself on his back with Luci on her knees beside his hip, tugging at his belt.

"Baby," he murmured, his hand going to still hers, slow this down, give both of them a chance to catch a thought.

"No talking," she returned, slightly breathless.

He aimed differently and did an ab curl to lift his hand to her face. "Babe."

She yanked his jeans down his hips and he was momentarily distracted by the sweet relief of his rock-hard, aching cock slapping free and then he was totally *not* momentarily distracted, but instead completely lost when she swallowed all of him she could take.

He fell to his back and his fingers instantly slid into her hair as he groaned, "Fucking *fuck*, you're good with your mouth."

She was.

Best ever.

By a long shot.

She blew him and he lifted his head to watch and honest to God, he wanted to spend a millennium watching Luci with her hollowed out cheeks pulling deep at his dick, her gorgeous head bobbing, but he couldn't.

She let out a surprised cry when he pulled her off and yanked her up over his chest.

"Hap!"

"Panties off," he bit out. "Now."

Her eyes flared and she scrambled to do what she was told.

It was fucking cute.

He didn't take a minute to reflect on how cute it was because it was also shit hot and he had to get a condom on, like, *yesterday.*

He got his wallet out, retrieved the condom, tossed the wallet over the end of the bed and got up on his knees, not even bothering to take off his jeans.

When he was on his knees, he vaguely saw his cap was sitting on her bed at the bottom edge of her pillow.

It did not vaguely register he liked that. He liked the fact he hadn't even noticed she'd tugged it off and tossed it aside. He liked something of his, something he wore all the time, resting like it belonged there on something that was hers, somewhere she went all the time.

This, his aching dick and hearing Luci's movements spurred him further to make light work of the condom.

Once it was on, he twisted to her then caught her around the waist.

She cried out a different way when he hauled her through the air to him.

And yet again a different way when he lifted her up, she wrapped her legs around him, and he drove her down on his cock.

Her head fell back and her nails dug in at either side of his neck.

Hap gritted his teeth at the sight, the stab of her nails that rocketed right to his dick, but more at the feel of her tight and slick and hot, sheathing him.

She dug her heels in the backs of his thighs, using them as leverage to fuck him, and he let her have that moment and let himself have that moment of watching her do it, feeling it, before he dropped her to her back in the bed and drilled her.

"Yes," she breathed, now digging her heels in to tilt her hips to take more of him.

Jesus.

He went at her harder, moving in to kiss her while he took her, but her chin dipped down sharply, she caught his eyes and whimpered, "Hap, *luce mia*."

Holy shit.

"Baby, are you co—?"

He didn't get that out as she spasmed around him, tossing an arm out to clutch at the comforter over her head, her other hand holding tight to his neck, her head pressing back into the mattress, sweet noises panting between her lips.

Yeah, she was coming.

He hadn't even got near her clit.

He gave her that, and it looked really freaking good, just with his dick.

Shit, he felt like he'd conquered a nation and then took her there to cut the ribbon to her new world.

And then it overwhelmed him and Hap was all about burying himself in her, his cock, his face in her neck, his grunts blasting her skin as he exploded, everything went black, all he could smell was Luci, all he could feel was her pussy clutching him tight.

He came down, shifting so his forehead was at her shoulder and he was certain he was taking weight in a forearm, but otherwise he didn't move.

He was inside Luci.

On top of her, on her bed, in her room, planted to the root inside Luciana after having the quickest orgasm he'd had since he was about seventeen, this after having the best sex he'd had since . . . ever.

Okay, right.

Coming here had not been his most sterling idea.

Fuck.

"Hap," she called.

He lifted his head and looked down at her.

She looked like she'd just come, done it hard, and was still feeling the goodness of that.

But still, she was terrified.

And again, Hap was unraveled.

So that was when he put his hand to her face and swept the pad of his thumb over her cheekbone before he drew circles with it at her temple.

"We'll figure it out," his mouth said.

Yup.

Coming here had been freaking stupid.

"We will?"

Hope had lit her expression, her words, the room around them.

Damn.

"Yeah, honey. We will," he murmured.

She smiled right into his face, bright and beautiful, and clutched him to her with all four limbs.

Pure joy.

So damned sweet.

Shit.

FOUR

Just to See Her Smile

Luci

"BABE."

Luci pressed her forehead into the bed, her fingers curled into the comforter at the sides of her head, her body rocking with Hap's thrusts, her mind centered on his cock filling her and retreating again and again and again, the sounds of their flesh connecting, the feel of his fingers digging deep into the swells of her behind.

No.

Oh no.

No, no, no.

George "Hap" Cunningham did not treat her like an untouchable goddess or breakable glass.

He fucked like an animal.

She loved it.

Loved it.

A squeeze of her cheek and a growled, "*Babe.*"

She tossed her head back and caught his eyes in their reflection in the glass at the foot of the bed, where they we facing, Luci on her knees bent chest to the bed, getting fucked, Hap on his knees behind her, fucking her.

Dio.

Fabulous.

"Watch," he ordered on a grunt.

It hit her she could see it all, and just how magnificent they were, right before the tingles shot up the insides of her thighs.

"*Bello,*" she breathed.

"Beautiful, do not come," he ground out.

Too late.

Her head arched back at an impossible angle so she had to come up to her hands in the bed and arch her back.

Suddenly she was fully up, just on her knees, Hap's arms around her, driving her down as he pounded up.

And she kept coming.

"You want me at your clit?" His words were coarse in her ear.

Gorgeous.

"N-no," she pushed out, trembling and still climaxing.

"Shit, you're cute," he grunted, taking her, *fucking her*, then gliding a hand over her shoulder, up the side of her neck, into the back of her hair.

He grasped it, shoved her forward at an arch away from his body, but still upright, holding her steady with his arm wrapped around her shoulder, his other one wrapped around her chest, fingers cupping her breast, and he grunted his climax while he pounded her through it.

And as he did, another wave hit her, leaving her pulsing around his driving cock and whispering out faint whimpers.

After a while, Hap bent forward, letting her rest her upper body to the bed, then he straightened and started stroking inside her gently as he ran his fingers over her bottom.

"Jesus, this ass," he murmured.

She smiled into the bed.

He caught at both of her hips, slid in and stayed put.

"You okay?"

She whipped her head around, cheek to the bed, but eyes aimed to him.

"I'm cute?"

"You aren't right now," he returned. "You're hot as fuck right now. Sadly, I can't do anything about that since you've very recently drained me dry."

She smiled at him.

"And she gets even hotter," he muttered, pulling out, using his hands at her hips to turn her to her back and then he landed on top of her.

The minute he caught her gaze, she announced, "We've been fucking for hours, Hap."

His lips twitched. "Yeah, babe. I know. I was there."

"As an Italian woman, there is no escape, it's coded in my DNA. I must get fed. But even more, I must feed you."

He did not look happy about the idea of leaving her bed.

And that made her happy.

"I'll make an antipasto tray, bring it up," she offered quietly.

"Luce, we got a problem."

Oh no.

No, no, no.

No problems.

The world did not exist. It was this bed and only her kitchen as she had to go to it to get food.

And then it would again only be this bed.

They could let the world in again.

Just . . . later.

To communicate this, Luci grabbed his head on either side and stated, "I don't want to hear of any problems."

"This was my last condom."

"*Dio mio*, we have a problem," she mumbled.

Hap burst out laughing.

Luci stilled and watched.

Hap was handsome. That muscle-packed body (even better without clothes, she knew that, she'd seen him in swim trunks, however she'd never seen his cock, and *that* was *delightful*). His merry brown eyes. His military-cut brown hair, short on the sides, longer on the top.

But laughing . . .

No, when Luci *made* him laugh.

He was beautiful.

Those eyes, merry and twinkling down at her when he quit laughing, their lashes blunt and profuse, were his best feature. And that said a great deal since all the rest were fabulous.

"How about this?" he started. "I hit the store, you make up some food. I can grab anything you need while I'm out. We'll reconnect here, eat, fuck, and then sleep until next week because I'm not twenty-two anymore, and you're killin' me."

"This is a plan," she agreed.

"You got beer?" he asked.

She was instantly insulted and didn't hide it.

He started chuckling. "Stupid question, you're Luce."

"I am," she retorted haughtily.

He bent and touched his mouth to hers before he drew away and said softly, "Get rid of this condom, get dressed, go out, back soon's I can."

"Deal," she whispered.

His gaze changed and when his mouth came back to hers, it was not a touch.

The other time had not been a fluke, the experience magnified by a haze of alcohol.

It was fact.

Hap was a great kisser.

He ended the kiss (sadly), rolled off but flipped her disheveled comforter over her and snatched up his jeans from the floor before he took his third walk to her bathroom.

She rolled to her side to watch him go and curled into herself instead of stretching like a cat.

Yes, he was attracted to her.

Yes, he wanted her.

Yes, he wanted *this*, fucking and bantering and eating, and fucking more.

And sleeping.

Sleeping until next week.

She pulled the comforter over her mouth so he wouldn't see her pleased smile if he walked back in.

She'd been able to extinguish it by the time Hap returned wearing nothing but jeans, his muscles bulging and shifting as he walked.

And watching him, Luci remembered when she first saw him that she thought he was *too* muscular. *Too* developed. *Too* big in that way.

She had been very wrong.

He found his T-shirt and tugged it on in that masculine way very masculine men had that was akin to wrangling the shirt to cover their bodies, uncaring how they stretched it and tugged it while they did so.

Luci enjoyed that show as well.

Shirt on, Hap sat on the bed to pull on his running shoes.

"You need anything else?" he asked.

"No, I went shopping this morning, so I'm fine."

He turned his head her way, still yanking on a shoe.

Yes.

So handsome.

Dio, those eyes.

"You got ice cream?"

Hmm.

"No," she answered.

"Then we are far from fine," he muttered, finished with his shoes, bent deep and kissed her again. He pulled an inch away and carried on muttering. "I'll stock you up. Do it quick. Be back soon."

"Okay, *caro*."

He gave her a wink.

She memorized it.

Then he pushed up off the bed but rounded it and nabbed his wallet then his baseball cap, shoving the former into his pocket and pulling the latter on as he sauntered out.

She loved the cap.

But she watched his ass as he walked away.

He had an amazing ass. She'd always thought that.

When she lost sight of him, Luci rolled to her back and stared at the ceiling before she rolled to her other side and bent her head back so she could stare through the reflection of the room in the windows to the dark and shadowy sea.

She had no idea what was going on.

She was not going to question it.

Hap said they'd figure it out.

And she believed him.

But she knew he would not take it there, take it there *again*, and then *again*, then leave to get more prophylactics and "stock her up," intending to come back and make love to her again and sleep together if he didn't intend to be with her to figure it out.

Make love.

Hap didn't do that, as such.

He still did.

It was unfair but natural to compare. She had not had anyone since Travis. And after she'd had Travis, the ones before no longer mattered.

So she let herself do that. Compare.

This once.

Travis made love to her. He never treated her like an untouchable goddess, but she was his wife, his woman. He was the kind of man who was gentle with women, all of them, including her.

Things between them sexually could get intense. Travis could definitely be creative. He had a high libido, as did she, and their sex life had been healthy and tremendously satisfying the length of their relationship.

But he had never dug his fingers in her ass while he took her pussy like he owned it, all the while ordering her to watch.

Eyes still on the sea, Luci finally stretched like a cat, feeling her lips curl up in a smile even she knew was sultry.

She should have known Hap would be like that. He took rough around the edges to extremes. She should have known he'd even fuck rough, dragging her around, lifting her through the air, positioning her where he wanted her, fucking her hard, knowing she could not only take it but want it, then giving her more.

The bigger surprise was how very much she enjoyed it. She didn't have to worry about pleasing him, if what she was doing was exciting him.

She didn't have to with Travis either. From the beginning, they'd been in sync, falling into each other and pleasuring each other's bodies like they were born to do it.

With Hap, he was in control. He dominated the bed. Even when she took his cock with her mouth, he shoved his hand into her hair like he was guiding her play.

And when he was done having his cock sucked, he just was and made that so.

She still knew she did it for him. The looks on his face she'd catch. The growls. When his touch would turn reverent, or possessive.

She smiled again, stretched this time to get any kinks out, then rolled out of the bed. She pulled on her panties, untied the tails of her top and shrugged it on, buttoning only the two buttons at her breasts.

She then walked downstairs.

As she made it to her kitchen, Luci thought about Sam (who would be angry about Hap and Luci) and Kia (who would not).

"They are not here. They do not get a say. Either way. This is me, my life, Hap, his life, and that is all," she declared as she opened her refrigerator.

And with that she put them out of her mind.

She was pulling out meats and cheeses she got at the deli that morning when she had the insane urge to call Pearl and let her know what had just happened.

She'd be gleeful and gleeful was much better than worried about her friend states away.

Hap would have to go back to Bragg and his work tomorrow (hopefully tomorrow night).

They would have talked by then (probably), started to figure it out.

Made a plan.

And made more plans (she hoped) to be together.

So, she could call Pearl with a much fuller report on Monday.

She had Andrea Bocelli playing low, the windows folded partially back so she could hear the sea, and she had made up a tray of olives, bocconcini, soppressata, prosciutto, chunks of provolone and pepperoncini when Hap returned.

He had to hit the doorbell. Her door automatically locked unless she hit the button to keep the latch open.

She went there, making her way thinking she needed to give him a key. She opened the door and froze when she saw he had six plastic bags of groceries dangling from his fingers, three on each side.

"I should have given you my market bags," she declared.

"Babe, step aside," he ordered.

She did.

He shouldered in and only then did she notice how full the bags were.

Had he been gone that long to do that much shopping?

"I told you I stocked up, *caro*," she called after him, closing the door and hearing the latch click.

"Apparently, I get hungry after a fuck-a-thon," he replied, lifting the bags and dumping them with loud thuds on her island.

Luci had a feeling he already knew this, but he was too much of a gentleman (of his sort) to share that.

She smiled at his quip as she walked his way but tipped her head to the side when she saw him looking around like she'd moved the furniture in his absence and this confused him.

His gaze finally came to her.

"Luce, it goes without saying, I'm a sure thing."

She stopped walking to him and stood still, threw her head back and burst out laughing, feeling the absolute fullness of it.

When her laughter was dying, she recommenced her trek to the island where Hap was still pulling out food but doing it now with his lips curved into a smile.

She studied the food coming out (chips, more chips, jars of dip, tubs of dip, a bag of peanut butter M&Ms, a bag of caramel M&Ms, a bag of peanut M&Ms, ice cream (rocky road), and then more chips).

Hap interrupted her perusal of the rather alarming junk food pile with, "Opera sucks."

She looked to him.

"Bocelli has the voice of an *angelo*," she retorted.

"Opera sucks," Hap repeated.

She grinned at him and called out, "Alexa, play Lada Gaga."

"Okay," Alexa's metallic voice said.

"Jesus, fuck, no," Hap stated as Lady Gaga started. "You got Alexa?"

"I have three Alexas."

He studied her then called, "Alexa, play Buckcherry."

"Okay," Alexa singsonged, and "Gluttony" came on.

"Hap, that's not relaxing," she complained.

He grinned wolfishly at her. "Baby, if you need more relaxation after coming for me for a full five minutes that last go, I'll fuel up and do it the right way."

She gave him a look that was mock annoyed before calling, "Alexa, play Tom Petty."

"Okay."

And "Saving Grace" came on.

"She can compromise," Hap muttered.

"Hap, *luce mio*, do you eat like this always?" Luci asked.

"Yup," Hap answered, loading up his arms with bags of chips before turning to her large cupboard where he knew she kept her chips, among other things.

There wouldn't be enough room in there. She had chips (not that many, but she had them). She also cooked, so she had a stocked larder.

She didn't tell him that.

Instead she asked, "How do you have that body and eat like this?"

"I have this body *so* I can eat like this," Hap explained, shoving chip bags in, forcing the space to accommodate his needs.

"You're going to crush the chips," she warned.

He turned from the cupboard, stating, "Best part. Tipping the bag to your mouth and eating all the crushed bits."

She'd never done that because she'd never blithely crushed chips.

But it was hard to argue. Chips were delicious, full ones, broken ones, so it probably went without saying bits tasted just as good.

She grabbed the ice cream and headed to the freezer.

"Babe," he called.

God, she loved that word aimed at her coming from his mouth after she'd spent a lot of time with him when they were both naked.

He'd always called her babe.

He called all women "babe."

Now, it was different.

"Yes?" she replied, straightening and kicking the freezer drawer closed with her foot.

She stopped dead when she caught the serious look on his face.

"We'll eat. We'll fuck. We'll sleep. But tomorrow, honey, we'll be talking."

"Of course," she whispered, studying his face hard, trying to figure out how he had been all happy-go-lucky Hap and now he was so very serious. "It wasn't a mistake," she blurted.

"No. It was not."

He said that firmly, enunciating each word clearly.

She felt her shoulders relax.

"What we did months ago wasn't a mistake. I thought it was then, I was wrong. But I'll never think this is a mistake. Not ever, baby," he said and then finished confusingly, "And I hope you never think it is either."

"I won't, Hap," she whispered. "Not ever. *Not ever*. Of course I won't." She shook her head. "Not ever."

He didn't say anything, but the muscle jumping up his cheek did.

Dio.

What was this?

"I'm glad, Luce," he finally spoke. "But we gotta get shit straight."

Luci lifted her chin. "I like shit straight."

He kept looking at her like he was trying to read her when she wasn't hiding anything so she just held his gaze.

Then he shook his head once, his lips twitched and he opened a bag of sour cream and chive chips and dumped half its contents on top of her perfectly constructed antipasto platter.

She did not say a word.

She didn't care.

She liked sour cream and chive chips.

She was hungry.

So she got Hap a beer, pulled out a bottle of wine, handed it to him and then went to open the beer.

She did the difficult work of popping the cap and then Hap was taken care of.

He did the work of pulling the cork and pouring the wine into a glass she slid in front of him and Luci was taken care of.

Hap took his beer and the tray out to the deck.

Luci took her wine and grabbed a throw blanket and followed him.

They sat on her double-wide lounge, under the blanket, murmuring to each other about nothing, just catching up on what had happened in the time they'd lost, all while they munched.

They decimated the tray. Hap had to get up to refill her wine once through it, and after it, he fucked her on her lounger under the throw, again while he was still almost fully clothed, but he demanded Luci be naked under him.

It was *delectable*.

He carried her to bed.

He then left her there as he went down to close the windows.

He was gone awhile so she suspected he tidied a bit too (Hap did that, especially putting food away, she'd noticed he was a stickler about food, though they'd left none of that, he still was known to at least help carry dishes into the kitchen).

She was near sleep, and fighting it, when he crawled into bed beside her.

Oh, but that simple act felt good.

When he settled at her side on his back, she wrapped him up tight.

And that felt better.

He sighed.

"Today, I am happy," she whispered into his skin.

He squeezed her with the arm he had around her.

"Thank you," she finished.

He bent his neck to kiss the top of her head.

Luci smiled yet again.

Then she fell asleep.

Hap

HOLDING LUCI TO HIM, HAP stared at the top of the windows, seeing nothing but dark sky beyond.

He was royally screwed.

But that was okay.

Because she was not.

She wanted it, he could give her this. He did give her this. And he'd continue to give her this.

Then, one day, when some good-looking guy who made more money than him or was more interesting than him or who didn't give a shit she played opera came along, Hap would be cool.

He wouldn't be able to hide the pain, but he'd mask the depths of it, and he wouldn't make it hard for her to scrape him off.

And he'd find a way to keep it cool and still be in her life, a part of the crew.

He was that guy from that Tim McGraw song.

And he was okay with that.

He was okay with anything.

Just to see her smile.

FIVE

He Would Call

Luci

THE NEXT MORNING, WITH HER espresso held up in front of her, Luci stood leaning her side into the kitchen island, staring out the windows at the sea.

Hap was still in bed, and since he'd done most of the work the day before, when Luci woke, she'd given herself time to enjoy lying beside him tangled up in his warmth before she left him to sleep.

She'd carefully extricated herself, got out of bed, went to wash her face, brush her teeth, put on a light moisturizer, pull a brush through her hair, don a blush satin nightie with delicate scallops of ivory lace at bodice and hem (her favorite) and shrug on her cream cashmere cable-knit robe.

She then went downstairs to confirm what she knew was true—she had the ingredients for Nutella pancakes and a packet of bacon.

Once she confirmed this, she wrapped her arms around her middle and hugged herself with joy that she had someone to make breakfast for.

And that someone was Hap.

Only then did she make herself an espresso.

Caffeine acquired, she commenced making the pancake batter.

That done, she made her second espresso.

Which brought her right there, with Hap sleeping in her bed upstairs, the ocean waves pounding their never-ending beat against the sand, everything all right with the world for the first time in a very long time.

Her lips were curved up as she lifted her espresso and took a sip.

She was lowering the cup when she caught movement out of the sides of her eyes.

She looked that way to see Hap, sleepy-eyed, wearing nothing but his jeans and a grumpy expression, lumbering down the stairs.

Yes.

Everything was all right with the world.

He was not a morning person. She already knew this. But usually it was because he'd over-imbibed the night before.

Luci would discover in short order why he looked grumpy that morning when he came right to her, took her cup out of her hand, put it on the island and yanked her into his arms.

"Why didn't you wake me?" he demanded, his voice slightly hoarse and still groggy.

"You did all the work yesterday," she reminded him. "I thought you'd want some sleep."

"You gettin' out of bed means we couldn't fuck before we both got out of bed."

She melted into him, placing her hands on his warm chest.

"Does that mean you didn't want sleep?" she asked.

"Do you. If I needed it, crash again after," he explained shortly, and bluntly. His eyes strayed to the countertop before they came back to her. "You could get up, make pancake batter, and I'd haul my ass downstairs when I got enough shuteye."

She was sorry she hadn't gone that route.

"I'll remember that for next time," she told him softly.

He grunted unintelligibly.

She took that and being in his arms as confirmation there'd be a next time.

And yes.

All was right in the world.

"Do you want espresso?" she queried.

"Do you have regular coffee?" he queried in return.

She gave him a look.

"Does that mean yes?" he prompted.

"I'm Italian. We invented *caffè*."

His lips quirked as he murmured, "Is that true?"

She had no idea.

But her people did it better than anyone in the world, so she felt it was safe at least to say they invented *excellent* coffee.

She decided not to respond.

Hap's lip quirk turned into a full-blown smile right before he bent to her and kissed her nose.

Luci froze.

Hap didn't feel it. He just gave her a squeeze before he let her go and sauntered to the coffee maker (a dual one she'd imported from Italy, rewired for American currents, both of which cost her a fortune, not to mention the appliance, which was far from inexpensive).

But Luci wasn't thinking about her fabulous coffee maker.

She was thinking that she would have never considered rough and ready Hap Cunningham to be the kind of man who kissed a woman's nose.

She'd known him years. It was not like he hadn't had women around their crew.

It was just that it was rare and they never lasted long.

Travis had teased him about this, but only once.

"If they get to meet you, they gotta earn it," had been Hap's firm and somewhat sharp reply that had shut Travis's teasing right down.

At first, Luci had been offended for all womankind at his words.

But at the look on his face, she realized what he meant from what he said wasn't what she thought.

Instead, it was the fact that he didn't bring women around them who did not mean something to Hap. If he didn't think that there might be a future. As you would not introduce someone to your mother and father or close family who you did not feel was important, who you did not want them to know and perhaps like, and perhaps start to make a part of the family, unless you thought they were special. Unless you thought they had staying power. And you definitely didn't introduce someone who had not proved to you they were special so as not to foist someone on the people you cared about who was not worthy.

In realizing this, at the time, those years ago, she'd wondered why the few who had proven themselves special to Hap had not gone the distance.

She'd then not thought about it, only wishing eventually he'd find his someone.

Now, that curiosity came back with a punch.

But those few women she'd seen him with, he'd shown affection, for certain, he hadn't shied away from it.

However, he'd never kissed any of them on the nose, not that Luci had seen.

It was an exquisite feeling. Like a surprise treasured gift. A man handing you a glorious diamond bracelet on any old day . . . just because.

She wanted to touch her nose. Seal the trace of his lips there so she could feel it forever.

Instead, she picked up her espresso and pivoted to face him.

"Do you need help with that?" she asked.

He turned from his stance in front of her coffee maker, holding the filter in his hand.

"Water goes in here." He stabbed his finger toward where the water went on the coffee maker. "Coffee goes in here." He snapped the filter up. "Hit that button and then magic."

"Yes," she murmured, lifting her cup to her lips to take a sip, but she watched him as she did so.

He pulled the tin of Illy to him and yanked it open with great force.

Hap would be the bull in any china shop.

Luci found it fascinating.

And endearing.

He'd shoved the filter in and flipped the switch when he turned to her. "Babe, you gonna feed me or stand there staring at my ass?"

She chuckled softly but denied, "I wasn't staring at your ass."

Well, not the entire time.

"Question still stands," he returned.

Hap was hungry.

Luci made a move.

She was dropping a dollop of Nutella in the center of some batter on her griddle when Hap called, "Luce."

She turned to see him sitting at one of the stools opposite her, across the island.

He had his long, thick, blunt fingers wrapped around a white mug resting on the counter.

"Our talk," he said gently.

She drew in breath, nodded and turned back to the stove, setting the Nutella aside and pouring more batter over the pancakes before she went to the frying bacon.

He didn't speak while she did this so she told the bacon, "You can start while I cook, *caro*, if you like."

She said that, but she didn't want him to start.

She didn't want anything to puncture this bubble of bliss they had. He'd talk of the outside world. Of work (and him going back to Bragg, which was not far away, say, like Australia, but it wasn't right down the street either). Of Sam and Kia. Of things not having to do with the sun shining and the ocean beating into the beach and the pancake batter bubbling and him at her island drinking coffee and his scent on her sheets upstairs.

But they must.

They had a future, she hoped.

She was looking forward to her future with some relish for the first time in a very long time.

They had to get on with it.

"Normally, probably for both of us, we'd give this time, get our feet wet, feel it out, before we brought anyone into it," he began.

She turned from the bacon, only halfway, but her head moved fully to look at him.

He had his focus fully on her in return.

"Go on," she urged.

"Baby, I gotta tell Sam."

She pressed her lips together.

The Code.

She returned to the bacon.

"Luce," he called.

"Do what you must," she told the bacon.

"Luciana, honey, look at me."

She pulled in another breath and did as he asked.

"We give this a couple of weeks, a month, two, then tell Sam, he'll go apeshit."

He was right.

"I know," she replied, and gave the pancakes her attention by flipping them.

"So he's gotta know. Next weekend. I'll tell him."

She again turned to Hap. "Next weekend?"

"Yeah. I'll come back out, let him know we gotta have a chat, we'll chat." He looked down at his coffee and started mumbling to say, "Maybe at Skippy's."

"I'll be with you."

His gaze lifted to her and he shook his head. "No, Luci."

"Yes, Hap."

"That isn't a good idea."

"For you? For me? Or for Sam?" she queried.

"For Sam," he answered.

"And why is Sam the priority in this scenario?" she inquired.

Hap shut his mouth.

Luci continued speaking.

"Kia will be there, as will I. We'll give him his *home turf*, as you Americans put it. You can take him out on the deck. Kia and I can stay inside. That way you'll have some privacy. But I want reinforcements, in the form of Kia, and I want to be there to offer support . . . for you."

He tipped his head to the side. "You gonna budge on that at all?"

"No."

His eyes danced with humor and he lifted his mug to take a sip.

"You have to go back today, yes?" she asked.

He nodded his head, lowering the mug. "Yeah."

"I'd like to see you this week, have more time to, as you say, get our feet wet."

She wanted to hold her breath when she said that but she didn't want him to notice her holding her breath, so she didn't.

"Already figured that out," he declared. "I'll see if I can get off a little early on Wednesday, come get you, bring you back. We'll have dinner along the way. If you can get away from the shop, you stay a couple of days, we'll come back Friday night or Saturday morning. But I'll have to work, babe. So bring shit to keep you occupied while I'm at the base."

She could not be happier he wanted her at his home, and even happier it wasn't just a night to show her the place, but instead a couple of days.

And she could definitely get away from her shop. She had other people running it, so she wasn't tied down to it. She went in often when she was in town, but they did all the work, so she was free to live her life.

Regardless of all that, she blinked at him. "That's hours of driving for you."

"I do it nearly every weekend," he reminded her.

"I can drive to Bragg, Hap."

"Yeah, then we'd have two cars when we come back, and I'd be following your ass rather than it bein' in the passenger seat of my truck."

He had a point.

"I like drivin'," he went on.

Good to know since he did so much of it and was offering to do more.

"And you can't Uber to Bragg," he finished.

"I can hire a driver," she told him.

"A what?" he asked.

"A driver. Like a limo, though I won't hire a limo, just a town car or something like that."

"To drive you to my suburban bachelor pad that I'm gonna have to spend tomorrow and Tuesday nights cleaning so it won't have you demanding I take you to a hotel?"

She smiled at him.

He studied her with curiosity, but there was something hidden in his gaze before he asked, "You can spend money on just about anything, can't you?"

Cautiously, due to whatever he was hiding, she replied, "It's just a driver. Sometimes, if I'm going to be gone for a while, I hire them to take me to the airport." When he said nothing, she added, "It's less expensive than parking my car there for weeks."

"Right," he muttered.

"It isn't any trouble, *bello*," she told him quietly.

"Probably should check the pancakes, Luci," he suggested.

He was right. So she did.

Though she couldn't help but think he was trying to take her attention away from him.

The bacon was ready to go to the plate she'd readied with paper towel on it. Therefore, she did that before she scooped the pancakes onto two other plates she'd gotten down. She added bacon and took them to the island to find Hap up, getting cutlery. He'd already got out the butter and syrup.

They settled in and Luci picked up her fork.

"Just let me come get you, yeah?"

His soft words made her turn her head Hap's way.

"If that's what you want, Hap, then of course," she agreed.

He grabbed her at the back of her neck, pulled her in and touched his mouth to hers before letting go and reaching out to slide the butter her way.

She felt odd about their exchange.

She did not feel odd about Hap wishing her to use the butter first.

And she definitely did not feel odd about how he expressed his gratitude when he got his way.

When she had her pancakes ready, Hap ordered, "Eat fast, Luce. You cheated me outta an orgasm this morning. I'm feeling payback."

Luci smiled at her pancakes.

She never ate fast. Food was there to savor.

That morning she set a personal record with how quickly she consumed her pancakes and bacon.

"I NEED YOU TO EXPLAIN something."

It was late afternoon. They'd spent most of the day in bed.

There'd been lovemaking. There'd been napping. There'd been kissing and caressing. There'd been whispered conversations. And they'd gone down to make sandwiches and retrieve chips and dips, the detritus of this on the floor beside her bed.

But mostly, Hap seemed content to spoon her across the bottom of her bed, under the comforter, their heads on her pillows he'd bunched there, holding her to him and watching the sea.

Another lovely realization about Hap. He not only gave sweet kisses on the nose, he was content just to hold her and stare at the ocean.

She was relaxed. Feeling more tranquil than she had in years.

It seemed Hap was in the same state.

So she didn't want to do what she was going to do next.

But she felt she must. It was the only thing weighing on her mind. Even Sam and what was sure to be his volatile, negative reaction towards Hap being with her didn't intrude.

This did.

Hap's arm resting along her waist curled in. "What?"

She turned to her belly and looked at him. It pleased her greatly after she did that he fell to his back so she could move into him, chest to chest, eye to eye, her hand curling around the side of his neck.

"Your aversion to me getting a driver," she stated.

That hidden look came into his eyes.

Luci stroked the underside of his jaw with her thumb. "I just want to understand."

He shifted his gaze to the ceiling and said nothing.

She was about to prompt him gently when his gaze came back to hers.

"You gotta know. It's actually a shock you don't know. Unless . . ."

He didn't finish his thought, so Luci asked, "Unless what?"

"Do you know how I grew up?"

Oh no.

That thing wasn't hidden in his eyes any longer.

It was locked there.

"Hap," she whispered, but said no more.

"I don't know what that means. Do you, or don't you?"

There were several things wrong with this for the both of them.

The first was what he was asking without simply asking it.

Had Travis told her about him?

The answer was no. Travis told her (almost) everything. Things about his brothers those brothers would wish to stay hidden?

He would never do that.

The second was that there was something to know about how Hap grew up, something he'd lock away, hide.

Which meant it was something bad.

And last, he did not feel comfortable with mentioning Travis, which had its own special list of problems.

"No, I don't know," she answered.

She wasn't resting on him long, considering at her words he pushed up farther to get his shoulders, not his head, on the pillows, taking her with him. This accomplished, he promptly shifted her to her back, partially rolling into her on his side.

In this position, he loomed over her.

But then he curled his arm around her waist and yanked her into his body.

And in this position, he was partially trapping her.

Dio.

It wasn't bad.

It was very bad.

Luci wrapped her fingers around his throat and slid them down to rest her palm on his collarbone.

"It does not make me feel happy that you experienced the need to trap me before you share about your childhood," she noted carefully.

"It wasn't a good one," he stated bluntly.

"I gathered that," she murmured.

"I grew up on a farm in Iowa," he shared.

"All right," she replied when he said nothing further.

"It was my grandfather's farm. Lived there with Gram and Gramps due to the fact my dad was in prison."

She felt her eyes grow wide.

"And my mom was a loser."

Oh no.

"Dad got out, got me, held up another liquor store about three months into his probation, got caught, went back in. I went back to my grandparents. I was six. This happened one more time, when I was eleven, though he managed to go for nearly five months before he knocked over a convenience store, and after that I stayed on the farm."

Luci curled into him and once there, pressed tight, sliding her arm along his until she had it around him, holding him like he was holding her.

Only after she'd done that did she see the expression on his face.

Disbelief.

Undiluted.

"*Caro*?" she called.

"A lot of reactions I'd expect from the different reactions I'd get when I'd share those nuggets, Luce. Not any of them has been someone pushin' close and holdin' on."

She was upset for him.

She was also insulted.

"You thought I'd pull away?" she queried.

"Babe, my father is a felon."

"And you are a soldier."

"What's your father do?" he asked abruptly.

"He does many things. He's an entrepreneur."

"Right," Hap muttered.

"And what does that matter?" she asked sharply. "You'd expect me to pull away because your father is a felon, I should expect you to pull away because mine is a successful businessman?"

"Luci, you're a fuckin' supermodel."

"*Former* supermodel."

"Like they call a former president, 'president' after he earns that title, same goes for a supermodel. You never quit bein' that."

It was rather funny how he put that.

Luci didn't laugh.

"Your point?" she pushed.

"You grew up with money. You got your own money."

"And?"

"And the house you'll see on Wednesday looks nothing like this one. Or Sam and Kia's."

"Yes, Travis was still enlisted when we met and married and we owned a home in Fayetteville that was not like this one either."

"Yeah, I went to that home, babe. And that didn't look anything like my place either."

She pushed up, having to press into him to do it, and got on her forearm to look him in the eye in order to share, "I'm still not seeing the point."

"There is no way, in fuck, when I got a workin' vehicle, I'd spend money on a fuckin' driver."

He was losing patience.

So was she.

"That's understandable, but *you* weren't going to," she retorted.

"Yeah, I know," he shot back. "You were gonna dump a few hundred on a ride like it was nothing, like you probably dumped a couple hundred on that nightie you had on this morning. I'm not complain', baby. That nightie is fuckin' sweet. But *no one* spends hundreds of dollars on a nightie."

"I do," she snapped.

"Right," he bit out.

"So you're telling me you have not progressed, like quite a bit of the rest of the world, to being capable of dealing with a woman who's successful in her career, and financially?"

"I'm telling you my dad was an asshole, my mom was a flake. I grew up on a farm with my grandparents in the time when small farms were being eaten up by big outfits or foreclosed on by banks. So we had nothin' but pride in our land, which eventually was lost. A three-generation legacy owned by a bank for about two weeks before they auctioned it off to a corporate entity who 'dozed the house my great-great-grandfather built so they could plant more corn."

Dio mio.

What a tragedy.

"Hap," she whispered.

"We turned the lights off when we left a room," he carried on. "We slept under three / four blankets because the furnace was cranked down to about fifty, because we couldn't afford to heat the house when we weren't conscious in it. We ate leftovers until they were all gone. Since Gramps would lose his mind if a banana got overripe, we had banana bread all the time because I didn't like bananas. Gram never gave up on tryin' to get me to eat 'em, but I loved banana bread and no way in fuck Gram would waste an overripe banana by just throwing it in the trash."

And Hap's attention to meticulously putting away food was explained.

"What did you do when you lost your farm?" she asked quietly.

"Gramps got a job haulin' around feed and seed at the feedstore. He was sixty-two. Gram got a job as a teacher's assistant. I made it my job to drink, carouse, give them shit, cause them grief, and generally make them live in fear they raised one son to be good for nothin', then they raised *his* son to be the same. We left a four-bedroom farmhouse to live in a two-bedroom apartment. It felt tiny. Because it *was* tiny."

"Oh, *bello*," she whispered.

"I enlisted, told them I did, Gram dissolved into tears. Cried for hours. She thought I'd land in prison like my dad. It wasn't a surprise. I'd planted those seeds. Gramps, he grabbed my shoulder and held so tight, I checked later. It made marks. Then he snatched me by the head and slammed our foreheads together and just stood there with me, breathing, for what felt like years. That was his way to share his relief I might not turn out to be a total asshole."

"You're not that young, angry man with an absent mother and father watching your grandparents struggle anymore, Hap. They're surely proud of you now."

"I know that," he bit out. "Though they were both dead before I made Private First Class."

So much sadness.

So much loss.

So young.

Oh Hap.

Luci again pressed close.

Hap kept talking.

"Dad's still alive. So's Ma. Until about five years ago, when I finally got my point across I was not down with the fact that they fucked away my childhood but felt entitled to hit me up for money or a place to stay, or I'll repeat *money* when they thought I had it to give."

"Did you . . . give them that?" she asked hesitantly.

"Fuck no," he clipped. "Didn't stop them from askin', which meant I felt like a dick I couldn't be the bigger man, take care of my folks, even if they didn't bother takin' care of me."

Well.

No.

"You should not feel badly because you refused to help them, Hap."

"Yeah, you find it easy to say no to your old man?"

"My father loved me. He nurtured me. He was proud of me, showed it and told me. And I'll admit, he even spoiled me. So yes, I assume I would have trouble saying no to him. The thing is, *he doesn't ask*. Not only because he doesn't need to, but *I'm his child*. He simply would not. Ever. Not *ever*. You don't do that to your children. Unless you were in the direst of straights that were beyond your control. You take care of your children until you die."

She stopped speaking and Hap just stared at her.

So she started speaking again.

"And I'm *unspeakably* offended that you'd think *I* would think less of you because of whatever decisions your father made, or your mother, or things you did as a young man. Or the fact you had a time when you didn't have money and lost everything, so you value it, and I must have a mind to that. That's all you had to say, and I would have a mind to it. As I hope you will have a mind to the fact I like to shop. I like nice things. I have the means to get them. I'll even desire to get some of them for you. But I'll do that in a way that does not make you uncomfortable, if you return that favor by not making me feel uncomfortable I have those means."

He seemed to be calmer, and was definitely holding her tighter, but there was something . . . *off* that she didn't understand when he asked, "This works with us, what's your dad gonna think when he meets me?"

Luci was not calmer when she asked back, "What do you think he thought of Travis?"

"Gordo didn't have a father who was a felon."

She had entirely no control over her voice raising, and if she had, she wouldn't have used it, when she asked, "So now you're insulting *my father*, assuming he'll judge you by *your father's* misdeeds?"

He rolled into her, trapping her full body this time.

"Baby, calm down," he whispered.

"*You just insulted my father!*" she shouted in his face.

"And the fiery Italian comes out," he muttered, eyes twinkling.

Damn the twinkle.

And yes. She was a fiery Italian. A *proud* one.

"Do not be charming when you've made me this angry, George Cunningham,"

Hap dipped his faced to hers and said, "I'm sorry. Gordo. Sam. A few friends. None of my girlfriends. They had your reaction. The rest. No. So I'm conditioned to people thinking I'm a piece of shit about to turn bad at any given moment. But I shouldn't have thought that of you."

Luci felt her eyes narrow. "None of your girlfriends?"

"Oh shit," Hap muttered, watching her closely.

"So that's why they didn't last," she declared flatly.

"Luce—"

"*Puttane!*" she suddenly spat. "*Stronzi! Che palle!*"

"Babe—"

"I actually *liked* one of them!" she yelled. "That blonde. I see her again, I'll scratch her eyes out! *Cazzo!*"

"Baby," his body shaking on hers and that word shaking with humor got her attention, "calm down."

"It is not okay, Hap, that people treated you that way."

"All right, honey," he said consolingly.

"You should be angry," she snapped.

"I'll let you do it. It's cuter."

He was being charming again.

She glared at him.

"You done?" he asked.

"No," she spat.

"You wanna fuck one more time before I have to hit the road?" he queried.

That got her attention, mostly the him hitting the road part.

All right.

Also the fucking part.

Luci turned her head to look at the sea.

She did want to have sex.

She did *not* want him to leave.

"Luci," he called.

She drew in and let out a big breath and turned back.

"Good to have that out of the way," he murmured.

"Yes," she said sharply.

"And thank you for bein' that woman."

"I've always been that woman, Hap."

"Yeah. Thank you."

That made her melt under him and move her hand to rest it on the side of his face. "*Bello*."

"What does that mean?" he asked.

"Handsome," she answered.

"*Puttane*?"

"It's a rude word for certain kinds of women," she muttered.

He grinned. "You can teach me all the rest later, Luce. Let's work off that anger of yours and then I gotta head out."

"I don't want you to go."

It just slipped out.

It was perhaps too much too soon.

She was very fortunate Hap didn't feel that way and showed her instantly by moving in to kiss her.

He pulled back and whispered, "I don't wanna go either, baby. But I gotta. Wednesday'll be here sooner than we think."

Only that made her smile.

She did that before she lifted her head and kissed him.

Things progressed delightfully.

But long before she'd wish, she was in her bomber lounge set (yes, also cashmere, and she would never share with Hap how much it cost), Givenchy slides (ditto on the cost), standing with Hap by the door of his truck, telling him to text her when he made it home.

He shook his head. "No text."

What?

"I'll call, babe."

Ah.

She smiled.

He kissed her smile but it was way too short before he broke it, put a hand in her belly and pushed her back.

"In the house," he ordered as he turned to his door.

"I'll wait until you leave," she replied.

He stopped in his opened door. "Get out of the chill."

"It won't take long."

Sadly.

"Babe, in the fuckin' house or I carry you in there."

She kind of wanted to force that.

Instead she gave him a look and then turned and very slowly walked to the steps.

She also walked up them very slowly.

However, apparently Hap could be more stubborn than she as he simply sat in his truck and stared at her through the windshield until she was inside her opened door.

She stood in it and waved as he reversed.

He lifted a hand, one finger pointed up, and flicked it to return her wave.

That made Luci giggle.

She only closed the door after he arced in her drive, pulled out and away.

She touched the button for release, and the latch clicked.

She rested her head against the door.

She'd just spent twenty-nine hours with Hap.

They'd talked.

They had a plan.

He'd bared his soul.

She'd exposed her quick temper.

And when he got home, he would not text.

He would call.

"Wednesday," she whispered.

And then she smiled.

SIX

Great

Hap

LATE WEDNESDAY NIGHT, HAP HIT the button to the garage door before he pulled into his drive.

"Is that your house, Hap? Oh my. I like it very much," Luci, at his side in his truck, exclaimed.

He couldn't see his house very well in the dark. But he didn't need to. He knew what it looked like.

The development was a newish build. He supposed it would be better once the trees filled in, say, in ten years.

Now, it wasn't special. The houses were close together. He liked the blue of the siding, he liked the parts that were brick.

But other than that, it wasn't only not special, it wasn't much of anything, outside a house.

He glanced at Luci's face in the dash lights before he swung in his drive.

She couldn't be inauthentic if she tried. She'd probably spontaneously combust in the effort.

And so, she looked excited at his nothing-special house.

That was because she liked him.

Which meant everything that came with him.

Which meant for Luci . . .

Done.

Hap did not know what to do with that.

They'd started this trek on rocky footing seeing as she'd clearly been waiting for him. He knew this when he'd barely pulled into her drive and she was already out the door, hoofing it down the stairs, carrying a big black tote bag.

He could not say it sucked that she'd been waiting for him and was so excited to see him, and go home with him, she was out the door and racing down the steps with her bag in hand before he'd even come to a stop in her driveway.

He could say it surprised him.

She'd dropped her tote to the gravel and thrown herself in his arms when he'd folded out of his truck.

He was a dude. A dude banging Luci, and Luci was Luci. So they'd made out in greeting.

Once that was done, he'd lifted his head and said, "You ever carry a bag again, I'm spankin' your ass."

She'd blinked up at him and asked, "What?"

"Babe, you got a bag, I carry it."

She looked to the house, then him. "But now you can just throw it in your truck and we can go, instead of you having to go up and get a bag I'm perfectly capable of carrying."

"It'd take five minutes."

"Five minutes we'd save, and three we could continue to save if this conversation doesn't go on any longer."

"I carry your bag, Luce."

She gave him a look that said she'd argue and the instant she did, he'd brace to argue.

As long as this lasted, he didn't have a lot to give. He didn't have lots of money. He didn't have a cush pad. He didn't drive a Mercedes.

But he could carry a fucking bag.

She thought better of it and he knew that when her body melted into his and she said, "Okay, Hap. You carry my bags."

"Awesome," he muttered.

She gave him a tentative smile and moved away.

He grabbed her bag, put it in the cab, and asked as she rounded the hood, "Everything locked down?"

She nodded, her long, thick fantastic hair sliding all over her shoulders and down her back. "Yes. All ready."

She'd climbed in. He had too. He pulled out and they'd been on their way.

It was awkward for the first five minutes, and then Luci started chattering.

Nothing new. Luce had always been a talker.

She did this until they hit a diner Hap liked that was halfway between him and her. She did this during dinner. She did this after they got back in his truck and headed out.

He had to admit, Luci at his side, listening to her throaty, sexy, accented voice blathering at him on a trip he took usually blasting out metal and not minding the time or distance, got a fuckuva lot better.

Now he was pulling into his garage with her at his side, his house spic and span for her visit, food in the fridge, clean sheets on the bed, and he was asking himself for the five hundredth time what the fuck he was doing, as he put the truck into park and switched off the ignition.

You take care of your children until you die.

Shit.

I like nice things. I have the means to get them. I'll even desire to get some of them for you. But I'll do that in a way that does not make you uncomfortable, if you return that favor by not making me feel uncomfortable I have those means.

Shit, fuck.

She made it sound like they could work.

She made it sound like they *did* work.

You take care of your children until you die.

And that was just . . .

Jesus.

It was just the most beautiful thing he'd ever heard in his life.

He got out, reached in and grabbed her bag.

She got out chattering.

"Oh, I'm going to do this. This is marvelous. This is *everything*."

He rounded the hood, hit the button to bring down the garage door and then looked at her.

She was staring at his peg wall that had some tools and garden equipment on it.

He had to admit, that wall was the shit.

His house was a disaster (until he cleaned it).

His garage was the bomb. Everything organized, maintained, in its place.

He didn't so much as have to spend five minutes looking for a screw if he needed it. He knew he had what he needed (because he also kept everything stocked, no being woken in the middle of the night by fire alarms that needed their batteries changed—he had the batteries and he changed them on a rota before those bastards even beeped they were kinda pissed).

His grandfather taught him that.

The thing was, he hadn't seen even a portable blower in Luci's garage.

"You do your own yard?" he asked.

She looked at him. "No. But in the future, as we get our feet wet, and continue to do so, are you going to allow me to carry on paying my landscapers to see to my beach grass and planters?"

Was she high?

"Hell no."

She smiled at him and tossed her head to his wall. "So I'll need a wall like this."

He'd give her a wall like that.

So you do got something to give, don't you, asshole?

Shit.

Fuck.

"You wanna get inside or you wanna go through my lockers?" he asked, jerking his head to the opposite wall where he had the bright red cabinets, drawers and lockers installed.

Luci looked that way and stated, "I like the red."

Of course she did.

"Babe, it's after eleven. Let's get inside so I can show you around, we can fit a quickie in, and I can pass out."

The smile he got from that was a lot bigger.

It also shot straight to his dick.

He opened the door, held it for her and she walked through it.

He followed her, right into the kitchen.

When he got the house, he'd been dating a woman for a while that he'd liked and thought would stick around, and maybe they'd build more, so he'd gone for some upgrades.

There were tile and hardwood floors, not linoleum and laminate. The countertops were granite. The cabinets whisper closed. The fireplace was gas. And there was some shelving, segmented, lined drawers and shit in the master closet he'd thought a chick would dig.

He'd finally gotten around to that woman finding out about his dad, this being when his father showed up, out of money and wanting Hap to believe he was half a second away from panhandling. He'd laid it on thick, even if he saw Hap had company, or maybe because he had company, and when things did not progress as he would have liked, his father had lost his mind.

Hap worked out so he could eat junk food. Sure, he did the protein shake gig, and was smart about fueling for a workout with decent food. But he was a stick-to-your-ribs, meat and potatoes (including potato chips) guy, had a physically demanding job where he was expected to stay in top shape, so he did.

Not exactly ancillary to that, he worked out to keep his mood level.

Luci was a fiery Italian.

Back in the day, Hap's temper could flash at a blink. It was ugly. It could get physical. And he'd thought he had no control over it.

He'd lived, aged and learned. The Army had helped . . . a lot.

His dad was a match though, and Hap was his tinder.

In other words, that visit had not gone well and the tell-all after it about his father to his woman had not gone better.

And his temper had scared the shit out of her.

Exit woman.

The story of his life.

Which brought him to now, Luci wandering into his living room that he had to admit had pretty boss furniture, since he liked to be comfortable but didn't like to piss away money, so he bought the good stuff that would last, not stuff he'd have to replace in a few years.

He dumped her bag by the opening from kitchen to living room.

"You have three TVs," she remarked.

He looked to the three TVs and back to her.

"Yup."

She turned to him. "Why do you need three TVs?"

He actually had five. One in his bedroom. One in his workout room. And the three there.

As far as he knew, Luci had one hanging on the wall in her white living room, another one for her guests in the downstairs suite.

And that was it.

Then again, her view from her bed was the ocean and even he wouldn't stick a TV in front of that.

"Sunday ticket," he explained.

"What?" she asked.

"Sunday ticket, Luce. I can watch three games simultaneously on three TVs."

For a second, she looked confused. It didn't last long. Her beautiful face brightened with humor and he caught sight of her perfect, white teeth.

Time for that quickie.

"I fear, next to the word 'man' in the American dictionary, there's a picture of you," she noted.

Okay, maybe not time for that quickie.

Time for a little more of Luci being cute.

He leaned a shoulder against the jamb. "Why is that a fear?"

"I actually don't know," she replied. "In fact, I think I'll call the dictionary people, tell them about you and suggest it if it's not there already."

He grinned at her.

She took in his grin before she wandered deeper into the space.

He thought this was going well.

But like it was calling to her, she made a beeline to the only photograph he had framed in the whole house, and Hap felt his body string tight.

It was set to the side, out of eyeline of the huge TV mounted above the fireplace, on his mantle.

She reached out and curled her long fingers around it, bringing it to her, and honest to Christ, it felt like her touching it was her touching him.

And he wasn't sure how he felt about that.

Hap only had her profile, but he still saw her face change. Go soft. Sweet.

He knew how he felt about that. He just wished he didn't feel it.

"Your grandparents," she murmured.

Yeah.

And him. On the porch. On the farm. Before it was lost. He'd been fifteen.

"You look like your grandmother," she whispered. She turned her eyes to him. "She was very beautiful."

She was. Sweet. Tough. No nonsense. Hard working. Strict. Hilarious. Strong.

And beautiful.

Luci's attention floated back to the picture. "But unlike you, she's very dainty."

"She wanted to be a ballerina," Hap told her.

She looked again to Hap.

"Then she met my gramps," he went on.

"I don't suspect she regretted it," Luci guessed.

"No tellin'. That wasn't somethin' she'd share, not to anyone. She made her choice. Cast her lot. Love makes you do stupid shit and maybe she regretted it a thousand times in the years they had together. I'll never know."

She kept hold of the picture but turned fully to him. "Love makes you do stupid shit?"

Yeah.

Like her being right there, holding the picture of him with the only family he'd ever had until he went into the Army.

Stupid.

"Workin' a farm isn't easy on a man, or a woman. She did not live the high life."

Slowly, almost methodically, Luci returned the frame to the mantle, saying, "The high life comes in many forms, Hap."

"There weren't any tutus near our farm, Luce. Or any spotlights."

She lifted her chin and locked her gaze with his.

"But there was her husband. And eventually you."

"I didn't make her life any easier."

"And still, you don't understand banana bread."

Hap went solid.

"Women have many ways of doing things," Luci said quietly. "If she knew you didn't like bananas, she didn't buy them to try and make you like them. She bought them to let them get ripe because she also knew you liked her banana bread. If you had little money, that was probably a treat. So she found a way to give you a treat. And then she did."

Hap's throat closed and his eyes strayed to that frame.

She'd do that, his gram. That was something she'd do.

And obviously something she'd done.

He just hadn't caught on.

Fuck.

"Her grandson, angry at the world because of his father, his mother, the hard life he watched his grandparents lead, enjoying banana bread. That's about the highest high life you can get," she finished.

And there was the second most beautiful thing he'd heard in his life.

He had no idea what made him say what he said next.

Maybe self-preservation.

But he said it.

"She met you, she would not like you. She'd think you were a fancy woman out slumming for shits and grins."

"And then I'd prove her wrong," she instantly shot back. "But right now, I'll prove *you* wrong. She'd never consider you slumming. She might think I was flighty or spoiled, and thus unworthy of you. But she wouldn't ever think I was too good for you."

"You don't even know her, babe," he pointed out, and she just shrugged.

"But I know you. Someone made you the man you are today. And both of those someones are right there," she stated, lifting a hand and jabbing a long fingernail at the frame. "Now are you going to give me a quick orgasm and pass out? Or would you like more time to try to push me away, fail and unnecessarily delay said orgasm and passing out?"

It shocked the shit out of him, but Hap ignored the invitation.

"I made their life hell, Luci."

"And still they kept you in it."

"An obligation. That's what people do in Iowa," he returned.

Shit.

Now it appeared he was pissing her off.

Luci pissed off was cute, but it wasn't a good thing because, although it was worth a repeat that it was cute, she said things when she was pissed that blew his mind.

"No. That's what grandparents do if they're good grandparents who love their grandchild. Look at them, Hap," she snapped on another jab of her finger at the picture. "They're smiling. I'm a model. I know these things. Those smiles aren't forced. You think she cried for hours because you went into the Army and she thought maybe you'd amount to something?" She shook her head. "You're wrong. She cried for hours, beside herself with happiness that you'd proved what she always believed to be correct. You were a good boy who would grow into a good man, that coming from what was inside you that she knew was there and they nurtured."

"That's a pretty big leap from a smile in a picture, babe," he retorted.

"Then you need to look really fucking close at that picture, Hap, because I see it. I see it because *I know you*. And I'm a woman. I know if I had a hand in making a man like you, the pride in that smile would shine through like the pride in her smile is *shining through*."

Hap again looked at the picture.

"Did you work with your grandfather when you had the farm?" she demanded.

He turned his attention back to her. "Yeah."

"Of course. And you decided on the Army after you lost the farm. What were you going to do before?"

He saw where this was going so he clenched his teeth.

She watched.

Then she whispered, "I see."

"Babe, maybe we should quit talkin' about this," he suggested.

"No, because, you see, you were going to work that farm."

She was right.

He opened his mouth to shut this down but didn't get dick out.

"And they knew it. And they were happy you were going to take on their legacy. And they understood completely that you acted out when your future was lost. And then you did what they'd hoped you'd do.

Adjusted your future and found a new path. One that is one of the most honorable you can take, even if it's also one of the most difficult. So yes, I'm sure they felt relief when you did that. But likely not surprise, except for the fact that you did it so quickly and didn't knock about aimless for decades before you did it."

"You make me sound pretty fuckin' great," he forced out.

"Because you are."

Yup.

There it was again.

Luci convinced they worked, they fit, saying shit that if he let it in would make him think the same.

"Luci, I am not great. I'm just a guy."

"So is Sam and I suspect you think he's great."

"He's an ex-NFL player who quit to become a soldier. Everyone thinks Sam is great. And by everyone, I mean everyone on the whole fuckin' planet."

"Because God gave him the talent to play football?" she asked incredulously.

"Well . . . yeah, and made him the man who'd quit it to serve his country."

"You serve your country," she returned.

Hap clenched his teeth again.

Luci tipped her head to the side. "Am I great because God made me beautiful and people would pay me large sums of money to take photos of me?"

He definitely thought she was great, and he had to admit that was one of the reasons why.

But the way she said that made it sound absurd.

Because it was.

He decided to stop talking.

"Now, your father is a felon, your mother is . . . I don't know, except she's an awful mother so," she fluttered her hand in the hair, "whatever. You lost your farm. You could have held up liquor stores. You could be angry at the world and take it out on other people. You could drink yourself to an early death. But no." She tossed her hand his way "You became you. With those circumstances, are you not great?"

"You've made your point, honey," he said quietly.

She hadn't, though she made sense, he just didn't feel like talking about it any longer.

But he hoped saying that would shut her up.

She lifted her chin. "Good."

"Can we go to bed now?" he prompted. "I'm wiped."

"You think I'm too good for you," she accused.

God dammit.

Hap pushed away from the jamb. "Luce—"

She lifted both hands and pressed her palms his way.

"Fine. Fine. We'll take up this conversation after you haven't been driving for hours," she declared.

"Not somethin' to look forward to," he muttered.

"Travis thought the world of you," she snapped, and his attention sharpened on her as his gut got tight. "Sam does. Kia does. When he's not being cantankerous, Skip does. Celeste. Thomas. Maris. *I* do. The only one who doesn't *is you*."

"Babe, can we talk about this *later*?" he growled.

She drew an audible breath through her nose.

When she let it out, her tone had changed. "Don't push me away, Hap."

"I'm not gonna push you away. In about ten minutes, I'd like to be as close as I can get to you, so let's move on to that."

"And don't be funny and tempting when I'm being serious."

He sighed.

Then he asked, "*Tempting?*"

"All right," she retorted. "*Hot.*"

Her not being cute would help a lot.

It really would.

He had no hope of that, though.

"It's you I'd like to get hot," he returned. "So is it okay with you I get on with that?"

"It's rather annoying you're such a good lover because I'm angry at you and frustrated with you, and I still want you to fuck me."

For a second, he was thrown.

Then he busted out laughing.

Through it, she ordered, "Bring my bag. I assume your room is up there?"

And then he watched, still laughing, as she didn't wait for him to confirm. She flounced toward his stairs.

When Hap lost sight of her, he went to the garage door, locked it, then nabbed her bag, shut out the lights and headed to the stairs.

That Tim McGraw song could gut a man who knew the pain of loving a woman he could not have.

It was just Luci who made that shit tougher than he could ever imagine.

As well as . . .

Fuck him running . . .

Fun.

SEVEN

My Happy

Hap

HAP WOKE TO THE SOUND of the alarm the next morning feeling great, smelling Luci on his sheets and . . .

Bacon.

He opened his eyes to a dark room.

He was the only one in the bed.

She was downstairs cooking.

Luci, in his kitchen, making him breakfast.

"Fuck," he muttered, rolling and reaching to turn off the alarm.

He lay on his back, lifted his hands and rubbed his face, feeling the stubble that had grown since yesterday morning.

He didn't want to shave.

He did not believe he was even thinking this, but he also didn't want to eat bacon.

His cock was hard and he wanted to bury it in Luci, feeling her skin against his, his face in her hair, her body wrapped around him.

He tossed off the covers, prowled to the bathroom, used the toilet, washed his hands, splashed his face with water, brushed his teeth and stabbed the floss wrapped around his fingers through his grill.

Rinse.

Pull on a pair of sweats.

Head to the kitchen.

And there she was in her sweater robe that was soft as kitten fur, his tee on under it (fuck him), hair gorgeous even if it was still a bedhead, eyes bright and happy and aimed at him.

"*Buongiorno, caro,*" she greeted.

He didn't hesitate in the stalk he had going on while replying, "What'd I say about leaving me in bed?"

Her smile grew wicked.

Yeah.

Fuck.

Him.

He grabbed her. Kissed her. He did the first rough. He did the last deep.

She tasted fresh and sunny and minty and happy.

Yeah.

Happy.

He'd never tasted that in his life.

It was beautiful.

Cosmopolitan, jet-setting, international supermodel in a nothing-special house, frying bacon for some guy who grew up on a farm, nearly fucked up his whole life, got his shit together simply to be a normal, average dude, and she was happy.

He broke the kiss, lifting his head.

"You don't have to make breakfast for me, babe."

Her eyes were a little fuzzy from the kiss, something he liked, and her body was relaxed into his, something he liked maybe more, though that was a tossup. "I like cooking breakfast for you."

"Did you cook breakfast for Gordo?"

It just came right out without thought, but Hap knew why it did.

Even giving her what she thought she wanted, he'd do everything he could to put anything at his disposal between them so she'd wake up and see she was destined for better, for more, for *happier.*

She felt Gordo slide right between them (or more to the point, Hap shoving the memory of him there) and he knew it because she was no longer leaning into him, giving him some of her weight. She'd tightened, even if she didn't pull away.

"Yes," she answered quietly. "But I'm not cooking breakfast for Travis. Travis is dead. I'm cooking for you because I'm *with you.*"

He let her go, stepped away and lifted his hand to rub the hair on top of his head while he studied the bacon in his skillet wondering now that he'd pull that shit, what was next.

He should apologize. That was a dick thing to say.

He stood staring at the sizzling bacon and did not apologize.

"That will break us, Hap," she declared, her voice stronger.

He dropped his hand and looked to her.

"You were avoiding speaking of him," she noted when she got his attention. "Now that you've seen I won't easily be pushed away, you're bringing him up to use as a tool to tear us apart, and I'll warn you, there is little I can imagine that would work in your efforts to accomplish that. But using my dead husband will."

"You've got to know that shit is gonna be on my mind," he pointed out, and there wasn't much to be said for him doing that except it was the truth.

"Then perhaps we can discuss it when we have time, this not being when you have to get ready to go to work," she returned.

She was now stabbing at the bacon with a fork, her chin tipped down, the line of her jaw strained.

"Luce—" he began, even though he had no idea what he was about to say.

Whatever it was, he didn't say it when her head jerked his way and he caught the fire warring with hurt in her gaze.

He did that to her. He'd intentionally made her pissed.

He'd also intentionally hurt her.

He'd done that.

And that didn't make him feel like a dick.

That made him feel like a motherfucker.

Shit.

"I loved him," she declared. "This is not news to you. I mourned him when he was gone, this is not news to you either. You witnessed it. You were there to help me work through it. In ways all my own, I will mourn him forever. More that is not news to you, as you know how much I loved him and you also know what kind of man he was, so you know he deserves that kind of grief because he earned it."

She paused, and Hap said nothing because there was nothing to say.

He did know all of this.

Luci kept going.

"I honestly don't know what to say to you to make you feel better about this. The truth is, we would not be what we are if he was here. We both know that. But he's *not here*. That was where life took us, Hap. *Us*, the *both of us*. I cannot say what Travis would say about us being together. It was not a possibility when he was alive. I would hope he'd want me to be happy. I would hope he'd want me to feel again what I felt last night when you were making love to me. What I felt this morning when I woke up beside you. What I felt when I came downstairs to cook you breakfast. But I cannot say for certain he'd be happy I was happy with you or if he'd be angry at us both. What I do I know is *he is no longer here*. So he does not get a say."

She drew in breath and this time Hap didn't get a chance to chime in because she didn't give him a shot.

"I also know I'm happy . . . with you. *With you*, Hap. Look at me and listen to me and please, God, believe me. I am not making breakfast for my dead husband. I'm not sleeping at his side. I'm not making love to him. I am absolutely not using you to be with him, to get back what I had with him, to play pretend to have some part of him back. I'm here *with you*. And if you can't get there with me, if you can't believe that, if you even *think* I'd use you like that, I'll find my way home and this will be done. I'll also find a way to us having some sort of relationship that won't make it hard for those who love us to be around us. But after what we've shared, you'll need to back off and give me time to get there."

She would end it.

All he had to do was tell her he couldn't get past Gordo and she'd end it.

That was all he had to say.

He stood there looking at her and said nothing.

"Why don't you take the day," she suggested after he remained silent. "I'll call a rental car company and have a vehicle on standby should you come home and wish me to leave. Now, if you don't mind finishing breakfast, I'm going to get dressed and take a walk."

She didn't wait for him to respond.

She tossed the fork on the counter and marched out of the kitchen.

Hap didn't move.

She'd given him his out. No screaming, shouting or tears. He'd crossed a line and she'd laid it down for him and left it to him to decide, promising that even if it was over, it wouldn't be *over*.

He had an out.

He stood still and stared at where she'd disappeared and stayed right there even after some time had passed, and he heard his front door open and close.

The only reason he moved was when he smelled the bacon burning.

He threw that out, cooked more, scrambled some eggs, ate them with the bacon then went up and showered, shaved and got dressed.

He came back down, made more eggs, left them and the rest of the bacon on a plate in the oven on warm and wrote a note to her to tell her where to find her breakfast.

Then he put a key under the mat at the back door and texted her the info on where to find it.

Finally, he locked up, hauled his ass in this truck and went to work knowing when he got home they'd be over.

But they wouldn't be *over*.

He was good with that.

And it killed him.

THAT NIGHT WHEN HAP GOT home, he walked into a tidy kitchen but the only thing he saw was the key he'd left for Luci sitting on the counter.

At the sight, he felt his throat get tight, his gut constrict like it wanted to force the bile in his stomach up his gullet, and his eyes shot to the living room.

The TV was dark. Luci was not to be seen.

But her black bag was sitting on the floor by the front door.

Christ.

Unlike the time between leaving her on Sunday and picking her up on Wednesday, when she texted frequently just because, and he texted her back, she had not texted him that day. Outside telling her where to find the key to get in, he also had not texted her.

But he figured she'd spent the day not like him, not feeling like an asshole and trying to convince herself it was for the best that she'd acted like that.

She'd likely spent the day just plain pissed at him for being an asshole.

He caught sight of her as she rounded the bottom of stairs, her purse over her shoulder, a suede jacket on, ready to roll.

Ready to roll.

Oh yeah.

She'd spent the day pissed at him for being an asshole.

And yeah.

He'd been right that morning.

This was going to kill him.

She stopped at the door and asked, "Shall I order a taxi?"

"Gordo was still here, but something happened to Sam, and what was going on with us went on with me and Kia, how would you feel?"

She shook her head sharply, instantly ticked, or *more* ticked, but she also paled, he could see it all the way across the room.

"Do not even speak of something happening to Sam," she snapped.

"Answer the question, Luce."

"That hasn't happened. That *won't* happen."

"Answer the question, Luciana," he pressed.

"It's impossible to say because it didn't happen that way," she fired back.

"No. You just *won't* say it because if it happened, you would not be where Kia is, okay with the idea of us not having been around when Gordo was here so not knowing how it was. You'd be pissed."

She tipped her head to the side angrily. "Are you saying I'm interchangeable with whatever woman was left behind by one of your buddies?"

Oh no she didn't.

Hell no.

"Now you've pissed me off," he growled. "You know what I'm asking, Luci. You just won't answer because you refuse to concede the point."

She looked to the door then back to him, and he knew she'd hunkered down for a fight when she did.

"So are you saying you care more about what Sam thinks, what Travis would think, than what I think or what you *feel*?"

"I'm saying you don't get to shut shit down just because you don't get it," he shot back. "You want what you want and you just want everyone to be okay with it when it's not okay. It's not black and white. Just what you feel or what I feel and people have to get it, and if they don't, they have to deal. There's people, dead and alive, people we both care about that are involved in this and that's gonna weigh on my mind. So this is not a 'deal with it, or don't, just tell me what you decide and then I'll go' type of sitch."

"Yes, and I did say we should talk about it when we had time to talk, not you bringing it up the way you did when we had no time to discuss it," she retorted.

"Sorry, I'm human and I'm trying to sort through important shit, and I might not measure my words if I'm feeling things deep. It might just come out. And when it does, I don't need, 'figure it out and let me know, whichever way you go, I'm good.'"

Okay.

Jesus.

Why was this coming out of his mouth?

He should just let her go.

It had been on his mind all fucking day.

He'd made his decision.

He would come home and let her go.

Just let her go.

So now what the fuck was he doing?

"You're right," she spoke up, her chin now lifted stubbornly. "If something happened to Sam, and you and Kia moved on to what you and I have, Travis and I would be angry." She bit the words out like she didn't like the taste of them. "*Very* angry. We'd feel betrayed for Sam."

He took a calming breath and evened his tone. "So you get where I'm at, honey, because I would not want to lose you. You or Gordo. And if it went that way, it'd destroy Kia. And that would be the most important of all. Are you hearing what I'm saying?"

She looked to the door again and he figured she did that to hide her expression from him.

Yeah, stubborn.

Hap gave her time.

When she took that time, a lot of it, he prompted, "Do you hear what I'm saying, Luci?"

She turned her attention back to him and she did not share she heard what he was saying.

He still knew by the look on her face she heard what he was saying.

She changed the subject to one that was even less comfortable. "It's important for me to know that you know that I'm very aware who I'm spending time with and I want to be with you, Hap. I'm not trying to replace Travis and using you to do that."

He hated that she thought he thought that.

He hated it worse that it was actually what he thought.

That wasn't her.

She would never do that.

And he knew it.

"It was a dick thing to say. It was a dick time to say it. You're right, I'm trying to push you away," he admitted.

And goddammit, he not only seemed to have no control over his mouth, the relief on her face made his stomach settle and his breathing start to come easier.

What she did next was even better.

Which made it worse.

"And I should not have put it all on your shoulders what would happen from there," she swung an arm out to indicate her bag by the door, "or had my mini-drama in making my point. I should have found another way to settle things so we both would not have had the days we both had. And instead, I should have waited for you to come home so we could discuss it."

"It was me that screwed that pooch, baby," he said softly. "You were making me bacon and I was being a dick."

"You don't fight fire with fire, Hap."

She had that right.

He was still in the wrong.

He wasn't going to push that discussion, because he could tell she was set on taking part of the blame even if she really had no part, so he'd get nowhere.

And it sucked because it was awesome that she could admit that he did something fucked up, she returned something fucked up, and she regretted it.

Yeah.

She made it seem like they could work.

"I'm sensing you're going to test me," she went on. "Test us. And I cannot fall down in proving that I believe in what I feel for you, what we can have. But I also now understand more of why you're thinking how you're thinking, and I'm glad I do, *bello*. I will be stronger. I promise you. Because, in truth, even if our pasts did not make this difficult, something would. That's simply life and no matter what, we'd need to prove to each other that what we can have will be worth any trouble we face along the way."

Hap had known her a long time. He knew she was beautiful. He knew she was funny. He knew she was warm, loving, affectionate. He knew she was loyal. He knew she was well-traveled. But even with her sophistication, she was as comfortable at a picnic table at a crab shack as she was in an expensive steak house. He also knew she was smart.

But he had not known her to be wise.

"Do you know what scares me the most?" he asked.

Jesus.

Fuck, fuck, *fuck*.

He just could not stop his mouth from running.

"What scares you the most, *luce mio*?" she asked gently.

"Fucking this up and hurting you."

And Christ . . .

Christ.

The look on her face that bought him nearly took him to his knees.

"You won't hurt me, Hap," she whispered.

"I want you to be happy."

"You're making me happy," she replied.

"Yeah, babe. Your bag packed and sitting by the door screams happy," he pointed out.

She walked to him and he let her. When she got close, she didn't get too close, but she did frame his face in both of her hands.

"You do know I did that to myself," she said quietly.

"I took us there."

"And I kept us there. We both didn't handle this morning very well, my Happy."

My Happy.

His nickname was Hap, which came from "Happy" because once he found the Army—once he'd found a new family that did not include his dad and his mom and their bullshit, and his grandparents and the loss of everything they knew and loved and worked so hard to keep—once he'd seen the man he could become and knew it was in his power to be that man, he'd been really fucking happy.

So he became that guy who would crack a joke to lighten a tense atmosphere and people would relax, or that guy who walked into a dud of a party and brought it to life by being loud and acting like an ass just so folks would loosen up.

But no one called him Happy.

The way she said it gave it new meaning and good Christ, it felt like that meaning settled in every cell in his body.

And the feeling was good.

"You cannot take it all on your shoulders, *caro*," she continued. "Especially when I contribute to fucking things up. Yes?"

He stared into her warm, brown eyes, which were staring deep into his.

"Yes?" she prompted, drifting her hands down to either side of his neck and curling her fingers around tight.

"Yeah, baby," he muttered.

A whisper of a smile hit her lips. "That was not very convincing."

He felt his mouth lift in a grin but he said nothing.

She kept hold on him and tipped her head to the side. "Shall I make dinner?"

"I'm frying us hamburgers."

She smiled and when she did, she lit his world.

Now, by letting this carry on, he was screwing *this* pooch and he did not care if he got chewed up in the process.

But if she did . . .

"I like hamburgers," she told him something he knew.

"I know."

Yeah, he knew.

He also knew she liked cheese melted on, American, as well as ketchup, mustard and pickles.

And he'd made sure he had all that for Luci.

What was he doing?

He had no answer to that.

What he had was Luciana, right there with her hands on him and contentment in her eyes that he did not come home and tell her to call a cab. Instead, they talked things through, worked things out, and he his damned self had taken them to a place where it seemed this could work.

So with nothing else for it, he bent in and touched his mouth to hers before he touched it to her nose, and then he rested his forehead against hers and looked from close into her gorgeous eyes.

Only then did he speak.

"No matter what, baby, know down to your soul you're the straight up best woman I've ever met and know I know that in a way you'll be that woman forever."

Throughout him speaking, her hold on him got tighter and tighter.

But when he stopped, she immediately stated, "Then we have nothing to worry about."

He could tell she believed that completely.

And it scared the hell out of him that she was wrong.

"I . . . CANNOT . . . BELIEVE THIS," LUCI huffed out, lying flat on top of him, Hap on his back in his bed, her naked body shaking with laughter, which he could feel even though his equally naked body was shaking with the same.

"Not shittin' you, baby. It was straight outta *Footloose*, and I won."

She threw her head back and he felt her hair glide over his arms wrapped around her as she busted out laughing even harder.

He kept it up with her, quietly so he could take in hers while she did it, and when she got some control over it, she asked, "Wh-what happened then?"

"His tractor rolled after he jumped from it so he had to tell his pops who got shit-pissed, hauled his ass to our farm, got in my gramps's face and demanded both of us be punished for playing chicken on expensive farm equipment."

She was still smiling, but she couldn't quite hide the warm concern in her eyes when he brought up his grandfather. She added to that sweetness by stroking his throat with her fingers.

"What did your grandfather do?"

"He assured the guy he'd find a fitting punishment for me, walked him to his truck, watched him drive away, walked up to the house and found me waiting for him in the hall, seein' as I'd been in the kitchen with Gram listening to all this going down."

"And then?" she pushed when he didn't go on.

He smiled up at her. "Then he congratulated me for not bein' a wuss and jumpin' off first and asked me if I got the girl."

Her body started shaking as her face lit up again. "Did you?"

He did.

He also got her virginity.

When you lived in a Podunk town in Iowa, playing chicken on expensive farm equipment for a date with a cheerleader was a sure bet to win the heart of said cheerleader.

As well as other things.

He did not inform Luci of the fullness of that.

"We dated awhile."

"I'm sure," she murmured, eyes dancing. "Did he punish you?"

Hap shook his head. "I honored the Cunningham name by keeping my seat and my wits even if it was doin' somethin' stupid. Gramps was like that. I figure he learned a lot from the mess that became my dad. That being there were a variety of lessons to teach a kid in any given situation, so he focused on priorities. Winning the girl or holding on to your honor by doing something daring, and keeping your shit even if it was also while doing somethin' fool and dangerous was more important than any tractor. Even though, if I did something to that tractor being stupid and playing fuckin' chicken on it, we'd have been fucked."

"I would agree with him," she declared.

"Obviously I did too. Especially then."

She gave him a big smile.

He rolled her off and rolled onto her, liking the feel of her under him just as much as he liked the feel of her on him, he was just ready for the change.

He took some weight into his arm but left the other one free so he could stroke the skin at her side.

In turn she stroked the skin of his back.

And just like he couldn't believe he didn't want bacon that morning, because getting it meant he didn't have Luci in his bed, he couldn't believe right then he liked the feel of them there, the way they were, more than he liked what they'd finished doing twenty minutes ago.

If this was something that could work, they could always have this. No matter how much time passed, no matter how old they got, no matter if something ugly happened that took away his ability to make love to her, or her ability to give that in return, they could always be skin against skin, laughing in bed, finding some way to hold each other, touch each other.

It seemed like nothing.

And yet it felt like everything.

That noted, apparently, even though he didn't have lunch and she shared she'd not had much of an appetite after what had happened that morning, they were hungrier for each other than they were for food.

That was why they were naked in his bed and the remains of dinner were still all over his kitchen.

He didn't even put the skillet in to soak.

Now here they were, in his bed in his nothing-special house, no turn of the head and there would be a wide-open view of the ocean.

And he wouldn't want to be anywhere else.

"What are you thinking?" she whispered.

He focused on her, head on his pillow, hair everywhere.

"I like you here."

Her fingers stopped roaming and her arms crossed his back, holding him close. "I like me here too."

She did. She didn't hide it. Even if he couldn't believe it, it was right there all over her face.

He slid his hand up and stroked her cheek with his knuckles.

"They might not like you . . . at first," he started. "But I'd have been proud to introduce you to my grandparents."

She tipped her head on the pillow and he knew she was teasing when she asked, "Because I'm a supermodel?"

He wasn't teasing when he replied, "Yeah. Because you're a supermodel. But mostly because you're Luci and they'd get you were that, but eventually they'd get you'd be happy living the rest of your days on a farm if the people you loved were there."

The playfulness left her gaze and she held on tighter, not only with her arms but shifting a long leg from under his and wrapping it around his thigh, saying only, "Hap."

"When I wasn't thinking today about what an asshole I'd been this morning, I was thinking what you said about Gram last night. About the banana bread. About the high life. And how, back then, I'd get pissed when they'd sit in that little kitchen in that little apartment after dinner, Gramps havin' his last cheap, crappy beer of the night, Gram drinking one of her cups of tea, and they'd laugh about nothin'. I didn't think there was anything to laugh about so that shit pissed me off. I knew they felt the loss of the farm. It was bad before it happened. It was bad when it happened. It was bad after it happened. But now I know, eventually they realized there was nothing they could do about it, so they moved on and they had everything they needed right in that little kitchen. No doubt about it, all that sucked. But in the end, they were good."

"I'm glad you've come to realize that, *bello*," she said.

"Yeah," he offered his understatement.

"Do you have other pictures of them?" she asked.

He nodded.

"Will you show them to me tomorrow night?" she requested.

"Maybe, if you don't hightail your ass out of bed first thing in the morning and instead suck me off or fuck me off so I don't feel the need to drag you upstairs and drill you even before you've swallowed your last bite of hamburger."

She burst out laughing again, digging her head in the pillow with her hilarity, her limbs tensing around him tight, her body shaking under the weight of his.

Hap smiled at her while she did, loving the look, the feel, the knowledge it was him that gave her that, not wounding her, not pissing her off, not doing some shit thing that would lead to her having a bad day.

And again, you got something to give, something that means more than shoes and views to Luci, and you know it. And straight up look at her, she thinks this is gonna work because if you got your head out of your ass, you'd realize it might just work too.

"Are we having hamburgers again tomorrow night?" she asked into his thoughts.

"Hotdogs," he lied.

"*Fantastico!*" she did not lie.

Christ.

Luci.

"Should we go downstairs and clean the kitchen?" she suggested.

"No," he answered.

She smiled but through it asked another question. "Should we go downstairs and get ice cream?"

"Shit yes."

Her smile got bigger.

He pulled her out of bed before he pulled on his sweats.

She pulled on his tee.

He'd seen her in some incredible clothes, but it was the God's honest truth she looked best in that.

He was going to hold her hand (yeah, hold her fucking hand) to walk down the stairs.

In the end he didn't because she jumped up on his back.

So he carried her down the stairs with his hands holding the backs of her thighs, her legs wrapped around his middle, her arms wrapped around his chest, her lips blathering nonsense in his ear, and her weight on his back.

And Hap knew he'd carry her like that across a desert to get ice cream. He'd carry her over a glacier.

He'd climb mountains with her on his back to take her to something she wanted.

He'd do anything to have her blathering nonsense in his ear, giving him her weight . . .

And getting her something she wanted.

THE NEXT MORNING HAP WAS not woken by the alarm.

He was woken with a hand wrapped around his cock that pulled him to his back.

Before he had his eyes open, he had Luci's wet mouth around his rock-hard dick.

He then learned something phenomenal.

Luciana swallowed.

After she'd taken him there, she came up over him, gave him her weight and aimed a satisfied look in his probably a lot more satisfied face.

"Better?" she taunted.

Challenge declared.

Challenge accepted.

He rolled her to her back and returned the favor.

When he'd finished her off with his mouth, was on her and looking into her soft, hazy eyes, he finally answered.

"Yeah, babe. Better."

EIGHT

Chicken and Biscuits

Luci

"BABE, I GOT SOMETHING TO go over with you."

Luci—sitting beside Hap in his truck on Saturday morning, heading back to the beach and to their talk with Sam and Kia in the afternoon, after having such a delicious day yesterday starting with orgasms and her cooking him breakfast, and ending with Hap making them spaghetti, going through pictures of him growing up, telling stories that did not seem tortured as they had done, then making love before falling asleep—did not want to go over something with Hap.

Especially when whatever it was, he sounded serious about.

She'd gotten him to a good place. If he wasn't exactly relaxed, he was no longer pushing her away.

She needed this easy, for now especially, as she was uneasy about what Sam's response would be, but more, what Hap's response would be to Sam's response.

And she needed this easy for him so he'd be feeling the good of them together to its fullest before he faced whatever reaction Sam was going to have.

"What's that?" she queried tentatively.

"Thursday."

She turned her head to look at him. "Thursday?"

"What I pulled Thursday morning."

Oh no.

They didn't have to go back over that. That was good.

Wasn't it?

She studied his profile seeing clearly it was not.

Merda.

"I'm not sure, *caro*, that we—" she began.

He interrupted her. "What I said, bringing Gordo into it, was uncool and we both know that. But what it did, making you go back there, talk about him and how you miss him and how you always will—"

"Hap—"

"I shouldn't have done that to you."

"It's just fact," she said softly. "And you would not feel the way you do about me if it wasn't."

"Yeah, I know," he replied. "And you got a lifetime of that. A lifetime of that loss. I don't need to be forcing it to the surface."

"*Bello*—"

"I loved him too."

She shut her mouth.

"You know that. I miss him too. Not like you, I get that. But I just want you to know I feel that, for me, for you, and I'm there even if we're like we are right now. I'm there when that hits you, however you need me to be."

Luci stared at Hap's profile unable to speak.

She would not be able to do that. If the shoe was on the other foot, he had lost a wife he adored and was moving on with Luci, but he continued to mourn his wife's passing in his way, she would need him to do that inside himself. To hide that from her. She was too possessive. Too selfish. She knew that about herself, even if she didn't like it. She'd want to be a bigger person, a better person, and she might be able to hide her feelings from him to give him what he needed, but it would hurt.

She'd never offer it, as Hap would say, straight out.

But he meant it.

He meant every word.

"I would not be able to do that for you," she blurted.

He glanced at her before looking back at the road. "Sorry?"

"I would want to, but I would find it difficult to support you in that way."

"Seein' as that's not the way it is, you don't have anything to worry about," he replied.

That was not the point.

She didn't belabor the point.

Dio, but she loved him.

"May I ask you something?" she requested.

"Shoot," he invited.

"If it was the other way around, not you losing a woman you loved, but if I'd found you first, not Travis, and I had lost you, how would you feel if Travis and I found each other?"

"I'd want you to be happy."

Not a moment's hesitation.

Not one.

"Do you say that because you know how I was with Travis?" she pressed cautiously.

"I say that because I'd want you to be happy," he repeated. Another glance to her before he looked back at the road. "Baby, why do you think I'm right here and you're right there?"

Luci turned her eyes out the windshield but not her attention.

I'd want you to be happy.

Dear Lord, she was going to cry.

"Luce?" he called.

She swallowed and stated, "I would find it in me to support you through the loss of a woman you loved, however you needed me to support you."

"Honey, look at me," he urged, taking up her hand, pulling it to his thigh and holding it tight.

She looked to him and he must have felt it because he didn't take his eyes off the road when he resumed speaking.

"That's not where we are. As sweet as that is, we've got what we've got. That's enough to deal with. There's no point to this conversation because we are where we're at and not anywhere else, and we got enough on our plates. It serves no purpose to take it anywhere else. You found Gordo. You lost Gordo. You want me. I'm right here. That's where we are. Let's just find our way through that minefield, yeah?"

You want me. I'm right here.

What did that mean?

"I just want you to know that the Hap you had before we started banging didn't go anywhere," he went on, a teasing tone now in his deep voice. "I'm there for you, babe. To eat your breakfasts and put up with you tellin' me I was hot even when I was sixteen and had shit for brains and a farmer's tan," he gave her hand a squeeze, "or however you need me to be there for you."

"You were a very handsome young man, *caro*," she retorted.

"I was full of piss and bullshit and didn't learn a woman could have an orgasm until I was nineteen and the woman I'd just banged laid into me for being a selfish fuck and kicked my ass out of her bed. So thanks, but you don't know what you're talking about."

Luci was now staring at his profile with a different reaction.

"You didn't know a woman could have an orgasm until you were nineteen years old?"

He shook his head. "Nope."

"*Incredibile*," she whispered.

"Nothin' incredible about it."

"That means more 'unbelievable,'" she shared.

"Ah," he murmured, now grinning.

"I'm very glad this woman kicked you out of her bed, Hap."

That made him roar with laughter.

She enjoyed watching him do that, and further enjoyed him doing it holding her hand, his fingers tensing around hers with his humor, but the minute his laughter turned to chuckles, she asked, "Did your grandfather not teach you these things?"

"Babe, I grew up on a farm. We had a couple of cows when I was younger, always had dogs. When I was maybe nine, one of our dogs went into heat, the other one was rutting with her and Gramps said, 'That's the way a baby's made, boy.' He didn't sound comfortable, even with just that. For me, I had no clue what he was talking about, but I knew I didn't want anything to do with the whole business. That was the beginning and end of my sex education until the not very comprehensive shit they shared in sex ed at school. That is, outside me hitting thirteen and finding a titty magazine under my pillow. I don't know who was behind that, Gramps or Gram. Whatever, it opened a whole world for me because I didn't even know *I* could have an orgasm until I jacked off to that magazine. I had no idea what to do with the hard-ons I'd been getting. One look at a pair of tits, it hit me. Thank fuck jacking off came naturally."

Luci laughed softly but she did it feeling something good and right fill her belly that had nothing to do with Hap being funny.

It was because Hap was being just that.

Hap.

Open and frank and amusing and self-deprecating in a way that was uniquely his and singularly charming.

"You?" Hap asked.

She faced forward saying, "Oh, I'm Italian. We're far more candid about many things, including sexuality. When I was young, maybe eleven, I walked in on an older cousin having sex with a waiter at one of my other cousin's weddings. I told my father about it and he said, '*Bellisima*, that is making love and it's not for you for now, but when it's your time, it's the most beautiful thing in the world.'"

"Definitely better than Intro to Sex: Two Dogs Fucking," Hap drawled, making Luci giggle.

"Yes. Definitely," she agreed. "Though I often looked back at that and realized my father was right. They were standing up and many would think it was sordid, but my cousin, Giorgia, had this expression on her face that was most attractive, and the man she was with was very handsome. They had no idea I was there, the moment was intense, there was only the other for them in it. She likely never saw him again, but she undoubtedly thought of him . . . fondly." She turned again to face Hap. "But because of that, and what my father said, when my time came, I didn't fear it. This is how I'd like to teach my children about making love. Obviously, I'd prefer they not see the act prior to me explaining its importance. But I would not ever want to make them feel it was base or shameful."

"You're talking to a dude who grew up in the Bible belt, Luce."

Oh dear.

"And?" she prompted.

His glance her way was longer this time before he looked back to the road. "It's not shameful, and I wouldn't want any of my kids to feel it was. Though there's a right time to talk about that, and I wouldn't want them to be anything but kids until that time was right. But if my baby girl got an eyeful before she was ready to process that in an adult way, I'd lose my goddamn mind."

That did not make her feel good and right in her belly.

That made her feel fiery and greedy and fiercely possessive. It made her want to crawl to him and take his mouth in a kiss that he'd remember the rest of his days.

Obviously, she could not do that as he was driving.

"Do you want children, *bello*?" she whispered.

"Yeah, baby," he whispered back.

Luci licked her lips and rubbed them together while she turned her gaze again to look out the windshield.

His hand squeezing hers did not make her look back because it felt like the warning it would turn out to be when he spoke.

"We feel different because we've known each other awhile, Luce, and because from when this started to where we are now took some time. But we're new, honey. Don't lose sight of that. You with me?"

She was not.

They were not new.

She knew new.

Hap had practically crusted her red sauce with freshly grated parmesan before handing her the bowl of pasta he'd made for her the night before. He did this without asking. And he did this because he knew she liked it like that.

That was not new.

The discovery he was exceptionally talented at cunnilingus was new.

They were not.

She understood the nuance he wanted her to understand.

She simply refused to allow it to hold her back.

No.

Them back.

"Babe, you with me?" he pushed.

She turned again to look at him and took a risk she knew was grave. But he was open and frank and this was too important.

He deserved that in return.

"I will not hide the fact I'm falling in love with you, George Cunningham."

His fingers flexed hard around hers, nearly causing pain.

However, she was not finished.

"And you would not be with me if you didn't feel the same. So yes, I do understand this new facet of *us* is very young. But the most important part of anything we will ever have is being friends, and that is *not*. I've loved you for a long time, Hap. That feeling is simply deepening to something fuller and richer, and I will not hide that I'm beside myself with happiness that it is."

"You're killin' me, Luci," he muttered, and she looked at him closely to see he did, even in profile, appear in pain.

"How?" she asked, not able to hide the alarm in her tone.

He did not speak immediately. It was as if he needed time to measure his words, make certain the right ones came out.

She had no idea if they were right or wrong in his mind when they did.

She just knew what they were in her mind.

"You make it sound like we can do this."

And he was making it sound like they couldn't.

"Well, we can," she snapped.

Another glance and, "Babe—"

"Sam will get on board, Hap, and if he doesn't—"

"It's not that."

"We . . . neither of us are unaware of how both of us felt about Travis and—"

"It's not that either."

"Then what is it?" she demanded to know.

Again with the hesitation, the searching for words, and Luci had learned quickly that there were instances when Hap found her quick temper "cute" and times when it was damaging.

She assessed now, losing patience with him he would not find cute.

So she kept quiet, even though it cost her.

It took too long, but he finally found his words.

"I just need to get past the idea you'll eventually figure it out."

"Figure what out?" she inquired.

He said nothing.

Luci gave him more time.

She really wanted to be patient, she simply found she could not.

"Figure *what* out, George?" she asked irritably.

"I'm an asshole."

"You're not an asshole," she shot back.

"And you got a quick temper."

She could not argue that.

Merda.

"And you're a supermodel," he went on.

She looked to the ceiling of the cab of his truck. "Oh, for the love of—"

"And I'm a farm boy."

She looked back to him. "I do not care."

"With a criminal dad and a never-there mom you just could not understand because that's so far from what you are, it's not even in your DNA."

"We've discussed this," she clipped.

"And he's gonna show, or she's gonna show. They've been away way too long so they've had plenty of time to significantly fuck their shit, so they're gonna land on my doorstep, one of them. And if you're with me, you might be there and you'll see the me they made, even if they had fuck all to do with raising me."

"And who's the you they made, *caro*?" she asked, not hiding her frustration.

"My temper, I don't hold it, will make you understand why I think yours is cute."

"So?" she asked. "Do you not think my temper comes from somewhere? My father's is explosive. If I did not know him to be the loving, caring man he is, it might even be frightening."

"I can guaran-damn-tee you mine has his beat."

Luci fell silent.

"I told you when I was young, that shit could get physical, baby," he said quietly. "And it's only the fact that my grandfather and the sheriff were good buds that I didn't have a juvie file a mile long and didn't hit detention repeatedly back in the day."

"That's not you anymore, Hap," she pointed out.

"One of them shows, I try to hold it, but they push it and it isn't pretty, Luciana. Trust me, honey. I go off and even I hate the me I become when I do. And it itches in my goddamn bones, thinking you'd ever see me that way. A way it's for sure to change the way you look at me."

She always found it very odd how things that were so obvious to those on the outside were so very concealed to those who were closer to it.

This time was no exception.

It just made her madder.

"You do know, Hap, that you've explained some of your childhood to me and it is not something I understand because I was not brought up that way. However, you've explained enough that if I was there, and you went off, as you say, on one of those two individuals who created a precious life and then left that life in order to carry on doing criminal or selfish things, I would think nothing but they deserved the power of your anger. Even your rage. They earned it and you should feel free to offer it to them however you see fit. I would probably think they deserved more than you'd give them. And last, you should be aware should this happen, *caro*, that you might not have the focus to give it to them because you'd be holding *me* back from saying a few things myself."

Hap stared straight ahead, continued driving and said not a word.

"Did your grandparents speak to you about your temper?" she asked.

"It bothered them," he said softly.

"And you felt they worried it meant you'd turn out like your father," she surmised.

"His first stint in prison was because he beat a man half to death for knocking over his beer in a biker bar. That being, he was pulled off that guy by some cops and therefore caught for a grocery store robbery for which he was wanted for questioning because he was tying one on to celebrate robbing that grocery store."

Hmm.

"And you think you have that in you?" she queried.

"A man sees his father in him, Luci," he whispered. "I figure good or bad, he searches for that. I don't know about the good. But I know about the bad."

"You're not your father, George."

He pulled her hand he was still holding to his stomach and pressed it there, using this like a tactic to soften the blow of the words he was about to say.

"You can say that until you're blue in the face, baby, and it won't matter. It just is what it is. I have him in me. He's a part of me. I see him in me when I get like that. And that's in a way that won't ever change."

"And there's nothing I can do to help you with this?" she pressed.

"I wish there was, but I don't see that happening," he replied.

"Well, then, I suppose when you're eighty-three and I'm still sitting beside you in your truck you'll realize then that I'll never figure it out and finally relax. It saddens me it'll take that long. But if I'm sitting beside you in your truck, I'll be fine with that."

He was now pressing her hand deep into the hard muscle of his abs and holding it way too tight.

Luci didn't make a peep.

He came to the realization of what he was doing so he released the pressure on her hand and moved it to tuck it into the crook where his thigh met his hip.

Luci turned to face forward.

"I want two children, a boy and a girl, the boy first," she announced to the windshield, and the pressure on her hand came back.

She ignored it.

"If I have two girls, I will be happy," she continued. "If I have a girl first, and a boy second, this will be disappointing, but I'm sure I'll be able to live with it. If I have two boys, my life will be over."

The pressure released but Hap carried on holding her hand.

"Your life will be over?" he asked quietly.

"If I can't dress at least one child in frilly pink dresses, I'll expire from sheer devastation."

He started stroking her fingers with his thumb, muttering, "Best find a crossroads to make a deal with the devil for at least one girl."

Luci grinned at the windshield.

"Though I want all boys," he added.

Luci frowned and looked back at him.

She ignored his lips turned up and squeezed his hand irately. "Do not even *say* that out loud. It might cause a *maledizione*."

"A what?"

"*Maledizione*. What is it in English? A spell, a bad one."

"A curse?"

"Yes, that. Don't speak of such things."

"Baby, you know you're gonna get what you get."

No.

She knew *they* were going to get what *they* got.

She believed in God. She was a good Catholic (okay, she tried to be a good one, thank God He was forgiving).

And she knew her God would not give her two beautiful, kind, loving, loyal men who made her happy only to take both of them away.

She *knew* this.

She also knew that He expected you to work at earning the goodness in life.

Travis had been easy.

Hap was proving difficult.

She did not mind.

In the end, God was going to give her the opportunity to have the best of both worlds.

This would not come without pain and suffering.

But then, what in life mattered if it didn't?

No?

She saw a sign go by as Hap drove.

"I'm hungry," she declared.

"Babe, we ate two hours ago."

"I saw a sign for Bojangles. There's one off this next exit."

"You want Bo's?"

He sounded intrigued.

Yes, she very much loved this man.

"I'm uncertain I can make it to the beach without chicken and biscuits."

"Yeah, I feel the same way."

Luci looked at Hap again. "You want chicken and biscuits?"

He glanced at her before looking back to the road and hitting his turn signal.

"No, baby. What you said earlier. I feel the same way."

She wasn't certain what he was talking about.

"A woman who can down two waffles and four smoky links and two hours later need chicken and biscuits," he muttered. "Yeah. I feel the same way."

Luci was still confused.

Until she remembered.

And you would not be with me if you didn't feel the same.

That was what she'd said earlier, after she'd told him she was falling in love with him.

It was like he sensed she understood this because he lifted her hand to his mouth and touched his lips to her knuckles before he dropped both their hands to his thigh.

And he kept hold all the while exiting. All the while navigating the roads to the drive-thru.

In fact, Hap didn't let her go until he had to pull out his wallet to pay for their food.

And Luci was just fine with that.

He could hold her hand as long as he wanted.

Hap Cunningham could hold her hand forever.

And she hoped, symbolically, he would.

NINE

I Wish

Luci

"WHAT'S GOING ON?"

Luci was pacing Sam and Kia's living room, their sweet, little dog, Memphis, trotting at her heels thinking it was a game, her eyes aimed out the windows to the deck where Hap and Sam were talking.

"Luci, honey, you both show, Hap barely says 'hey' before he asks Sam outside . . . *what's going on*?"

Kia's question came at her again, and Luci stopped pacing to look at her friend.

Memphis yapped.

Both women ignored her.

Kia was showing now, slightly, and like many women, she was even more beautiful carrying a child than when she was not.

Luci thought of this only briefly.

"Hap came to me last Saturday to work things out," she announced.

"Yeah, I guessed that when you two showed here together," Kia replied, watching her closely.

"He wished to find a way to take us back to where we were before we . . . you know."

Kia nodded. "I know."

"Instead, we made love and spent most of the rest of the weekend in bed."

Kia's eyes became huge.

"He drove out to come get me on Wednesday. I've been with him at his home until today. Now he will be with me at my home until he has to leave tomorrow," Luci told her.

"You're together?" Kia breathed.

Luci straightened her shoulders and wished she could smile, but she was too worried about what was happening on the deck, so she could not.

"Yes, *cara*, we're together," she confirmed.

Kia's face grew bright with happiness, a smile growing wide on her mouth before her expression darkened and she turned her head to look out the window.

Luci looked out the window as well.

Body language was *not good*.

Both men seemed tense. Hap was talking. Sam's face was made of stone.

Merda.

"Yes, Hap is very concerned how Sam will take it," she muttered in answer to Kia's unspoken comment.

"Maybe I should go out there," Kia muttered in return.

"I do not think Hap would welcome that," Luci told her.

"Honey," Kia called, and Luci pried her eyes from the men on the deck to look at her friend. "Are things going well?"

She could not say they were going *well*.

She could say she thought she was getting somewhere.

"He's an exceptional lover."

Kia's smile came back. It was hesitant this time, but it was there.

"Well, that's good."

"He has issues that are not mine to share, *cara*, but even though some of them have to do with Travis . . . and Sam, most of them are all Hap's."

"Oh man," Kia mumbled.

"We're working through them," Luci stated, and even she heard the defiance in her voice. Then again, she felt the same in her heart. "But when we're not, he's lovely, Kia. You know how he is. He's Hap. He's funny and he's sweet and he's loving. He's also honest and forthright and that's so very refreshing. And he makes me dinner and tells me stories of growing up in Iowa." She drew in breath and let it out, sharing, "*Bellisima*, he makes me happy."

Kia studied her a moment and then replied, "Good." Her head tilted a bit before she went on to ask, "But . . . I don't get . . ." She shook her head and carried on, "It's kind of new, so isn't it kind of soon for Hap to be taking it there with Sam?"

"He thought, and I have to admit I agree, that if we let too much time pass with us as we are now without sharing with Sam, he would be even angrier, thinking we were keeping it from him."

Kia sounded like she didn't want to say her next. "I have to admit, I agree with that too, even if it isn't right and you don't owe that to Sam."

"Hap feels he does, and since he does, I'm here to support him while he does what he feels he must do."

Kia's gaze was still sharp on her when she noted, "I can't tell from what you're giving me if I'm happy for you."

Luci forced her face to soften. "You can be happy for me, my friend." She tipped her head to indicate the deck. "I'm just worried about what's happening out there."

Kia's words were now cautious. "If Hap allows Sam to—"

Before she could finish that, Luci butted in. "He won't. He'll find it difficult if Sam reacts badly, but he cares deeply for me. He'll be upset but he'll move past it. No." She shook her head. "It's not that. It's how *I* will feel if Sam hurts Hap, and in doing that, hurts me by hurting Hap and standing in the way of our happiness."

"Yeah," Kia murmured, her eyes drifting back to the window. "I won't be too happy if my man pulls that crap either."

"It'll be all right," Luci assured, and Kia looked again to her.

"That's my line."

It was at that, Luci finally smiled.

Her smile didn't last long before she tensed and looked to the windows.

At what Luci saw, she instantly moved to the door.

She was just arriving there when it was opened by Hap, his angry eyes searing into her and his voice was gravel when he declared, "Babe, we're going."

Memphis yipped her greeting to Hap, but Hap ignored her, and Luci only glanced at a now pale Kia before she found her hand seized and she was pulled out the door.

She was being led quickly along the deck when Sam called, sounding just as angry, "Hap, we're not done."

"We so fuckin' are," Hap bit out, dragging her toward the ramp at the side of the house that led to the drive at the back.

Luci looked back to see Sam had his feet planted, his arms crossed on his chest. Kia was out with him, her hand on his biceps, her head tipped back to look up at her husband, but Sam's eyes were on them and his face was no less stony.

Luci was angry at him even not fully knowing what was happening, but she had to see to Hap.

So the only thing she gave Sam was a look of disappointment, a short shake of her head to further share that, and then she hurried along to catch up with Hap as he pulled her around the corner of the house and down the ramp.

He took her right to her side of the truck, opening the door, and before she could even lift a foot to climb in, he had her in his arms and he dumped her in her seat.

He also slammed the door.

Luci let out a stunned breath.

It was then, through the window, she fully caught the look on his face.

Dio.

This was the temper he'd been talking about.

She watched as he prowled around the hood and angled in beside her, even that movement feeling violent, and switched the ignition like he held grave hostility toward his truck.

He, however, did not turn around in the drive or pull out in a spray of gravel or a peel of tires like she expected him to do. He drove with iron control, carefully, deliberately, and again Luci found herself falling a little more in love with him because, even if he was clearly immensely angry, and perhaps would let some of that loose with his driving if he was alone, he was with her so he did not.

She assessed her options and decided against saying anything, allowing him his thoughts as they made the short drive to her house.

They'd stopped there when they'd arrived at the beach in order to bring in their bags before they'd gone to Sam and Kia's.

So now they had nothing to take up when he parked in front of one her two garage doors.

"That bay is empty, *bello*," she said quietly as he used great force to shove the truck into park. "I'll get you the remote."

"Right," he bit out, turning off the vehicle.

She got out.

Hap got out.

He prowled to the foot of her stairs before her but stopped and swung his arm in an exaggerated move of gallantry to indicate she should precede him up the steps.

She scurried to do so and used equal haste in unlocking the door.

She'd just brought her keys and her phone, both she kept in her pockets, so she didn't need her purse. Therefore, when she went in, she went to the kitchen and tossed the keys on the counter, pulling the phone out of the back pocket of her jeans to do the same.

She did this saying, "I also need to get you a key."

"Yeah," Hap stated, and she turned to see him stalking to and up her stairs.

When he disappeared, she looked to the sun shining on the sea in hopes that vision would calm her, as it often did.

This time it did not.

Then she hurried to the stairs and up them.

She found Hap in her bedroom, hands in the pockets of his jeans, standing at the windows but with his side to them, also staring at the sea.

She gave it a moment, but he didn't turn to her.

"Would you like time?" she asked gently. "Or would you like to talk about it?"

He finally gave her his attention, but did it only twisting his head and shoulders her way.

"Or would you like to shout?" she added another option.

"I wish . . ." he began, but he trailed off, said no more, and looked back to the sea.

"You wish what, *luce mio*?" she queried, taking a few more steps into the room.

"What does *luce mio* mean?" he asked the sea.

"My light."

"Your light," he muttered.

"I didn't call—" she started.

He twisted again to her and interrupted. "I know. You'd never do that. To him or me."

He was right. She would not. She called Travis *cuore mio* (my heart) or *tesoro* (treasure) and sometimes *vita mia* (my life), but she never called him her light or even *bello*.

She fell silent.

Hap looked back to the sea.

Luci took another step toward him and prompted, "You wish?"

"I wish they were alive."

She wasn't expecting that, and getting it, even not exactly understanding who he was referring to, just the words made her entire frame go solid.

Hap kept speaking.

"I wish they were alive. I wish I could take you to Iowa and walk into a restaurant with you on my arm and they could meet you. I wish they could see the man I became, the woman I earned being that man. I wish they could see that it was worth all the effort and headache and pains in their asses to believe in me. I wish they could see that in the end, I didn't let them down."

He was speaking of his grandparents.

Oh, Hap.

Her Happy.

So much regret.

So much melancholy.

She unlocked her frame and moved across the room to stand with him. Once there, she gingerly lifted a hand to put it on his chest.

He didn't move, his body stayed tense, strung tight, a vein pulsing up his neck, a muscle twitching in his jaw.

She said nothing, just stood there with him as he battled whatever demons were plaguing him.

"I wish," he went on, "they could come visit here. Stay downstairs. Have nothing to do but walk the beach, or Gram helping you cook and them opening the windows and falling asleep to the sound of the waves."

"I wish that too, *amore*," she whispered.

He didn't nod, didn't glance her way, he just kept speaking.

"I wish I could sit with Gramps and buy him decent beer and you could have wine and Gram could have her tea and we could just sit on the deck, talking and laughing."

"I wish that too, Happy," she said softly.

Again, no acknowledgement of her words, he simply kept going.

"I wish I could buy them a little place, wherever they wanted to be, here with me, or in Iowa, or in Florida, I don't give a fuck. Somewhere they liked. Somewhere where there were no worries. Gramps would demand that he mow the lawn and Gram would can and make jam, but they'd do that only because they wanted to, not because they had to. Nothing weighing on them. Nothing heavy. Nothing suffocating."

She shifted a bit closer and pressed her hand into his chest.

"And I wish they'd come. One of them. Both of them. I don't give a shit. But I wish they'd come when you were there. At my house. I wouldn't lose my shit. I'd open the door and let them get a load of you and then tell them to fuck off."

He was now speaking of his parents.

So she shifted even closer and murmured, "Oh, Hap."

"I actually wish they'll come just so they can see you, see the man they had no hand in making, who made a woman like you fall in love with him, then shut the door in their faces."

Luci wished that too.

But before she could share that, suddenly, he looked directly into her eyes and the feeling burning in his made Luci forget how to breathe.

"I didn't lie. If something happened to me, I saw you lose Gordo, I wouldn't want that for you. That would kill me again, a thousand times, just the thought of it fucking *destroys* me, Luci. I'd want you to move on. I don't care if it's a man, a woman, a dog, a fuckin' alien, whatever you needed to make you happy, I'd want that for you. I'd want you to find that. My spirit would lay restless or wander lost until I knew you were happy."

Not expecting this, or the depths of emotion behind it, a noise came from her nose as the tears spilled over her eyes, but Luci said nothing.

"But I would pine," he whispered and made another sudden movement. So sudden, she jumped as his hands caught her on both sides of her head, pressing in, and his eyes were all she could see. "If I lost you, I would *pine*. I would drink myself stupid, trying not to feel. I'd waste every second, every breath of my useless life if you were no longer in it. I'd be pissed, at God, at man, at the sun, at every-fucking-thing, that you were taken from me, and I'd never get over it. I would *pine*, Luci. There would not be another for me."

And as sudden as his movements, Luci was understanding.

Understanding *all* the reasons he tried to push her away.

Understanding just how deeply Hap Cunningham was in love with her.

And understanding, the man he thought he was, why he feared that and why he wanted to protect her from it.

She lifted her hands and caught his wrists, holding tight, begging, "Don't say that, Hap."

"It's true. I knew it the minute you leaned into me that first time you kissed me. A room lights up when you walk in it. A shit day becomes golden the second you smile. I tasted you on my tongue and I was lost forever."

And there was that look that she'd never fully comprehended explained.

That was the most beautiful thing she'd ever heard in . . .

Her . . .

Life.

But . . .

Still.

Fat, wet drop after fat, wet drop slid down her cheeks as she moved her hands to hold his head like he was holding hers, pressing in, and she hissed, *"Don't say that, Happy."*

"It's true, baby. I get I need to share your heart with him and I'm okay with that. But you're the only one who will ever have mine."

A sob burst from her throat as she pleaded, "Please, *please*, life is so unkind. Don't say that, darling."

"You gotta know."

"I'd want you to be happy."

"That would never happen."

Brokenly, she beseeched, "Please don't say that to me."

His thumbs slid through the wet on her cheeks, and he whispered, "You gotta know." He angled his head, touched his mouth to hers with his eyes wide open, staring into hers, and again repeated, "You gotta know."

Luci closed her eyes and more wet was forced out, coursing down her cheeks.

And then she tipped her head back and Hap's lips were on hers, his tongue gliding in her mouth.

She arched her body into his, doing this completely, giving him her weight, and his arm moved around her shoulder blades, his other swept down her back, her bottom, to her thighs. He lifted her up, swinging her lower half to his side, and carried her to the bed, all the while kissing her gently, but deeply.

On the bed, after all that emotion, she thought it'd go fast. Hungry. Frenzied.

But Hap didn't let it.

He drank from her mouth and roved his hands over her body, taking his time. Even when he rolled over her and pulled her sweater over her head, it was tender and sweet. His mouth then on her neck, his fingers unbuttoning the shirt she wore under her sweater, his lips tracing the path he opened.

He gently tugged the shirt over her shoulders and Luci helped him take it off. Even if his work was languid, she felt the pulse of promise and tried to quicken his pace, but she got distracted when his mouth closed on her nipple over her bra.

She arced into the touch, the feel.

Then she gave herself over to it. His hands light and restful and beautiful slowly warming her to a soothing, exquisite heat.

Her bra was gone and she had no idea when he'd taken it off when he got up on his knees, straddling her thighs.

She started to push up, watching him tug his sweater and tee over his head.

Once it was gone, his wide, muscled chest exposed to her, he looked down at her and ordered quietly, "Lie back. Arms over your head."

"I wish to touch you."

He put a hand to her chest and gently pushed her back, commanding, "Do as you're told, baby."

She did, because his command was exciting. She did, because that was what Hap wanted. And the instant she did, his fingers went to the button of her jeans. He undid them and slid them down, taking her panties with them, pulling off her boots and socks at the bottom.

She then fought squirming or preening as his eyes roamed her naked body. This battle proved harder when his hands did the same, leisurely. And it was nearly impossible when he added his mouth, those lips, his tongue.

"Hap,' she breathed.

He took his time opening her thighs, and she watched as he dipped his head and felt as he lapped at her between her legs.

"*Hap*," she whimpered, eyes rolling back, moving her arm to cup his head and hold him to her.

He lifted up and kissed the strip of curls between her legs.

She looked down, and he whispered, "Arms over your head, Luci, keep them there, honey."

She stared into his eyes and what he was doing, what she was feeling, what was happening suddenly dawned on her.

Luci nodded and moved her arm back over her head. His gaze grew soft and lazy before he went back in, lapping and licking, gently suckling, softly nibbling, his fingers trailing on her hips, her belly, up to cup a breast and rub her nipple with his thumb. All easy, slow, like they had centuries.

Hap made love, but he did it fucking.

But Hap was not making love to her now.

Luci knew what it was.

He was worshiping.

She felt it in every stroke of his tongue, every trace of his fingers.

It wasn't restful, it was *reverent*.

He didn't want her to touch him because he wanted this to be that.

Adulation.

Exaltation.

Luci fell into it. Cocking her elbows toward the ceiling to clutch at the comforter with her fingers, she offered her body, her sex, to his ministrations, giving him the only thing he wanted in return—her noises, her writhing, her whimpers and pants.

"*Amore*," she breathed, so close, feeling the burn like a banked fire, spread for him, smoldering.

He came to his knees between her legs and she opened her eyes, finding it difficult to focus on him.

But she did and he was pulling his wallet out of his pocket.

"Just you, *bello*, please," she begged.

"Shh, baby," he shushed. "Lift your knees high and wide, stay open for me."

Luci did as asked, feeling the thrill of doing that for him instead of disappointment he'd pulled out a condom and put the packet between his teeth. His eyes on her darkening now with hunger, the condom dropping into his open palm as he bit his lip when he yanked his jeans to his thighs and his hard, thick cock sprang free.

She whimpered.

He tore open the packet.

"You're so goddamn beautiful," he growled.

"I need you inside me."

Done rolling the condom on, he wrapped his hand around his cock and bent to her, catching the back of her knee in the biceps of his other arm and planting his hand in the bed.

This did not make her happy. It kept him away from her.

"Closer, *caro*," she whispered.

She felt him as he fed himself to her.

"*Closer, caro, please*," she whimpered.

Slowly, he slid inside.

Her eyes closed, her neck arched and her hand came up blindly to find him. It did, clamping at the side of his neck.

"Back over your head, Luci."

She righted her head and opened her eyes to look at him. "Happy."

"Over your head, honey."

It took effort, but she did as told, and only then did he move.

She bit her lip at the gorgeous feel of him gliding inside and a low snarl rolled between his lips when he saw her do it before he grunted, "Fuckin' beautiful."

"Faster," she pleaded.

He slid his free hand over her side, her belly, and down, and found her clit with his thumb.

She jerked, the beauty of that tearing through her, and she panted, forcing her eyes open, pulsing her hips to meet his torturously slow thrusts, the rolling of his thumb driving her mad.

"Hap."

His head was bent, watching her take him, his eyes roamed up and his mouth muttered, "Fuckin' fuck me, so goddamn *beautiful.*"

Yes.

He was worshipping her.

"*Hap,*" she forced out, her body trapped by the position, what he was doing and his commands, the movements she could make were desperate as she tried to deepen their connection, drive him to give her more, the sensations surging through her overwhelming.

"Baby, come when you come," he urged, going slightly faster (but not fast enough) and thrusting definitely harder (*just* hard enough).

"My darling," she breathed.

Unable to stop herself, she moved her free leg to wrap it around his buttocks, feeling them tense and flex with his drives, just that bowing her back as she struggled to move her hips to meet his thrusts.

"Let go, Luci."

She was dazed, gone, unable to focus, nothing but a body suspended, ready to fall, holding back because she wanted him to go with her.

He thrust faster, deeper, rolling his thumb harder. "Let go, Luciana."

She cried out, tensing her calf around his ass, locking him to her, her back curving up, her head jolting to the side, her lips parted, whispery noises escaping as she clamped her pussy around him and fell, only to glide through the air, not in freefall.

Just free.

Flying.

"*Yes,*" she breathed.

"Christ. Jesus. *Fuck yes,*" he grunted.

It took her a while. Hours or minutes or decades, she had no idea, before she realized the fullness of what he was giving her.

She came back to earth in time to feel him pounding inside, the muscles of his chest and neck popping, the expression on his face so dark and ravening, if he was not Hap, it would be frightening.

And he was giving her this too.

He'd watched her.

Now she would watch him.

He shifted his arm so he'd let her leg go and his weight came to her, his hands shoving under her, up her neck, into her hair, fisting. She curled her other leg around his back, clutching him, her breaths forced out with each of his powerful thrusts, mingling with his grunts of effort.

"Call it," he growled.

"Come, darling," she purred.

His head shot back, his body straining, his lips opened, his fingers in her hair tugged down, shocking a pleasured cry from her mouth and his hips bucked into hers as he came inside her, giving her his offering.

She knew, giving her everything.

His head fell forward, his forehead in the side of her neck, and she released the comforter to wrap her arms around him.

But he stayed inside and this, she'd learned, was Hap. He stayed connected for as long as he could, not sliding out until he had no choice, and even then he kept close.

It took him a while to recover and she still heard the labor of his breathing when he asked, "You okay?"

She most definitely was.

"Yes, *bello*," she whispered.

He kissed her neck but kept his face there and did what he did, keeping them connected until he naturally began to slide out.

Only then did he pull away, but only to shift her to her side and press in behind her, wrapping one arm around her to pull her closer, the other he slid under her head to cushion her, and he lifted to kiss her shoulder before he buried his faced in the back of her hair.

Luci stared at the unceasing beat of the sea.

Now it soothed her.

She sighed.

"Be a minute, then I'm back," he muttered, touching his lips to the back of her neck before gently pulling away to leave the bed.

Luci didn't move. Didn't think. She heard the toilet flush but it was part of the real world, outside of what they'd just done, what they'd just shared, what Hap had just given to her, so she refused to process it.

The only thing she processed was him coming back, moving her to bunch pillows under their heads, one for her, several for him so he could watch the ocean without obstruction. He then pulled her into his arms, curled his legs into hers, and the world was right again.

"You gotta check in at the shop?" he asked.

She shook her head slightly. "Not today."

"But soon?"

Sadly, she had to nod her head, this she also did slightly. "Yes, Happy."

"Monday," he decreed. "Tuesday, I got some exercises I gotta do with the boys this week, I can't get away early. You drive to me. I want you home when I get there."

She felt her lips curve. "All right, *caro*."

Hap fell silent.

Luci didn't break it.

Hap didn't either.

Until he did.

"Nobody but me?" he asked the back of her head quietly.

She knew what he was asking.

Nobody but him since Travis.

"Nobody but you," she answered, also quietly.

"Nobody but you since we kissed, honey, but before that . . ." He didn't finish his sentence. But he did go on. "Minute I get back to the base, I'll make an appointment. Get the all clear, you on birth control?"

"I'll make an appointment."

"Okay, baby," he murmured, using his arm to pull her deeper into his body.

Luci sighed again.

Hap was silent.

Luci didn't break it.

After a time, Hap did.

"Talkin' to him, feelin' his anger, even thinking I got it, I could deal with it, I would feel the same, I know we're tight and this would be a tough spot, but he'd get past it because I'd eventually get past it, something happened."

"What, *bello*?"

"You're my religion."

Luci closed her eyes.

Yes.

She'd been right.

She'd just been worshiped.

"I'm all about God," Hap continued. "Grew up Christian. We went to church on Sundays. My gram was devout. And okay, I fucked around a lot at church because I was me. But I believe. And what I believe is, He made you and He gave you to me, so He'd get where I'm at."

She opened her eyes and said, "Yes, darling, He'd get where you're at."

His arms gave her a squeeze. "I thought that, and Sam was sayin' shit I knew he would say and it hit me. Him saying I had no business bein' with you was like him sayin' I had no business believing in my God. I needed to believe in *his* God. And that wasn't only whacked, it was just wrong."

"Yes, it was just wrong," she agreed.

"I tried to explain that to him, without the religion part, even though I think he'd get me. Kia is his religion. He nearly blew it with her, took off on one of his gigs, and she left. When he got back and she was gone, he called me. Never seen the man panicked. Never heard that coming from him. She was gone and he was undone."

"I remember."

"So, he'd understand."

"Yes."

"I tried to tell myself this was new for him so he might not understand where I was at. Tried to tell myself we didn't have a lot of time in, so I had to get that he wouldn't understand how deep I was. Tried to keep my head there so I wouldn't lose my mind. But he told me I had to let you go. He told me I was confusing you. He told me you were looking for Gordo—"

Luci's body jerked and she moved as if to pull away and bound up, but his arm banded around her belly and he shoved his face in the back of her hair.

"Cool it, baby. Cool it. Cool it. You knew he'd go there. *I* went there. You knew he would. Cut him some slack."

She drew a sharp breath into her nose and forced herself to relax.

Hap kissed the side of her neck and settled in behind her.

His voice held some humor when he continued, "Though, that's when I lost it with him. Told him he could say dick shit to me, but that was insulting you, and we were done. Then I made us done and hauled our asses outta there."

"You can imagine, feeling that was an insult to me, how I feel as it was also an insult to you," she pointed out.

"Yeah." Definite humor in that. "I can imagine."

She twisted her neck to catch his gaze. "I'm not finding things funny, Hap."

"Baby, he can think what he thinks for as long as he thinks it. He can even not get over it, which he won't. Kia'd have his ass in a sling, and he'd never lose you. Not ever. The man has lost a lot. He also would never lose me. But as long as it takes him, it takes him. And where are we?"

She stared into his eyes.

He gave her a shake of his arm. "Where are we, Luciana?"

"Together," she whispered.

"Yeah," he confirmed.

"I'm still angry at him."

Hap gave her a gentle smile. "I figured you would be."

"You were . . ." She hesitated, took in a breath and then guided him there, "In a bad place about your grandparents."

His expression went as gentle as his smile and he bent in to give her a brief kiss.

When he pulled away, however, he didn't go far.

"Regrets suck," he muttered. "You are . . . the things you've been saying . . ." He shook his head, looked to the sea, then returned to her and whispered, "Baby, you've been helping me see things differently. And now that I see me like you see me, I just wish I hadn't pissed so much life away so they could have seen it too since it was always there. I just didn't get it."

She had no control over the moan that floated up her throat and out of her mouth.

And then they weren't spooning.

Hap turned her into his arms and held her as she wept into his chest.

He said nothing. He didn't try to hush her tears. He did eventually begin to stroke her hair.

But other than that, he let her cry it out.

He also let her burrow closer when she'd burned it out, his arms tightening around her to hold her there.

She sniffled and told his chest, "I have something else to teach you."

"Great," he muttered, but she smiled because she could tell with just that one word he was teasing.

She stopped smiling because what she had to say she knew would be hard for him to believe.

But it was crucial she guided him to believing it.

She tipped her head back and he dipped his chin down so he could look into her eyes.

"Hearts don't work the way you think they do, darling."

His arms spasmed around her.

She just pressed closer.

And kept speaking.

"There aren't rooms that people fill or pieces you give away. If you love someone with all of your heart, you just do. But you can love many with all your heart. Like I love my father. And Sam. And Kia. And my friend Massimo. And Celeste." She slid her hand up his chest to the bottom of his throat and pressed lightly. "Like I love Travis. And like I love you."

He dropped his forehead to hers and whispered, "Baby."

"It's true. He had more time with me, but in the end, I hope, I'll have more time with you. But he won't have more of me, like you won't have more of me. You both have all of me and always will."

"You know I loved you before he died."

She nodded, her forehead rolling against his. "I know."

"Not like this, I couldn't go there, but still like this, honey. Somewhere deep I wouldn't go."

This was news.

"Really?"

"Luci, you're you."

That made her smile. "This is true. I am me."

She saw his eyes smile back, he gave her a squeeze, a quick kiss, and then pulled his face an inch away.

"So . . . we're good," he noted.

"We're good," she agreed.

And finally, she was thinking they were.

And again, she felt happy.

"We're doin' this," he stated.

She smiled again, but a lot bigger this time. "We are."

He took in her smile before he lifted his gaze back to hers. "So how you feel about hitting the crab shack?"

"I feel like that's the best idea I've heard all day, except my idea of swinging through Bo's. But the crab shack is better, even than Bo's."

That got her his smile before he kissed her again, not briefly this time.

Then he dragged her out of bed.

She was pulling on her panties when it struck her that he was still wearing his jeans.

"Can I put in a request?" she asked.

"Hit me," he invited, reaching to nab his sweater from the floor.

"You on your back with your arms over your head, totally naked."

He tipped his head to the side, openly intrigued.

"You gonna go down on me?"

"Well . . . obviously."

"Babe, you're good with your mouth."

She struggled her bra on. "So are you."

He assumed a look of such supreme male satisfaction that it made her wonder if she should take her bra off again.

"You get in your flow, and I gotta fuck your face, even with my arms over my head, and you got no problem with that, I'm in."

She'd stopped mid-straightening the twists in her straps so she could fully experience the lovely shiver his words caused.

He'd just finished tugging down his sweater when he saw her arrested and therefore asked, "You feelin' like goin' to Skip's in your undies?"

"Not particularly."

"Then get a move on, gorgeous. I'm feelin' the need for a sandwich and then getting home so I can get naked for my woman."

Now that . . .

That got her moving.

TEN

Paper and Memories

Kia

I WAS READY FOR MY stubborn husband when his stubborn ass got home from his run.

So the instant he walked through the door, I asked, "Are we going to Luci's now so you can apologize to Hap?"

He gave me a scowl as he trudged his big, sweaty body across the living room to the stairs and replied, "I'm hittin' the shower then I'm going to the grocery store."

Avoiding me.

Because his stubborn ass knew he was wrong.

He just wouldn't admit it.

I moved to the foot of the stairs and called to his back, "We don't need anything at the store."

He made no sound or movement to indicate he heard me, just turned left at the top of the stairs toward our room and disappeared.

"You're being stubborn, Sampson Cooper!" I shouted.

At that, I heard our bedroom door slam.

"And annoying!" I yelled.

To that, nothing.

"Bah!" I huffed and walked to my laptop sitting on the kitchen bar.

I was not surprised at his reaction to the news of there being a Hap and Luci. Nor his stubbornness in the hour-long, heated discussion (okay, fight) we'd had after Hap and Luci left. Nor his declaring our discussion (yeah, fight) was done and making that so by changing into his running gear and taking off (he did that a lot when we fought, mostly because—it was sweet, though not when we were fighting—he hated fighting with me so that was his way to put an end to it, that and the grocery store). Nor the fact that he was still feeling obstinate when he returned, even though he'd been out running for over an hour.

I was still pissed.

Sam, of all people, should get it.

Why didn't he get it?

I jabbed through the website I'd been cruising and considered buying a baby crib that cost eight thousand dollars, just to teach him.

The problem with that was, Sam was loaded. He was a high school football coach, but he'd been an NFL superstar and then did other stuff that I was glad he no longer did, but it had paid well, so he was rich as sin. He wouldn't blink at an eight-thousand-dollar crib. He didn't blink at anything I bought. If I wanted it and didn't get it, but he heard I wanted it, he got it for me.

I wasn't exactly broke either, seeing as I was married to him, and Sam was definitely a "what's mine is yours" type of guy, even if he wasn't exactly a "what's yours is mine" type of guy. And this was not because he didn't need what was mine, but the buckets of cash I had were from a life insurance policy my dead first husband took out on himself incidentally while he was also insuring me due to his plan to have me murdered.

Yes.

Things had been a little crazy,

Fortunately, life had evened out.

Not to mention, Sam was insanely excited I was having his baby, in his badass, ex-professional football player, ex-special forces, ex-mercenary kind of way, of course. We got an Amazon package just yesterday that had *three* baby books of *names*.

Just names.

He had a legal pad in his office upstairs that had four whole pages of names written on them (three for boys, one for girls, the boy thing was perplexing him, it was cute, that was, it was cute yesterday, when I wasn't ticked at him—we'd find out the sex soon so at least he could pare that down).

So if I bought an eight-thousand-dollar crib, he might click through the site and ask why I didn't buy the twelve-thousand-dollar one.

He was baby crazy.

Which kind of shocked me he was fighting with me, because for the last few months he'd acted like I was the first woman to successfully conceive a child in the last millennium. It was a wonder he didn't carry me everywhere and have the entire house padded so I didn't bump into anything and get a bruise.

I guessed that meant he was pretty displeased Hap was going for it with Luci.

But really, we were all adults, including Hap and Luci, so I did not get why Sam thought he had a say.

I mean, I knew he was as close as a brother to Gordo, even if I'd never met Gordo. I also knew Gordo had died in Sam's arms. It broke my heart and I hated that for my husband (*really* hated it), but Gordo's death nearly broke Luci, and her healing enough to try to find love again was something to celebrate.

Dammit.

I was deciding the crib really was cute when Sam stalked into the kitchen wearing a sweater and faded jeans, the former looked nice on him, the latter made me want to jump his bones, even pissed (yep, the jeans were that good, or more to the point, Sam's ass was that good).

"I'm buying an eight-thousand-dollar crib for Carly," I announced as he swiped his keys off the counter.

"She's not gonna be named Carly," he growled.

"I like Carly."

He stopped in order to blast me with his stare.

And again, I wanted to jump his bones.

What could I say? My hubby was hot, even pissed. I thought that before I'd met him, when he was my celebrity crush. I *definitely* thought that now, after I thoroughly enjoyed him knocking me up, and all the other times he'd done naughty things to me.

"She's gonna have a name like Kia. A pretty one. An unusual one. One that not half the other girls in her class have," he declared.

That was sweet.

I didn't share that sentiment partly because I was gearing up to get on him again about Hap and Luci but mostly because the door to the deck slammed open and I was forced to jump in shock and twist in my seat.

Skip was there.

And he looked mad.

Uh-oh.

"Skip, whatever it is, I don't wanna hear it," Sam stated.

"Well, you're gonna hear it," Skip stated, slamming the door shut behind him and marching in.

"You wanna not slam our fuckin' door?" Sam somewhat suggested (the "somewhat" part being that it was actually a demand).

I stopped myself from rolling my eyes since Sam did that same thing to our bedroom door not fifteen minutes ago.

It was then I saw Skip had a white envelope and he was digging in it.

He stopped by me and slapped a photograph on the counter by my laptop.

"Joey. Joe. Joseph Patrick McShane."

I studied the picture.

Joey, Joe, Joseph Patrick McShane was a good-looking, dark-headed man in navy whites.

And beside him in that picture was another man in navy whites, that man being a much younger Skip.

Both of them were smiling.

I wasn't sure I'd ever seen Skip smiling.

At least not like that.

I held my breath.

Another picture was slapped beside it and in it Joey, Joe, Joseph Patrick McShane was wearing jeans and a plaid shirt and had his arm wrapped around a very beautiful dark-haired woman wearing a very pretty flowered sundress.

Oh no.

"She was Rebecca. Becky," Skip said. "Rebecca Dolores Skerritt McShane."

He knew all her names.

Oh God.

"He was my boy," Skip told Sam, his eyes glued to my husband. All of a sudden he pounded his chest with his fist and I jumped again, then tensed. "*My* boy. My brother. My Gordo to your Sam."

"Skip," I whispered, not surprised but still not liking the past tense.

Sam said nothing.

"She was his," Skip went on. "They started dating before he joined the Navy. She was sixteen. He was seventeen. She was that girl. That girl who was all girl but who was also one of the boys. That girl who laughed easy and loved hard and stayed true no matter *what*."

As lovely as all that sounded, I didn't like where this was going.

My eyes slid to Sam to see his face set in granite.

It was clear he didn't like it either.

Skip's voice lowered. "Loved her, Joey did. We all did, but she was his moon and stars and sky and breath. She loved him back the same. I don't talk about it, so I never told you about it. Tried to bury it so deep, even lied by omission, not mentioning it when shit went down in the next generation. But here it is. Never seen a love like that, until I saw Gordo with Luci. Never seen a love like that, until I saw *you*," he jabbed a weather-beaten finger at Sam, "and *Kia*." He jabbed his finger at me.

Sam kept silent, but Skip did not.

"He didn't die in the line of duty. Nope." He shook his head. "He got cancer. You know, my sister had ALS. And after what happened with Joey, I never thought I'd think this, even after I lost my sis the way I lost my sis. Never thought I'd say this out loud, but true to Christ, I wish she'd gotten his cancer. I wish she was just her one day and feeling weird and went to the doc and was told she had two months to live and then that was it for her. She'd get weak and endure immense pain and waste away and then there was nothing. I wished that, Sam. After watching what that disease did to her, I wished that for her. I wished it was fast instead of being so *goddamned slow*."

I slid off my seat to my feet and Skip's head turned my way.

"Please don't touch me, sweetheart. Please," he whispered.

God, he was killing me.

"Okay, Skip," I whispered back, but stayed on my feet at the ready.

Skip looked back at Sam and his tone was lower, more level, when he shared, "We didn't expect it, Becky and me. We didn't expect what happened after Joe was gone to happen. Truth be told, it wasn't like I never thought it. Never thought I wished I had a girl like Joey's. So pretty. So sweet. Funny. Able to take a ribbing and give as good as she got. Tough as nails and soft as silk."

He dug into his envelope and pulled out one last picture, putting it beside the others and tossing the envelope aside.

It was a shot of slightly older Becky with her arms around a slightly older Skip's middle, her front pressed to his side, his arm around her shoulders, her head on his chest. Her smile was happy.

His was guarded.

"We fell in love," he said quietly.

"Skip," Sam said low.

"Didn't mean to. Didn't even want to. She didn't either. It just happened, few years after we lost Joe. We'd lost touch. We found each other again. It wasn't about Joe. It was about us."

He paused.

I held my breath.

He continued.

"I made it about Joe."

Oh God.

"Man—" Sam started.

"This life, this shitty mess that is life, it's a struggle, Sam," Skip told him. "It's pain and it's loss and it's heartbreak. It's disease and it's death and it's fighting to carry on. It's hard, Sam, *hard*. Every day is a battle. Every . . . *damned* . . . *day*. Only way to make it through is to latch on to any good you can find. Latch on and do it tight. Sink your nails in and *don't . . . let . . . go*."

Sam stared at Skip.

Skip stared at Sam.

I stared between the both of them, no longer wondering why Skip was so grouchy all the time.

At least that mystery was solved.

I just wished he was hilariously cantankerous because that was him.

I would never wish this.

Not on anybody.

Especially not Skip.

"I let her go, Sam," Skip whispered, and I had to start deep breathing so I wouldn't cry. "It was the stupidest damn thing I've done in my life, and I've been pretty damned stupid, son. And I've regretted it every day. And the biggest regret I have is that I broke her heart. I broke her, Sam. Joe did that and it destroyed him before the cancer took him, and he didn't have any control over it. But when I did it, I did have control, and I did it anyway. And I knew there wasn't another woman for me. I knew it. I still let her go and I paid the price, and that price was steep, believe me. Because I was right. There was never another woman for me. Thirty-five years, she was the one then, she's the one now, she'll be the one the day I die, and I let her go."

"You need to find her, Skippy," I said softly, and he turned his head toward me.

"She died of a stroke three years ago, Kia."

I put my hand over my mouth and looked to Sam.

Skip looked to Sam too.

"Hap and Luci came to the shack and they were happy. I've seen that before from our girl but never from our boy. He's blind in love. Lost to it. And the only thing that's making that less than all it should be for them is me asking if you knew and Hap tellin' me you weren't best pleased."

He leaned into his fist on the counter, eyes locked on Sam.

I slid my hand down to my throat and held my breath again.

"They know the pain of life. The loss. The heartbreak, son," he said quietly. "Let them have their happy." He pushed off his fist but knocked his knuckles into the counter. "I'm leaving those for you. You think on things. But I want them back. It's all I have left . . . of either of them. You think on that too. Because when life boils down to paper and memories, you'll want all you can get of that last."

And with that, he turned on his foot and strode right out.

I watched him go then turned to my husband.

"Honey," I whispered.

Sam looked to me. "Tell my wife I love her."

Slowly, I closed my eyes.

Gordo's last words.

"Baby," Sam called.

I opened my eyes.

"I want more for him."

"I . . . sorry?" I asked.

"Hap," he answered. "He deserves more than to be second best to a dead man."

"He deserves to have what he wants."

"He deserves more."

"How can you have more than Luci?"

"She loved him like you love me."

"And then he died."

Sam shut his mouth.

I kept going.

"They've been together a week and Hap came to you to tell you so you wouldn't think they were hiding things. He knows what you were to Gordo. What Gordo is to you. What Gordo was to Luci. Can you honestly know that man longer than I've known that man and not know he would not be on our deck, explaining he and Luci were falling in love, if he did not believe he was getting what he needed and intent on giving her the same?"

"You don't know."

"I know your thinking is colored by your brother's girlfriend settling for something she didn't want after she lost Ben. She is not Luci. Luci's older, wiser, knows what she wants, knows how precious life is, love is, and she's very much in love with Hap."

"It's been a week."

"And I fell in love with you over breakfast the first time we met. Do you not believe that?"

Sam shut his mouth again.

"When did you fall in love with me, honey?" I whispered.

He didn't whisper, or hesitate, when he answered, "Over breakfast."

God, I loved my husband.

I smiled at him.

He took in my smile then looked down at the pictures.

"I hate that for Skip," he murmured.

Yes.

I loved my husband.

"Me too," I agreed.

I watched his wide chest expand then he let out a breath and looked at me.

"I'll go talk to Hap tomorrow."

Oh yeah.

I really, *really* loved my husband.

"Need you right here, Kia," he stated.

It was my turn not to hesitate.

I rounded the bar and went to him.

The second I got close, he folded me in his arms.

So I did the same with him.

"I struggle," he said into the top of my hair.

I tipped my head back. "With what?"

"With you, especially pregnant. I wanna wrap you up in cotton wool. Get itchy, you goin' out in a car by yourself. Get jumpy, I'm at work, expect you to text you're home, and you're late tellin' me you got home."

I didn't know he felt that.

I didn't like he felt that.

At the same time, I did because it shared how much he felt for me.

It was time to start communicating more effusively with my husband.

I gave him a squeeze. "Nothing is going to happen to me, baby."

"You had a hit out on you when I met you."

Well, that was quite the drama.

I pressed closer. "It's all good now."

"I lost Ben. I lost Gordo. I watched my mother lose her son. I watched Luci lose Gordo." His hold on me tightened. "I'm holding on to happy."

I was so down with that.

"Hold on all you want, Sam, I'm not going anywhere."

He bent his head and kissed me.

He lifted away, thought better of it, and bent in again.

It got heated.

He started shuffling me backward.

I broke the connection of our mouths. "I thought you were going to the grocery store."

His lips twitched. "Don't be a smartass."

I grinned at him.

He kept shuffling me.

"So, about that eight-thousand-dollar crib," I teased as he rounded us at the corner by the stairs.

"Get what you want. I've contacted an architect. We're adding on to the house."

I planted my feet.

"Babe," he growled.

I lifted my brows. "We're adding on to the house?"

"We havin' more than one kid?"

Absolutely.

"Yes."

"We need more room."

"That's construction, and mess, and construction workers, and dust, and noise, and *construction*."

"We need more room, Kia."

"We can find another house."

His voice was steel when he declared, "I'm not leaving the house where you fell in love with me."

That was super sweet.

But still.

"We fell in love over a breakfast table in a hotel in Lake Como," I reminded him.

"We started the fall there. We *landed*," he gave me a squeeze, "*here*."

Okay.

Well.

I couldn't argue that.

Actually, I kind of could since there was Crete and Indiana in between.

But I just didn't feel like it.

And the bottom line truth was, we did, indeed, land right here.

"Whatever. I'll move in with Luci while they're building."

His expression turned stormy. "You're not moving away from me."

"You can come with."

His eyes lifted to the ceiling.

I went solid.

"Where's Memphis?"

Memphis was our King Charles spaniel.

Memphis was cute as heck and totally social, even with Skip, who that day had been angry, but he was typically seriously grumpy.

Memphis was only not social when she was feeling like napping or when she was doing something she shouldn't be doing, like chewing one of Sam's running shoes.

It was a new thing of hers.

Sam figured she sensed I was pregnant and was acting out to get my attention.

I figured it was something else entirely.

What could I say?

She was no longer a puppy.

But she loved her dad.

And she sensed I was pregnant, so she wanted to make sure she didn't lose his attention.

Sam went solid too, except his lips muttered, "Shit."

"Memphis!" I shouted.

"*Yap!*" Memphis shouted back from upstairs.

"What are you doing?" I yelled.

"*Yap, yap, yap!*" Memphis told me.

"She was snoozing on our bed when I went in to take a shower," Sam told me. "Then she was snoozing on the rug in the bathroom that's outside the shower, so I nearly broke my neck when I got out of the fuckin' shower."

That would be funny if I didn't have to say what I had to say.

And, by the way, it proved my theory that our furry little girl wanted her daddy's attention.

"Did you put your shoes in the closet?"

"No."

"Then kiss at least one good-bye."

"*Yap, yap, yap!*" Memphis yelled.

"And you want another dog," he reminded me.

"Maybe I'm rethinking that."

"*Yap!*" Memphis chimed in.

Sam grinned at me.

I remembered what we'd been doing.

So I pulled from his arms and raced up the stairs.

"Dammit, Kia! Don't run on the fuckin' stairs!" Sam shouted from behind me, and I heard his heavy footfalls as he chased me.

My husband loved me.

That was good.

Because he, Memphis, and the baby inside me were my world.

Luci

JUST AFTER DAWN THE NEXT morning, with windswept hair, her arms wrapped around her holding her cardigan closed, Luci moved across the deck to Sam and Kia's back door.

She knocked. She had to do it loud because it was early, they'd likely still be asleep, but she knew Sam would hear her.

She stopped knocking and turned to the surf, the wind blowing in her face, taking her hair back, eyes seeing the sun not very high over the sea.

She drew in a breath, turned again to the door, and saw Sam coming down the stairs wearing dark track pants with a light stripe down the side, pulling down a long-sleeved white tee.

He came right to the door, his expression gentle but inscrutable, and immediately opened the door.

"Luci, babe, get in from the chill," he murmured.

"Thank you."

His big body gave a slight jerk. "For what?"

"For not letting him die alone."

That big body went utterly still.

"Thank you, Sam, for bringing him back to me," she whispered.

"Luci," Sam whispered back.

"He loved you, but he would love you *so much more* if he knew how you were going to take care of me."

"Babe, come in from the chill," Sam urged quietly.

"Now you have to let me go."

Something moved over his face. A pain she understood. A pain she'd lived with for years. A pain that had buried itself deep inside her and would always be there, even if she'd learned to live with it.

A pain, his brand of it, that Sam was learning to live with too.

Yes.

She'd been right when she'd had her thought that morning after waking in Hap's arms.

This wasn't about "The Code."

Or it was about "*a* code," just not the one she thought it was.

For some men, duty and brotherhood never died.

Sam was one of those men.

And Luci understood it, for if you kept it alive, you could fool yourself into keeping what you loved alive, even after it was indisputably lost.

She lifted her hand to press it to her heart. "We will keep him alive in here." She reached out and pressed his chest over his heart. "And in here. It is not how we would want him to be with us. But it's all we have and having had Travis for the short time we did, we both know it's better than nothing."

Sam's fingers curled around the back of her hand and held tight, now pressing her hand into his chest.

But he said nothing.

"Your job is done, *caro*," she said softly. "And you did it well. Now you must let me go."

"I was gonna go talk to Hap today," he shared.

"Good. This will bring him great relief."

It also brought her great relief, but she didn't tell him that.

"If anything happens to me, promise—" Sam started.

Luci turned her hand and curled her fingers into his with all her might, leaning into him and hissing, "Nothing is going to happen to you."

"Promise me you'll take care of her," he finished stubbornly. "Promise me you and Hap will look after her."

She pounded their hands on his chest once. "Nothing is going to happen to you, Sam."

"Promise me, Luci, you'll look after Kia and our baby."

She stared into his eyes.

Dio.

Life was so unkind.

"You don't even have to ask me that," she told him.

He closed his eyes.

Luci squeezed his hand.

He opened his eyes.

"Nothing is going to happen to you, Sam," she whispered.

"I know," he replied.

She gave him a small smile.

He used her hand in his to guide it around his back and then he let it go and pulled her into his arms.

He engulfed her in a hug and Luci pressed into his big, strong body, wrapping both her arms around him, holding close.

"I miss him," she said to Sam's chest.

He held Travis to that chest as he died.

He held Travis to that chest after he died.

He held Travis to his chest when he carried him home.

His voice was thick when he replied, "Me too."

She tipped her head back and caught his eyes. "*Grazie, il mio bell'amico.*"

"It was my pleasure, sweetheart," he whispered. His study of her face became acute. "You happy?"

Luci felt her face gentle. "I woke up in his arms. He told me I was his religion last night. And he was not hungry, but I was, so he swung by Bo's on the way here yesterday."

Sam's head ticked and his eyes registered surprise then warmth at the "religion" comment.

He was smiling by the end.

"So yes, Sam," she continued. "Though, I'm not happy, as such. He's making me happy."

"Good," he muttered.

"Now, I must go. He doesn't like it when I leave him alone in bed in the morning."

His smile got bigger and he gave her a squeeze, saying, "I bet he doesn't."

She shot him a return smile and squeezed him back.

Then she moved her arms from around him so she could catch his head in her hands. She went up on her toes to kiss each cheek and pulled away but didn't let go.

"I love you, Sam. So very much."

He placed his hands on her neck and kissed her forehead, somewhat like Hap kissed her nose, if not exactly like Hap gave her that.

"I love you too, Luci," he replied after he'd pulled back.

She let him go and stepped away. "We'll see you later?"

He nodded. "Yeah." He looked down the beach toward her house and back at her. "You walk here?"

It was her turn to nod.

"Babe, I'll walk you back."

"Not necessary. It isn't far."

"Luci—"

"Sam, I'm good." She stared straight into his eyes and the inflection in her tone was much changed. "I'm good, *caro*."

It took him a while to come to terms with that in all its many nuances.

Then he nodded once again.

Only then, she knew, did he truly let her go.

And let Travis go.

Odd, but she felt no loss. She thought she would. She thought this would be difficult.

Instead, it was beautiful. Precious. A treasured memory made that she would never forget.

She gave him another smile and a small wave as she turned and strolled to the walkway to the beach.

Luci moved at a much faster clip on the way home. Or as fast as the sand would let her white Keds take her.

She hit the gate to the switchback stairs at the side of her deck and punched in the code that unlocked it. She swung the latticework door open, walked under the arch, and made sure the latch caught behind her.

She walked up the stairs, eyes to her feet, but lifted her head the instant she hit the top.

She then halted.

Hap was leaning against the side of a closed window in the opening made by a panel he'd folded back. He was wearing much the same as Sam, except not track pants, but navy sweats, and not a long sleeve white T-shirt, but a cream, thermal, three-button, long-sleeved Henley.

He had his arms crossed on his chest and his bare feet crossed at his ankles.

"Couldn't help yourself, could you?" he asked.

She grinned and moved toward him.

The minute she made it to him, he uncrossed his arms and pulled her into them.

She gave him as much of her weight as she could with two hands at his pecs.

"That go okay?" he asked, concern unhidden in his eyes.

"Yes. Sam will be over sometime today to talk with you."

She was right.

He was relieved.

He didn't hide that either.

"You maneuver that or did Skip?" he queried.

"He'd come to that conclusion before our talk so my guess . . . Skip."

"Right."

She had very good friends.

She had Hap's arms around her.

The sun was shining and the waves were crashing into the shore.

So maybe life was not *that* unkind.

Luci kissed him under his chin.

When she was done doing that, he inquired, "You gonna make me breakfast, or are we gonna go back upstairs and fuck, then you make me breakfast?"

She didn't even have to think about it.

"I choose option two."

"Excellent," he muttered, curling an arm around her shoulders and drawing her inside.

He kept it around her shoulders when he folded the window back into place and made sure it was secured.

And he continued to keep it around her shoulders when he walked them upstairs.

He removed it when they made it to her bed.

But then, of course, he needed it, and his hands, and other parts of him, to bring her even closer.

ELEVEN

His woman. His girl. Luci.

Hap

HAP WALKED IN HIS BACK door and was instantly accosted by his woman.

Though, he was accosted in a way he'd never been accosted by anyone before.

She had hold of his head and was kissing every inch of his face she could reach.

He put his hands on her hips and laughing asked, "Jesus, babe. What the fuck is going on?"

She pulled away and his breath stuck at the look of unadulterated joy on her face.

"Kia and Sam had their ultrasound today. It's a boy!"

His stomach warmed, his mouth smiled, and his lips said, "Fuckin' brilliant."

"I know!" she yelled, dancing away from him and into the kitchen. "We're having champagne to celebrate."

He was not having champagne.

Champagne did not go with the tacos he was making for dinner that night.

And he hated champagne.

He didn't tell her that.

He wandered into the kitchen after her.

It was Wednesday, a week and a half after their roller-coaster weekend at the beach.

Last week, she'd come to him on Tuesday, as ordered, left on Thursday, and Saturday, he'd used the remote she'd given him to park in her garage. He had to wait all of half an hour for her to get home from the shop late Saturday morning.

On Sunday, since she'd arranged things with the women who worked her store, she'd come back with him. They were returning again on Saturday.

He had no idea how long they could go on like this.

He also didn't care.

He was realizing that Luciana was a woman who lived in the moment.

Since she'd pulled his head out of his ass, those moments were fucking great.

So he was sticking there with her.

And he had a strong feeling he'd be down with that even if it lasted fifty years.

"I'm gonna get outta my fatigues then I'll get on dinner," he told her, head in the fridge, grabbing a beer.

"I can make dinner, Happy."

If they were out, among people, she called him Hap or George.

When they were alone, not all the time, but a lot of the time, she called him Happy.

She was big into endearments, and he figured that was part of it, adding the "py" like she might add an "ie" to his real name to be cute, sweet, familiar.

Mostly, he figured she was making a point.

Since it was a good point that meant good things for her, he was down.

"You make breakfast, I make dinner," he reminded her, popping the cap on his beer.

"It doesn't seem fair you work all day and then come home and cook."

He sucked some back, swallowed and shared, "I like cookin'."

For her.

He liked cooking for her.

He didn't share that distinction with Luci.

Her eyes were on his beer. "You're not going to drink champagne with me, are you?"

"Nope."

Her shining eyes came to his. "More for me."

"Yup," he said, went to her, kissed her nose and then walked through the living room, loped up the stairs and changed into jeans and a tee.

But he took his phone out before he walked back downstairs and made the call.

"Hey," Sam greeted.

"Yo," Hap replied. "Heard the news, daddio. Awesome."

"Yeah."

Hap also heard the smile in Sam's voice.

It was gone when he continued, "Listen, brother . . ."

Hap listened but Sam didn't say anything else.

So he prompted, "What?"

"Got about four hundred names written down, but I . . . Hap, buddy, I can't get around it."

"What?" Hap repeated.

"Now we know he's a boy, we're namin' him Benjamin Travis."

"Yeah you are."

Sam was silent.

"Strong name," Hap went on. "Didn't know Ben, but Gordo would be fuck-ton honored, dude. Beside himself. And Luci'll lose her shit, she'll be so happy."

"You're cool?"

He sounded dubious.

Hap dipped his voice low. "Remember, Sam, I loved him too."

A second's hesitation, then, "Yeah."

"I won't tell Luciana. Should come from you."

"Thanks, brother."

"Happy for you, Sam. You and Kia. He'll be beautiful."

"Yeah." Sam cleared his throat then said, "Kia's still pissed you two aren't gonna be here for Thanksgiving tomorrow. Mom isn't too happy either."

"Makin' Luci Gramps's brined bird and Gram's mushroom sausage stuffing, Sam. No way Maris and Kia'd let me horn in to do that for Luce at your place. Though, like we told you last weekend, you're all welcome here. We'll have plenty."

"My thoughts on the matter, even though my wife won't get there with me because it's all about family for her, is that you want your woman all to yourself."

His grandfather's brined turkey and his grandmother's stuffing were the shit.

But yeah.

Sam knew where it was at.

"We'll be back on Saturday."

"Don't bring leftovers. I nearly got a hernia carrying the bird Kia bought up the stairs. It's like she thinks she's gonna feed my whole team."

Hap laughed.

Then he said, "Listen, bro, gotta go make dinner for my woman."

"Let you go. See you this weekend?"

"Absolutely."

"Later, brother."

"Later, man."

Hap disconnected and sucked in a deep breath.

He let it out and went downstairs to make dinner for his woman.

HAP WALKED IN THE BACK door and the first thing he saw was the Christmas tree in the living room.

Last weekend it had been Christmas trees-a-fuckin'-go-go.

On Saturday, her two trees. One, a huge, butt-ugly silver one that had white and clear (yeah, *clear*) ornaments in her living room that he gave her no end of shit about. One, an equally butt-ugly, but smaller and narrow gold one that had pink ornaments made entirely of feathers (yeah, *feathers*) in her bedroom that he also gave her no end of shit about.

Onto Sunday and his place, where they got a real tree and he dug out the box of decorations he hadn't opened in forever.

The ornaments from Iowa he'd inherited from his grandparents.

Half the time Luce had been near tears, the other half bursting with excitement and Christmas cheer when he told stories as they unearthed the ornaments and they trimmed the tree.

Except for the near-tears parts, it had been the bomb.

And his tree, with its old, mismatched ornaments, was gorgeous.

He'd also bought some boughs so Luci could decorate his mantle, stringing them with lights, and nestling the new frames she'd bought in them.

She'd framed pix of his grandparents and pix of him with his grandparents that she dug out of the ones he showed her.

When she was with him, she had all day on her own and she liked to take long walks to keep fit, but other than that she didn't have a lot to do but talk on the phone to her friends, clean his house (which she did), keep his larder stocked (which she did), do their laundry (something else she did) and shop.

But those pictures were her having the means to do something for him in a way she was clued in to how he'd feel about it.

It worked.

His house never felt like a home.

It wasn't the tree.

It was Luci and those pictures.

So now it did.

It was when he smelled what he smelled that he turned his head to the right.

Luci was cooking.

"Luce, I do dinner," he announced.

"Well hello to you too," she replied from her place at the stove, shifting shit around in a skillet, steam swelling from a big pot on another burner.

He went to her, gave her a quick kiss, pulled not too far away and repeated. "Luciana, I do dinner."

She gave him a fake pouty look.

It was cute.

"But Happy, I *needed* my mother's *spaghetti alla carbornara* tonight. *Needed* it."

He looked down at the chunks of pancetta frying in the pan and his stomach let it be known on the rare occasion he allowed her to cook, she cooked gen-you-wine eye-talian, and that shit was life.

"All right, baby," he muttered and kissed her again. He turned to head out. "I'm gonna change. You cool with eating in front of the game?"

"When's football season end again?" she asked his back.

"July," he lied.

He looked over his shoulder at her and chuckled when he saw the expression of horror on her face.

"Tell me you're kidding, George Cunningham," she demanded to his departing back.

"February," he answered.

"*Grazie Dio.*"

That made him chuckle again.

He went up and changed and came down again to find her draining pasta.

"Got a call from Massimo today," she told him as he headed to the fridge for a beer.

On his way, Hap saw her wineglass mostly empty, so he detoured to fill it and asked, "Yeah?"

"He started his house thirty years ago. He's decided to do a special show, in February. Fashion Week. I checked my phone and it doesn't clash with your Super Bowl."

He'd got his beer, popped the cap, and turned his hips to the counter and his attention to her.

"You tellin' me you're gonna go?"

She was dumping skillet contents into drained spaghetti in the big pot as she answered, "I'm telling you that I'd like us both to go as Massimo is featuring models from his entire career. The oldest is Siobhan. She's fifty-two."

"Fifty-two. Over the hill."

She turned a glare at him.

He grinned at her and took a drag from his bottle.

"He wants me to walk. Will you go with me?"

Would he go to New York, watch her walk a catwalk, kiss a variety of cheeks, and generally hold court in her world, all (except the catwalk) on his arm?

If he needed leave and didn't get it, he was going AWOL.

"Only if I get a front row seat at this show."

She dropped her wooden spoon, clapped her hands then rushed to him and threw herself in his arms, jumping up and down in them.

"Massimo would put you nowhere else!" she cried, then kissed him. When she pulled away, she announced, "This makes me *very happy*."

His meaning in life.

Serious.

"Good, baby," he muttered.

She shot him a sunny smile and returned to her pasta.

"Shoot me the dates by text and if I need leave, I'll request it tomorrow."

"All right, *bello*."

He watched her cook, wearing jeans and a sweater with bare feet in his kitchen.

This was his life.

Christ.

This was his life.

And it was good.

"BABE, COME CLOSER."

She didn't.

She rode him, wearing nothing but a sexy, lacy little bra, and she did it slow.

"Luce, go faster and *come closer*."

He was on his back on the couch, naked, his arms over his head, hands stuffed in the cushion by the arm of the couch, and she was on his dick.

The game had not been boring.

Luci cupping his junk in the second quarter and giving him a look that told him what she wanted to do with it, he didn't care what he was missing.

Her hazy eyes found his as she slowed her roll.

Slowed her fucking roll.

She was killing him, all of her, that little bra, that hair, that face, her sweet, tight pussy a wet, hot tease.

"Babe," he growled, pulling both hands from the cushion to grasp her hips and get this show on the road.

"Arms over your head, Hap," she warned.

"Go faster, you'll get what you want."

She leaned into him, face to face. "Arms over your head, *caro*."

He stared into her turned-on eyes in her smug face, knowing she was playing with him, and thought, *fuck it*.

He rolled her and drilled her.

"Hap! No fair!" she cried.

"Wrap your legs around me."

She was taking his cock hard, so now biting her lip, her nails digging in his shoulders, liking what she was getting but not about to admit it.

She pulled herself together, slapped his arm and repeated, "No fair."

What she did not do was wrap those long legs around him.

"Right," he replied, pulled out, knifed up to his knees and felt his cock jump when she cried out in a way he liked after he flipped her to her belly then hauled her up on her knees in front of him.

That ass.

Damn.

He thrust hard and deep.

Her head reared back, hair flying everywhere.

Fuck yeah.

"Ride that now," he grunted.

"Yes, darling," she gasped, slamming back into him.

He mounted her, hand in the couch at her side, other hand slipping over her belly down and in, going at her clit.

She started panting and bucking.

Wild.

"Yeah, baby, fuck me," he encouraged, meeting her moves, the wet, sweet noises of their connection fucking *music*.

She started rippling around his dick.

Her warning.

"Don't come," he ordered.

"Hap," she breathed.

"Don't come, Luciana."

She exploded, trembling under him, her pussy clenching, milking his dick, her hot little noises spurring him on.

Fuck, she was awesome.

He pushed back up, grabbed her ass on both sides and watched his slick cock take her, fucking hot, totally beautiful, until he arched into her, shooting hard and deep, his eyes closing, a guttural noise bursting from his balls, hurtling up his chest and out his mouth.

He came back to the world and fucked her gentle, watching her take that too. Moving his gaze, he saw the softness of her face in profile with her cheek to the couch, tendrils of her hair obscuring his view she didn't bother pulling away.

So Hap reached out and did it for her.

She made a mew of gratitude, and again he wondered if he liked this better than what she just gave him. That look on her face. Knowing he did it for her and how much.

When he started losing it, he pulled out, nabbed his tee, shoved it under her so if she leaked, she leaked on his tee and not the couch, and rolled her before he lowered himself to her.

"Good?" he asked, but he didn't need to.

Her expression was still soft, sated, partially dazed, and her fingertips were moving over his skin lightly, like he had braille stamped everywhere and she was fascinated by what she was reading.

"No fair," she replied, trying and failing to assume a pouty face.

He grinned at her.

"That isn't our deal, Hap."

"Baby, do not even try to tell me you didn't get off on that."

"I was getting off on what I was doing before."

"You got off harder taking me on your knees. You love getting fucked on your knees."

Her eyes narrowed.

Yeah, she loved it.

"If I used my hands when you told me not to, what would you do?" she asked.

"Pull you over my thighs and spank your ass then probably fuck you on your knees."

She squirmed.

He fought his grin at feeling it and put his lips to hers. "You want that, use your hands next time I'm doin' you like that."

Her gaze slid to the side. "Ugh."

He pulled back an inch. "How hard you come?"

She rolled her eyes.

"That hard?" he teased.

She glared into his eyes. "You're annoying."

"I love you."

Her body went still under his.

He'd never said it straight out like that.

She knew.

But he'd never said it.

"Though, just shot inside you with two handfuls of your ass, so I'm feeling sentimental."

Her eyes got big.

Then they squeezed shut as she busted out laughing and finally wrapped him in all her limbs.

He grinned down at her as she did.

Nope.

This . . .

Luci laughing hard.

This was the best it could get.

When she was done, he asked, "You want me to clean you up?"

"I'll do it, *amore*."

He kissed her, long and wet, before he helped her to her feet.

He gathered her clothes first, handing them to her, before he pulled on his jeans and sweater.

He was flat out on the couch when she returned, dressed, and collapsed on him.

He curled his arms around her and tangled his legs with hers.

She burrowed closer.

She passed out halfway through the fourth quarter.

He carried her to bed.

He was never so happy to miss most of a game.

THE MUSIC WAS PUMPING, THE flashbulbs were popping, and Hap

felt his gut drop when she came out on Massimo's arm.

The dress was shocking red. All lace. A complicated top. It fit her beautiful body like a glove to her knees where it bulged out and trailed behind her five feet in a wide swell of delicate red lace.

She led with her hips, smiling big and white, her hair huge, her makeup heavy, her hand tucked in the crook of Massimo's elbow, her head turning side to side as she worked it down the catwalk.

That was his woman.

That was his girl.

That was his Luci.

She came abreast of him, looked right at him and lifted her elegant hand with its blood-red fingernails to her ruby red lips and blew him an exaggerated kiss before her smile went wired, and he would swear to his dying breath she lit up that whole damned place.

Bulbs popped in his direction, but he didn't care. On her way back, when she leaned slightly in front of Massimo to catch his eyes again, he jerked up his chin.

She threw that huge head of hair back, and even in that massive place that was filled with thunderous applause at the finale of a show even he thought was the shit, you could hear her loud, throaty laughter.

That was his woman.

That was his girl.

That was his Luci.

SHE WAS TWO INCHES TALLER than him, trailing a spread of heavy red lace, some of which was now gathered and hooked to a button at the back of the poof at her knees, her fingers wrapped tight around his arm, when they strode into the party.

People clapped, gasped, shouted, and two came up immediately, impatiently taking turns to kiss her cheeks.

It was the proudest moment of his entire goddamned life.

"This is First Sergeant Hap Cunningham, my man," she murmured.

Handshakes.

Chin lifts.

"Please meet George. George Cunningham," she introduced.

Nodding heads.

Clapping of arms.

She was eventually swept away.

Hap didn't mind.

He got to watch her in her element.

It was an amazing show. There were hundreds of beautiful people in beautiful clothes there, at least fifty other models, male and female, several of them famous, like Luci, but she reigned supreme.

They loved her.

Worshipped her.

He knew that feeling. Though his devotion was a different kind, it was still all about Luci.

And anyway, the minute she was gone, they descended on him like he was a rock star, gushing how Luciana looked *fabulous*. How she seemed *so very happy*. How they hoped she was *back*. How they made such a *handsome couple*. How deeply they *thanked him for his service*.

And shock of shocks, all of that was genuine.

It wasn't until a half an hour in when he was alone for the first time that he heard a meant-to-be-overheard, sniped, "Well, she definitely has a *type*."

He was in his dress uniform, at Luci's request.

He started to turn his head to find the woman who'd said that when he heard, "Of course she does. Gorgeous, muscled, red-blooded American heroes are *everyone's* type, *dahleenk*, if you have any taste at all."

Hap didn't know who'd made the first comment.

But a tiny old woman who was in the most ridiculous outfit he'd ever seen said the last.

She squinted through a massive pair of insanely ludicrous glasses at a thin woman in black with a streak of red lipstick on reedy lips and went on, "You shouldn't be wearing black. Although Massimo stamped next season indisputably in *scarlet*, it seems to me you should be wearing *green*."

The woman in black got red in the face and scuttled away, the woman she was with following her.

The old lady stopped in front of him and peered up at him.

"I'm glad you turned out not to be a schmuck," she announced.

"Let me guess," he replied. "You're Pearl."

She did a mini-bow, straightened and said, "I see, yet again, my reputation precedes me."

"Luci thinks you're the shit."

She did. Pearl Bazer was the person in New York, outside Massimo, she most couldn't wait for him to meet.

"That's because I am," she retorted.

"I like your outfit."

"Liar. You hate it."

"It's interesting."

"I'm old as dirt. Interesting is all I got left, sonny."

"I feel the urge to spot you. I'm afraid your necklace is gonna send you flat on your face. How much does that thing weigh?"

"I'm too old to work out and too stubborn to die so I gotta stay in shape *somehow*. I do it by accessorizing."

Hap started laughing.

He wasn't done when she declared. "Luci was right. I like you."

He wrapped his arm around his stomach, his other he laid at the small of his back and returned her bow.

"However, you're in the presence of a lady who lacks champagne. I don't know what the Army thinks of this, but it's my notion you're dishonoring your uniform."

He gave her a grin, a salute, and asked, "You want me to bring two glasses? You seem like a woman who knows how to double fist."

She busted out laughing, reaching up to grab hold of his biceps as she did it, her shoulders shaking, her head hanging, and he decided Luci was right.

She was the shit.

Suddenly, her head came up, she appeared all serious, even if her eyes behind those crazy glasses were still dancing. "I invented the double fist." She shooed him with her hand. "Run along, soldier. A citizen is in need."

He didn't run along.

If there was any human in the world he'd do this to, outside his woman, it was this old broad.

So he bent down, kissed her cheek, and muttered, "At your service."

Then he shot her a wink and moved to find a bar.

He'd given his order when a man said, "You survived Pearl. You're ready for battle."

He looked to his side to see a dark-headed, good-looking, tall, fit guy in a really nice suit, nice shirt, no tie, standing there.

"I'm considering recruiting her," Hap returned. "I have a feeling even with those glasses she's an excellent shot."

The man smiled and offered his hand. "Henry Gagnon. Devotee of Pearl, friend of Luci's."

Hap took his hand and shook it, replying, "Hap Cunningham. I like Pearl and I'm just Luci's."

The man broke the connection, muttering, "Just Luci's."

"Yup," Hap confirmed, then asked, "Henry Gagnon?"

"Yes."

"Dude, friend of mine has a coffee table book of yours. You got talent."

Gagnon inclined his head.

Classy fucker.

"That probably doesn't mean a lot coming from a grunt," Hap noted.

"I think that's something people have trouble understanding. Anyone who enjoys your work, and shares that, it means a great deal. More than you can know." The man's lips curved. "And it doesn't hurt to know I received the royalties from your friend who bought the book."

"We'll start a library of them," Hap joked.

"Obliged," Gagnon replied.

Hap turned to the bar to gather Pearl's glasses and his beer, a beer he'd ordered to stay in the bottle.

"Old fashioned," Gagnon said to the bartender and looked to Hap. "You hold on a second, I'll help you with those."

"Thanks," Hap murmured.

Gagnon got his drink, took one of Pearl's champagne flutes and moved away from the bar beside Hap.

"No way to take the awkwardness out of it," Gagnon began. "Pearl put Luci on the spot with me as her audience, and Luci shared about you two the last time she was in New York."

"Fantastic," Hap mumbled.

Gagnon stopped, and Hap stopped with him. "She's radiant. You did that. I haven't seen her like that in years. If I was that kind of guy, I'd hug you."

He did not know this man.

But still, that felt fucking good.

"Glad you're not that guy because I'm not that guy either," Hap told him. "But nice you noticed, better you give a shit."

"And I'm glad the stars aligned."

Hap cocked a brow "Come again?"

"For you two. I don't need to know the story, but warning, Pearl will force it out of Luciana and share to a small, select cadre of those she feels deserve the information, and since I was there that night at dinner, I've no doubt I'll be one. I'm just glad the stars aligned for you to find each other and the story didn't end at Cipriani three months ago."

"We hooked up during the day."

Gagnon smiled small, but still all class, and they started walking again as Gagnon said, "Don't kill the dream. The stars always shine somewhere."

"Don't kill the dream?"

Gagnon looked at him. "You almost fucked it up with Luciana. I *did* fuck it up with the woman I loved. You two surmounted a big obstacle. You're giving me hope. Don't kill it."

"Gonna try to win her back?"

"She married someone else. I have to start fresh."

Rough.

"The sun is a star, brother."

Gagnon halted a lot more abruptly that time, a look of shock on his handsome mug.

Then he shook his head and muttered with open disgust, "I've been shot at while taking pictures of ISIS and I'm having a conversation out of a romance novel with a virtual stranger at a post-show Fashion Week party."

"Time to go, bro," Hap advised, starting them walking again. "I'd suggest arm wrestling, but we might get champagne on our clothes."

Gagnon laughed.

"What's funny?"

They'd made it to Pearl and Luci was with her.

"Baby," he murmured, moving in to kiss her cheek.

When he shifted back, she gave him bright eyes then she gave the flute in his hand the same. "Is that for me?"

"Pearl is double fisting. I'll go back and take care of you."

"I'll just have some of this," she said, taking his beer, putting it to her red lips and sucking back a draw, full throated.

Fucking *fuck*, but he loved this woman.

He grinned at her as she handed back the bottle.

"I now want beer," Pearl announced, holding the glass Gagnon obviously gave her.

Hap offered her the second.

She shook her head then tipped it to Luci.

He gave it to his woman.

Once she had it, she leaned into his side, tucking her hand around his arm.

Second proudest moment of his life.

Serious.

"Okay, she's taken care of," Pearl declared, eyes on Hap and Luci. She turned to Gagnon. "Now what are we going to do about you?"

"Mm?" Gagnon asked distractedly over the rim of the glass that he had raised to his lips, his attention aimed over Pearl's head.

Pearl twisted to look behind her.

Luci craned her neck to look.

"Who is that *vision*?" Pearl breathed.

"I don't know," Luci whispered.

Hap caught sight of the blonde everyone was looking at and leaned toward Gagnon. "Dude, *hup*."

It looked like it took a lot of effort for Gagnon to give him his attention.

"Sorry?"

"Old broad and former supermodel matchmaker radar just pinged, brother. You're up shit's creek," Hap said under his breath.

Gagnon took in Luci and Pearl then mumbled, "Fuck."

"Who is she?" Pearl demanded.

"I don't know," Gagnon answered smoothly, his gaze straying back to the cool, curvy blonde in a dress Luci would tell him later was made of blush satin and bugle beads (the fuck?).

Pearl waited a beat.

Then two.

Then said impatiently, "Well, my boy, *find out*."

"You better go," Luci advised.

"And now would be a good time," Pearl pushed.

"Let him play his game, women," Hap grunted.

"Bluh," Pearl forced out.

Luci rolled her eyes.

The blonde went on the move.

"Excuse me," Gagnon murmured.

Then, without saying good-bye, he moved with the grace of a big cat through a room crowded with uppity people.

All Hap could think was he'd be good in the bush.

Then it happened.

The blonde tripped, spilling champagne everywhere, crying out, as did the others that were around her.

Gagnon had made it close enough to catch her, full body, with just one of his arms, before she hit the deck, not spilling a drop of his own damned drink.

Agile, suave and gallant . . .

As.

Fuck.

Hap was impressed.

"You have got to be fuckin' kidding me," he stated, trying hard not to bust out laughing.

"How sweet," Luci drawled.

The blonde took one look at Gagnon, her face went pink, then her mouth moved as she said something before she pulled from his hold and dashed away, shouldering through the crowd.

"You have got to be *fuckin' kidding me*," Hap repeated, his words shaking with laughter.

"*Dio mio*," Luci murmured, those words amused too.

When Gagnon hesitated, Hap shouted, "Do you need to check your horoscope, bro?"

Many turned to look.

But Gagnon shot him a shit-eating grin.

Then he pushed after her.

"That's the way, brother," Hap muttered.

"Horoscope?" Pearl asked.

He looked down at her. He then took a drag from his beer.

And after he swallowed it down, he said, "I'm thinking the stars are aligned tonight."

Luci curled her front into his side, giving him her weight.

The wrinkles on Pearl's face rearranged in her version of a huge-ass smile.

It was one of the most beautiful things Hap ever saw.

He didn't share this.

He took another draw from his brew.

IT WAS TWO DAYS AFTER they got back from New York.

Just two.

They were laid out on his couch bingeing *Altered Carbon* on Netflix (for the second time, the show was the shit, they both thought so). There was enough junk food on the coffee table, this their dinner, to take out a battalion.

It was getting late.

After nine o'clock.

And the doorbell rang.

"What the fuck?" Hap muttered as Luci used his chest to push up and look over the back of the couch.

She turned her head to look down at him. "Are you expecting some-one?"

"No."

He was going to ignore it when the doorbell rang again.

"Maybe it's someone with a mistaken delivery of pizza and we can take it and then not answer the door the second time when they come back after they realize their mistake," she suggested.

He glanced at the coffee table, where on top of the mess was an empty bag of cheddar cheese Ruffles that Luce had not ten minutes ago upended the last crushed bits into her mouth, then he looked back at his woman.

"Babe, how in *the fuck* can you want pizza?" he asked.

"Is there ever a time when it's okay not to want pizza?" she asked back.

He could not answer that because there wasn't ever that time.

The doorbell rang again.

"Shit," he murmured, sliding her off and coming out from under her.

He took his feet, walked to the door, didn't see anything out the high windows, but got up to them, checked side to side and the doorbell rang again.

He looked down.

And his chest seized.

He should have known.

They'd taken pictures of him. Of Luci blowing the kiss to him. Of them at the party afterward. They'd even posed for some.

He hadn't seen the pictures anywhere.

That didn't mean they hadn't been printed somewhere.

Like it had a mind of its own, his hand reached out, unlocked the deadbolt and opened the door.

"Ma," he whispered.

She smiled up at him, but her attention wasn't on him. Her eyes were darting beyond him, into the house.

"Georgie."

It all happened in a flash.

One second he was standing there, staring at his mother.

The next second he was catching Luci on attack, arm around her belly, and hauling her back.

"Babe," he said in her ear, plastering her to his front.

"Get the fuck out of here!" she screamed at his mother.

"Honey," he whispered.

"You have no business here. You have no business even looking *at this magnificent man! Go! Leave! And don't ever come back!"*

This magnificent man.

Nice.

"George?"

His mother's call was tremulous.

He forced Luci behind him and shut the door enough his body was fully blocking the opening. He felt Luce at his back, and he looked into his mother's eyes.

"Two choices," he stated. "Leave. Or cops."

Then he stepped back, pushing Luci with him, and shut the door.

He locked it.

He turned, hands clamped on Luci's waist, and shuffled her backwards.

"She *dares*!" she shouted, heated gaze laser-aimed at the door.

"Cool it, Luce."

"She saw us in the papers. We were in the papers. Massimo told me. So, she *dares*."

He pressed her against the back of the couch. "Luciana. Look at me."

She turned blazing eyes to him. "She's ugly! Hideous! That woman is not your mother."

His mom was actually a good-looking woman.

He didn't debate that.

"Baby." He got in her face. "Calm *down*."

She hissed in a breath.

Hap took her in.

"Christ, serious *as fuck*, I pretty much need to fuck you really motherfucking hard right now. Prepare, Luci, you're not gonna be able to move for a week," he announced.

Luci blinked.

"Get upstairs. Get naked. I'll put away the food and be up ASAP," Hap ordered.

"But, she's—"

"She doesn't exist, Luce. She is not of our world. This," he squeezed her waist, "and this," he took her hand and pressed it flat to his chest, "is our world. Now are you gonna get naked, or what?"

"You . . . you're not angry," she observed.

"What do I have to be angry about?"

She stared at him.

"And anyway," he continued, "you flying at her like an Italian she-devil is anger enough for the both of us."

Her lips twitched.

He fought a grin.

He stopped fighting his grin when he realized she wasn't doing as she'd been told.

"Baby, a man's woman moves to take down his estranged, middle-aged mother on his doorstep, he gets in a certain mood," he educated her. "You gonna help me out with that?"

She sounded a lot calmer when she offered, "I can help you put away the food first."

"And take away me knowing you're waiting for me naked in my bed? I don't think so."

She added her other hand to his chest, leaned in and whispered, "I love you, Happy."

"Not as much as I love you."

"I have a feeling I love you more."

Hap looked deep into her eyes and stated, "Luciana, that would be impossible."

Her eyes got wet and she sniffed.

"Go upstairs," he ordered quietly.

"Okay, *bello*."

He touched his lips to hers.

She slid her hands up to either side of his neck and gave him a squeeze.

Then she let him go, sidled out from in front of him, and he turned to watch her strut like she was on a catwalk (her normal gait) to his stairs.

When he lost sight of her, he put away the food. Made sure the back door and door to the garage were locked. He turned out the lights. Went to the front door and opened it.

No mom.

No car.

His mom or dad, you mention cops, they didn't fuck around.

They vaporized.

He didn't give it a thought.

He closed and locked the door.

Then he walked up the stairs to his woman.

His girl.

Luci.

EPILOGUE

Life Was Beautiful

Luci

SHE HAD HIM IN HER mouth, her hand wrapped around him working him too, her other hand cupping his sac, gently squeezing.

She lifted her eyes and felt a spasm all over, but stronger in one particular place, as she saw him on his ass with his broad back to the headboard, his legs spread, knees cocked, feet to the bed, his powerful arms lifted over his head, holding on, his eyes dark and hungry and locked on her.

He wasn't holding on to the headboard as one of their games.

He was holding on to have an unobstructed view of her work.

"Come 'ere," he growled.

Gaze still to his, sucking hard, Luci pulled up, following the movement with a tight stroke of her hand, giving his balls a firm squeeze, and she watched the muscles strain in his pecs, his neck, one jumping in his hard jaw, those in his biceps bunching.

"Luciana, *come here*," he ordered thickly.

She licked the tip, showing him her taking in his pre-climax pearl of offering.

His expression intensified, his gaze burning.

"Luce," he warned.

She let him go and climbed up.

Or more aptly, climbed *on*.

Except to wrap his arms around her, Hap didn't change his position at all.

As she knew he would do, he let her fuck him for a time, taking it, enjoying it, watching her do it.

Then he took her to her back and made her orgasm there before he let her watch him do the same.

For her part, Luci hastened this by digging her nails in his ass and dragging them up his back, forcing him to arch into her, fill her completely, and explode inside her with a rough, muted roar.

After, she held him close.

He nuzzled one side of her neck with his mouth as he stroked the other side with his thumb.

Eventually, he moved his lips to the hinge of her jaw. "I'm gonna go check."

Of course he was.

"All right, *amore*."

He lifted his head and looked into her eyes.

But his eyes.

Dio mio, he was handsome.

"You gonna snooze?" he asked.

Of course she was.

She smiled at him.

He grinned, kissed her nose, then took her mouth and kissed her there, long, wet and sweet.

He pulled out and away, tossing the soft sheet over her as he left their bed.

Hap walked naked to the bathroom.

She rolled to watch and only when he disappeared did she stretch languidly and turn to her other side.

He came back, and she felt the bed depress with his weight at her back, felt his arm move under the sheet and heard his quiet, "Tip, baby, yeah?"

She did and closed her eyes, her lips curling when she felt the warm cloth move between her legs as he washed her.

"All good?" he asked when the cloth went away.

"Yes."

She felt his lips skim the point of her shoulder. "Love you, Luce."

"Love you too, Happy."

He moved away.

Luci's eyes opened, drifted closed, opened again, and then closed as she fell back to sleep.

SHE OPENED HER EYES AND the first thing she saw was her left hand laying on the butter-yellow sheet.

On it was a band of diamonds, three tiered, the two outer layers, the stones were small, the inner layer, they were much larger, all of this set in yellow gold.

No engagement ring.

She didn't want one.

Hap had not been happy.

It took some time to explain she wasn't making a point, it was that she wanted their marriage rings to symbolize the exquisite simplicity of their lives.

They'd chosen lovely, matching narrow bands.

But on the day, when Kia had handed her the band she was to put on Hap in that precious moment, it had been far wider, bolder.

And when Hap had slid hers on her finger, it had been filled with sparkling diamonds.

She lifted her eyes to the framed photo on the nightstand at Hap's side of the bed.

She was in ivory. A Massimo (of course). Sleeveless. A deeply plunging vee neckline, gathered crossover, natural waist, a full, ethereal, tiered skirt of floating gossamer flounces. Delicate. Stylish. Sophisticated. Angelic.

Hap was in his mess dress.

They were standing tight to each other's side, their arms around each other's backs and were both looking to the side, laughing at something Skip had said.

Behind them was a field of corn.

She heard a high-pitched giggle and that was what pulled her from the bed.

She reached to the bottom, grabbing then shrugging on the boldly printed silk robe, closing it and tying it at her waist, the deep slits in the sides and opening at the front making the bottom waft about her legs as she walked across the cool stone to and through the opened doors of the Juliet balcony.

She stopped, resting her hands on the balustrade. The beautiful blue waters dotted with sailboats, leafy green swells of mountains at the sides, mingled with the terracotta roofed buildings adorning the fringes of Lake Como was her view.

She didn't study it.

She looked down to the veranda below.

Sam, wearing a pale-blue linen shirt and jeans, had hold of nearly three-year-old Bash, her darling, her baby, little George Sebastiano, wheeling him through the air as Ben danced around his father's long legs, pulling at the denim, crying out for his turn.

She swept her gaze down to the end of the veranda where there sat a wrought iron table. On it, it appeared there was fruit, slices of cheese, pastry, toast, crystal pitchers of juice, silver-topped French presses, bright-colored stoneware, cutlery glinting in the sun.

Celeste sat with head bowed to Talia, Sam and Kia's little girl, who was in her lap. Talia was reaching to a strawberry.

Kia sat across from them, next to Thomas, also wearing a beautifully printed robe and leaned back with her coffee cup in her hands, her head turned, her face filled with laughter at whatever Thomas was telling her.

Luci swung her attention to the other end of the veranda where the steps started that led down to the vine-covered arches at the edge of the lake where they kept their gleaming Riva Aquarama with its ivory cushions.

As she suspected, Hap, in jeans, a tight tee, with a baseball cap pulled down on his head and running shoes on his feet had an abundance of pink frills with white details stuffed secure in his arm, pudgy legs tucked to his ribs, a little white hat on her head.

Daddy's little girl.

TeeTee.

Vita mia.

Little Luciana Vita, their six-month-old baby girl.

"Mama!"

Her eyes went direct to her son, who was upside down against Sam's side, but still waving frantically up at her.

Luci smiled and waved back.

Sam flipped him around and he squealed.

Her smile got bigger, but she felt it and her attention turned.

Her husband was two steps down, but he'd stopped, tipped his head back, and under the bill of his cap he was looking up at her even while his daughter was slapping his throat, an indication she wanted him to keep moving.

When Hap took Luci out on the boat, he went fast, held her close, the wind whipping her hair, making it fly in her face, his face, and often she would laugh. Laugh and laugh. For no reason except she liked speed. She liked the beauty of Lake Como. And she loved being with her husband.

When Daddy took his baby girl on the boat, he held her tucked tight in his lap and he went slow.

Vita still laughed and laughed for no reason, except she loved the wind in her face and being with her daddy.

Luci lifted her fingers to her lips and blew him and their daughter a kiss.

He shook his head, grinning, but eventually tilted up his chin.

Then he resumed his descent.

Luci stood where she was and watched, her eyes trained precisely where they needed to be.

The gleaming boat made its appearance, sedately trailing white foam against the deep blue of the lake, the man in the cap with a precious bundle of pink frills in his lap, his fingers wrapped firm around the ivory wheel, father and daughter gliding into the sun.

And life was beautiful.

The End

The Favor

A short story from The Unfinished Heroes Series
featuring Deacon and Cassidy of Deacon

DEACON BARELY GOT IN THE front door before he heard stampeding little feet and a screech of, "Dad*daaaaaaay*!"

And *boom*!

Pepper hit him like a bullet shaped as a four-year-old girl.

He swayed back, righted himself, cupped a hand on her head over her thick, soft, dark hair and watched as, a lot slower on her feet and a lot less steady, not to mention a lot quieter, Ruth followed her big sister.

On the move, he swung Pepper up into his arms and deposited her on a hip, all the while she shrieked with glee like they didn't do this every day, something they did.

Still on the go, he scooped up Ruth, who giggled softly and latched on to his tee with a fist while he strode to the kitchen to find their mother.

In the kitchen Deacon did not find their mother, his wife, his Cassie.

He found their friend Milagros.

"*Hola*, Deacon," she greeted with a smile.

"Hey," he replied, glancing around for his wife.

"Sorry, we were supposed to be gone by now," she told him.

His eyes shot back to her.

We?

Gone?

"Note for you from Cassidy," she said, tipping her head to the counter where an envelope lay. "The girls are coming with me to have dinner with Manuel *y mis hijos*."

"Enchiladas!" Pepper shouted.

"Tamalaysh," Ruth whispered.

Deacon tightened his arms around his girls as he dropped his eyes to the note.

On it, he could see, was written, Deacon Deacon.

His lips twitched.

All was good.

Used to Deacon not saying much, Milagros clapped her hands in front of her, announcing, "All right. We've got the car seats in. Jackets, girls. Let's go. *Vamanos, mijas*."

Processing the order that was not exactly verbalized, Deacon turned his head and kissed Pepper's cheek, muttering, "Be good for Milagros, baby."

She giggled, gave him a kiss on the mouth and replied, "I always am, Dadday!"

She never was.

He shot her a grin, hunkered down to put her on her feet and still in a squat with his hold on his two-year-old, he turned and kissed her cheek.

She laid her hand solemnly on his.

"You be good too," he said.

"I will, Daddy."

Christ, *daddy* was the most beautiful word in the English language.

Right after *husband*.

But Ruth would be good.

Pepper was her mother, in looks and personality. Boisterous, fun-loving, full of energy and bossy, she was Cassie head to toe. Cassie had named her and it seemed with that she'd claimed their eldest in every way she could.

Ruth, named by Deacon, was like her mother in looks, but her father in temperament. Quiet. Contemplative. But a risk taker. If there was something to try or discover, she was all in. But she did it introspectively. It was the experience, not the thrill, that engrossed her.

Deacon helped his girls with their jackets and walked them out to Milagros's car, then buckled Ruth in while Milagros dealt with Pepper.

"Love my girls," he said into the back seat.

"Love you too, Dadday!" Pepper cried.

"Love you, Daddy," Ruth replied, looking him direct in the eyes.

He gave them a wink before he pulled out of the door, closed it and moved around to accept Cassie's friend's kiss on his cheek.

"Manuel or I will have them home by eight," she promised.

It was nearing six.

Two hours for whatever Cassie had planned.

He nodded.

She smiled, got in the car, and with all three females in the vehicle waving at him, she drove down the lane.

Deacon watched her turn out on the street before he jogged back into the house, straight to the kitchen, and ripped open the envelope. Even though his Cassie could get creative, he was relatively certain what he'd find.

In it was a folded, lined piece of paper that had nothing on it but a huge 11 written in black Sharpie.

Yup.

His wife was a boss.

And yup.

That was what he thought he'd find, or a shorter version of it.

He grinned, and refolding the paper, he shoved it in the back pocket of his jeans as walked back to the front door.

He did not run to cabin eleven.

But he didn't fuck around getting there.

This meant he didn't waste time looking around the setting of cabins at the end of the lane that made up Glacier Lily Cottages, which he and Cassidy rented to skiers, hikers, photographers, nature enthusiasts and whatever folk wanted to spend time in a kickass cottage by a river in the Rockies.

He didn't need to look around.

After six years living there, and years before that spending the little downtime he let himself have in cabin eleven, doing it wondering why in the fuck Cassidy did not have a man, not to mention wishing he was the kind of man who deserved to have her, he knew every inch of the place.

In those years, he'd constructed the laundry nooks that had stackable washer/dryers in each cabin. He'd put in the new double-glazed windows so renters had more peace, more privacy, and he and Cassie could cut down on heating bills. He'd built the convenience shed with the industrial washer and dryer so Cassie and Milagros didn't have to lug bedding up to the shed by the house. This also allowed them to offer towels to their guests (something they didn't used to do). All that shit now housed in a clean, cool area that was handy. There was also the gazebo he'd built before they were married, which was where they were married, not to mention where he'd asked her to marry him.

So yeah.

He knew that place.

It was not hers the first time he'd found it.

It became hers and she made it all hers.

Then it became theirs, and she made it that way too.

He had a job outside Glacier Lily, Cassie looked after the girls and worked the cabins.

But it was still theirs.

His wife wanted her husband in her life in all ways she could have him. She made no bones about it. There was no yours and mine. There was *ours*. Our home. Our business. Our money.

Our daughters.

He dug belonging somewhere, to someone, after knocking loose for so long.

But that last part was by far the best.

Only part better was belonging to Cassie.

He jogged up the path that led up the hill to eleven, which was the most secluded of the cabins, removed, surrounded by trees, why he'd chosen it back in the day but why it was useful for the purposes he and Cassidy used it now. That and a heavy dose of the good kind of nostalgia.

He went to and through the open door.

He locked it behind him.

He walked right to the bedroom they always used, the one he'd always used when he was alone, and stopped in the door.

And there she sat on the side of the bed facing him. She was wearing faded jeans, worn blue Chucks, a brown shirt that said Maxwell Construction on it in yellow over a tight pale-yellow thermal. Her dark hair was down. She had no hint of makeup. Her tits and hips were bigger after giving birth to two babies.

And she was what she'd been the first time he'd laid eyes on her.

The most beautiful woman he'd ever seen.

"You're not naked," he noted.

She smiled.

Fuck yeah.

The most beautiful woman he had ever seen.

"Get naked," he ordered, moving into the room.

His Cassie Boss could seriously boss.

But she was also really good at doing what she was told.

DEACON WATCHED AND THRUSTED AS she found it.

Cassie's head was turned, cheek to the sheet on her knees, legs spread, ass in the air, arms cinched at her wrists behind her back with black, silk rope.

His Cassie liked to be tied up and other manner of all things kinky.

It wasn't the best thing about her, but it sure as fuck made the list.

She was gorgeous normally. Movie-star gorgeous. Double-take gorgeous. Knock-a-man-back gorgeous. Bring-him-to-his-knees gorgeous.

Coming, she was fucking *magnificent*.

Even so, he had trouble not staring at her ass, especially while he was fucking her.

His wife had a stellar ass.

"Baby," she gasped, "come."

"Who's tied up?" he asked.

Her eyes were closed, her cheeks flushed, her lips wet, her shining hair all over the bed, but still she smiled.

"Do you get to boss when you're tied up?" he continued, thrust hard, stayed inside and rolled his hips.

She bit her lip and her eyes opened only for him to watch them roll back in her head.

Good.

Orgasm two.

Time to let himself blow.

He did that. Giving it to her like she liked it, which was how he liked it, and eyes locked to her hands bound behind her back just above her ass, Deacon groaned as he shot inside the sweet, wet heat that was his Cassie.

Nirvana.

Every damned time.

He fucked her gentle after he came down and untied her wrists as he did it.

She stretched her arms in front of her then curled her hands under her cheek, all while she swayed into his slow thrusts.

They didn't talk much when they connected like this. Years together, it wasn't about it being practiced, rote. It was all good. Brilliant. It was just they were so in sync, their communication was nonverbal.

Eventually, he pulled out, rolled her to her back, lowered himself on her, then tossed the comforter over them.

She pressed up and he took the cue, rolling them to their sides where she immediately tangled herself up in him, doing it snuggling deep.

He wrapped his arms around her and pulled her in deeper.

"What's the occasion?" he asked the top of her hair.

Cassie tipped her head back and looked at him. "Occasion?"

"Cabin eleven."

She smiled. "I miss it."

"Yeah," he replied. "It's been a whole three weeks since you forked our girls on Milagros and arranged for me to come bang your brains out in eleven. I was worried it'd ceased to exist."

She burst out laughing, and he loved it when she did that. Particularly when he made her do it, and even more particularly when she did it tangled up in him so he could feel her tightening all around.

When she quit laughing, she admitted, "Okay, I have an ulterior motive."

"Mm-hmm," he muttered.

She scooched closer. "I want to ask a favor."

Deacon sighed.

The cabins needed something.

He'd failed to note earlier the new insulation they'd blown in last autumn.

And the new fridges they'd put in that summer after Cassie found some website that had really fucking good ones for really fucking low prices, but they were dinged or scratched in places you couldn't see. Apparently, no one wanted a new fridge that was dinged and scratched.

Those fridges "completed the look" (her words) of her years-long redesign of the cabins' kitchens.

They also used less energy, which did not suck.

"No, you can't put hot tubs on the back porches of all the cabins," he told her.

She got a faraway look and he instantly wanted to kick his own ass.

Instead, he gave his wife a squeeze and growled, "Cassidy."

"Hot tubs would be rad."

Jesus.

"We're not putting hot tubs outside each cabin."

"A communal one," she pushed.

"No."

Her eyes lit. "One for us?"

That he'd consider.

He communicated this to her by grunting.

She added a bright smile to her bright eyes, but she didn't say anything.

"So . . ." he prompted.

Suddenly, she became serious.

"Okay, keep an open mind," she said to begin.

At this, Deacon frowned.

If he had it in him to give, he'd give it. She knew that. He'd told her that. Repeatedly. Then they'd lived that for years.

What could this "favor" be that had her preparing him when the only time he'd said no to her (and meant it) was when she wanted to have Pepper's ears pierced when she was two, and he'd wanted Pepper to be of an age she could somewhat intelligently make decisions about needles being poked into her body for non-medical reasons.

Cassie got his aversion to needles and didn't push it.

They agreed to give their daughter the option on her seventh birthday.

"Baby," he whispered, not liking her hesitation.

"Promise to have an open mind?"

Jesus.

"Do you have to ask that?"

She pushed into him and replied quietly, "I do when I'm going to try to talk you into having another kid. Ruth is getting so big. Pepper will be in school soon. And I'm just not ready to live in a house without a baby in it."

His chin shot into his throat.

Um . . .

What?

"You do not have to ask that shit, and you definitely do not have to act weird about it or explain it," he growled.

"Dea—"

"You want another kid, we'll have another kid," he went on.

His wife blinked.

"Three things on this earth I give a shit about, you and our girls. I got enough in me to give a shit about a fourth if that fourth is something made of you and me."

"You love Milagros," she said softly.

"I like Milagros. I respect her. I love *you* and *our girls*."

"You love Raid," she kept at him.

He couldn't deny that, but he sure as shit wasn't going to confirm it verbally since she was missing his point.

She snuggled into him, mumbling, "You so love Raid."

"Whatever," he mumbled back. But he spoke normal when he said, "Ditch the birth control pills."

Her eyes widened, "Like . . . *now*?"

"I reckon we got just under an hour before the girls come home so you're not leaving this bed. But yeah. Later. After the girls are down."

"God, sometimes I forget just how much you love me," she whispered, staring at him in wonder.

But now she was pissing him off.

"I'm not giving you a kidney, I'm givin' you a kid which, incidentally, is a kid you'll be giving *me*," he clipped.

He saw that she immediately caught on she'd poked the bear.

"Okay, Badass," she said soothingly.

Deacon was not soothed.

"Just to be clear, you needed a kidney, I'd give you a kidney," he continued.

She now appeared like she didn't know whether to laugh or start weeping.

"I know," she forced out.

"You really wanted hot tubs, I'd get you hot tubs."

"Baby," she breathed, pressing even closer.

"You're it. You're my life. You're the reason I breathe. You're my wife. You're my savior. My life had no meaning until you entered it."

Her voice was choked when she ordered, "Stop."

He didn't stop.

"And you know all that shit, so don't act like you don't know how much I love you. You fuckin' do."

"Yes, I do," she whispered.

Only then did Deacon shut up.

Cassidy knew her husband, so she gave him time.

Then she said, "I'd give you a kidney too."

"I would not allow that."

Another blink, this one different.

It was what he'd named in his head the "Oh Shit Blink."

"You wouldn't?" she asked.

As per his norm, he ignored the Oh Shit Blink and prepared for one part of all they had that was just like everything else.

Something Deacon goddamned cherished.

Beautiful war.

"No way you'd walk around with one kidney after givin' me the other one. You can do it if it's *my* kidney that you needed, because if you didn't get it you wouldn't have any, which would mean I wouldn't have you. But not givin' me one of yours. Something happened to the last one you had, I'd not be down with that."

She pulled slightly away. "So, you'd walk around with one kidney after giving me the other one, but you wouldn't let me do the same for you?"

"Fuck no."

She pulled farther away.

He yanked her back.

She knew him so she didn't push that.

What she did was declare, "That's crazy."

"It fucking is not."

"I should be able to give you my kidney," she snapped.

"Baby, you carried and pushed out two beautiful girls for me, and you're up for goin' for round three. You're not giving me a kidney."

"I cannot believe you won't let me give you a kidney."

"I won't need one, so there's no reason to be pissed about it."

"It's the principle, Deacon."

"I don't care, Cassie."

"If you need a kidney, I'm giving you a kidney!" Now she was near-on shouting.

Right, this had now officially gotten out of hand.

Not to mention, it was fucking ridiculous.

"Babe—"

"No way!" she cut him off. "Welcome to the new millennium, Deacon Deacon! Where the damsel gets to save the dude in distress if that's the way it goes."

Time to contain this.

He cupped her jaw in his hand and dipped his face to hers. "And what if something happened to you? What would our girls do?"

"And what if something happened to *you*? I'd be Rebecca."

His head jerked. "Who?"

"Rebecca!" she shouted. "From *This Is Us*, except without the marrying the new guy part. *Definitely* without the marrying the best friend part. I'd be lost. I'd be *gone*. I'd never get over it."

"Baby, you gotta quit watching that show," he muttered. "It fucks you up."

"Because I'm Rebecca!" she yelled. "And you're Jack! We're *the best* together. We're a unit. We come as one. We're Deacon and Cassidy. We're just a *we*. You can't have *one* be a *we*. You lose one, you lose *everything*. We wouldn't be called *This Is Us* if we lost you because there is no *us* without *you*."

That felt freaking phenomenal, but . . .

Jesus Christ.

"Cassie, baby—"

"And our girls would be Kate and Kevin and Randall. They'd be *all fucked up* without their daddy. Forget it. In thirty years I'm not going to endure some hideous visit to a rehab center and have all our shit rolled out in front of some stony-faced counselor. No way! I couldn't hold us together if we lost you. So you are totally getting my kidney!"

"Okay, baby, I'll take your kidney."

She glared at him then huffed out a breath. "Okay."

"All right," he murmured.

"All right," she pushed out.

"I'll also give you another kid," he went on.

"Great," she blew out.

"I want another girl," he told her.

She shook her head. "You have to pass on the badass gene."

"Ruth is totally gonna be a badass."

That made her crack, though she hid it behind more boss. "You're giving me a boy."

"'Fraid you can't boss that into being, baby. We're just gonna have to take what we get."

She stared at him.

Then she stated, "You're it, Deacon. You're the reason I breathe. You're my husband. I was put on this earth for you. I can't exist on this earth without you."

He slid his thumb over her cheekbone. "Don't say that."

"It's true. I know how much you love me, but I'm not sure you have any clue how much I love you."

"Considering you threw a hissy fit to give me a kidney I don't need, I think I caught on," he replied.

"Don't joke," she bit out.

"I'm not," he returned.

She studied him.

Then she lifted her hand to his at her face, curled her fingers around and turned her head to kiss his palm.

Deacon drew in a breath.

Then he let it out.

The breath in was Cassie.

And the breath out was still Cassie.

Because she'd resurrected him.

And also because she loved him just as good as she got, and from him, she got everything.

She turned to face him again but held his hand against her skin.

Even with her holding on, he stroked her cheek.

"Only you could throw a fit about giving away a kidney," he muttered.

"Tomorrow, you're checking the wiring of every appliance, big or small, in our house. It was the Crock-Pot that did Jack in. Since we'd both totally go back into the inferno to save the dogs, we need to trash anything that might conceivably set the house on fire."

"That's it," he declared. "You are not watching that show anymore."

And she wasn't.

Christ.

A Crock-Pot?

"By the way," she replied, he knew ignoring his statement—his woman lived for that show, cried every damned time, he did *not* get that shit. "If we have another kid, we have to get another dog."

"Done."

She smiled at him again.

He frowned at her.

"Where *are* the dogs?" he asked.

"The run. We needed alone time."

Right.

Speaking of that.

"We got maybe half an hour for another fuck. You up for that?" he asked.

She rolled her eyes, mumbling, "He has to ask."

He rolled her to her back, asking, "You bring any more toys with you?"

She looked at him and repeated, "He has to ask."

Nice.

He felt his cock spring back to life.

"I got to play first, baby. You get to play this time," he murmured, going in for a lip brush.

"You *so* love me," she crowed.

"Yeah," he said in all seriousness.

She gazed into his eyes.

Then she said, "Yeah."

The End

More Than Everything

A novella tying up a Loose End from the The Honey Series
featuring Diesel, Maddox and Molly from The Greatest Risk

ONE

Empty

Diesel

DIESEL DROVE HOME IN HIS truck after beers with the boys, allowing his dick to go partially hard thinking about what waited for him there.

Molly was with her sister down in Tucson. Apparently, bridesmaid dress shopping took all weekend. Then again, the diva gene had skipped Molly entirely, but triple timed her sister Holly, and since the woman was getting married, this shit had reached extremes.

So he and Maddox should be thankful finding the perfect bridesmaid dress wasn't taking three weeks.

This meant he was alone with his boy, Mad, from then, Friday night, to Sunday evening.

This was not an unusual circumstance, but since they'd found Molly and added her to their lives, it was rare they didn't sleep in their huge California king with limbs tangled as their normal threesome.

Molly could go away, to be with her parents up in Flag, or her sister down in Tucson, but she wasn't gone long, maybe a night. And if she was gone, Diesel and Maddox slept like they did before she'd come into their lives. In the same bed. Usually after a great fuck.

But not tangled.

Not even touching.

And D could go away, to visit his family in Indiana, where Maddox wasn't welcome, but Molly was, so Molly stayed home in Phoenix with

Mad, and Diesel took off on his own.

And it was just the way they rolled that they had their alone times with just one of their three. D and Molly. Molly and D. Molly and Mad. Mad and D.

But this was a long stretch of alone for him and Maddox.

It was lunacy, but D had to admit to a certain level of anxiety and that had nothing to do with the thoughts he was letting harden his cock, these centering around the activities Maddox could get up to later that night in using it.

That anxiety had to do with their play a few weeks ago with Mistress Sixx as an observer at the Bolt.

"And that's just fuckin' stupid," he told his windshield as he drove.

It was.

It had been Maddox and Diesel before there was a Molly.

They'd met. They'd connected. They'd *really* connected. They'd done their thing together as Mad and D. They'd done it together as a team with Mistresses. They'd done their thing together as a team taking a sub. They'd moved in together in the little house they now shared with Molly. They'd agreed practically in the same breath after they'd had Molly and gone back for more, and more (and more), a lot of the time taking that going back for more out of play, that she was going to be a part of them . . . permanently.

From the beginning it had been Mad and D.

So he didn't know what his problem was.

What he did know was what tonight would bring.

D fucked Molly, with Mad, with Maddox just watching, with Maddox in the living room watching TV, with Mad out of the house at the gym, whatever. Mad fucked Molly the same. Mad fucked *Diesel* the same. And D fucked Maddox the same.

So D and Maddox going at it with their woman gone was not a problem.

It was just that, in a small, three bedroom house with three people living there, it was rare you got alone space.

D didn't really need it. He didn't mind being alone, but he preferred company.

Molly didn't like it. She liked her boys close.

But Molly . . . now, their woman was a talker. She could chat in the Olympics and go for gold. Her musical voice babbling in the house was one of the sweetest sounds there could be.

Diesel was also wordy. He thought something, he said it. He had a lot of thoughts. That was just him.

Maddox was not the same. He was quiet. Listened good. Didn't talk much.

And he liked his alone times. Getting the quiet. Getting his chill on.

So much, D would often grab Mol and hit the grocery store. Take in a movie. Go somewhere and share a drink or have a meal. All so Mad could get his chill.

This meant D knew what was on for that night.

He'd show after spending a couple hours with his buds from work and Mad would be in his chill. Diesel would get there, get them both fresh beers, hang with Maddox in front of the tube, catch the last of a game, sucking them back, being quiet, letting Mad have his zone.

Then they'd go to bed. They'd fuck (and D didn't care which way this went, him all up in Mad or him taking monster cock from his boy—it was righteous however it went, and that "however it went" would be that it was righteous always). They'd sleep (not tangled up). They'd get up and fuck again.

Then onward to have their Saturday.

Without Molly.

That was what was bringing on the anxiety.

He was worried he didn't know how to be alone with Maddox anymore.

No. That wasn't right.

All had been good and would have remained good if Maddox hadn't taken it there, as in *there* that night he was going at D at their sex club, the Bolt.

On the surface, since then, nothing had changed. They ate together, watched TV together, slept together (with Molly intertwined in between), woke up together, fucked each other and Molly, worked each other at the Bolt (but not Molly, they never worked her at the Bolt, she was theirs and no one got a good look at her).

But something had changed.

"Get it outta your head," he growled at his windshield. "It's Mad and D. Mad and D and Molly. Like it always has been. Like it always will be. Nothing's changed."

So yeah.

Beer and the game and a good solid fuck and sleep.

Tomorrow, maybe they'd catch a movie.

All normal, as it always had been and always would be.

That was all Diesel let stay in his head as he drove up the drive he and Mad had modified when Molly had moved in.

They'd widened it, put in the carport at the side as well as the door to get into the garage from the port. He and Maddox parked their trucks under the port. Molly parked her white Ford Escape in the garage.

Since Maddox owned it before he met Diesel, he and Mad had lived in that house together nearly two years before Molly came along and they hadn't touched anything unless it needed to be fixed.

But after Molly . . .

They made it right for their girl.

New wood floors, the real thing. Breaking down walls and losing a bedroom to give her a great room with a new kitchen. Gutting the guest bath and master and putting in all-new. Using part of the dead bedroom space to build her a big closet.

It was where most of any extra money got to, and almost all of their vacation time, making that place a place that would make Molly happy and neither man gave that first shit.

It made her happy.

That was all that mattered.

Now it was just as she wanted, even to the point the yard was the shit.

But since her sister got engaged, Molly had been hinting around about their commitment ceremony and nudging about kids.

They'd talked about it. They had it down. They had their agreement. They all knew and were down with what they'd decided for their future.

They'd commit, do it in front of family and friends (or Mol and Mad's families, not D's—not that D's wouldn't be invited, in all likelihood they just wouldn't show), and when it was time for kids, they'd both go at her after she got off the Pill and it wouldn't be hard to know what popped out.

Maddox was dark, black eyes, black hair, lots of it, *everywhere*. Brown in his skin. Molly had auburn hair and from the pictures of her as a kid they knew she grew out of freckles. So if the kid was made of Maddox's seed that dark would probably win out. Diesel had light-brown hair and light-blue eyes.

If the baby had Mol's coloring (and D had to admit, he hoped for a little girl along the way with red hair and freckles), they'd do a DNA test.

So whoever knocked her up would have to go in gloved for as long as it took to knock her up the second time around.

If they decided more than two, and could afford it, they'd have to decide on four, so they could keep Molly happy, giving her all her Maddox she could get *and* all her Diesel.

It was time, he thought as he pulled his red Ram in beside Mad's white F-250. They'd had Molly now over two years. They needed to make a move, for her, for them, toward a commitment that went beyond their three, toward a family.

But D could just see his parents' faces when he came out with the fact that Maddox was not his hanger-on roommate who really needed to move out now that D had found Molly. But instead was his boy, D was Mad's boy. They were a unit. They were not a couple, but came in three. And that was how it always would be.

Yeah.

He could just see that.

Which would be them saying serious vile shit to him that'd knock around in his head for, oh . . . he didn't know.

Fucking eternity.

Right before they disowned him.

He couldn't even think about where his older brother would take it.

He'd lose his mind and it would be far from pretty.

His little sister would show, though, with smiles and big boxes filled with presents.

And she'd try to take his back and she'd go to the mat for that.

Instead of splintering at losing D, in order to back his play, Rebel would break apart their family.

That particular thought heavy on his mind, Diesel got out of his truck, beeped the locks and headed to the door at the side of the garage with his keys in his hand. He unlocked it, moved through, locked it behind him and went through the empty space that was half where Molly parked and half of the other half was usually empty but the half that wasn't was filled with big plastic tubs precisely packed with Molly's bountiful holiday decorations and a whole load of other shit.

Truth was, both men with long cab trucks, they'd never been able to fit their vehicles in that little garage. It barely fit the length of Molly's Escape. So the carport had been necessary two years before they met Molly. Four, counting how long Maddox had lived there.

He went in the back door and saw down the wide hall that served as the family entrance Maddox's black head at the end of the couch where he was lounging with a bottle of Bud on his flat stomach.

"Yo," he called and turned to toss his keys in the pottery bowl on top of a table there.

Molly pitched a fit if they didn't throw their keys in that bowl. This was mostly because, if they didn't, both men would habitually lose them which met with calls for all-out efforts to find the fuckers so they could go to work.

And this drove Molly insane.

He was realizing Maddox didn't respond to his greeting as he turned back to head down the hall.

And found himself slammed chest first into the wall with a strong forearm shoved in his shoulder blades.

Before he could say a word, Maddox jammed his crotch against D's ass and even through two pairs of jeans he could feel that colossal monster rigid against his flesh.

His partial hard-on went instantly super-powered, chafing painfully against his fly.

"Mad," he murmured.

"Spread," Maddox ordered, his deep, abrasive voice grating against D's ear, that ride scoring down his back right to his ass which automatically clenched like it was taking a driving cock it liked a fuckuva lot.

What had done it for him when he'd first laid eyes on Maddox was his face and his body.

The man was seriously fucking easy to look at. He was just extremely good looking, but his face goddamned shouted, *Don't fuck with me!* And since Diesel had wanted nothing but to fuck him and take that in return, it was a total turn-on.

Add to that, Maddox's tall, broad-shouldered, strong, compactly muscled body was the shit.

And he had a great fucking head of hair.

What nearly had D dropping to his knees even before he'd seen the meat his boy packed and hiking that shit out to swallow it down his throat was hearing Mad's voice.

Shit, from word one it had always gone right up his ass.

Diesel put his hands to the wall but not to push away.

To brace.

And he spread his legs.

Still shoved up at his ass, Maddox reached around, popped the button of his jeans and slid down the zip.

His boy was not one to fuck around, ever, especially when fucking.

So he didn't then, reaching right in and freeing D's hard, straining length, wrapping it in a tight fist at the base.

"You get hard on the way home?" Maddox asked.

"Yeah," D pushed out, his entire focus on his cock and the hope that Mad would start pumping it.

"Yeah," Maddox whispered, further tightening his fist and Diesel gritted his teeth as Maddox pulled hard down the length.

Fucking beautiful.

Best handjobs he'd ever had started with the first Mad had given him after he'd let his boy lay him out during a wrestling match on their second date. A match they'd had to decide who'd get to fuck who. And after he'd won, Mad had made him lie still on his back while he knelt between D's spread legs and pumped his dick until he flooded all over his stomach (seeing if he'd pass that test, precisely why D'd let him win—he'd passed). They ended with the last one he'd had, which was three mornings ago when Mad had jacked him off in the shower while Molly was on the phone handling the final details of this weekend with fucking Holly.

But right then, that was all he got before Maddox ordered, "Don't move."

Then he disappeared.

Diesel absolutely did not move.

Again, as it was with Mad, it didn't take long.

Diesel's hips swayed as Maddox yanked his jeans down until they caught at his spread thighs.

"Lose the tee," he commanded.

D moved his hands from the wall to take hold of the hem of his T-shirt. He pulled it up and off and dropped it to the floor.

"Hands back to the wall," Maddox demanded.

Diesel obliged.

Both Maddox's hands landed on either side of his spine at the middle and moved down to his ass where he grabbed hold and a grunt shoved up D's throat as he spread him viciously.

"My man," he forced out, fighting his legs trembling, pressing in at the wall for a different reason, that being in order to stay standing and focus on something other than spontaneously coming.

Maddox said nothing.

But his hands massaged D's ass cheeks, doing it hard, maybe hard enough to leave bruises with the pads of his fingers, before he slipped them lower, palms right under the bottom curves. He shoved up, tipping D's ass out.

"Fuck," he groaned, his balls drawing up, his cock swelling so bad, he knew soon it'd begin aching.

Then Maddox's hands were at the insides of his thighs, shoving them apart, straining them against his jeans, as D felt his man push his face through and latch on tight, sucking his balls into his mouth.

Fucking, fucking *awesome*.

D tipped further as a rumble rolled out his throat and he pulsed into Maddox's rhythmic sucking.

"Yeah, fuck yeah, Mad, take those," he encouraged roughly.

Maddox did, giving it to his boy, always giving, sucking harder.

"Christ, fuck," D bit. "You got a mouth on you."

Maddox's hands slid up to his ass, he released D's balls, pulled him apart and his mouth was *there*.

"Jesus," D clipped, his body bolting before he pushed back as Maddox tongued him.

Fuck, he did not know what got into his man tonight. Maddox was not averse to eating out Diesel's ass but the occasion was usually not a getting-home-from-drinks-with-the-boys-starting-the-weekend fuck.

That kind of attention at the back, a man needed serious attention at the front.

Yeah, his dick was now aching.

"Maddox, my man, need one of our hands on my cock."

And that need at the moment was a *need*.

Diesel's body bolted again as Mad bit deep into the flesh just at the side of his crease and muttered, "No."

Then he went back to tonguing.

Christ.

This was going somewhere, fast.

So Mad had to get there with Diesel.

Fast.

"Okay then, need you to fuck it," he huffed.

And lost Mad's mouth in his ass but not at his ear. Instead he felt the head of Maddox's cock slipping through his crack.

"Gotta earn it, D," he growled. "Now, go. Get yourself lubed. Naked. Bed. On your knees."

The cock left his crack and Maddox stepped away.

Slowly, Diesel pushed away from the wall and turned toward his man.

Mad had his cock out of his jeans and was stroking the wide, long length.

And yeah.

If that was the first sight he'd had of Maddox, even before getting his voice, that monster cock, he'd have been on his knees.

But right then, if D was another guy, Maddox would catch his neck, pull him in and kiss him before he repeated his order to go to their room and position. Just like he did to Molly before she carried out an order. Something Diesel had seen a lot. Something that, watching, set something else in D to aching.

Because D was not that guy.

They did not kiss.

Unless Mol asked them to when one of them was inside her and the other was watching.

Or on the very rare occasion where Mad got him there.

As in *there.*

Where he'd taken him at the Bolt.

But right then, the harsh darkness in Maddox's attractive but cruel face was not about D not giving him that, even though D knew he wanted it and just how badly.

It was about him wanting D to get his ass to their bedroom so he could earn a hard fucking.

D yanked up his jeans, ignored his forgotten tee, and didn't bother doing his jeans up since he'd be taking them off. He just held them up as he moved down the hall, into the great room, down the other hall to the end.

Their bedroom.

He dropped his boots and jeans on the floor and went to the nightstand to rifle through the variety of toys that jumbled with remotes for different kinds of appliances until he found a tube of lube and generously took care of business.

He then got on his knees in the bed where he knew Maddox would want him.

Close to the bottom end.

Better to shove D over and fuck him standing.

Or other.

Maddox being Maddox, it wasn't about D kneeling there, hard, desperate and wanting and making him wait, something Diesel would not hesitate to do to Mad.

He came in not a minute later and stopped at the side of the bed so Diesel could watch him pull off his clothes.

The thirty seconds that took was bad enough.

Fuck, his boy had a body. Power packed, that muscle. Heavy fur on his chest, down his boxed abs, bushing real thick around his big dick, covering his thighs and calves. Molly had to wax the skin at the small of his back and his crack so his hair didn't pull while D was fucking him or Molly was taking his ass with a strap-on (he could take pain, seriously, but that wasn't pain—it was irritating as fuck).

But other than back to ass, from pecs to ankles, he was furred.

It was seriously fucking hot.

D watched as Maddox crawled into the bed on all fours, prowling to his boy, his eyes lifted to D's face, his mouth aimed right to D's dick.

That dick jumped and his ass squeezed tight in preparation for what was coming but his eyes didn't know where to go. Watch his boy suck down his cock or watch that tight ass move across the bed.

But all he got when Maddox arrived was the tip of his tongue tracing up the underside of D's dick, coming right to the head before he got up on his knees in front of D, face to face, and caught him behind the back of the neck.

Diesel's entire body tensed to pull away but Maddox just fell back, taking D with him as he went down on his ass and kept going. He cocked his knees, brought them high, spread his legs, and as the pressure on his neck directed him to where Maddox wanted him to go, D felt his mouth wet.

Now on his back, Maddox used his other hand to lift his cock off his stomach and hold it positioned before he forced D's mouth to throat it.

Something he did.

Deeply.

Fuck yeah.

Yeah.

D blew his boy, plunging up and down on that monster, meeting Maddox's fist that stroked the length D couldn't take and loving the ache in his dick now that he was giving this to his Mad.

D opened up and took as much as he could get, sucking hard, his cheeks hollowing out on each pull, getting off on the noises he was forcing from Maddox's chest, seeing his abs constrict, the lines get tighter, the veins snaking down the flat plain from lower abs to cock popping, tasting precum on his tongue.

Then with a rough tug on his hair he was out.

He looked up that body.

"Fuck me," Maddox growled.

D didn't make him ask again.

He moved. Mad drew his legs well back. D positioned, held Maddox's black eyes and drove into tight heat, marveling at the fact he didn't blow taking that fine ass at the same time watching the muscles of Maddox's neck all the way down to his pecs stand out at the penetration.

He'd prepared too, so the passage was slick for D to drive in and again and again, Mad's back cradled in his spread thighs, his hand pulling hard at his own cock, his other hand gripping his balls, squeezing and pulling those as D fucked him and watched a goddamned fucking spectacular show.

"Feel good, D?" Maddox rumbled.

"Fuck yeah, Mad," D pushed out, and it looked good too.

"Earn it, boy," Maddox ordered.

D put his hands to Mad's knees, spread him farther and used them for leverage as he lifted up and started punching into his boy's hole.

He watched Maddox's teeth clench, felt his ass do it, and Mad dug his head into the bed and punished his own dick and balls with a brutal jacking as he took D's fucking.

"Yeah, fuck, *yeah, fuck it*," Mad ground out, milking D's dick with a rhythmic clenching as D fucked his ass.

Fuck, with that, as whenever he pulled that shit, Diesel wasn't going to last long.

"I'm gonna blow in you," D warned and Maddox's head instantly righted.

"Yeah, you are, then you're gonna take it when I blow in you."

"*Fuck*," D grunted, that being all it took.

He jacked into him, shooting cum up tight, hot, sweet ass.

And barely finished jetting, he lost that heat, found himself shifted parallel to the bed, face in the mattress, up on his knees, a monster of a cock rammed up his ass.

Fuck, almost better.

"Give that to me," he groaned, rearing back into it.

"I'll give it," Maddox growled, cranking into his ass.

D could go at his boy but the man up his ass fucked like a Mack truck that was late on delivery.

And Diesel did not ever keep him guessing that he got off on every goddamned stroke.

"Shit, fuck, shit, Christ," D bit out. "That ass feel good, my man?"

"Always, D," Maddox grunted.

"Thrash it, motherfucker."

His invitation was accepted and he took it tough and tried not to let all he felt into his head when he heard his boy let go and shoot his always huge load deep inside D.

D stayed still and loose, rocking with him as Maddox drove into him through his orgasm and he decelerated when Maddox started pulling out to the head and gliding back in to the root as he slowed his roll.

Diesel closed his eyes when Maddox finished his last glide, filling him full, then reached around and cupped D's junk.

"We're gonna clean up, pull on our clothes and have a beer, D," he said in his coarse voice. "But when we go to bed, my man, advice, you do it lubed. You with me?"

Keeping his eyes closed, suddenly knowing what they'd be doing this weekend, and wanting it as bad as he'd wanted that fresh cum up his ass, which was to say a fuckuva lot, he muttered, "I'm with you, Maddox."

"Good," Mad grunted, pulsed his hips against D's ass, and D shut his eyes tighter.

Because he liked it.

He liked fucking Mad and blowing him and him eating D out and he liked Maddox's monster driving up his ass.

But he liked this best of all.

Knelt before his boy, full of his cum, full of his cock.

One.

Connected.

Maddox pulled out gently and Diesel didn't move a muscle except to open his eyes as the bed jarred and he watched his boy walk to the cush bathroom they'd given Molly in the little house in the middle-class neighborhood where they lived, seeing his own cum sliding down the back inside of Maddox's shaggy thigh.

He'd been right.

A good solid fucking, two ways.

Just not after a beer and the game.

The beer and the game came after.

So he'd just given it and got it real fuckin' good.

And after, Maddox buried inside him, he'd had everything.

So why did he feel so goddamned empty?

TWO

Do You Feel It?

Diesel

DIESEL'S EYES OPENED WITH A pop as a large cock drove home up his ass.

"Maddox," he groaned as Mad rolled into him, taking him from his side to his stomach before hauling him up to his knees, still buried deep.

"All fours," Maddox growled and D pushed up, feeling the blood pound into his dick, thickening it, making it rise, with what was inside him, instantly making it ache.

Like a warning, Maddox slid out slow and glided back in slower, hesitating a beat as D stayed in position to take him before it *began*.

Their grunts exploded into the room as Maddox drove D up the bed to the point he was up on his knees, both his arms braced, one hand against the wall, the fingers of his other curled over the top of the headboard and holding on in a way he worried he'd split the wood or punch right through the wall. Or the headboard would, the loud banging had to be cracking the drywall.

His rigid cock was slapping up against his stomach, his balls swaying wildly, neither getting any attention. Maddox had an arm angled across his chest, fingers curled into his shoulder to try to hold him steady and his other hand was wrapped around the front of his leg, the pads of his fingers digging into the inside of D's thigh.

"Jesus, fuck, buddy," he huffed out, just as Maddox groaned, driving deep again, and again, and once more, in a way D knew his back was arched against the orgasm and both their hips swayed violently with his climaxing thrusts.

D felt Mad's forehead rest on his shoulder blade, the heat of his breath against his back as his own chest heaved with the effort of taking a savage fucking before he took that same kind of fist around his cock. Mad pulled out the back in a way that made Diesel grunt, and he was whipped around to face Maddox with Mad using D's dick. He had to go with the pull or he'd have pain that didn't hurt so good or just lose the fucker.

And then Maddox was down on him, pulling him deep into his mouth, fingers fisted around the base yanking him out with each stroke, and there it was.

Christ.

Head falling back, Diesel rolled with the rhythm of one of Mad's talented blowjobs.

Maddox eventually clamped a hand on his ass to hold him stationary for the draw and release until D could take no more, landed a hand on the back of his neck, curled it around and, with breath hissing through clenched teeth, he shot down his boy's throat.

Maddox kept stroking, swallowing, stroking, swallowing, just stroking as D closed his eyes and felt the gentle pulls of Mad's wet, hot mouth and tight lips before Maddox slid him out, lifted up to his knees in front of D and grabbed a fistful of his hair at the back of his head.

"I sleep with your cum inside. *You* sleep with my cum inside," he abraded his order.

"You got it, bro," D said quietly, and Maddox let him go instantly, moving away.

Since Mad didn't plug him, this meant they'd have to change the sheets before Molly came home. Two men in her life, her being their submissive, all of them with libidos that were so far off the fucking chain, the chain was a distant memory, she was a dab hand at cleaning up cum.

Still, not cool to make her sleep in sheets or have to change ones that she hadn't had a hand in making dirty.

Diesel settled on his back, pulling the covers up to his waist, feeling Maddox settle in too, before he realized he'd have a wet spot that would be annoying and it'd drive him Maddox's way, so he turned to his side toward his man, then to his stomach, and saw in the shadows Maddox lying on his back.

"What was that?" he asked low.

"Told you to sleep lubed."

"Man, you fuck like a jackhammer but—"

"You didn't like it, why were you hard as a rock when I took you down my throat?"

D decided not to respond.

"You pissed I didn't take you there when I was inside you?" Maddox asked.

"I'm not pissed. You know I roll with you when you're in the mood. It's just—"

"What?"

"It's just that—"

"What?"

"I'd tell you what if you fucking let me finish talking."

Maddox didn't speak.

Diesel didn't either.

"Bro, you wanna finish, finish," Maddox clipped.

He wanted this?

"I'm not just a fuckin' hole you can drill into," he bit out.

"Yeah you are."

D came up on his forearms feeling a fire light in his chest.

"Say that again," he demanded, his deep voice nearly as rough as Mad's normal speaking tone.

Maddox rolled his way and got up on his forearm too. "D, I fucked your ass to get off then I sucked your cock to get you off. It's not something we haven't done a hundred times before. You aren't sitting there, hard and needing to jack your own junk to shoot your load. So what the fuck are you complaining about?"

"How about next time you just drill that hole that's yours to shoot into and I'll take care of myself."

"Don't be fuckin' stupid."

Diesel thought back from then to the minute he walked in the door and tossed his keys in that damned bowl.

"You're on another planet," he said.

"For fuck's sake," Mad hissed. "We both just came hard. Why are we fucking fighting?"

"I don't know, Maddox. Maybe because you just used me like a whore then seemed to remember who the fuck I was and gave me a guilt blowjob to cover shit up but it doesn't hide the fact your mind is somewhere else. And I've known you a long time, bud. You go somewhere else when you get pissed and don't use your fuckin' words to hash it out. And wherever you were, you were already there when you slammed me against the wall and pulled out my cock earlier. But don't use my ass to work out your issues, D. Use your mouth and I'm not talking about giving another blowjob or deigning to grant me the boon of tonguing my hole."

"So giving me your cum and taking mine earlier was just me working out some issue, yeah?"

"I don't know," D shot back. "You tell me."

"I don't have a goddamn issue."

"Fuck, this is going nowhere," Diesel muttered, falling off his forearms, turning his head away and shifting his upper body so Maddox had his back.

"Yeah, brother, turn your back on me. That's it."

He looked over his shoulder at Maddox's shadow still up on a forearm. "We gonna talk whatever shit you're chewing on out?"

"I'm not chewing on any shit, D."

D let turning back away from him and punching his pillow be his response.

After a while, he felt Maddox settle in and Diesel stared angrily into the dark wondering how the fuck he was going to get back to sleep.

After another while, Maddox stated, "For the record, I'm pissed *now* you took my mouth at your ass and twisted it to shit. I know how much you like it and now what I thought was pretty fucking hot is not that. It's twisted to shit."

"Don't make this about me."

A shorter while but he took it before he sighed, "It's always about you, D."

Had he lost his mind?

The man just nearly fucked him into the goddamn wall without a word, without a meaningful touch, without anything but holding him steady to take a fucking.

Fuck, if it wouldn't make him look like an eleven year old throwing a tantrum, he'd get up, clean the motherfucker's cum from his ass and sleep in the guest room.

Instead he closed his eyes and remembered what Molly told him about how people didn't breathe deeply enough. How she said it was relaxing. Why all those people who did yoga because they were actually into yoga, not because they used it to get great asses and wear clothes that made men notice they had great asses, were all chilled out.

So he focused on breathing deep.

That shit was actually working and he was about to fall asleep when Maddox said quietly, "It sucks 'cause it's not cool but it's true that I was glad Mol was gonna be outta the house for a while because I wanted to connect with you. Feels like we got disconnected somehow and I was trying to reconnect."

Diesel took in another deep breath and blew it out, saying, "Well, bro, fucking works great but not sure Mol would appreciate a man-size hole in her wall 'cause one of her men fucked her other man through it."

"Did I hurt you?"

He sounded freaked.

D turned back to him.

"No, my man," he said quietly. "You know I can take it. You also know I like it like that. But even if that's as connected as we can get, it didn't feel like connecting."

"Do you feel it?" Maddox asked.

D knew what he meant.

"Yeah," Diesel admitted.

"We gotta work on that, D."

"Yeah," D agreed.

He heard Maddox let out a deep breath.

Then Mad did it.

Like he could do it. Not often. But Maddox could do it. Do it like Diesel loved it. Like D very, *very* rarely gave it back.

Gentle, he whispered, "Go to sleep, baby. We'll talk more in the morning."

"Just to say," D started to joke, "the jackhammer on steroids gig far from sucked and the blowjob was your usual stupendous."

There was a smile in his rough voice when he replied, "Good to know. Now go to sleep."

"Rest good, Mad," he muttered.

"You too, D."

And with a Molly-sized space in between them, it took a while, but both men fell asleep.

THREE

Remember?

Maddox

THE NEXT MORNING, MADDOX STOOD at the kitchen sink wearing his old, lost-cause pajama bottoms with a coffee mug held up in his hand, his eyes aimed out the back window.

The long, narrow stretch of grass out there was so green it looked like it should be in Ireland, not Phoenix. And the old cinderblock fence around their yard had been built onto so it was as high as city code would allow and stuccoed a warm beige.

Didn't matter they'd made that wall look nicer, in front of it, the line of shrubs Maddox and Diesel had planted were growing thick and high, and in another year or two, they'd completely obscure the wall, growing higher, further fencing them in, keeping others out, muting noise, giving them a refuge of privacy.

That lawn was so green and those shrubs were growing that fast in this climate because Diesel tended that yard and those shrubs like he was hoping they'd be photographed for a magazine. Weed killer. Fertilizer. Judicious pruning.

But he didn't want it to be photographed for a magazine.

He wanted it to be a nice place where his Molly and his Maddox could hang out.

They had a covered back patio that ran the length of the house and they used it. They were outside people. Even in the heat of summer in the Valley of the Sun, they were out there under the ceiling fan, sometimes with the misters on, when it got dark turning on the strings of old-looking, Edison-bulb lights, throwing back beers and shooting the shit.

After they'd gotten the house done, but before they'd gone deep in doing the yard, since they didn't have a lot of room to put in a full pool, Diesel and Maddox had dug a spot where they put in an outdoor soaking pool to use to cool off, laze around and fuck in at one side of the patio. It was partially covered by the patio overhang, partially in the sun and had a nice water feature that shot spray into the pool. It could also be heated and had jets so it could be used as a Jacuzzi in the winter.

Mol had placed huge urns around it that had been distressed to look old, like they were from Roman times or something, these disbursed around pool and also the short, squat, thick-trunked stand of five palms that had been the only feature of the yard when Maddox bought the house. They also had pads that they could sit in or lay on at the sides.

They spent a lot of time in and around that pool.

At the other side of the patio was a kickass built-in grill. It had burners with it so you could full-on cook out there. And a small bar with outdoor stools surrounded it so that whoever wasn't grilling could hang close to whoever was.

Only when they had that shit sorted did they see about the rest of the yard, front and back.

Their neighborhood was seriously regentrifying, but their house was still straight-up the best on the goddamned block.

Maddox had bought it six years before in a bank auction when the old owners had defaulted, and it was almost criminal what he'd paid for it. Practically nothing. Not even six figures. This was especially since it was in good shape. The old owners hadn't gutted it, like some who'd defaulted had.

It still wasn't a palace.

Since Mol, they'd poured money and as much of their free time as they could into it.

Molly was the practice manager of a big medical imaging practice. D made good bill working road construction for the city. Maddox was foreman for a large landscaping and pool company that serviced all of Phoenix and the surrounding areas. They all pulled down decent wages.

But they hadn't taken but two vacations together since they'd had Molly, these to go up to Denver and visit with D's sister Rebel, and they'd agreed no big birthday or Christmas shit.

All so they could sort the house.

Now it was sorted.

And now it was time to consider the future.

He looked down in his mug then over to the coffeepot.

It was full and the liquid in it was nearly black.

Due to D's inability to jolt himself into the land of the living without sucking back explosive amounts of caffeine, Maddox, and then Molly, had learned to like serious strong coffee.

At one point, Maddox had suggested they get a Keurig so they could all have what they liked, but Mol had lost it, carrying on about the environment, how those pods were piling up, choking landfills so bad they'd be coming up garbage disposals before they knew it.

She'd been so off on one, and so cute doing it, in order not to piss her off by laughing at her, D had given Maddox a look before he'd hooked their woman at her waist, hauled her in his lap and promised her they would never buy a Keurig on threat of death.

Then they'd taken her mind off it when Diesel started making out with her and playing with her tits while Maddox spread her legs and went down on her sitting in D's lap until she came.

The Keurig had never been brought up again.

But that morning, Maddox had just flipped a switch because Molly had set them up before she left like her boys couldn't make their own coffee.

She was that way. *They* were that way.

They took care of each other.

He looked down at his cup that he'd had to pour an inch of French vanilla creamer in to cut the joe.

He was going to take a sip.

But instead he held the mug out and looked down his bare stomach to his pajama bottoms.

He'd had them since before D. They were so old and used and worn and had been washed so much what once was flannel was now soft and thin, like cotton. The back hems were ragged and hunks of them had worn away from Maddox walking on them or dragging them.

A few months into Molly living with them, she set about domesticating them. In other words squeezing the bachelor bullshit out of them. In doing this, she'd gone through their clothes to get rid of crap that should have been tossed years ago. And she'd put those bottoms in those piles.

Before she chucked that shit out, though, she'd asked them to make sure there wasn't anything in those piles they wanted to keep.

Maddox didn't give that first shit about anything in those stacks. Clothes were clothes. You put them on. Washed them. Put them on again. Tossed them out when they got stained, misshapen, or worn out. So he didn't care about those pajama bottoms. He figured if Mol didn't like them, they could go and he'd buy new.

But even if she didn't throw anything away without asking, Diesel had gotten pissed those bottoms were in those piles.

He'd yanked them out, bunched them up in a fist and bit, "Throwin' these out is like throwin' Maddox out."

He'd then stalked away, going to the bedroom where he put them back in the drawer.

Molly had been stunned.

To soothe her, Maddox had explained it to her.

But D doing that, what Maddox had felt had been entirely different.

Because the morning after their second date, the date Maddox knew Diesel let him win at a wrestling match so he could test how good Mad was with his hands, his mouth, his cock, the morning after the first night they'd fallen asleep together and slept beside each other, D had lurched into the old kitchen they'd had before they'd built their great room.

There he'd found Maddox sitting at a kitchen table that was now long gone.

And Mad had been wearing those bottoms.

D'd walked up to him, fisted a hand in his hair, yanked his head back and took his mouth in a kiss that was so hot, when it ended, the only reason Maddox hadn't asked him to move in immediately was that Diesel had caught the fact that his kiss had woken Mad's junk up.

So he'd hauled Maddox out of this chair, bent him over the table, yanked those pajama bottoms over his ass, and fucked Maddox dry.

Mad didn't mind. He was into pain. He'd come all over the floor under the table taking him and he'd done it hard.

But it was the first time he'd had Diesel's cock.

With those bottoms around his thighs.

Diesel was like that when they were beginning.

Yeah, he was a dude. Maddox was a dude. They were both bi. Loved cock, ass, tits and pussy. But D could be demonstrative back then. Kiss and give him looks where his blue eyes were warm or his face was expressive.

But four months in, when Maddox had asked him to think about moving in, Diesel's expression was shocked. Like that hadn't occurred to him. Like he didn't understand what it meant that from their second date, which was their first fuck, they'd spent every night together, woke up together in one or the other's beds, played together when they rocked a sub or took on a Mistress and spent every minute they weren't working . . . together.

They hadn't ever had the conversation about being exclusive.

They just *were*. From the second date. Both knowing instinctively that going for another cock was the height of betrayal.

But the man looked for all the fucking world like it never occurred to him he could share a home, and a life, with his man.

Maddox should have known then.

He should have clocked that and put the work in back then.

He didn't because Diesel had answered his suggestion of thinking about moving in with the words, "What are you doing this weekend, bro?"

And that had been it.

D had moved in that weekend.

And that had been when it changed.

Almost the night he'd moved in, the door closed on certain things they'd had in the beginning and didn't reopen until Maddox saw Diesel giving it to Molly two years later.

He'd missed it. He'd tried to push it, and been thrown back. He'd gotten pissed about it and tried to passive-aggressive the motherfucker which had not been a sterling idea (this being suggesting he take up the proposal of a Dom who'd made an approach, offering Molly and D the opportunity to watch, something Diesel was violently opposed to and didn't mind shouting that really fucking loudly, so in the end it was a play that meant Maddox and Molly nearly lost him).

That had told Maddox what he needed to know.

He was D's, D was his.

Molly might allow a new pussy in the form of a one-time-only Mistress working over one, the other or both her boys (never a sub) because she seriously got off on watching that kind of thing, and that was solely her prerogative.

Even though, that line being drawn, no cock could be added to the equation, whatever door Diesel closed because that motherfucking family of his fucked with his head all his life, was just that.

Closed.

Diesel needed it. He needed to think it was two sexed-up guys who got off on a lot of shit, including fucking each other, but they were hetero and the emotional stuff, the soft stuff, that was saved solely for pussy.

And Maddox took that because that was how Diesel came.

Until that scene at the Bolt with Mistress Sixx.

The kiss they'd shared.

Getting Diesel in the zone he let Maddox make love to him . . . for a while.

Diesel could get into that zone with Maddox, not even realizing what he was doing, giving it to him like that, without mouth to mouth, of course.

But Maddox had to work it and good to take Diesel there, and even when he got a little, some switch in D eventually would flip, he'd close down and in the end it was rough and often brutal.

Which was what had happened at the Bolt.

But with Sixx's response to watching it—Mistress Sixx, fucking *revered* in the scene, the soft look on her pretty face, the sorrow in her eyes when she'd looked into his after the scene was over, knowing she got it, knowing she knew what Maddox needed, wasn't getting and how vital it was—something triggered in Mad.

And now he was finding it harder and harder to let it lie. To sacrifice what was his due. To allow D to stay in that place in his head. Not to wake his shit up, show him what he was missing, what he was withholding from Maddox, and get it through his thick skull his family in Indiana was a pack of vicious bigots who had no place in anyone's life, but most especially not Diesel's.

And if none of that happened?

He looked to his coffee.

Back to the pot.

And then to the yard.

All around him was them—*them*—the three of them. Even his pajama bottoms couldn't be thrown out because of the memories they held. Molly couldn't leave for two days without stocking the fridge and setting up the coffeepot for her boys. And you couldn't step a foot anywhere in that house without a reminder of what Diesel and Maddox had worked side by side to give to their woman.

If one part of the three that made them drifted away, Maddox wanted to think he could keep Molly and continue to make her happy. But he knew there was no hope of that.

She'd never forgive him for letting D go. And she'd never forgive D for going. Or she'd never forgive either of them if Maddox couldn't take it anymore and he took off.

They'd disintegrate.

It had to be their three.

But Maddox didn't know how much longer he could take it.

He also didn't know how to confront D with it. He'd allowed it to go on so long, he couldn't even begin to get a lock on how to try to get into his head and sort it out.

Mostly, he couldn't stand the fear that gripped him at the possibility that, if he tried, Diesel would entirely shut down, completely lose his shit, flatly refuse to take them there, stubbornly become enraged Maddox was trying and then he'd cut ties in a way they couldn't be mended and he'd go.

Maddox knew Molly felt it. She knew what was not happening, what Mad was not getting, how deep the need to have it ran, and it destroyed their Molly, but she was not that person who could wade in.

She was a sexual submissive, *their* sub, but she wasn't a doormat, in sex or in life. She didn't let them walk all over her, or anyone do that.

But she was a submissive in play and the truth was, she had hints of that in regular life. There were women like Sixx who were strong and rocked that shit, it was beautiful, awesome. And there were women like

Mol, the kind of women who attracted men like Maddox and D, who were strong in quieter ways, took care of her men in her ways, but who needed her men to look after her in all other ways.

She needed Maddox to sort shit out.

Diesel needed Maddox to sort shit out.

And last night, waiting for his boy to come home from having beers with those dickheads he called friends but were all homophobic assholes, maybe not as bad as Diesel's parents and his waste-of-space older brother, but if you could say it, even just razzing the other guys or trying to make them think you had a big dick, you had the bigot in you, Maddox had gone off the rails.

The shit they did early was fucking great.

But in the midst of it, when Diesel had gone rigid like he was preparing to bolt when he thought Maddox was going to kiss him, then later, settled in with a beer and all the bro after they'd both been inside each other, Maddox had let it get under his skin and he'd fucked up.

Woken his man and angry fucked him and D, taking that jacked-up fucking, obviously didn't miss it.

And being Diesel, he called him on it.

Not knowing how to talk it out, never his strong suit in the first place, Maddox had instead gotten pissed and denied he had a problem.

Which was a lame-ass move.

That was not the way to connect. That was not the way to get in his head.

But Christ, he didn't know the way.

He sucked back some coffee, studied the yard and heard him coming before he saw him stagger into the kitchen.

Even with his weighty thoughts, Maddox couldn't bite back the smile.

Diesel's light-brown hair was totally messed up. His blue eyes were glazed. His huge, built body was uncoordinated, like he was drunk.

He had on a pair of gray sweats cut off just above the bulge of his lower quad and nothing else.

Maddox was no pushover. At six foot one, he took care of his body and had a physical job.

But he knew Diesel had let him win that first wrestling match because

Diesel was a beast. Six-three with heavy muscle from the solid slope of his trapezius at the back of his neck to the swell of his calf.

And those sweats were hanging low on his hips, the muscles of his abs and obliques so significantly defined that V that led to his groin could almost be described as a tunnel.

And behind those sweats, surrounding his gorgeous dick, he was shaved.

When they did their BDSM gig, Maddox allowed Diesel to work him because Maddox got off on it, got off on the service, got off on the unexpected, got off on the pain, and Diesel was fucking inspired with that shit.

He'd let his boy work him, but part of that play meant whatever he did earned retribution and Mad got his back.

But in that area of their lives, even if he took it, Mad owned D.

They both owned Molly.

But Maddox owned D.

And recently he'd discovered that he liked that cock shaved.

So once a week, D's ass was tied to the bed and Maddox shaved around his cock before he sucked it, ate him out and then fucked him tough.

That time was a couple of days away.

And now that it had begun, they all looked forward to the ritual.

Maddox turned to watch Diesel reel to the coffeepot, lift a hand, get a mug from the cupboard and pour his coffee black.

Years they'd been together and Maddox still had no clue how the guy could suck it back like that. Molly and Maddox went through practically a bottle of creamer a week to drink D's joe.

But no creamer for D.

It was black.

He lurched to the table, pulled out a chair and sat down heavily, one foot on the floor, knee bent, but leg splayed to the side like he couldn't hold it up, one leg out, heel to the floor, like he couldn't be bothered to cock it.

Too bad Molly wasn't there. Her man spread like that, she'd feel obliged to blow him alert, something she did often.

Diesel lifted the coffee to his lips, threw some back and Maddox felt his mouth twitch because D didn't even wince at the heat from that huge swallow.

"It's a wonder you can feel anything in your mouth. Got to have burned all sensation away with years of sucking back your morning coffee like that," Maddox noted.

D's eyes were fixed to the floor, not avoiding Maddox's, just because that was how he was in the morning, when he mumbled, "Trust me, I can feel shit with my mouth."

That made Maddox smile.

"You good?" Maddox asked.

Diesel slightly lifted his mug and muttered, "I will be."

Then he took another sip.

"We should call Mol," Maddox told him. "Check in. See how things are going down there."

Diesel lifted a big hand and rubbed the top of his hair making the thick mess an even bigger mess before his hand dropped to his thigh like he couldn't hold it up anymore.

"Yeah," he agreed, and sucked back more joe.

"We can wait until you're at least a quarter human," Maddox told him.

"Obliged," D murmured.

Maddox grinned again.

He'd gone back to the pot, glugged more creamer into his mug, refilled his cup and resumed his position at the sink, leaning his ass against it to enjoy the always entertaining show of Diesel becoming human when the call to Molly became one they would take, not give.

His phone on the counter rang and it was their girl.

"Mol," he muttered, snagging his phone, taking the call, hitting speaker and walking to the kitchen table, greeting, "Hey, baby."

"Hey, Mady," she replied as Maddox set the phone to the table and sat down at corners to D.

"You got me and D, you're on speakerphone."

"D's up?" she asked.

"Yup," Maddox answered.

"Is he alive?" she asked.

Maddox chuckled and looked to D who was staring at the phone like he didn't know what it was, but at least the sides of his lips were turned up.

The caffeine was kicking in.

"He's at least breathing," Maddox told her. "How are things down there?"

"Well . . ."

She trailed off.

Maddox stopped looking at the phone and started glaring at it as he felt his neck muscles get tight.

Molly had a great family. They'd been a little confused at the way of things in the beginning but they managed to pry open their minds, this happening as they witnessed Maddox and Diesel and how they treated Molly.

After that got through, it was all good. They traded off Thanksgivings at her folks or Mad's (and Mad's folks, including his little sister, were live-and-let-live people—they'd all loved D from the beginning and when Molly had come around, that same shit happened immediately). They got both guys birthday presents. Sent hilarious Christmas gifts, like matching hideous sweaters for the three of them.

Holly was included in that.

She was a good gal.

But she was also totally high maintenance and could be a pain in the ass.

Especially Molly's ass.

"What's up?" D barked and Maddox's eyes shot to him.

Caffeine eventually woke him.

But anyone fucking with Molly would make him instantly alert.

Fucking *fuck*, but he loved that guy.

"Okay, well, um . . . she's already picked out my bridesmaid dress," Molly told them. "She had it picked out before I got here. I just have to go this morning and try it on to see how she feels about it."

"Good," Diesel bit out. "So you're comin' home later today?"

"Actually . . . no," she said, but didn't say anything more.

"Molly, spit it out," Maddox ordered.

"Okay, well, Dylan is . . . not a big fan of Holly's bridezilla. He's been getting up in her face to calm down. I think this weekend was more sister time to play off me to make her feel better that her going off on one with this wedding was an okay thing to do. The problem was, as Mom was following me down here yesterday, they had it out and Dylan put his foot down. He said if she didn't get her head out of her ass and stop spending so much money on what amounts to a day in their lives, they were going to have problems."

Dylan was Holly's fiancée. Good man. Loved Holly. Doted on Molly like she was his little sister. Treated D and Maddox like bros.

No clue how it came about, because by the look of him—all poster boy for the boy next door—you'd think he'd be the opposite. But stereotypes went both ways. Dylan didn't blink when he'd learned Holly's sister lived with and slept with two men, that was how it was, not a phase—a relationship that had traction and would extend through the future.

For Dylan, it just was what it was.

Fuck, Dylan had asked D and him to be ushers at the wedding.

Maybe it was because he was a history professor at U of A.

Gotta love those liberal college types.

"I'm not thinkin' that was the way to go," Maddox muttered.

"Well, no, but you see, what I didn't know and you don't know until right now is that Mom and Dad gave her a budget and she's exceeded it by about seven thousand dollars."

"Jesus Christ," Diesel clipped.

"I know," she said softly. "So her and Dylan have to cover that and she's not even done planning. So then she um . . . she um . . ."

She trailed off.

"Molly," Maddox growled.

"Well, you know Mom met me last night so she could follow me down for this weekend so she could be there too. But when we showed, Holly was a mess, crying and carrying on and saying she didn't know if she could marry a man who doesn't *get* how *important* a wedding *is* for a woman. And then she told us she'd told him that it would all be good because she'd talk to Mom and Dad about it and get *my* budget for a wedding, because obviously I'd never have one, and everything would be okay."

The air in the kitchen could not be cut with a knife.

It'd take a chainsaw.

"Say that again," Diesel demanded, which was good because Maddox was so ticked, he couldn't get his lips to move.

"You heard me," she whispered, then took a beat and spoke normal. "Dylan called her a selfish bitch and stormed out, which she thought was insanely out of line. I think she expected Mom and me to agree with her but I took one look at Mom . . . and you know how she gets red in the face when she's drinking? Well, it was like that. And she just took off. Walked out before she said anything she'd regret and stayed in a hotel last night."

"And you're still there because . . . ?" Maddox prompted irately.

"Because she's my sister."

"Come home," Diesel ordered.

"Honey, I calmed her down and we talked—"

"We might not get a bullshit vanilla wedding but whatever we have will be what you want with flowers and cake and a beautiful dress and shit like that and she knows that so throwin' your lifestyle out like that is not on. Come home," Diesel demanded while Maddox stared at him.

He was on board with that.

He'd always been on board with that.

But Maddox could not describe the depths of relief he felt hearing Diesel say that with the power he put in the words that he was still on board with that.

"I told her that after Mom left and I got her to calm down," Molly replied, "And she realized she was over the line. It was like the haze of wedding fever lifted and she got it. She apologized to me and called Dylan and they talked for about two hours while I talked with Mom, and then Dad because Mom called him and he was pissed, then Mom again. And now we're about to go have breakfast with Mom so Holly can sort things out with her and then we can go look at this gown. But I think I should stay. We have to go over what she has planned and cut out seven thousand dollars, something that's probably going to take a lot of work. But in the end, she just . . . needs me."

Good down to her soul, their Molly.

The one individual in that scenario who had the right to lose their mind was her and she was the one who calmed everyone down.

"You need us, we're there. You need to leave, go. More shit happens and you get upset, don't drive. We'll come down and get you," Maddox told her.

"It's all going to be okay now," she assured.

"If it's not, you heard me," Maddox replied.

"I heard you, baby," she said softly.

Maddox drew in a breath.

"So how are my boys doing?" she asked, moving them away from that subject.

"We're good," Diesel grunted.

"What are you up to?"

Maddox and Diesel locked eyes.

Then Diesel said, "Maddox nearly fucked me through the wall last night. No worries, baby. There might be drywall damage, but if there is, we'll fix it."

They heard her pretty laugh through which she said, "Too bad I missed that."

D dropped his eyes to the phone in a way Maddox couldn't read. "We'll reenact it when you get home."

Apparently he was over it if he was joking about it.

Or at least Maddox was going to go with that.

"Awesome," she replied. "So while the cat's away, the cocks play?"

"Pretty much just fuckin' each other's brains out," Diesel shared casually.

"Don't get too much in, save some for me," she said.

"Always ready for Molly," Diesel told her gently.

"Love you, D."

"Back atchu, Mol," D replied.

"Love you, Mady," she went on.

"You know you got it back, baby," Maddox said.

"Okay, gotta let you go. I'll call tomorrow before I hit the road. 'Kay?"

"Call whenever, if you want, we're here," Maddox ordered.

"I know. But I'll probably be busy. If I can, I'll connect later. Now gotta dash."

"Later, babe," Maddox said.

"Later, Mol," Diesel said with him.

"Later, boys," she replied.

The screen muted and Maddox again looked to D.

"We gotta take care of that for her," Maddox told him.

He meant making moves on their future.

Diesel knew what he meant.

So D sucked back more coffee, and after he swallowed, he murmured, "Yeah."

"House is done, bud, pool, yard. She won't want anything big but we gotta give her what she wants and be ready to cover it."

Diesel nodded and took in more joe.

Maddox felt his stomach tighten as he threw out, "And we got a future to plan for."

With that, he meant building a family.

D knew what he meant with that too.

Diesel's eyes came right to his.

"Yeah," he said softly.

On board.

Commitment ceremony.

Kids.

Still soft, Diesel said, "She needs a ring."

Diesel, absolutely not the shopper unless Mol was there (not that Maddox was but he could buy himself a pair of jeans and had opinions on couches and shit) offered, "I'll look into those."

Diesel nodded again, set his cup aside and watched his hand do it.

Then his gaze came direct back to Maddox.

"Come here," he ordered quietly.

In that voice, with that look on his face, you'd have to bolt him down with chains to keep his ass in the chair at corners to D's.

But he was not chained so he got up and barely took a step before D's long arms were reaching out.

He grasped Maddox by the hips and pulled him around so his ass was to the table, D shifting in his chair to face him, his head tipped back.

He didn't take his hands off Maddox's hips when he asked, "You sleep good?"

"Nope," Mad admitted.

"Me either," Diesel muttered, his eyes dropped and he couldn't miss Maddox's meat pushing at the bottoms, something that had started to happen at "come here" and culminated the minute D got his hands on him.

But something shifted in his gaze as he stared at Mad's junk.

Mad read it and his balls drew up, his chest warmed, and D's fingers moved into the elastic waistband, pulling the bottoms down to Mad's thighs, his cock snapping free.

Diesel took hold and Maddox tried to watch as he bent forward and swallowed him.

But the instant he had that mouth, his head dropped back and his hands went behind him to brace against the top of the table because D had a hot, wet mouth, power behind his pulls and could seriously suck cock.

Christ.

Right before he blew, Diesel popped him out and pushed his chair back, getting up.

D left him there and went to open a drawer and Maddox knew what that was about.

Who they were and how they all went at each other, certain things needed to be convenient pretty much everywhere.

So he watched as D turned from a drawer, his sweats now tucked under his balls, his hand greasing his dick with lube, his other hand carrying a condom.

D caught his eyes and came back to Maddox. He whipped him around, bent him over the table and Maddox felt that slick cock bump his ass as D reached around and rolled a magnum condom up his dick.

D just got it to the stem when he positioned and drove in.

Chest pressed to the table, head back, Maddox took the so-serious-in-their-fucking-beauty-they-were-almost-spiritual thrusts of D's cock.

But he felt his legs shake when D's chest came down to his back while his hips bucked against his ass.

"Remember?" he asked.

The pajama bottoms.

The dry fuck.

Cum all over the floor.

The morning after their second date.

When it began.

"I remember. No lube that time, though, and no condom," Maddox grunted.

"Yeah, we're gentlemen now, though, bro."

Maddox torqued his neck to look over his shoulder at D's face and grinned a grin that looked cruel on the harsh face God gave him but D understood was actually hungry as D pounded in.

"We're good," Diesel whispered.

Fuck.

Fuck.

He hoped to fuck that could be believed.

"Yeah," Maddox growled.

"Gonna make you come now, my man," Diesel warned.

"Go for it."

Maddox thought he'd then do what he did. Pull away, lift up, hold Mad's hips and watch his cock ram him.

He didn't.

The table moved and they moved with it but Diesel stayed chest to back as he took Mad's ass and stroked his cock until Mad jerked back. Pressing his shoulders into D's pecs, he gritted his teeth and shot into the condom seconds before D grunted in his ear, drove home and came up his ass.

He mentally prepared for D to pull out, go bro, end it, put a line under it, communicate clearly to Maddox what this was and who they were.

He didn't and Maddox had to prepare more when Diesel ran his hand up his side, in between chest and back, over his shoulder, up his neck and into his hair, cupping his scalp, pressing him forehead down to the table.

Not a domination.

Just post-fuck touch.

Jesus.

D's lips came to his ear as he flexed up his ass and a low noise sounded in Maddox's chest.

"Wanna take in a movie today?" he asked.

Maddox closed his eyes and pushed out, "Yeah. Go out to breakfast now, though."

"Yeah," Diesel agreed and flexed again.

Fuck.

Shit.

Did what happen last night penetrate?

Was Diesel thinking on things?

Thinking them through?

"Shower first," Diesel growled.

Maddox opened his eyes, turned his head and caught D's gaze.

They should slow their roll. There were a lot of reasons Molly was theirs, including her sexual appetite. Two days without her men, she'd come home with needs they'd need to assuage.

He knew that.

D knew that.

Still, what came next out of his mouth came right out of his mouth.

"Fuck yeah," he growled back.

Diesel smiled.

That smile.

In the very beginning, the body had caught his eye. And that face, a man's face, all man, lumberjack or linebacker.

Yeah, when Maddox first saw him, he wanted to fuck that body looking at that face then he wanted to *dominate* that body, and while doing it, if he was looking at that face, that definitely would work.

But when Diesel had smiled, that had been it. Maddox had known it was going to be a fuckuva lot more because he was going to make it that way.

D slid his hand down to the back of Mad's neck, gave it a firm squeeze, but that was all he got. No kiss. Nothing else.

That said, he slowly lifted away and carefully pulled out.

But he stayed close and it was D that slid the condom off.

Diesel yanked his sweats over his junk as Maddox lifted up and righted his pants, watching Diesel open the cupboard and toss the condom in the kitchen bin.

D then sauntered to the table where Maddox still was, snatched his mug, and from up close said, "More coffee, Mad. Then meet you there."

D went to the coffeepot.

Maddox watched him go, wondering if he'd fucked some sense into his man last night.

He didn't ask.

He didn't push.

For now, he thought his best play was to let what just happened stand.

So he headed to the shower.

FOUR

Right Here

Diesel

"IF THERE'S A MEDICAL CONDITION that's the opposite of balls dropping, that just happened to me," Maddox muttered as he and Diesel walked out of the jewelry store.

They'd had breakfast at Snooze. They'd taken in a movie at the Fashion Mall. Then they'd taken this unusual opportunity of both of them being at a mall to hit a jewelry store to look at diamond engagement rings for Molly.

Neither of them had ever bought a significant piece of jewelry for a woman before.

D'd had girlfriends prior to Molly and he couldn't say he'd gone the chocolates and flowers route often, but he could get his romance on. At a festival once, he'd even bought a long-term girlfriend he'd had in his twenties a silver necklace with a heart pendant that he thought she'd rock, he'd been right and she'd loved it.

Maddox, he knew since they'd talked about it before and after Molly, also had his share of babes. But he was not the romantic type so even Molly got her flowers and little nothings that she acted like they were everything from D on Valentine's Day and her birthday, though D made Maddox sign the cards.

Maddox had never given a woman flowers or jewelry.

Red asses, spectacular orgasms, foot rubs, but not roses or silver, definitely not gold and diamonds.

Even though D knew a dozen red roses were highway robbery, but worth that dig when Molly caught sight of them, he still had not been prepared for what it would take to put a ring on her finger.

At least not one that made a statement.

And they had to make a statement.

For Molly.

"I hear that," Diesel muttered back.

And he did.

He heard it, but it was worse for him.

They all made good cake, but D's salary was the lowest of their three.

He tried not to feel that.

It wasn't an issue for Mol or Maddox, then again, they made more than him so it wouldn't be.

And usually, he could ignore it, seeing as Molly took care of their finances and was sure to make it equal across the board. She had online access to all their bank accounts and paid bills based on whatever schedule she had in her head that made it fair for all of them. She budgeted for groceries and other shit they needed and had debit cards from both D and Mad's accounts she used when it was their turn to take the hit. And she was the one that transferred money into all their savings so they could pay for shit for the house, though now those accounts were just getting bigger with nothing to spend the money on.

Except a kickass commitment ceremony for Molly.

And a ring.

For Molly.

But even if Maddox couldn't drop that load on his own without feeling the pinch, it was times like these that Diesel knew he'd feel it more and was reminded he was low man on that totem pole of giving them the lives they were living.

Then again he was that in a lot of ways.

He'd spent years burying that fact and working hard to bury it deep.

And it did not feel real great that shit was suddenly surfacing.

"We gotta go bigger than Dylan," Diesel told him through a throat that seemed to be closing as they moved down the wide hall.

They did this dodging teenagers who needed to learn better manners. Also old-timers who'd made the mall their walking track. Not to mention the women with strollers who wielded them in a way that it was clear they thought they'd popped out a kid and the world owed them right of way not only when they should get it, walking down the hall, but when they waltzed out of a store not even looking if they were gonna slam their kid into someone.

Fuck, he hated the mall. It was almost worse than the airport in its lack of "We're all in this humanity thing together" zone, firmly entrenched in its "I got shit to do and I don't give a fuck you're breathing and probably got shit to do too, the world revolves around me" zone.

"Yeah we do," Maddox agreed.

Diesel had no idea what size ring Holly had and he wasn't going to ask Dylan. But he *was* going to make note of it next time he saw Molly's sister.

That said, he also had no idea how they were going to manage buying their girl a better rock than her sister had and not just because the fuckers were insanely expensive, but because Molly managed their money.

She'd see ten thousand dollars gone, for sure.

She'd even notice a monthly payment.

"How we gonna do that shit?" Diesel asked, skirting two women, both with monstrous strollers that looked more like dog houses on wheels, both of them looking at each other and gabbing, neither of them looking where they were going.

"No clue," Maddox mumbled, purposefully pressing into Diesel to veer them off the course they were on so they'd take a set of stairs, not a ramp, in order to avoid the flow of traffic—elderly and pushed on wheels—coming their way.

"Have you thought about skincare?"

Diesel turned his head when it came clear someone was in his space asking him an asinine question, and he looked down at the woman who was shoving a small, condom-size packet in his face.

"Even men need to take care of their skin," she shared, lifting the packet farther toward him as she walked with him.

He stared at her and kept walking.

"He's not interested," Maddox answered for him.

"He should be," she replied. "And you should too."

Diesel looked to Maddox. "What's happening?"

Mad started laughing and kept walking.

"It'll only take a minute for me to show you the miracle of . . ." she called after them.

But they just kept walking and did it not listening, so fortunately she drifted away.

"I hate the fucking mall," Diesel muttered, which made Maddox laugh harder. Diesel scowled at his man. "When did they start jacking shit on you in the walkways?"

"Um . . . I don't know. Nineteen ninety-eight?" Maddox answered.

"That should be illegal," D told him.

Maddox spoke, continuing to grin like he thought Diesel was hilarious. "You need to get out more, my brother, and not just to sports bars."

"Not if some chick is gonna shove a prophylactic packet of male skincare in my face."

Maddox started laughing again, D quit grumbling and they walked and rode escalators in silence to Maddox's truck in the underground parking.

They did this while D mentally made the decision to kick in on whatever ring Maddox picked (obviously), no matter how deep it dug, but he was not going back to the mall to help him pick it.

He could order a vase of roses or pick out a necklace at a booth at a festival.

But he was never going back to the mall.

And it was when he had his ass in the passenger seat and slammed his door that he realized they'd gone out to breakfast. They'd gone to see a movie. They'd gone to look at engagement rings for Molly.

And it had all been good.

It wasn't awkward. They shared a life. They'd been sharing that life for years. If they didn't let anything fuck with it, they were comfortable in it. They had things to talk about. Molly's sister's bullshit. Who was gonna check the salt in the water softener (Maddox). Who was gonna take Molly's Escape to get the oil changed (D).

They were just Maddox and Diesel.

Like always.

Mad had started up, pulled out and begun to negotiate toward the ramp that led to the exit when he said, "I could get a loan from my folks. They'd help us out, knowing we're good for it, especially knowing what it's for, catching them on the flipside."

He was talking about Molly's ring.

And he was right.

His folks would do that.

Maddox's mother was counting down the days until one of her children got busy and started to give her grandkids. Even though Mad was thirty-four, and his little sister thirty-one, it was only last year they'd downsized from the home where Maddox and his sister grew up to a house in a development with three golf courses.

But they'd gone for a three-bedroom, which was one bedroom they didn't need but they got it, "So Bob can have his man cave and the grand-babies can have a room when they sleep over," Erin had said.

She didn't even care if the kid who came out of Molly was Diesel's. That was the woman Erin Vega was. Hell, Erin was so grandbaby crazy, she'd talked to them about finding a surrogate before Molly had even entered the picture.

That thought made something tighten in his lower gut, something that hadn't hit him back when Erin had brought that up, because then it was straight-up not an option in Diesel's mind.

But Erin had been okay thinking it would only be Mad and D together raising a baby. Same with Mad's old man, Bob. When Molly had come along, neither of them had acted like they were relieved, just curious, not confused, *curious*, and like always, welcoming.

And they weren't hippies or in-your-face liberals or shit like that.

They just wanted their kids to be happy.

Sure, Bob had shared early on over beers with D that, "The first couple boys Mad had around, I wasn't sure how I felt about that. But whatever. I love the Rolling Stones. My father hated Mick Jagger. Thought he was a skinny, drug-addled waste of space. We got into rip-roarin's about it. Not once. All the friggin' time. I mean, he's a rock 'n' roll singer, not the leader of a cult I'd joined. But he's also a genius I admired. Dad didn't have to like ole Mick, but he didn't have to get in my face about it. And I remember after one such go 'round tellin' myself I'd never do that to one of my kids. But have to say, I started to get that way with Maddox having girls, and guys, and then girls, and then guys and me thinkin' what the hell? But then I realized I don't have to get it. Just Maddox does."

Just Maddox does.

Remembering those words, D's gut felt tighter.

And as for Erin? She simply didn't care. From the beginning. Like she didn't care her daughter had blue hair and a year's worth of tattoo parlor piercings in her body.

"Far's I can see," Erin had said the only time she'd mentioned anything like that about her kids, "me and Bob did it up right. Both Maddox and Minnie feel all kinds of all right being just who they are. And what works for my babies works for me."

D's gut got even tighter as more thoughts hit him and these thoughts hit him harder.

Not thoughts, exactly.

Memories.

Memories of Tommy Barnes.

A year older than him in high school, both of them on the football team, offensive line. They got on, pals, best buds, went on double dates, hung out all the time.

Including that time in the back of Tommy's pickup out in the fields by that huge stand of trees where they went often to drink beer, smoke pot, look at the stars, talk about the babes they'd banged and otherwise shoot the shit.

It wasn't like D hadn't had thoughts, thoughts he jacked off to a lot, thoughts he hid and they messed with his head, until that night when he kept catching Tommy's eyes straying to his crotch.

The drunker they got, the more Maryjane they smoked, the more Tommy's eyes on his junk made that junk stand up and take notice until the feelings he was feeling he couldn't deal with. That made him get pissed and he grabbed Tommy by the throat and shoved him against the side panel of the bed of the truck.

He got in his face, Tommy looked in his eyes, and before D could say anything, both of them close, breathing hard in each other's faces, Tommy's hands had gone to his jeans and he'd shifted up to his knees.

D didn't even think.

Tommy got out a condom and handed it to D before he moved

around, giving Diesel his back, yanking his jeans and shorts over his ass.

D just put on the condom and went in.

Tommy had come all over the side panel the minute he took D's cock and D didn't last long up that tight ass.

After that two minutes was up, they'd both knelt there in the bed of the truck in the moonlight, connected, breaths coming deep and fast, and he was about to threaten Tommy with what would happen if he said dick about what had just gone down when Tommy spoke quietly.

"Our secret, man. No one knows. Never. Not ever. Swear it."

He'd then shifted D out of his ass, turned toward him, pulled off the condom and knelt in front of him, sucking down Diesel's softening dick.

Not surprisingly, that visual of Tommy, a big, muscled, good-looking son of a bitch with a sculpted ass that was right then bared to Diesel's gaze, rhythmically swallowing down D's dick, and just the feel of Tommy's mouth around his cock, that cock sprang back to life in a nanosecond. And ten minutes later Tommy took D's load down his throat like he'd been waiting for it for years.

And D had given up that load knowing he'd waited for that, and what had gone on before, for what felt like centuries.

From that night on, they'd still hung out, double dated, and fucked . . . a lot. Tommy liked D up his ass but D could get him in the mood to give as well as take.

And it had always been their secret.

It remained their secret even after Tommy was caught in a raid on a gay bar in Indianapolis when he was twenty-two and his personal secret came out.

"D?"

Diesel jerked when Maddox called him and then he blinked because they were out of the garage, on Scottsdale Road, in the sun, and he was so up in his head, he hadn't noticed.

He lifted a hand, flipped down the visor and the Ray-Bans he'd put up there before going in for the movie fell into his hand.

He slid them on and looked out the side window.

"Do you want me to ask my folks about the loan?" Maddox asked.

"Sure," D muttered distractedly.

This was met with silence.

Silence that Maddox broke.

"Brother, what's on your mind?"

"Tommy."

Yeah.

Fuck.

That just came out.

It just came *right out*.

He didn't share.

Ever.

He had nothing to share, nothing to give.

Nothing.

Nothing but his cocky, good ole boy self, creativity with giving orgasms, ability to take whatever was dished out to get his own, and as much love as he could shower on Molly, doing that along with Mad.

"Say what?" Mad asked.

"Tommy. Tommy Barnes. First ass I had. I was seventeen. He was eighteen. It was at night in a field in the back of his pickup after about ten beers and two joints."

When D quit talking, Maddox gave him time to keep going, and when he didn't, Mad prompted, "Yeah?"

"After that, I fucked him, he fucked me and we did it as regular as we could get away with it. Mostly I fucked him and he blew me. Loved sucking cock, Tommy. Loved taking it too."

D shut up again.

Maddox didn't say anything. Even when he stopped at a stoplight, he didn't say shit.

Maybe this was because, in all their years, D had never told him this and now he had no clue why D was spouting this shit.

No, probably because of that.

When the light turned green and Maddox turned right on Camelback, D started talking again.

"Bar got raided in Indy. They said it was about drugs being dealt there but it was a gay bar and it was in Indy so everyone knew that was bullshit."

"Right," Maddox said low.

"He was outed, Tommy was."

"Bet that didn't go well," Maddox noted.

"It totally did."

He could hear the surprise in Mad's, "What?"

D looked forward, out the windshield, but not to Maddox. "His parents disowned him. Said they never wanted to see him again, and they said that to anyone who would listen, including Tommy. Everyone in town had an opinion and there was a consensus that Tommy was a pervert. Shit was said everywhere, it was ugly. Tommy just packed up and took off. Moved to Chicago. Didn't look back. As far as I know, and it's been at least ten years, he's never gone back. He didn't act like he was run out of town. He acted like he couldn't wait to go. Like he was finally free."

Maddox gave it another beat before he asked, "So you never saw him again?"

"Saw him, yeah. For about a year, went up every few weekends to hang with my bud and also get my rocks off. My parents thought I was in Cleveland banging some girl. Every time I went he told me to get the fuck out of there. He knew where my dad was at, the shit that came out of Gunner's mouth."

Nothing for you there, man, Tommy had said. *It isn't about narrow minds. It isn't about closed minds. It's about hate. You don't love the parts of a person you get that fit into your view of the world. You love all of a person and if you don't, you don't love them at all.*

"D," Maddox said quietly.

"About a year in, he got a job, a good one. They transferred him to Boston. He still lives there. Got two kids with his man. They got married last year."

"So you're still in touch," Maddox stated flatly.

That made D look at him. "Not hiding that shit. It isn't like we're best buds anymore. We mostly lost touch and did that a long time ago. He just calls every once in a while. Checks in."

Maddox had nothing to say to that.

"Maddox, it isn't that big of a deal," Diesel reiterated.

"I was still in touch with the first cock I had and you didn't know it, would you think that was a big deal?" Maddox asked tightly.

"You *are* still in touch with Gavin. He was over for dinner last month."

"Yeah, so you know about it."

"I left because of him," Diesel announced.

"Come again?"

D looked back out the windshield. "The great Hoosier state. I left after Tommy got transferred to Boston. Took everything I'd saved, packed up my truck and took off to Phoenix. I didn't pick Phoenix because of the year-round sun or me liking saguaro or shit like that. I picked it because it was the farthest away I could get."

"'Cause you had no one's ass to fuck that was within driving distance that might not get you caught?" Maddox guessed. "But the bottom line was, you wanted ass to fuck and not get caught fucking it."

"No," Diesel returned instantly. "Because I was suffocating, it was going slow, but I knew if I stayed a part of me would die and what was left, even as much as I got off on it, it wouldn't be worth living anymore because I was a selfish fuck. I wanted it all."

The air in the cab got heavy and Mad left it at that for a few beats before he said, "That isn't selfish, Diesel."

"How you think Gunner's gonna be when he rolls up to our commitment ceremony?" Diesel asked.

"I think Gunner's gonna get his head out of his ass, and if he doesn't, he's not invited."

"He's my brother, Mad."

"He's a cocksucker, the bad kind, D. He treats everyone like shit, even you, and he doesn't even know you're bi. That also includes Rebel, who's a damned handful but she's golden to her core. No one can dislike that girl. She's Molly in little sister form whose hearts and flowers can turn to kicking ass because she's got more moral fiber than anyone I know and isn't afraid to shout the walls down when she feels like someone's fucking over someone she loves or doing the wrong thing."

Their conversation was weighty, but still, D had to smile about the truth of that.

"We're gonna put a ring on Molly's finger, D. We're gonna commit in front of God and family and everybody. We're gonna make babies with our girl. We're gonna build a family," Maddox declared. "And if those assholes aren't all in with that, they're not in at all."

His last words rang so close to what Tommy had said years before, Diesel felt a chill hit the back of his neck.

"Yeah?" Maddox pushed.

"What do I have to give to all that?" Diesel asked.

"Sorry?" Maddox asked back, his graveled voice now gritty.

"Built-in babysitters. Lots of Christmas presents. Big Thanksgivings. Huge-ass graduation parties. And that's all you and Molly and your people. And then there's me. I got nothing to give but me."

"And Rebel, and if you don't know this, it shocks the shit out of me, but she's three aunts, two grandmothers, and a couple of dozen nosy but well-meaning cousins all rolled into one," Maddox returned.

That also was the damned truth.

And he wanted to smile at that too.

He just couldn't.

He turned his head to look at Maddox again but he didn't get to say what he intended to say.

Maddox was still speaking.

"And if you do not get that even if you didn't have Rebel, you'd be enough, you'd be all we needed, then Mol and I are seriously falling down on the job."

That hit him low in the gut and right in the throat.

He looked back out the windshield. "We need to quit talking about this."

"We needed to *start* talkin' about it about four years ago. Now we're here, last thing we need to do is quit."

He again turned his eyes to Mad. "I'm serious, bro. You need to let this lie."

Maddox glanced at him, back to the road, and let that sit until he turned on his signal to go left on 44th.

"For now, brother," he murmured after he stopped at the end of the line of cars waiting to make the turn.

Diesel shifted his gaze out the side window.

That feeling hit him in the gut and throat again after Maddox made the turn and they were nearly to Indian School Road.

It did because Mad said quietly, "Thanks for tellin' me about Tommy."

D wanted to pass it off with a "whatever," but that wasn't in him. Not then. All his cocky had left the building.

He felt weird.

Exposed.

Raw.

Wrong.

And he had since that scene with Sixx watching.

Blurting that shit about Tommy hadn't helped.

He didn't know what would help.

Except maybe Molly getting home and them getting back to where he felt right. Secure. Good.

He waited until Maddox turned into their drive before he declared, "Think we should lay off the fucking until Molly gets back. She'll be rarin' to go and we need to be ready for her."

Mad pulled his truck in beside Diesel's, shifted into park, switched off the ignition and turned to D, resting his forearm on the wheel.

"Man, if you think you're gonna tell me about the first ass you took, the first cock you took, the first man's mouth wrapped around your dick and you think you aren't gettin' me stakin' my claim to all of that, think again. We get in there, I'm goin' at you, brother. We can rest up for Molly over a beer later and lay off each other tomorrow, but only after my cum's deep up your ass."

"Seriously, Maddox—" D started, and Mad's hand snaked out, catching him at the back of the neck.

He held hard and leaned in.

"That body's mine," he growled. "You're tired, I'll hold. You're raw, I'll hold. You're slippin' into your head about shit that's crystal clear to everyone but you, no fuckin' way, D. You don't hold me back like that, not like that. You know who owns you and you think about it for a second, you know, tellin' me about Tommy, even if it's ancient history, your man's gonna stake that claim."

That shit hadn't occurred to him.

Nothing had before it all came rushing out of his mouth.

But giving it a second to think about it, Maddox did not lie.

Still, D pulled at the hold and felt his face get hard. "I didn't tell you so you'd—"

"I don't give a fuck," Maddox bit off. "You keep this up, I'm gonna strap you down and switch you red then fuck you until you make a permanent dent in the bed and you'll be in no condition to help me take care of Molly when she gets home."

D stared into his eyes and kept pressing against the hand at his neck but otherwise didn't move until his whole body jerked when Mad's other hand shot out and gripped his junk.

Then he smiled that hot, nasty smile and D, already hard, only got harder taking it in.

Mad didn't miss it or the opportunity to do something about it.

He dragged the apple of his palm tight along D's length as he dug his fingers in at D's neck and his smile turned into a hotter, nastier sneer that made Diesel's balls draw up.

But all he said was, "Yeah."

Then he let him go, got out of the truck and Diesel watched him walk to the door.

You love all of a person and if you don't, you don't love them at all.

He had that from Molly.

It fucked with his head, but he had that from Maddox too.

He gave it back to Molly.

And he knew it fucked with Mad's head he couldn't give that back to Maddox.

And that fucked with D's head.

"Christ," he exploded, eyes on the side garage door Maddox had disappeared through.

The man needed to lock his truck and D didn't have the key.

"Fuck," D muttered, threw open his door, jacked his body out of the cab and stalked after Maddox, his hard-on rasping painfully, which meant spectacularly, against his fly.

He barely made the door to the garage when the locks on the truck beeped.

Maddox was waiting for him to get out.

You love all of a person and if you don't, you don't love them at all.

Diesel entered the garage to see Maddox had made it to the inner door and was holding it open, looking at him.

"Switch?" he asked, brows up, mouth twitching.

"Fuck you," Diesel muttered.

Maddox chuckled and it was as rough as his voice.

So of course that went right to his dick.

"You try to hold that door open for me, I'm gonna punch you in the throat," D warned.

At that, Maddox let out a deep, harsh belly laugh that made Diesel wonder how his fly was holding in his junk, he was now so hard, it was a miracle his dick didn't punch through the zipper.

Maddox walked through the door two steps before Diesel made it to him.

D lifted a hand and caught it before it closed and he walked in behind Mad.

It was fucked, but without hesitation, he followed Maddox to the bedroom, hoping he'd earned the switch.

He had.

Maddox

ON BARE FEET, MADDOX WALKED down the hall to their bedroom silently.

He stopped in the door.

The room was dark. The sun had gone down after he'd left earlier. But the Edison bulbs outside along with some muted moonlight coming in the big window that had a view to their pool illuminated Diesel's big body in the bed.

Naked, on his stomach but shifted slightly to his side, back turned to the door, sheets tangled around his calves, one long leg partly hitched, flesh so raw, Maddox could see the welts in the shadows, plug snug up his ass.

D was out.

He would be.

They'd had a marathon session where Maddox had forced three out of him, to Maddox's one.

Another man or another time, he'd walk into that room for more together time that might not include fucking, instead of walking away from it alone.

But he walked away from it, pulling his phone out of the back pocket of his jeans.

He hit the kitchen, nabbed a beer, popped the cap and headed out to the back patio.

It was August. The heat was definitely still on the Valley and would keep it in its grip for another two months, at least.

Maddox had grown up in Phoenix. Unlike ninety-five percent of the population, he was comfortable in what he was wearing at that time of the year. Jeans and a tee.

It wasn't like he didn't feel it. It was just that he not only didn't mind it, he loved it.

He'd been other places. The minute the temperature dipped below seventy, he hated it.

Lower than that? Trussed up in parkas and scarves and gloves and shit?

Not his bag.

He sat on a slider that had a view to the French doors, put his feet up on the ottoman, engaged his phone and muttered to it, "Call Molly."

He put it to his ear.

"Hey, Mady," she greeted on ring two, sounding sleepy.

He was surprised.

It wasn't late. Maybe seven thirty, latest eight.

Shit, that sister of hers was running her ragged.

"Did I wake you?"

"No, it's just been a big day."

"Tell me about it," he urged.

"Is D there?"

"He's passed out."

He heard her soft, sweet laughter then her quiet, "You so totally aren't saving any for me."

Maddox grinned.

"I'll share in total tomorrow when I come home," she went on. "If I tell you, I'll have to tell Diesel or you'll have to tell him and I might as well tell you both. But we'll just say, the dress works, but cutting seven thousand dollars from a wedding spend is hard work to the point it might be impossible."

"Sorry, baby," Maddox murmured.

She was Molly, so she switched in right away and her tone was different when she asked, "You okay?"

As always with his Molly, he didn't beat around the bush.

"You know Tommy Barnes?" he asked. "D's Tommy?"

Her tone was vastly different, the alarmed variety, when she repeated, "D's Tommy?"

"His first dude, started it all for him. Back in high school."

She was silent.

Totally.

"You know him," Maddox said, not knowing what that made him feel but he did know it wasn't good. "He told you."

"I've never heard that name in my life," she replied. "He's never mentioned him. He's never mentioned his girls. That's not true. He did once, saw it bugged me, so he hasn't done it again."

That was D. All about Molly.

"And none of the guys?" Maddox asked.

"Nope," she answered in a way he knew she was also shaking her head. "But he shared with you?"

"Just came right out with it in the truck on the way home from a movie this afternoon."

"Whoa."

"Yeah."

"It's Holly and Dylan and the wedding," she decided.

Maybe.

More like Sixx and knowing she witnessed that kiss Maddox laid on him during their scene.

"And Sixx," Molly went on.

Maddox grinned again, reminded like he frequently was of one of the many reasons he loved their girl.

And then she gave him more.

"You guys aren't right," she declared.

"I'm tryin' to make headway with that," Maddox told her.

"Knew you would, honey," she whispered.

Yup.

Totally loved her.

And total pressure.

Because it was on him to do more than make headway with Diesel.

"Is it working or are you trying to do that simply by fucking our D until he passes out?" she asked.

"Seein' as he gave me his trip down memory lane with that Tommy guy, I'm thinking it's working."

"Of course, and that's good, so maybe . . . baby steps?" she said tentatively.

"Yeah," he agreed. "Though I get the feeling from him it was a giant leap, not a baby step. So I'm gonna let it go and lay off for a while."

"Mm-hmm," she murmured.

"Couldn't read that, baby," he told her. "Give me more."

"I don't know, Maddox. I mean, we've never pushed him, except that once, when you suggested letting that Dom work you, and that didn't go too good."

That was an understatement.

"But, I think he's been opened up now," she continued. "I think that's what's behind the change in him these past few weeks. And I don't know if it's in a good way where we can get in there, or a bad way, where if we try to push, he'll shut down."

"I'm where you are, Mol," Maddox agreed.

"Did you hear what Sixx said to him?" she asked.

"When?"

"After that scene, after you guys brought those baddies down at the Bolt. When we were saying goodbye in the parking lot. Did you hear her tell him that the scene you two had was beautiful?"

Maddox lifted the forgotten beer he was holding between two fingers to his mouth and took a draw, his eyes moving from the doors to the pool.

He should turn on the light. When that pool was glowing, it looked the shit.

"Mady, did you hear me?"

He swallowed. "I heard you, baby. And yeah, I heard her."

"I think . . . he was . . ." He listened to her pull in a breath. "I think he took that in. Like, she's a . . . I don't know. Like a counselor. Like an objective observer. Something like that."

"You think we should get Sixx to observe again?"

The way she spoke next, he knew she was shaking her head. "I don't know. But he respects her. He likes her. She was like, one of us almost immediately, not, you know *one of us*, one of us. But she *got* us. She felt natural being there. I think he felt that too."

"I think you're right."

"Did you? Did you feel that from her?"

Truth be told, he'd be happy never taking another Domme, never going back to the Bolt to do their gig public, just having what they had at home. When D played him, he got all he needed. When he or they took Molly, the same. What they had together, the three of them, was it for him and always had been. He couldn't say he didn't enjoy it when they let themselves get worked by a Domme so they could get off and Molly could watch and get off too. But he'd be good without it.

So in the beginning, he could take or leave Sixx.

But after their scene, when she'd looked right in his eyes, put her hand on his chest and he knew how deep her empathy ran to where he was at, having his boy like he craved having him, but for too short of a time, way too short, and having to give that up . . . for D.

Yeah.

She'd felt natural then. Not one of them, *one of them*, but an integral part of that scene that took some of the bitter out of the bittersweet.

Not much, but since the bitter stuck in his craw, even a little bit helped.

"I had to work my way up to it, baby, but she was solid and I can't lie and say it didn't mean a lot she got it," he told her.

"Yeah. You being D's Dom, her being a Domme, you're like, mind melded or something."

He chuckled.

"I think we should just feel our way, honey," she said softly. "I think right now, if he's opening up, he'd be easy to spook and that'd be bad."

He didn't want to give it to her, but he had to.

"Fucked him angry last night, Molly. He told it true, nearly fucked him through the wall, but I did it because I was pissed he pulled the bro after having drinks with those assholes he works with. Coming home, I went at him, let him have me, it was good, and then he goes bro. Pissed me off."

"I see that," she said gently.

"I took care of him but he saw through it and we fought."

"Oh, baby," she whispered. "Did you tell him why you were angry?"

He did not.

"Just told him I thought we'd disconnected and I was trying to re-connect."

"Well, that's one way to put it," she muttered.

"I want all of him, Mol," he told her.

"Of course you do," she said in a soothing, musical coo. "I want you to have all of him too."

"I'm not a patient man," he reminded her.

"You're the most patient man I've ever known."

He blinked at the pool, his chin jerking in.

"Just stay patient, Mady," she carried on. "A little while longer. We'll get him there."

And if we don't?

The question lay unspoken between them as Maddox took another swig from his bottle and moved his eyes back to the door when he sensed movement.

In his cutoff sweats, Diesel was making his way to the fridge.

"He's up," he told their woman.

"Yeah, and Holly's opening another bottle of wine. I'll let you go. Tell D I said, 'hey,' and I should be home around two or three tomorrow. Mom's leaving earlier because she's got farther to drive so she's not stopping around. I'll text when I'm on my way."

"'Kay, baby. Try to have fun, tell your family we said hello and see you tomorrow."

"I will. You too. And love you."

"You got that back," he replied.

"'Bye, honey."

"Later, Mol."

He hung up and watched Diesel pop the cap on a beer.

He continued to watch as Diesel came to the door, through it and walked out, closing the door behind him as he lifted the bottle and took a pull.

He moved to the chair opposite Maddox and eased in.

Maddox felt one side of his lips snag up.

"You took that plug out, bro, you're gettin' more of your monster," he warned.

Diesel adjusted his ass in the padded slider in a way that Maddox knew he still felt his man's switch and his ass was definitely full.

"Not my first rodeo with you, Mad. Who were you talkin' to?"

"Molly," Maddox answered. "The dress worked. The seven thousand dollar cuts are not. And Holly's opening up another bottle of wine."

"Right," Diesel mumbled before he took another swig.

"You good?"

D's eyes came right to him.

"Claim staked, asshole. Midway through orgasm two, I forgot Tommy's name."

Maddox grinned at him.

D held his eyes and Maddox felt the grin freeze on his face.

"You didn't have to do that," Diesel said low.

He said that.

What he meant, or what Maddox hoped like fuck he meant, was, *It's only you. It'll only ever be you. There's no one else for me, never was even when I had other cock, and never will be.*

"You complaining?" Mad asked.

"Nope," Diesel said, and again lifted the bottle to his lips, his gaze sliding away.

Maddox took his own draw.

They fell silent.

Mad broke it.

"Molly'll be home around two, maybe three."

"Miss her," D mumbled.

"Yeah," Maddox agreed. Then he called, "D?"

Diesel's gaze came back to him.

Fuck.

Should he say what he wanted to say?

Before he made the decision, his mouth started moving.

"Took a lot of ass, took a lot of cock, it's still only you and it'll only ever be you."

D stared at him, face blank, eyes working.

"That's it," Maddox went on, feeling slightly sick. "All I'll say."

D continued to stare at him.

And then he looked away.

Maddox downed a big pull, suddenly wishing the beer was bourbon.

"Wouldn't want to be anywhere else."

At Diesel's words, Maddox went still.

"But right here," D finished, not looking at him.

Instead, he slouched down in his slider, put his feet up on Maddox's ottoman, not touching, but after what he said, he didn't have to.

Baby steps.

He'd pushed a little further.

And there they were.

Together.

"You hungry?" Maddox asked quietly.

"That a casserole Mol left for us in the fridge?" D asked back.

"Yup, bro, bake and good to go. Ready in thirty."

Diesel looked again to Maddox. "Workout you put me through, I could eat three of those things."

Seeing as Diesel didn't do stove or wooden spoons, the only thing he could handle in the kitchen was the coffeepot, Maddox took the hint, lifted his feet off the ottoman and hefted himself out of the chair.

"Will you need another beer by the time I pre-heat the oven, slide that fucker in and come back out here?" Mad asked.

"Is my name Diesel Joshua Stapleton?"

"Unless you had it changed without fillin' me in on that info."

"Then yeah on the beer."

Grinning again, Maddox headed to the French doors.

If he went in to do something and Molly was out there with him or them, he'd kiss her before he went.

A time that seemed ages ago, he would have done the same to D.

Now that option wasn't open to him.

Stay patient. A little while longer.

He'd wait.

And while he did . . .

He'd hope.

FIVE

Welcome Their Girl Home

Diesel

THE NEXT AFTERNOON, DIESEL SAT slouched in the couch opposite Maddox, both of them at angles, both their feet on the coffee table, both of them with beers resting on their abs.

He'd woken to a plugged ass, the flesh still pleasantly sore, an empty bed and a note on the kitchen counter by the coffeepot that he'd been able to read halfway through his second cup. A note sharing that Mad was at the gym.

This was not a surprise or an indication he was escaping Diesel. They'd learned a long time ago that Mad needed alone time at the gym.

They were all members at the same place, but if Mad went with Diesel and/or Molly, they'd talk his ear off and Maddox was that guy who liked focus when he worked his body. He blasted heavy metal in his ears and got in the zone. He didn't want his man or woman jabbering at him while he was lifting or pounding it out on a treadmill, and with Mad around, always a listening ear, somehow neither of them could stop that shit from happening even knowing Mad liked to be in the zone.

Molly and D often went together, but Maddox always went alone.

So at the time, Diesel didn't think twice about Mad being at the gym.

Somewhat caffeinated, D made one of three things he could make in the kitchen, oatmeal (the other two being toast and nuking a jar of cheese to pour over corn chips), belted it back and put on his running gear.

He'd been intent on toughing it out for thirty minutes, but in early morning heat after ten years he wasn't used to (and that was saying something since he worked daily in the shit, but at least he didn't have to run when working), he barely made twenty.

To make up for it, he punished his abs on the weight bench he declined in their den that they'd made workout space and did chin ups on the bar he and Mad had secured in the ceiling until his abs, arms, chest and back burned (both bench and bar doubling when shit got interesting, that being when it got sexual).

Since he was drenched in sweat, when he was done, he went out and mowed the lawn.

Getting in his own zone, and with Molly coming home, he also pulled out the blower and tidied every inch of yard and patio, yanking out the power hose to blast the lawn furniture so if Molly went out, she wouldn't get any of the infamous Phoenician dust that always clung to the air and coated everything around on her clothes.

He set the furniture out in the sun and it was dry in ten minutes.

He was putting it back when Mad got home.

Mad checked in with D, took a shower, Diesel finished up on the patio and took a shower after him. They ate huge sandwiches made from the dizzying variety of cold cuts Mol left for them like she'd be gone for three weeks, not two days. Then to rest up, both of them, done in from a weekend of fucking and a morning of working out a different way, parked it in front of the TV and baseball.

D's eyes slid from Maddox's bare feet on the coffee table, up his long legs in his jeans, to his dark-blue tee that was tight on his pecs, loose at his stomach, practically cutting of his circulation at his biceps.

Then his gaze hit Mad's profile.

He hadn't shaved that morning or the one before.

D liked the beard and not just because it looked good, but because it felt good.

Molly felt the same.

Maddox, being the Dom he was, liked to give it.

He also liked to take it away.

He stopped thinking of the stubble Maddox had that was two days for him, but six for any other guy, and thought about that morning.

A Sunday morning trip to the gym was not totally out of the realm of possibility for Maddox, but Sunday mornings for their three usually was about all of them out on the patio with coffee and different sections of the paper. Quiet, together time which eventually fed into Mol or Mad making breakfast, something they'd eat out on the patio. They usually didn't start their day until the clock was well past striking ten.

D had gone to sleep the night before experiencing the not-so-awesome feeling of both looking forward to having that just with Maddox and dreading it after he spouted all that shit about Tommy, worried he'd keep going, why he'd do that and what would come of it.

Not that the results of him sharing the little he had about Tommy had been bad. The sesh with Maddox in their bed had been Mad's usual brilliance when he got down to business that he intended to last a while. Lots of pain. Lots of penetration any way he could take it. Phenomenal orgasms, as many as he could pull out.

D just felt naked, and not the good kind, after giving it up about Tommy.

And somehow he knew Maddox had sensed that and the trip to the gym was not about getting away from temptation so they could rest up for Molly or keeping his body in shape because he (and D and Mol) liked it like that.

It was about giving Diesel space.

That was Maddox.

That was his man.

And it was occurring to Diesel that Mad had been giving it up in a lot of ways for D since the beginning.

A lot of ways.

For a long time.

And D did not give that back.

It's always about you, D.

Maddox had said that Friday night, when they were fighting.

It's always about you.

Before he could wrap his mind around that, all it meant, and the fact that all it meant was not only true, but not good, the sound of the garage door going up set D's eyes off Mad and down the hall to the back door.

He felt Maddox's gaze and looked back at him to see him grinning at D.

"Molly," Mad muttered, curling up, putting his beer on the coffee table and strolling down the hall with that loose-hipped gait he had that was so Maddox.

All about the confidence

All about the chill.

All about being comfortable in his skin.

It was then D realized that it wasn't Maddox's face, his body, his voice or his huge dick that did it for Diesel in the beginning.

It was that confidence.

It was that Maddox was who he was. He did not give that first shit what anyone thought about him. If someone said something—which fortunately no one had, Mad had learned a long time ago to narrow his life only to those who he wanted in it, taking on D's family in the remote way he had to do that since they didn't visit often, but they still seemed to loom large, at least to Diesel, when Maddox took on D and taking that shit because it came with D—Diesel suspected if he was in the mood, he had it in his power to let it go. But D knew, if he was in a different mood, Maddox had it in his power to fuck that someone up.

Either way, he'd be okay with it because that was Mad.

Diesel curled up to his feet, set his beer aside and followed him, hitting the door that Maddox was holding open for him and seeing Mol's Escape already parked inside, the garage door going down.

Maddox didn't hesitate to walk to her as D took hold of the door, stopping in it and holding it open with a shoulder while he crossed his arms on his chest.

Molly exploded out of the car and threw herself in Maddox's waiting arms, crying, "Mady!"

That was all she got out.

Molly all Molly in a little flouncy dress with a short but full skirt, what looked like a short sleeve shirt on top, all of it with a pattern of little birds on it, Maddox didn't bother saying anything in return.

He just pulled her body up his and took her mouth.

They went at it, and even though watching them made that tight feeling hit his gut again, D couldn't stop the sides of his lips turning up.

When Maddox ended it, he did it pulling Molly's thick hair away from the side of her face and murmuring, "I'll get your bag, baby."

"'Kay," she said, all Molly, meaning all smiles.

He let her go and she aimed that bright smile D's way.

It hit him where it always hit him, right in the chest, warm and sweet.

Then she launched herself his way and he had to unfold his arms to catch her since, when she made it to him, she jumped up and wrapped her arms around his neck. He turned his back to the door, she wrapped her legs around his hips, and she didn't even get out his name before he took her mouth and walked her in the house still doing it.

She was the sweetest kisser he'd ever had. Even after years, their Molly was timid with her tongue, but greedy taking her man's, and the contradiction never failed to score right through his cock.

He was almost to the couch before he broke their kiss, grinned down at her, and greeted, "Hey, baby."

The smile was back in place. "Hey, D."

He dropped her to her feet at the front of the couch and she immediately dropped her purse that was hanging on her shoulder to the coffee table.

They heard her bag hit tile and both turned to see Maddox was in, her weekender at the end of the hall, and Maddox's eyes were on their woman.

"Beer?" he offered.

"Please," she answered.

She bent and dug in her purse as D twisted around her, falling to his back on the couch in a lounge where his body was taking up the space, his shoulders to the arm, and the second she had her phone free, he grabbed her hips and yanked her on top of him.

She stretched out, settled in, smiled into his face again and he had no choice but to smile back.

"Drive good?" he asked.

"They need to make it three lanes all the way," she answered her standard answer anytime she went or came back from Tucson. "Arizona drivers drive way too offensively for two lanes *ever*."

"We'll start our petition about that after you wind down from the trip," he teased and the smile stayed pinned to her face.

And that was Molly.

She worked with doctors, they could be a pain in the ass, but she never let it get her down.

The drive to Tucson was always busy and full of jockeying for position, she found it stressful, but she never let it get her down.

For D she had to pretend Maddox was just a friend on the rare occasion any family member of his (but Rebel) was around, and she never let it get her down.

Maddox had the confidence, the chill, the ability not to give a shit about anything or anyone who didn't matter.

Molly had the strength of will to keep on keeping on no matter what hit her, she left it where it needed to be the minute she walked over the threshold into the home she shared with the men who were her life.

It was D who had the baggage.

It was D who weighed them both down.

Maddox moved in at their sides, handed Molly her beer, she took it while D reached out to get his at the same time shaking off his thoughts, and Maddox retrieved his own before throwing himself on the other end of the couch.

This time, Molly there, he settled in a tangle with D's legs, as well as Molly's, as Molly sucked back some brew.

She pressed into D to put the bottle to the floor and engaged her phone, eventually turning it D's way.

"This is the dress," she declared.

He looked at the snap.

"Shit," he whispered

On her phone was a picture of her in a long, very light pink dress that seemed to have lots of material and a high neck where the material latched onto a string that wound around her lower neck, but her shoulders and arms were bare. There was a sweet slit in the front and a belt at the waist gathering all that material to her body. It was feminine, innocent, almost angelic.

Absolutely Molly, from hem to collarbone.

"Baby, gorgeous," he said quietly.

He felt her kiss his jaw and that was the only reason his eyes moved from the photo to her to see her shifting so she could reach out and show Maddox.

D knew the instant Mad clapped eyes on it because he said, "Jesus, fuck."

"I take it my boys approve," Molly noted.

Approve wasn't the word for it and he hoped like fuck Holly and Dylan were having their reception somewhere with a private space big enough to fit three because he had no clue how he was gonna get through a ceremony without having her while she was wearing that dress and he knew from Mad's tone he felt the same.

"Approve is one word you could use," Maddox said.

Yup.

He felt the same.

She collapsed back on D, but he felt her feet burrowing into Maddox's thighs, and she looked at the picture of herself.

"I'm the only one who gets this style. The other three are in something else and their color is dove gray. It's totally gonna work," she murmured.

D cared nothing for what the other chicks were wearing.

He was just glad Holly had taken care of her sister and not dressed her up in something heinous.

She tossed her phone on the coffee table and pressed into D again to retrieve her beer as Diesel asked, "You best those budget cuts?"

She slugged some back and looked at him.

"So, get this, she had eight different kinds of hors d'oeuvres being passed around. We cut it back to six, and that saved sixteen hundred dollars right there," she declared.

Sixteen hundred on snacks?

"Christ," he muttered.

She looked to Maddox. "And we scaled back the table flower arrangements from the massive size to the middle massive size and saved another thousand."

"Sounds like you got on the right track," Maddox remarked.

She turned her attention back to D. "We also switched up the brand of champagne she picked for the toasts and saved another five hundred bucks."

Diesel was getting the idea that the ring for Molly's finger wasn't even the half of it.

Not near.

Even with her parents in to give her some cake.

Shit.

"We hit a snag because she refuses to cut back on the bridesmaid gifts she's buying," Molly went on. "But I managed to talk her out of the shoes she was going to wear, which cost twelve hundred dollars. I found ones she still loves, but isn't going to spend twelve hundred dollars on to wear once, because the ones she picked scream, '*bridal*,' and she'll so totally not ever wear them again. The ones I found, they're awesome, they'll work with her gown, but she might also be able to wear them again and they only cost three hundred dollars."

D could not imagine a three hundred dollar pair of shoes. He wasn't even going to attempt to imagine a twelve hundred dollar pair since that shit was impossible.

"And the DJ package was cut back from Studio 54 to Nice Wedding in Tucson and that saved another four hundred," Molly continued, and at that, D chuckled.

"So you made a good dent in it," Maddox noted and Molly looked back to Mad.

"We had it out over the guest gifts. She's determined to give everyone a little pot with a succulent in it or a personalized split of champagne, both *way* expensive. But Mom found some things on Etsy that were really cute, and tons cheaper, so she's going to think on it."

There was humor in his voice now when Maddox repeated, "So you made a good dent in it."

Molly did a thing with her head that was both nodding and shaking that was so fucking cute, Diesel could barely stand not trying to kiss her through it as she shared, "She's got a little less than three grand to go and bridesmaid gifts to buy. I told her maybe for her shower, she should ask for donations to the wedding, but she said she wanted people to be free to give her what they want her to have."

Translation, D thought, Holly wanted the presents.

Molly kept talking.

"So I don't know where it's gonna go from here. But yeah," she smiled again at Maddox, "we made a dent in it."

"How much money did your folks give her?" Diesel asked curiously.

Mol looked back to him. "Twenty K."

Diesel blinked.

Maddox spoke D's thoughts.

"Holy fuck."

"I know," Molly agreed, cuddling herself and her beer into D's chest. "We're so totally doing something in the backyard. An arch with sunflowers on it. A vat a chili, bowls of Fritos and grated cheese. Tin tubs of beer. Done. We'll use the rest for our honeymoon."

Diesel looked toward Maddox.

Maddox shook his head once, agreeing with D's unspoken statement.

D turned his eyes back to Molly.

"You're gonna have better than that, baby."

She maneuvered her beer to her lips still snuggled into him, sucked back a bolt, dropped the beer to his chest and tipped her head back to look up at him.

"Why?" she asked.

"Why?" he asked back, feeling his brows draw together.

"Yeah, why?" she replied. "I love sunflowers, chili and beer. They've got red and orange ones that are stunning. Sunflowers, I mean. It'll be amazing."

"Only one you're gonna get, sweetheart, you need to do it up big," he told her.

She snuggled deeper, her feet moving on Maddox, and shot him another grin.

"We'll do the honeymoon up big," she declared.

"We'll do that too," Maddox announced, on the move and D looked from Molly to Mad, who was running his hand up the back of her thigh.

Apparently it was time to stop talking about Holly's wedding, and whatever they were going to do for their ceremony, and properly welcome their girl home.

He was surprised Maddox let it go as long as it did.

Fuck, he was surprised *he* had.

He watched Mad's hand disappear up her skirt and D's gaze went right to her face so he could watch it get soft.

She didn't disappoint.

She then shifted, hitching up her leg to hook her calf around his hip which meant Diesel felt Maddox's wrist brush his hardening cock as Mad's fingers probably dipped in the gusset of her panties, and D could guess that because Molly's pretty face got softer but her gorgeous green eyes got hot.

Time to get down to business.

"Mouth, baby," D whispered, Molly turned hazing-over eyes to him and offered him her mouth.

He set his beer on the floor, grabbed hers and joined the two, all as he took her mouth.

Maddox shifted further and so did Molly as Maddox moved her from lazing down his side, her back to the couch, to lying down his front, her knees bent deep, thighs straddling his hips.

Diesel sucked her sweet tongue deep into his mouth and gladly took her little moan, biting back his own groan when Maddox's chin nudged his now rock-hard dick as their man shoved his face between her legs.

On a soft huff, she was forced to break the kiss, her eyes half-mast, cute, hot, sweet, so D nibbled her lower lip and went in with his hands, pulling her skirt up and diving into her panties, palming her round ass.

"You *did* save some for me," she whispered.

"Fuck yeah, baby, always," he whispered back, lifted his head, took her mouth again and slid her panties over her ass.

Maddox moved out, pulled her up to her knees on either side of D's hips, and took over pulling her panties down her thighs, over one knee and down the calf, then the other and they were gone.

Mad went back in between her legs and D kissed her, swallowing her mews and moans, his hands roaming the soft skin of her ass and the backs of her thighs as Mad ate her out and D's ass and balls tightened, feeling her excitement build and build, tasting it, loving it.

Eventually, when he heard Maddox growl, "D," with practice, he knew what that meant.

His hand moved in and he stopped kissing her, started playing with her clit as Maddox moved over her, over them, and she turned her head and took Maddox's tongue while she ground into D's fingers.

D dove inside, now thumbing her clit, finger fucking her, and she rode him, Mad breaking their kiss to go in at her neck.

But his eyes lifted to Diesel's when his teeth were nipping her earlobe, her earring sucked into his mouth, and Diesel raised a brow.

Maddox let her ear go and grunted, "You."

Brilliant.

To facilitate that happening, Maddox moved back and undid D's jeans, yanking them down his hips.

D removed his fingers, tangled his other hand in Molly's hair to turn her mouth back to his and Maddox positioned Diesel's cock, driving Molly down on it.

Having that slick, tight wet, he groaned down her throat and had to tighten his hold on her hair to keep her mouth to his instead of her head slamming back as he surged up and started fucking their baby.

She took over, riding him, sitting up, bouncing, her dazed eyes barely focusing on his face. Maddox's hands slid from her waist to her front, undoing the buttons at the top of her dress. He pulled it apart, yanking down her bra, going at her tits, all with his face shoved in her neck, all as she rode D's cock.

It was a fucking great show.

"*God,*" she breathed, head falling back, bouncing faster, taking him harder.

D went in down below, under her skirt that was splayed out around his hips, thumb to her clit, thrusting up to meet his baby's bounds.

"Fuck, you're beautiful," he growled, watching and latching on with his other hand to her hip, using it to pound her down on his cock.

Maddox's head came out of Molly's neck.

"Roll," he ordered and disappeared.

Diesel pulled her down to him, chest to chest, and flipped their girl. Having her softness under him, her beautiful hair spread all over the couch, her face looking like that, her eyes misty and lost in what her men were giving her, her lips swollen and parted, he took it up about seven notches and pounded in.

Her fingers went into his hair and latched on.

"Baby," she whispered.

"Yeah," he whispered back.

"Harder," she begged.

He gave it to her, anything she wanted, always.

Fuck, God, the feel of her, her smell, looking at her how she looked when she took him, he could fuck her for years, decades, centuries.

"Hold," Maddox ordered.

Gone for her, trembling with the effort, D buried himself inside Molly, held his body still, held her eyes and watched them get hotter as he felt Maddox moving in from behind.

"Go," Maddox grunted.

D pulled out and took cock up his ass.

His entire frame spasmed, Molly's did the same under him, and he fucked as he got fucked, Maddox leveraging his body in one hand in the couch, pummeling D's ass with his monster.

"Fuck yeah," Diesel groaned.

"Love you, love you, love my boys," Molly chanted breathlessly, lifting her knees, rounding them both with her legs, and D knew she was digging her heels in Maddox's hips, using that hold to lift herself up and take Diesel deeper.

Christ.

So.

Much.

Better.

"I-I can't hold," she pushed out.

"Don't," D and Maddox said together.

She let go, arching back, crying out, her pussy clamping on to D's driving dick, Jesus, even more gorgeous. Impossible. Amazing.

Molly.

Maddox moved his hand from the couch to wrap both around the backs of Molly's knees and he drove deep up D's ass as D pounded Molly through her orgasm, his face now buried in her neck.

"Fuck him, fuck me," Molly whimpered through her orgasm.

Too much, her slick cunt, that monster driving hard, her lyrical voice rough in heat.

Fuck.

"Gotta blow," D groaned into her neck.

"Go," Maddox ordered.

D arched into their girl, back into his man, exploding, shooting deep inside, jerking with it, his ass clamping down on the huge cock moving inside, making him buck through a mind-scrambling orgasm and do it for a long time. Until he collapsed on Molly for a beat before he pulled his weight into a forearm and found her eyes.

Her arms around his shoulders, she lifted her head and kept her eyes open even as she touched her open mouth to his.

He held her gaze and grunted into her mouth as he kept taking Maddox's fucking, doing it almost the best way there was. Buried in their baby.

"I love how you fuck our D," Molly said to Mad still looking at D. "Love feeling you moving inside."

That did it for Maddox, he drove in, forcing a grunt straight from D's ass through his gut up his chest and out his mouth right into Molly's, her hands darting up to grip his hair tight and hold him to her as he arched again into Maddox's climax, panting while he took his man's load, feeling Molly pant against his lips just because she liked knowing he was getting it.

Maddox thrust his cock deeper, shuddering against D as he shot his cum, pounding into him in jerks until he settled, buried, D's ass full of his monster, Molly's cunt full of D, and Maddox rested his forehead on Diesel's shoulder.

D pressed a kiss to Molly's mouth and she let his hair go and rested her head back as D asked quietly, "You good, man?"

Mad pulsed up his ass and D hissed.

"Do I feel good?"

D grinned at Molly. "Uh . . . yeah."

"You good, baby?" Maddox asked and his tone said that was directed at Molly.

"Yeah, honey," she answered.

"I get that pussy next," Maddox told her and the bright in her face, the heat in her eyes, said she was all for that. "My man," he called.

D turned his head and saw Maddox's cruel beauty inches from his.

His gut dropped, his chest went funny and his throat got dry.

"I'm at her pussy, you're at her mouth," Maddox laid it out.

The feeling vanished and Diesel grinned at him. "Works for me."

"First," Mad's gaze moved back to Molly, "gonna feed my babies."

"Yay," Molly whispered.

Slowly, Maddox pulled out the back and got off the couch. He leaned in, laid a long one on Molly while Diesel watched up close. Then he straightened away, grabbed a handful of D's ass, two fingers finding their way inside through the slick of Mad's own cum and the lube he'd left behind, making D clench his teeth at that goodness, and Mad gave him a squeeze.

With that, Mad slid his fingers out, let him go, hitched up his jeans and walked away.

Diesel turned to Molly and laid his own wet one on her before he disconnected their mouths and their bodies. But he made his way down hers, kissing her throat, the indent at the middle of her collarbone, her chest before he covered her tits with her bra. He then kept going down, dropping a kiss on the strip of hair between her legs then he touched his tongue lightly to her clit.

She shivered and slid her fingers back into his hair.

He looked up her body at her pretty face.

"You want me to clean you up?" he offered.

"I'll do it," she said.

"You touch that weekender, Maddox'll be fucking you with your ass red," he warned.

She grinned at him, slid off the couch and he got up to his knees on it, pulling up his jeans as she bent in and kissed his mouth.

"How long is it going to take before you realize that threat is not a deterrent?" she asked softly before she moved away, bending to grab her panties from the floor before she went.

He did up his jeans, got off the couch and growled when he saw her heading to her bag where Mad had left it.

Her gaze came to him and her hands went up. "Okay, okay, jeez."

With that, she left the bag alone and bounced away, her little skirt swaying side to side, and he watched it as she went.

When she disappeared, his eyes moved to the kitchen and he saw Maddox had been engaged in the same pleasant pastime.

Probably feeling his gaze, Maddox looked to him with a wicked gorgeous smile on his lips.

"You want me to clean you up?" he offered.

"Fuck off," Diesel returned, moving toward Molly's bag.

Maddox chuckled.

D bent and nabbed her bag.

He was on his way to follow Molly to their room, drop her bag and clean Mad's cum from his ass when he stopped because Maddox called his name.

"That dress," Mad said low when he got Diesel's attention.

He got him.

If Molly looked that good in a bridesmaid dress, what would they get when she walked to them to commit officially?

They'd get it *damned* good.

Like always.

"Tomorrow, phone your folks," D ordered quietly. "And she can have sunflowers if she wants, but if that's all she wants, she's gonna have twenty K worth of them and still get a honeymoon that's gonna rock her world."

"Agreed," Maddox muttered.

D nodded even though he had no idea how they'd pull that off along with a ring, started to move again but stopped when Mad again called his name.

And that shit happened to his gut when he saw the look on Maddox's face.

"Your ass, her pussy, my world," Maddox whispered.

He'd heard that before, or versions of it, but it was all the same. And he'd heard it more than once.

The latest, before that time right there?

That night at the Bolt when Sixx was observing.

Diesel stared into his man's eyes.

It took him a while and it took him a lot, too much, more than it should.

It should come easy.

But he forced it out on a grunt.

"Same."

Then he got his ass out of there, to their Molly so order could be restored, just them, dinner, TV, more fucking, togetherness, nothing deep.

Just everything.

Everything that meant anything.

SIX

Without Him

Diesel

DIESEL MOVED IN THE BACK door and tossed his keys in the pottery bowl on the table.

He went right, through the workout room to the small room attached to it, and dumped his workout bag by the washer.

He didn't do anything with the sweaty stuff inside. Molly would have a conniption if he did. She had a thing about laundry and part of that thing was that Mad nor D were allowed to touch it, or according to her, they'd fuck it up, though he couldn't imagine how. You tossed the shit in with some soap, turned the machine on, when that was finished you shoved the wet clothes in the dryer, took it out, put it away . . . done.

Not according to Molly.

D felt no driving need to do laundry so he didn't argue.

He also didn't do dick with his sweaty gym clothes.

Instead, he moved out of the room, back through the workout room, down the back hall into the great room and was about to call out, seeing as both Molly's Escape and Mad's truck were there and D had hit the gym after work so he knew they were home but they were nowhere to be seen.

He didn't call out.

He looked out the French doors to the patio, and when he noted they weren't out there, he turned his head toward the hall that led to the bedrooms.

He started that way but stopped, eyes at the end to the opened door to their room, hearing the noises coming from there.

Apparently, Mol and Mad were working out a different way.

He turned back toward the kitchen, on his way to get a beer, when his eyes fell on Molly's laptop on the island.

He stopped again and stared at it a beat before reaching to the back pocket of his jeans and pulling out his phone.

He went to texts, saw the group one on the top, in that position seeing as he'd told Molly and Maddox he was going to the gym after work, and they both replied in their ways (Mol: *Okay, honey, see you when you get home.* Mad: *Right. Later*).

D went to the text under that, not a group text, that one just from Mad, and he opened it.

It was a picture of a ring and a link to a website where you could buy it.

Under it Maddox had texted, *This is the fucking one.*

It had been a week and a half since Molly had gone down to Tucson.

As expected, Maddox's parents had been all in to float them a loan for Molly's ring. In fact, D had another text string that was a lot of emojis of hearts, happy faces and blowing kisses from Erin, that was how excited she was they were buying Molly a ring and getting down to business.

The picture on his phone was the fifth one Mad had sent to him in the last week and a half.

And it was the only one that was perfect.

A square diamond with the sides rounded off, elevated from the base, entirely surrounded by smaller diamonds, with even more of the stones embedded in the band as well as some scrollwork type stuff the website called "filigree." It was classy, pretty, feminine, substantial without being flashy, and very Molly.

It was also nearly thirteen thousand dollars.

D moved to Mol's laptop, opened it, powered it up and got a beer while it was chugging. He went back to it and put in her password.

Then he logged into the websites he wanted.

His bank account.

And Maddox's.

Clicking between the two, he felt a weight hit his gut.

Mad had nearly four K in savings.

D had a little over two.

Not only did this not equal thirteen thousand dollars, it clearly shared the discrepancy between his and Mad's earning power.

He logged out of both accounts, shut down the laptop, clapped it closed and turned his head to stare out the window over the kitchen sink after slugging back some beer.

How they were going to find seven thousand dollars to cover Molly's ring and the money to give her a fantastic honeymoon, D didn't have a clue.

He was all in for Erin and Bob to kick money their way so they could get the ring without Molly knowing about it.

He wasn't in at all with them owing Mad's parents seven grand.

But that ring was perfect in the way that now, D knew, no other ring would do.

"Fuck," he whispered as his phone rang.

In order not to disturb what his man and woman were doing in the back, he quickly took the call as he moved toward the French doors to the patio.

But he saw who the call was before he put the cell this ear.

"Yo, Mistress girl," he greeted quietly, shifting through the doors and closing them behind him.

"Hey, D, how's things?" Sixx asked.

D pulled up the good ole boy and said through a forced smile, "Movin' and groovin', like always. Wake. Work. Fuck. Sleep. Rinse. Repeat." He heard her soft laughter as he eased himself into a slider. "How's things with you?"

"Good . . . great, actually. Wake. Work. Fuck. Sleep. Rinse. Repeat. What could be bad about that?" she replied.

He'd been taking a swig while she talked.

He swallowed it and said, "Not a damned thing."

"It's been a while," she noted.

It had.

After their gig at the Bolt, they'd seen her and her man a couple of times, accepting her invitation to go to the gladiator games her man, Stellan, ran out east, having Sixx and Stellan over for dinner.

Since then, they'd gone their separate ways.

Sixx texted every once in a while, being a smartass and keeping a connection. He'd texted back, returning the smartass and the connection.

But that was it.

As far as he knew, she didn't keep in touch with Molly or Maddox like that.

Though he'd never asked.

"Yeah," he agreed, but said no more because there wasn't anything to say.

"Listen, I need to ask a favor," she told him.

"Shoot," he invited.

"I've got a job, and I'm sorry it's not more notice, but I've got to do what I've got to do tomorrow night. I need backup. Just eyes and ears, making sure things are copasetic. It isn't dangerous. But it could take some time, an hour, most two. If you can help out, I can pay in cash."

Pay in cash.

Diesel sat straighter in the slider.

Sixx was a private investigator. She worked in-house at a law firm, but also took on private jobs. He and Maddox had helped out with one when she was on the case of a drug-dealing, flesh-peddling asshole at the Bolt. It had been serious cool, a major high, and they'd done nothing but pass information, give her cover and act as muscle when she needed it.

Still, it was tons of fun.

"What's the job?" he asked.

"It's a client for the firm. I need to do a bit of breaking and entering and on-the-spot hacking. It has to be at night. It has to be tomorrow since the person I'm B and E'ing will be otherwise engaged. But the locale is populated and I'm not totally sure when he's going to come back. So I need someone on the outside while I'm on the inside and my normal backups are otherwise engaged."

"I'm in," he stated immediately.

"Not a Bolt night?"

He looked to his knees.

They'd only been back to the Bolt once since Maddox had worked him with Sixx observing. They usually went two nights a week, the first for D to work Mad, during which he earned his retribution, which would happen the next night.

After that one time they'd gone, and how disconnected he'd been during that particular shesh, not one of them had even suggested they head to their club and he wasn't so up his own ass he didn't know why.

Molly and Maddox were looking after him.

They knew the scene before had fucked with him.

So they weren't pushing it.

"Nope," D said shortly.

"Cool," Sixx replied. "We'll meet up tomorrow. I'll text you the address. Around eight. Like I said, you should be done at nine, latest ten. That work for you?"

"Yup. You need Maddox too?" he asked.

"No, just one of you. Though appreciate the offer."

"It'll be me. You need us again, Maddox can have the next go unless it's fucking someone up, then I'm calling it."

He heard her laugh again and he envisioned her face as he listened.

She was nearly as pretty as Molly, but in entirely the opposite way. Tall, angular, short hair, all edge.

"Stellan and me'll have to have you guys over for dinner sometime soon. I'll talk to him about it, we'll set something up," she said.

"Look forward to that, and I'm sure Mol and Mad will too."

"Great. I'll let you go and send the addy via text. See you tomorrow."

"Right. Tomorrow. Later, Mistress girl."

She didn't sign off.

She asked, "You doing okay?" in a tone that stated clear she'd somehow read that he was not.

Diesel took another slug of beer, looking at the yard before he answered with a lie, "Awesome."

Sixx didn't respond for long beats, and when she did she didn't hide she was thinking he was full of shit.

She also didn't push it.

"Okay, D. Later."

"Yeah," he replied. "Tomorrow."

With that, he disconnected in case she changed her mind about pushing it, dropping his phone hand to his thigh, lifting his beer hand to his mouth and throwing back another bolt.

When he took the bottle from his mouth, he held it in front of him, studying it like he'd never seen a bottle of beer before in his life.

And then it wasn't the bottle of beer he was seeing.

It was that ring. Molly in her bridesmaid's dress. Sunflowers. Molly under him with her auburn hair all over the couch, Maddox at his back with his cock planted inside.

Maddox over him at the Bolt with his tongue in D's mouth.

He blinked hard, pushed himself up and muttered irately, "You gotta get your shit tight, man. What the fuck is wrong with you?"

And with that, he walked into the house. He went to the kitchen and put his beer and phone on the island.

Then he walked down the hall.

He stopped in the door, put his shoulder to the jamb and stood there, watching Maddox moving inside Molly, both of them naked, going at it missionary, her arms around his shoulders, the fingers of one hand cupping the back of his head, her legs around his hips, their mouths as attached and active as their privates.

It was beautiful, completely. Their nude bodies, their movements, all the ways they were connecting, the noises they were making muted by their kiss.

They'd be happy without him.

They'd still have it all . . .

Without him.

In tandem, they broke that kiss and turned their heads to look at Diesel.

"Don't mind me," he said quietly.

"Come here, honey," Molly urged.

"Nope," he said on a gentle smile to their girl.

"Come here," Maddox commanded.

Diesel looked into his eyes.

"No."

He watched those black eyes flash then he watched Molly flatten a hand on the side of Mad's face, pulling his attention to her.

"He wants to watch," she whispered.

"Whatever," Maddox muttered irritably, and before Molly could respond to the irritation, he kissed her again.

He hadn't stopped moving inside her throughout and he kept doing it, D kept watching, pleasantly feeling himself go from semi-hard to fully erect, until shit got critical.

Only then did he move forward, toward the bed.

He gained both their attention but whispered, "Don't look at me."

Molly shoved Mad's face in her neck.

Mad pounded into Molly's body as her head arched back.

D sat at the side of the bed below their hips.

"Hitch a leg," he ordered quietly.

Maddox bent a knee, digging it into the mattress, going at her harder.

Instantly, Molly cried out with her orgasm, her legs visibly tightening their hold on her man.

That was when Diesel reached in.

Gripping Mad's balls, he gave them a squeeze and then he watched, now achingly hard, as Maddox's back, neck and head arced, his mouth opened, and the sudden sound of the grunting roar of his climax struck the room like a blow.

"Yes," Molly breathed as Diesel rhythmically wrung Maddox's balls dry, Mad finding that rhythm and using it, bucking into Molly with each clasp, a sharp groan accompanying them, mingling with Molly's whimpers, the dents at the sides of his ass clenching in and releasing along with the tempo.

Diesel watched, having fallen into it, his hand around those balls, that ass moving, Molly's legs circling the show. He was so spellbound by it all, Maddox had stopped buried inside their woman, and D kept massaging those balls, holding their weight in his hand, memorizing the feel, what was hitting his eyes.

He moved his hand and slid it flat along the inside of Mad's outstretched thigh, then back up, over his ass and along Molly's shin from ankle to knee, fascinated with the path his touch was taking, the feel of them against his skin.

Suddenly, his eyes moved from Molly's knee to Molly's face and he saw her looking over Maddox's shoulder to D.

Mad had his mouth working at her ear.

But Molly had her gaze locked on D.

And what he saw in it made him straighten immediately from the bed.

"I'll order a pizza," he declared, striding toward the door.

"D," Molly called.

"Diesel," Maddox said.

He ignored them and walked out of the room.

He had Molly's laptop open but hadn't even booted it up when Maddox prowled into the kitchen wearing jeans and nothing else.

He got close, smack in D's face, as nose to nose as he could get two inches shorter than Diesel.

It took a lot out of him, but as Mad invaded his space, D didn't move a muscle.

"What the fuck was that?" Maddox growled low.

"What the fuck was what?" Diesel returned, also quiet.

"You know what," Maddox clipped.

"If I knew what, I wouldn't ask," D pointed out.

Maddox jabbed a finger to the hall that led to their room without taking his eyes off D's.

"*That.*"

"You tell me you didn't get off on me squeezing you dry, I'll call bullshit," D retorted.

"We both wanted you in on that," Maddox shot back.

"It was your gig."

"It's never our gig, it's *our* gig," Mad snarled.

Diesel shook his head. "Man, I just got back from the gym where I didn't fuck around. I wasn't feelin' it. But that doesn't mean I'm not in to watch and maybe lend a hand when the time came, which is what I did."

"You got home ten minutes before, took a fuckin' call and only showed when the festivities were nearing an end."

"So?"

"So, why didn't you come back when you got home?" Maddox asked.

"Does it matter?"

"If it didn't matter, I wouldn't ask," Mad used D's earlier syntax to hurl it back, and Diesel, having a thin hold on his temper, felt it start to prick through.

"That's not the first time I wanted nothing but to watch," Diesel reminded him.

"I called you in," Mad reminded D.

Diesel kept at the trip down recent memory lane. "And I said no."

"I own you, Diesel," Maddox declared. "So that's not your call."

"When I'm not feelin' it, it's not *your* call."

"When you're not feelin' it, you don't come to watch and you don't get so hard, you make an instant fade mark in your jeans," Maddox fired back. "So it *was* my call, asshole."

That was true.

Still.

"What's up your ass?" Diesel growled.

"Not you. That's one thing that wasn't up my ass," Maddox replied.

"You want my cock, drop the jeans and I'll oblige," Diesel returned.

Maddox's black brows went up and he called him on his earlier lie. "So you're feelin' it now?"

"Fuck you," Diesel spat.

They scowled into each other's eyes and they did this so long, D was concerned Molly'd finish cleaning up and walk in on them.

It wasn't like none of them fought. They fought. All of them, Mad and D, Mad and Molly, D and Molly.

It was just that, out of respect for the one not involved in the fight, they didn't do it out in the open.

Suddenly, Maddox backed off, not much but he wasn't in D's face anymore.

He turned his head to the side and D watched a muscle jump up his cheek through his now heavy beard because he hadn't shaved since Molly was away for the weekend.

Diesel took in a calming breath and started, "Maddox—"

Mad turned back to Diesel. "You haven't fucked me since you bent me over the kitchen table that Saturday morning Molly was in Tucson."

He hadn't?

Shit.

No.

He hadn't.

Diesel swallowed.

He'd taken Maddox's dick, repeatedly.

He had not given that back.

He'd never gone so long without fucking Maddox since . . .

Hell, he'd never gone that long without fucking Maddox.

"Buddy," he said quietly, "I'll get some food in me, you get some recuperation time, we'll—"

Maddox cut him off. "What is it?"

Diesel felt his head twitch to the side. "What's what?"

"You're deep in your head, D, again, and . . . *fuck*," he hissed the last, looking away before looking back again. "I'm here," he said awkwardly. "You ever wanna talk, I'm . . . uh, here."

Diesel stared at him.

It was on the tip of his tongue to joke that it was hard to miss he was there since Mad was standing right in front of D and a couple of minutes before the man was right in his face.

Instead he said low, "I checked our accounts, brother, and we don't have the money for that ring. We don't even have half of it between the two of us. And it's that ring. We both know it. Molly has to have that ring. And we can't afford it."

Maddox's chin jerked slightly into his neck as his black eyes stared unblinking into D's.

"You're thinkin' about Mol's ring?"

"We got a little over six K. Your parents float that loan, we'll owe them without being able to pay them back for a long fuckin' time."

"They'll be cool with that, D," Maddox said.

"I won't."

Maddox said nothing and he did this studying D.

Then he nodded. "You're heard. But just to say, talked to George and he says you can usually get them to swing you a deal. Fifteen percent off, sometimes even twenty."

George owned the company Maddox worked at. The man was loaded, his wife dressed like the woman of a man who was rolling in it, so he'd know. And that was good news. If that panned out, that'd help.

They were still in the hole.

"We still don't have enough," D noted.

Maddox nodded again. "We'll think on it. Yeah?"

Diesel nodded back, thinking a windfall of five hundred dollars in cash from Sixx for two hours of checking the coast was clear would also help, but not much.

Though if she had other jobs she needed assists with and they paid that kind of cake . . .

"You better be ordering boneless wings!" Molly called down the hall.

This was Molly Speak for, "Whatever you two are talking about after Maddox hightailed his ass out of the bedroom after making love to me needs to stop because I'm almost there."

She put up with a lot, Molly did, and she did it well, and it was not just shit like doing all their laundry because she had on her hands two men who had no interest in doing it "right" (whatever that was).

There was a shitload more.

D turned his attention to the laptop and hit the on button.

Maddox shifted so he was back to the island, hips resting against it beside D.

Molly entered the room wearing cute little short shorts in T-shirt fabric that had a pink drawstring and tiny pink hearts on a gray background and a skintight pink tank that clearly showed the lace of her bra. Both of those, with her hair a messy knot on top of her head, a bunch of it falling down her shoulders, swollen lips, rosy cheeks, lazy eyes, otherwise known as Molly's after-sex face, made D's dick start feeling it for certain.

"Buffalo with extra ranch dressing," she ordered.

"Gotcha," D said as she walked right to his side.

She grabbed hold of his tee at his abs and got on her toes as he turned his head and bent his neck to touch his mouth to hers.

When he was done, she grinned up at him but the searching look in her eyes made him grin back at her fast then look again to the laptop.

Out of the sides of his eyes, D caught her scraping her fingernails lightly through the hair on Mad's chest and going on her toes to get a lip touch from him before she moved away, asking Diesel, "Good workout?"

"Not as good as yours," he teased.

She laughed softly as Diesel pulled up the pizza website.

He logged in and started clicking through as Molly brought Maddox a beer.

"God, you're taking a year doing that," Molly complained and D turned his head to see her leaning her side into Maddox's front, facing D, Mad's arm loose around her waist, her head tipped back to look at Diesel, a grin on her face.

"Hungry, baby?" he asked.

"Starving," she answered.

He grinned back then turned his attention to the laptop, muttering, "I'll hurry."

"I know you. It might take seven years for you to tap out two fingered, 'We want extra ranch,' in the note section," she complained.

He looked at her again. "I can order pizza."

"I'd be done by now," she replied.

"And I'd be done by now too, sweetheart, if you weren't yammering at me."

Maddox chuckled.

Molly rolled her eyes.

That was so cute, like anytime she did it, D fought taking a further break from finishing on the computer in order to kiss her, but since feeding their girl was clearly priority, he decided to finish on the computer.

He did that, pulled up the map that showed when the delivery guy was on the way, then reached out and nabbed his forgotten beer, turning toward them, leaning a hip against the counter and announcing, "I've got plans with Sixx tomorrow night. She needs backup on some job."

Maddox's head cocked sharply to the side.

Molly's sweet green eyes got big.

"Say what?" Maddox asked.

"That call I took after I got home. It was Sixx. She needs some help tomorrow. Says it'll take an hour, the most two. I'll be home, latest, around ten."

"I . . . uh . . ." Molly started but trailed off.

"You think maybe we should talk about this?" Maddox asked without stammering at all.

In fact the man looked ticked.

"About what?" Diesel asked back then stated, "You can do the next job, if she's got one. But I'm calling it if she needs to fuck someone up."

"Is it dangerous?" Molly asked carefully.

Ah.

Right.

He looked to her. "No, baby. She just needs someone to keep an eye on things while she uh . . ." he decided against sharing about the B and E, "does what she has to do. It's not dangerous."

"Why's she asking you?" Maddox inquired and D looked to him, beginning to get ticked himself.

"Why wouldn't she?"

"When'd you become her partner?" Maddox pushed.

"I'm not her partner," he answered shortly. "Her usual backup is busy so she called me."

"I don't get it," Mad stated.

"You don't have to get it," Diesel returned angrily. "Clearly she trusts me. Thinks I have my shit tight. She's in a bind, needs to do what she's gotta do and needs someone with her, so she asked me. It was a cool thing to do considering she *definitely* has her shit tight so it's kinda nice to know she thinks the same about me."

"I wasn't sayin' that, D," Maddox said slowly.

"So what were you saying?" Diesel demanded heatedly.

"Please don't fight," Molly whispered and got both her men's immediate attention.

It was law. Straight up. No breaking it. Unspoken but they all knew.

If any of them were into it with another, the one not in it did not wade in.

Ever.

Just like they didn't fight when the other one was around, when a fight started when the other one was around, that one did not get involved in the discussion.

D watched Molly's cheeks get even pinker before she turned in a way that was openly deliberate. She lifted both hands and rested them on Mad's bearded cheeks, again going up on her toes but also pulling him down to her.

There, she kissed him, mouths open. D could see her glistening pink tongue and Maddox's.

She broke the connection abruptly and didn't let a beat slide by before she had her hands on D's face, yanking him to her, again rolling up on her toes, pulling his mouth down on her.

She slid her tongue inside and he tasted her usual sweet but he also tasted hints of man and beer.

Maddox.

Maddox in his mouth.

She broke the kiss and looked him right in the eye before she took a step away from both of them.

"I'm grabbing a beer. I'll be out on the patio," she mumbled.

Then she did just that.

Escaping their fight.

Giving them space.

But most definitely making her point before she went.

Both men stared at the French doors long after she closed them behind her.

It was D that broke the uncomfortable silence and cut through the tension.

He looked at Mad and explained, "It's five hundred dollars cash, this job with Sixx. We need it. I'm not involved in anything she's doing. She needs eyes so she can enter some guy's place and do what she's gotta do. I'll be gone two hours tops. But we need that money for Molly's ring. *I* need that money for Molly's ring. So I'm gonna tell Sixx, if she's got other gigs, I'm in. Especially for that kind of cake."

Maddox's brows had risen at one particular part of his speech.

"*You* need that money for Molly's ring?"

"Equal, brother. And right now what we got in our savings to put toward that buy isn't equal."

Maddox stared at him, that muscle in his cheek flexing.

He was a man. A man with a huge dick. So he got him.

He affirmed this verbally.

"I hear that, D."

"Right," Diesel replied.

"And I wasn't sayin' what you thought I was sayin'," Maddox went on. "I know you can handle yourself. But Sixx is a badass and if that job at the Bolt is anything to go by, she gets involved with some serious players. Drug dealers. Pimps. She doesn't blink at that shit. But that's her job. That's what she does. You don't have that experience and it isn't that you aren't sharp and fit and aware. It's just that you have to clue into the fact that, if anything happened to you, me and Molly would feel that. You gotta do what you gotta do, I get that. But whatever you do, even if you're doing it somewhere else, me and Mol are always along for that ride."

Me and Molly would feel that.

Diesel looked away from his man and took a swig of beer.

"You know that, right?" Maddox pushed.

Diesel looked back at him and answered quietly, "Yeah, man. I know that."

"So don't get pissed, tomorrow, I check in before we hit the sack," Maddox finished.

They all started their days early. Both Mad and D with jobs where they worked outside in the Phoenix heat, in order to work during the time when it baked, but not as bad as it did in the late afternoon, their days could start at six or seven.

The good part about that was they were usually done around two thirty or three.

The bad part about that was, with the physicality of their jobs on top of early start times, they couldn't get around going to bed early.

Molly had arranged her schedule at work so it was as close to theirs as it could be, that being seven to four.

This meant at least two of them were in bed at nine every night, mostly because at least two of them fucked before they went to sleep.

He'd probably come home either to both of them out, or both of them in bed, but awake, waiting for him to come home.

Considering Maddox seemed to be able to man up, Diesel had to try to kick in to do the same.

"I've needed some space lately. Shit in my head," he said low. "It didn't occur to me you'd feel that as me pullin' away because honest to

God, I didn't realize I was. When I'm at a place I can actually wrap my brain around what that shit is, we'll talk it out. In the meantime, totally lame, but totally true, one hundred percent true, buddy, I promise. It's me. Not you."

The relief that Maddox allowed openly to wash through his face made Diesel's mouth fill with saliva.

"Okay, bud," he said softly. "I can give space."

Diesel jerked up his chin.

"And I'm there when you're ready," Mad continued.

Diesel looked him in the eyes and for that, gave him a full nod.

Mad's full lips embedded in his thickening beard twitched. "And good call, not pointing out to Molly we have three bottles of ranch dressing in the house."

Diesel burst out laughing.

Maddox chuckled along with then.

Right.

There they were.

They were good.

Good.

For now.

SEVEN

More than Everything

Diesel

"ONLINE," DIESEL SAID INTO THE transmitter in his hand, his eyes on the laptop on the seat beside him in his truck as a picture filled a quarter of the screen, replacing static.

"Right. Thanks," he heard Sixx say in the earbud in his ear.

Yup.

Earbud in his ear. Little transmitter that looked like a miniature microphone in his hand which was bluetoothed to a new app that Sixx had downloaded on his phone. A laptop on his passenger seat that had a split screen on it, four views, all of them now showing pictures since Sixx had successfully installed the last camera in the hallway that led to her target's apartment door. A cord plugged into the laptop reaching out through a crack in his window in order to get the camera signals.

Another view was inside the elevator. And another was in the lobby. The last was at the door to the elevator bay from the underground garage.

Sixx was *tricked out* in kit on this sleuth shit.

It was fucking *fantastic.*

He also had a slim-line pair of binoculars and a file holding an eight by ten glossy of a guy's face and a piece of paper with the make, model, color and license plate number of a car, both he'd already memorized.

His truck was positioned across the road, opposite the entry to the parking garage to the apartment building. He was seated where he was because the guy was out in his car. D should be able to spot him driving in.

If not, added insurance, there were cameras everywhere and no way, unless he was Spider-Man and went in through his window, could the guy make it into his apartment without D being able to give Sixx the heads up.

On the bottom right of the laptop screen, he watched Sixx break and enter.

Right, not so much breaking as picking, but she entered and the door wasn't shut before he heard in his earbud, "I'm in."

"See that," he said in the transmitter, deciding he was going to ask her to show him how to pick a lock. "Have fun."

"Always do," she replied.

Reaching out to the binoculars because a car just then turned into the parking garage, he checked it out.

Chevy.

He was looking for a Ford.

The cool stuff over, Diesel settled in, alert, watchful of the front door he could also see, scanning even the cars that passed, checking the faces of anyone who appeared on the cameras.

He figured it'd get boring but the complex was a cush one off 1st Avenue. It was after eight thirty, but there was heavy traffic, car and foot, so there was always something to keep his eye on. And considering if he fucked this up, Sixx was caught and the guy was able to do the impossible—subdue her and call the cops—she'd face a felony charge, the stakes were high.

Even sitting in his truck, it was a rush.

So much so, fifteen minutes slid by and it felt like five.

"Anything good?" he asked in the transmitter. "Like an inspired porn collection?"

Sixx was laughing when she replied, "Dude's b-o-r-i-n-g. But I'm in on his computer. Maybe he's into Japanese sex anime."

"I'll keep my fingers crossed for you," Diesel returned, speaking while thinking Sixx laughed a lot.

He was also thinking he used to do that.

A lot.

When he was with Tommy, before and after he left town. They yucked it up all the time, when they weren't fucking.

He didn't laugh much when he wasn't with Tommy.

But he did when he arrived in Phoenix.

He'd had no money. No job. Was living in a shithole while he tried to get a life started.

And still, he felt light for the first time in his life.

Light.

Easy.

Free.

Life was good.

He ate crushed tortilla chips in salsa for breakfast lunch and dinner because it was all he could afford and he did this for months, until he scored a job that didn't get him out of that shithole, but it did allow him to go to a burger joint for dinner.

And still.

Life was good.

From age twenty-two to twenty-eight, when he'd met Mad.

Then finding Maddox. Making him smile that cruel smile of his. Laugh that gravelly laugh. Doing both along with him.

That was more good.

Adding Molly and giving her the same.

That was all good.

He'd just simply had it good for the last decade.

And it all ended that night at the Bolt when he knew at the beginning of the scene how Mad was going to play it and he did just that, ending the scene displaying Diesel on his back on a padded table, sucking him off then fucking his ass while their mouths were connected.

Nope.

Not fucking his ass.

Making love to him.

After that, the laughter hadn't died but it didn't come as easy anymore.

Why?

They had it good. Nothing had changed.

So . . .

Why?

On that thought, his phone rang, he saw who it was and considered not taking it. Not because he didn't want to talk to the caller, he always wanted to talk to her, but he had to keep tight for Sixx.

Still, she was only twenty minutes into a job that would take at least an hour and he had nothing to do but keep an eye out.

So he took the call and put it on speakerphone.

"Yo, sis," he answered.

"This is not a voice from beyond the veil. This is me. Live and in Denver. Wondering why the hell I never hear from my brother," Rebel returned.

He grinned at the computer screen.

Rebel.

Now Rebel could always make him smile.

"Wassup?" he asked.

"Wassup?" she repeated back to him.

"Yeah. Wassup?"

"Diesel, I haven't heard from you in over a month," she declared.

"I was unaware I had to report in to my baby sister."

"Okay then, I'm now making you officially aware you have to report in to your baby sister."

"Reb, baby doll, the phone goes both ways."

"Yeah, and I just said into mine, 'Call my asshole brother who doesn't stay in touch,' and we're rapping now, aren't we?"

Anyone else, he might get pissed.

Rebel, not a chance.

First, she was hard to get pissed at. She might be more about cinnamon than sugar, but she was still all sweet.

Second, she was just busting his chops since that, apparently, was what baby sisters were born to do.

Still, his baby sister had it down to an art.

Diesel looked through the binoculars at a car entering the garage (not their guy), but did it asking, "So, are you gonna tell me what's up?"

"Are you sitting down?"

Shit.

"What?" he asked.

"Mom wants a family Thanksgiving," she announced.

Fuck.

"She's ticked you haven't been home in a while," she continued.

Shit.

"That would include you and Molly," she went on.

Fuck.

"So," Rebel continued, "while she's burying herself even further in denial about who Maddox really is to you and Mol in order to buck up and phone you to ask you and Molly for Thanksgiving, at the same time making it clear Maddox is not welcome, but trying to do that politely, I thought I'd give you a heads up so you could think of a good excuse to tell her you can't go without it being something like, 'I'm bi, Ma, you don't dig, you can go fuck yourself.'"

Diesel blew out a breath, staring hard at the feeds on the laptop screen.

"D, you there?" Rebel called.

"We're looking at rings for Molly."

Christ.

What was the matter with him?

Shit just kept vomiting from his mouth.

"Oh. My. *God!*" The last word was squealed with so much excitement, his sister lived in Denver, they were separated by masses of land that included mountain ranges and deserts, and he could still feel her thrill whisper across his skin.

He wanted to smile at that.

He wanted to get all puffed up like a man about to stake his claim to his future knowing he had it all.

He didn't.

"I'm leaving them," he let out.

Fuck!

"What?" she whispered.

Time to backtrack.

"Listen—" he began.

That's as far as he got.

It was a wonder with Rebel and what just came out of his mouth that he got out the "L" sound.

"How are you buying Mol a ring in one breath and leaving them in the next?" she demanded to know.

"Right, Rebel, I'm in the middle of something right now and—"

"Oh no. Hell no, D. Are you and Maddox looking at rings for Molly?"

"I can't talk about this right—"

"Are you?" she snapped.

"I'm gonna need to shut that down," he told her, feeling his gut start aching to the point he felt sick.

"Are you crazy?" she asked, sounding like she thought he wasn't crazy, he was straight-up certifiable.

He checked out another car through the binoculars (not their guy) as he replied, "Babe, seriously, this is not a—"

"You know, if you can't tell them, I will. I'll be happy to do it, D. I'll take that hit for you and, unlike you, I'll enjoy it. And straight up, since we're finally here, talking about this, you'll lose Dad. You'll lose Gunner. And neither are big losses. Especially Gunner. He's a bully. He's been a bully since we were little kids. He'll be a bully until the day he dies, which will be alone, unloved, and wondering where he went wrong, not understanding you can't be a total dick to every being who crosses your path and have a single one of them give a damn about you. Mom, she'll freak and she'll listen to Dad's shit, but after a while, she'll get over it. And when she does, she'll go against Dad. She can be weak but she has her times of being strong. And those times have always been about her kids. So she'll get there. She will, Diesel. You'll just have to give her space and wait it out, and in the end, you'll have the only one worth something. That is, not including me. You'll always have me."

"You're not talkin' to them," he growled.

"Because you're doing it yourself?" she asked.

"No," he bit.

"And what? What, D? You're gonna leave Maddox and Molly because your father and brother are bigots?"

"Like I've been sayin', right now, I can't talk about—"

"You can't do that. You can't leave them."

"They got each other and if they want, they can find someone else who they don't have to deal with his bullshit."

He said it and it only made him feel sicker.

Her tone had changed entirely, gone gentle, soft, when she said,

"Honey, they don't want anybody else."

"It's more than just Dad and Gunner," he told her.

"Tell me the more," she urged.

"I don't got time and I don't got the headspace right now. I'm in the middle of something."

"This is important, Diesel."

And that was when he lost it.

Yup.

On his baby sister.

"*You think I don't know that?*" he barked.

She was silent.

He drew in a big breath.

Another one.

He scanned everything with his eyes.

He blew out one last breath into the silence Rebel let fall before he said soft, "That was outta line."

"I need to come down and have some quality time with my big brother," she replied.

He shook his head even if she couldn't see. "I gotta sort out my head on my own."

"Why?"

"It's just how I gotta do it, Reb."

"I know." That was a whisper.

A whisper even over the phone line he could hear was full of sadness.

Even anguish.

And D felt even sicker.

But Rebel?

Rebel didn't keep him guessing what was behind it.

"Because you are who you are. You've always been who you are. And they've always been who they are. So you felt like you had to hide. You felt like you had to go it alone, even surrounded by people, people who love you or who are meant to love you. You never felt safe to reach out. And I want you to feel safe to reach out but you're conditioned to go it alone for fear of what might happen if you open up and let the truth out. You have Maddox and Molly and me and we all love you. We want you to feel loved. Feel safe. Feel able to share anything with us. But I get it, D. I hate it. But I get it."

Diesel was suddenly breathing heavily, like he was bench pressing above his weight, but instead he was putting everything he had into listening to every word his sister said and watching everything around him so he didn't let Sixx down.

He shouldn't have taken the call.

Too late now.

"And you care what they think of you," she carried on. "I get that too. That's what sons do. That's what little brothers do. You look up to them. Whether they deserve it or not, it's the way it is. And you want them to respect you. And you know they won't when they learn and you haven't gotten to that place where you realize they don't matter and that's precisely the reason why they don't. They don't deserve *your* respect for precisely the reason they'll retract theirs."

"Baby doll," he whispered.

"But listen to me," she said fiercely. "Please, God, Diesel, *listen to me*. When you find that one, that one who's *the one*, it means everything. *Everything*, Diesel. But you didn't find the one. You found *the ones*. That means you're in the unique position to have *more than everything*. More. Than. *Everything*. There isn't more than everything. But you . . . Diesel, you have that. Don't let that go, big brother. It's so precious, it's unspeakably precious. It's so rare, it's nonexistent, except for lucky people. People who deserve it. People like you. So, please, God, do not let that go."

She barely finished her last word when his phone binged with a text.

He looked at it.

Maddox.

All good?

"Mad is texting, Reb. I gotta go," he said to his sister.

"Right," she replied quietly.

"Love you, babe."

"Growing up in that house, it was only you, Diesel."

He shut his eyes.

"We were so out of place," she kept at him, "it felt there wasn't a place on this earth for us. Until I found my place, until you found your place, I only had you."

And he'd only had her.

And Tommy.

He opened his eyes and scanned, murmuring, "Baby doll."

"I want you to have everything, D. So it goes without saying, if you can lay your hands on even more, I want you to have that too."

Diesel didn't reply.

Rebel didn't remain silent.

"Love you, big brother."

"Thanks for warning me about Mom's call."

"Always."

That was all there was and that was Rebel. When she was done, she was done.

And she was done.

He heard her disconnect.

Then he ran his thumb over the phone.

Transmitters. Earbuds. Cameras. Sixx is the shit. So you aren't getting a turn, he texted to Maddox, putting the conversation with his sister in the back of his head.

It felt like seconds before he got back, *Right, bud. Have fun. Stay safe. Tell Sixx hey. We're hitting the sack in a few.*

They'd probably fuck. They didn't do it before he left. He didn't do it with either of them before either. And a day never went by when at least some of that action didn't happen.

He also hadn't made good on his promise to do Maddox the night before.

And Maddox hadn't pushed it.

Christ.

Will do. Later, Diesel replied then threw the phone on the seat by the laptop, swallowed the sick feeling still in his gut, did a scan, and engaged the transmitter.

"Still good?" he asked Sixx.

"No Japanese sex anime," Sixx replied.

He read that as her not finding what she was looking for.

"So, not good," he surmised.

"I'm taking a deep dive. Can you give me another half an hour?"

"Absolutely."

"Thanks, D."

He left her alone to focus as he focused.

Surprisingly, even though he suspected it would, the boredom never crept in. It was a Thursday night but people were out and about, getting home for the evening, driving in, walking up, strolling down the halls. There was so much happening, even as more time passed, there was no way not to stay alert.

Half an hour later, Sixx said in his earbud, "I need another ten."

"You got it," he replied.

Though she didn't.

Five minutes later, the dude's car drove in.

He put the transmitter to his mouth. "Man's home. Just drove in. Get out."

"Roger that," she said.

Roger that.

Feeling heavy from just about everything, but most recently his chat with his sister, that still made him smile because this gig was the shit.

He gave her some time to focus and then he gave her a blow by blow.

"He's not to the garage door yet and your hallway is clear." He waited. "He hit the garage door and he's through. Hallway still clear."

He waited and saw her come out of the apartment.

She locked the door, boogied down the hall, reached up and grabbed the camera she'd mounted.

Static on that box on the screen.

He caught her in the elevator, looking right at their guy who was coming out going up as she was getting in to go down.

She nodded to him.

The guy nodded back having no clue the stranger he'd just nodded to spent the last hour plus in his pad.

"Totally the shit," he muttered.

She grabbed camera three (elevator), camera two (garage) and camera one (lobby) and she was out, hoofing it to D's truck, all while D put the binocs in their case and zipped the transmitter in its. After the lobby camera went out, he powered down the laptop, slapped it shut, wound up the cable neat and had it all ready for her as she climbed in.

She took the stuff after she shut the door. When she stowed it in its bag, he gave her his earbud.

But he didn't want to.

James Bond never had a kickass pickup.

But Diesel rocked that shit.

He turned to the wheel and started her up in order to drive Sixx to where they'd left her car.

"Get what you need?" he asked.

"Nope."

He tried to keep the hopeful out of his, "You need to go back?" And that hope was not all about another potential five hundred bucks.

"I had lots of time in there, D. This guy is not a mastermind and thus able to hide his shit. He's an average Joe. So average, it's a wonder his vanilla self didn't blend into the background so he was invisible as I walked by him getting off the elevator. His ex is going to have to get creative about reasons to take him to the cleaners with this divorce. The man doesn't even have condoms in the house . . . *anywhere.*"

What newly single dude didn't have condoms?

Anywhere?

Jesus.

"Bummer," D muttered, pulling into the road.

"You win some, you lose some," Sixx replied, like it was all the same to her.

Then again, it was. She got paid either way.

D had too. He had five crisp one hundred dollar bills in his wallet.

Another bit of goodness about the woman, Sixx paid in advance.

"Just to say, you got other gigs you need eyes or anything, you know my number," he told her.

"Glad to hear that since my usual backup is pregnant and she's about to go offline at her husband's decree. He's in the family business, I work with him too, but they have their own jobs so going solo makes his time tight. You got good instincts. Thanks for the rundown when he was coming in, by the way. So yes. It isn't regular I need an assist, but it happens and that's not rare. So I'll be taking you up on that."

Brilliant.

"Be obliged you teach me how to pick a lock," he shared.

"Then we'll add some field trips on our schedule," she replied immediately.

Stellar.

"Bored with the day job?" Sixx asked.

He worked road construction.

It didn't suck.

But there were no transmitters.

"Just good with the absence of neon orange vests but the presence of a shitload of cash for doin' practically nothing in my wallet," he told her.

"Practically nothing to you is peace of mind allowing focus for me, D," she replied. "That's worth more than five bills, but I don't think I'd get away with any more on my expense account."

"You get a golden goose, definitely hit my number."

She laughed and he let himself grin at the windshield.

He dropped her at her car and she stood in the open door saying, "Tell Molly and Maddox I said hello and we'll find a time for that dinner party soon, D."

"They say hey back and yeah. Look forward to that," he replied.

She didn't move from the door. Just stood there, looking through the cab at him.

And then, proving the goodness never ended with Sixx, she said quietly, "You can hit my number anytime too, D. I'm always there for you at the other end of the line."

She didn't back that up with shit, getting in his face about knowing something was bugging him, pushing him to share.

She just dipped her chin, stepped out of the door, closed it and strolled on her long legs to her Cayenne.

He watched her swing in and didn't start moving until he saw her headlights go on.

Since they were both headed east, she followed him down Camelback but turned left on 44th to head to Paradise Valley while he turned right on it to skirt Arcadia and head to the area that didn't have nineteen hundred square foot houses that cost eight hundred grand.

D parked beside Maddox's truck, hauled his ass out, beeped his locks and let himself in the house.

He was not surprised the little lamp on the table by the door was lit.

That would be Molly.

He dumped his keys in the bowl and turned the lamp off.

He was also not surprised the under cupboard lights in the kitchen were lit.

That would be Maddox.

He flipped those off before heading to bed.

The hall was dark. The back bedroom door open, the room beyond it dark.

He hit it and saw through the moonlight Molly cozied up to Maddox's side, both on their stomachs. The covers were up to her shoulders because the AC was cranked down, even at night, ceiling fan on. The fan was white noise they all needed, but also breeze and AC that Mad needed since his body ran hot in sleep which was why the covers were up to Mol's shoulders, but only up to his middle back.

Neither moved as he came in but he saw Molly was wearing a nightie which meant Maddox hadn't fucked her before they fell asleep. If he had, she'd be naked. Her choice, before-sleep fucks meant she stayed in bed, her men cleaned her up and then she passed out.

So there'd been no fucking.

That was interesting.

D moved to the walk-in and dumped his boots and clothes in the dark.

As he walked back out into their room, naked, he had a strange urge to walk right out, go to their guestroom and sleep there.

Leave them be.

By force of habit, his feet took him to his side of the bed.

He hadn't even reached to the covers when he saw Maddox's head and shoulders come up, turned his way.

"Good?" he whispered.

"Yeah, buddy," D whispered back, carefully pulling back the covers to slide in.

He was in on his back in bed and still, Maddox hadn't lowered down.

The moonlight was shining in the windows, silvering the room.

Through it, they held each other's eyes.

And fuck, even in the dark, the man was beautiful.

His harsh face smoothed out in the shadows, he wasn't more beautiful, just a different variety.

D's cock pulsed as it started to get hard.

He shifted to his side, toward Maddox, and Molly moved, turning her head slowly his way.

"D?" she muttered groggily.

"Go back to sleep, baby," D murmured.

"Mm," she hummed, all drowsy, reaching out with limbs to tangle him up with them.

"No, sweetheart," D said, his eyes still locked on Maddox. "Mad and me are gonna go to the other room."

At his words, the air in that room got thick and warm.

Molly's head came up.

Then her body moved, coming his way, sliding over his.

He didn't hesitate and slid under her, knowing she didn't just grant permission.

In her way she gave an order.

Her men were gonna do what they were going to do, but in doing it, they weren't going anywhere.

"D," Maddox whispered.

Diesel wrapped his fingers at the back of his man's neck and shoved his still lifted head down.

Then he moved in. Shifting his hand, D bared his teeth and scored the skin of Mad's neck, down, over the contours of muscle on his shoulder blade, down, along his spine, down, he took a bite at the right cheek of his ass.

Maddox growled.

D's dick, already hard, twitched.

"Spread," he grunted.

Maddox opened his legs.

And D's dick thumped.

Diesel shifted in and moved his mouth to the small of Maddox's back, reaching between his legs.

He wrapped his fingers around that monster and stroked up the long, rock-solid length, *hard*.

"Fuck," Maddox groaned, his body tensing everywhere as Diesel started on a handjob against the mattress, gliding his lips to just above the top of Mad's crease, a place his man was exceptionally sensitive, where he licked and then sucked. "*Fuck*," Maddox bit out, starting to move his hips to ride D's fist.

D drew on his flesh, moved his mouth, nibbled his ass cheeks, stroked his cock, then shifted away. Fisting back to the root, he tightened, lifting up.

Mad came up on his knees.

Molly emitted a little moan, and it was no wonder.

Maddox on his knees was a thing of beauty.

D's cock started throbbing.

Maddox began to come up on his hands but Diesel reached out his free hand and bent over him, his cock brushing Maddox's ass, making D shiver, Mad's body jump. He wrapped his fingers around the back of Maddox's neck and pushed.

"Down," he ordered.

Maddox went down, ass still in the air.

"Stay down," D commanded.

Maddox didn't move.

His hand between Mad's legs, Diesel recommenced stroking.

The weight was heavy, as always, hot to the touch, also as always, those veins popping out so dense, D could trace them even with a closed fist.

Lost in the feel of his man's meat, the sight in front of his eyes, he rumbled, "Fuck me, love this cock," tightening his hold around the thick, long length.

Maddox said nothing but his body tensed further as it started trembling.

D went in with some ball massage.

In response, Maddox flexed his feet, digging his toes into the bed as a low, ragged noise rolled up his chest, that noise skating along D's dick.

Christ, his man.

Fuck.

Diesel let Mad's balls go, palmed his ass and shoved a thumb inside.

Mad bit back his grunt.

"Love this ass," he muttered, fucking him with his thumb.

Maddox couldn't tense enough to hold back the trembling any longer, or his movements. He took the thumb, fucking D's fist.

"Yeah, show me you like it," Diesel encouraged, watching the show having to brace himself to hold back from positioning and powering inside just to give his cock what it needed, give himself what he needed.

Maddox went faster, reaching out his hands to push against the headboard, his back muscles shifting and contracting with the movement.

Nice.

"Yeah, brother," Diesel whispered.

"More," Maddox whispered back.

D removed his thumb, drove in two fingers, watching Maddox's head as he did, enjoying as it jerked back.

"Fuck yeah," Maddox growled, fucking himself, fucking D's hand.

Diesel was so into the show, he jolted when Molly wrapped her fingers around his dick, coating it in lube, greasing him, preparing him.

She did the job and moved silently away.

The instant she was done, he couldn't wait any longer. Diesel removed his fingers and replaced them with the tip of his cock, so when Maddox reared back, he took D.

Heat.

Tight and slick and fucking amazing.

Maddox's head shot back again on a grunt and he came up on his hands.

"Down," D hissed.

Maddox went down and Diesel went at him. Pulling his hand from between Mad's legs, going around his side and latching onto that big dick to stroke again, without his arm as an obstruction, he thrust deep.

"Yeah, Christ, fuck, *yeah*," Maddox groaned, rearing back into the cock up his ass.

Diesel watched that fantastic body taking his in the moonlight, felt that huge, steel shaft in his hand, the clench and release as Maddox took D up his ass, and he loved that cock, that ass, that body.

But the truth of it was . . .

He loved that man.

"Up," he clipped. "All the way."

Maddox pushed up to sitting on D's dick and D pumped up into him, slow, steady, enjoying the glide, sliding a hand up Mad's ridged abs, tweaking a nipple, up, to his throat, closing his fingers around the muscles there, feeling his heart beat against D's palm, strong and fast.

Molly moved in and twisted both Maddox's nipples. In response, he clamped down on D's dick and the slow steady glide disappeared as Mad started riding wild.

God.

Fuck.

Yeah.

Goddamned beautiful.

Every inch of him, inside out.

Diesel slid his hand up, clamping under Maddox's bearded jaw, shoving his head back until it hit D's shoulder, growling, "Yeah, baby, ride that cock. Ride your man up your ass. *Ride me.*"

Diesel pulsed up as Maddox drove down, giving him more, getting more, watching over Mad's shoulder, down the wide, furred chest, the defined stomach as he jacked that gorgeous monster cock, Mad's thighs spread wide, Diesel's knees and thighs between them, Mad's balls slamming into Diesel's flesh.

Beauty.

Pure beauty.

Perfection.

Absolute.

"Christ, fuck, *Christ, fuck,*" Maddox grunted, his ass clenching, milking D's cock, practically hauling it up with him as they fucked, all of it scrambling D's brain at the same time centering it, fixing it, staking it right there.

In that moment.

Connected.

And then it happened.

Lost in what was happening, D twisted Maddox's head and there it was.

They looked into each other's eyes right before Diesel seized Maddox's mouth.

He shoved his tongue inside, tasting warmth and Mad, jacking up into his man, fisting his dick fast and hard, and swallowing down the snarling rumble as Maddox arched back into D and blew his cum straight up his own chest, shuddering full body even as he kept up the ride.

He sucked D's tongue hard right before D's hips slammed into Mad's ass and his world wiped clear of everything but that suction on his tongue and the release of his seed jetting deep inside his boy.

The orgasm swept him up in something he wasn't sure he'd ever felt and he bucked up into that tight like he'd do it for days, lips locked, fist clamped hard and still unconsciously rhythmically pumping Maddox's dick as he groaned and growled into Mad's mouth, shooting cum . . . and more, more, Christ . . . *more*.

He drifted back to himself finding he was suckling at Maddox's tongue in his mouth, Mad's hand was cupped around the back of his head holding D to him, his fingers wrapped around D's at his cock, slowing D's roll, and he was sitting on D's dick like he could do it for a year.

D began to move his head away and that hand cupping him became fingers clenched in his hair.

"Fuck no, baby," his gravel sheared at D's lips. Then he caught hold of Diesel's lower one with his teeth and bit hard enough D could taste blood. He let him go and repeated, "Fuck. No."

D looked into Maddox's eyes as close as they could get.

"Get my plug, Molly, darlin'. Holdin' D inside me tonight."

"Okay, honey," Molly whispered instantly.

D felt the bed move with Molly but he held Maddox's gaze, not only because Mad had a hold of him and he couldn't move it, but also because it hit him then what he'd done.

He'd just made love to Maddox.

Yeah, he'd fucked him on his knees with his ass on offer before he'd pulled him up to join the ride.

But that wasn't play or a savage fuck that practically forced a man to come.

He'd made love to Molly on her knees and with her riding his dick, her back to his front and the other way around.

And that's what he'd just done to Mad.

"Maddox—" he started, putting pressure on that hand in his hair and trying to pry his fingers from his boy's cock.

"No, D," Maddox said low. He shifted in and D tried to stay loose as Mad touched his lips to D's. Then he whispered, "Yeah," and ran his tongue along D's abused lower lip and D couldn't beat back the shiver that caused. Dripping approval now, Mad whispered again, "Yeah."

More aware of what was happening than D, Maddox pulsed up and Diesel lost him at the back.

Molly was there and she didn't waste time sliding Maddox's plug home.

She then circled front, pulling off her nightie before kissing Maddox's throat, doing it gliding her hands through Mad's cum on his chest. Then she moved to D, kissing his throat, transferring that cum to D's chest. Taking D's mouth, she pressed close, wriggling, getting Mad's cum on her. She shifted and took Maddox's mouth, snuggling into him, coating herself with more cum.

She was not being stealthy.

Her point with Mad's seed was crystal clear.

They were his. Both of them.

In all ways.

And it was not the first time D had Mad all over him, but this time, he felt it on his skin with a heat so hot, it seared like a brand, at the same time like an ointment, sinking into the muscle, the flesh, the blood, down to the bone.

She broke away, put her hand over Maddox's in D's hair, her other to Maddox's head and pressing them together.

Needing no encouragement, Maddox took D's mouth.

Not having the opportunity to get his head together, like his orgasm, when their mouths met, Diesel's world wiped clear and he pulled his hand from Maddox's cock. Lifting his other, he gripped his man on both sides of his neck and went at his mouth, taking, taking, Christ, *devouring*.

Maddox gave that back.

They changed positions, front to front, chests crushed together, their cocks brushing, D groaned against Mad's tongue, Maddox pressed closer and kissed him harder, his beard scraping D's skin. He felt Molly's hand light on the base of his spine and slide lovingly up, in the back of his head knowing she was doing that to Maddox too.

God.

Shit.

More than everything.

Yeah, fuck yeah.

Right there, in that bed, their three.

More than everything.

Maddox broke the kiss but immediately put his mouth to D's ear.

"Molly," he said.

Deep in the zone, he said nothing, just turned in unison with Mad.

Maddox pulled her into position, her back to their fronts. Like a practiced dance, D went in from the back, dipping into her panties, curling around, finger fucking her, Maddox at the front, working her clit, both of them claimed a nipple, both of them had their mouths working her neck.

She came within minutes, wet to the point of dripping when they began after watching her men go at each other, soaked and quivering by the time she cried out her climax.

Maddox didn't even allow her recovery. She was still panting when he took her down to her back, then forced Diesel down with her, on his side, covering her side.

Then Maddox came down, on her other side, practically burying her, tangling his legs in D's over Molly's, his arm over her, curved around D, yanking them closer so they were a mound of hot, sweaty, cum-covered bodies in the middle of the bed.

They could tangle, especially after a threesome.

But not like this.

Not even in the beginning.

Never like this.

D was a part of it and he still couldn't tell where he ended and Molly or Maddox began.

"Now, my babies, sleep," Maddox ordered.

"Okay, Mady," Molly instantly, her tone openly happy, agreed.

Diesel said nothing.

"'Night, Molly," Maddox said gently.

"'Night, honey," Molly replied.

Maddox's hand slid down to D's ass and gripped. "'Night, D."

"'Night," he grunted.

Maddox chuckled and squeezed D's ass.

Yup.

Maddox too.

Happy.

D shut his eyes.

Tight.

What the fuck had he done?

"Love you, Mady," Molly whispered then pulled out all the stops, "Love you, my DD."

She rarely called him DD, unless she was in a super loving mood. Not that he didn't like it so she avoided it, just, he guessed, that "D" was already a nickname.

"Love you, Mol," no hesitation before Maddox carried on, "Love you, Diesel."

D screwed his eyes shut even tighter.

He'd never said it.

To Molly yes.

Not to Mad.

"Same, both," D grunted.

Maddox clamped on his ass harder, jerking them even closer.

Shit.

Shit.

Right.

What . . .

The fuck . . .

Had he done?

Molly let out a happy sigh and Diesel breathed deep.
Tomorrow, he'd deal.
Tomorrow, he'd pull his shit together.
Tomorrow, he'd figure it out.

EIGHT

A Meeting of the Hearts

Maddox

EARLY THE NEXT MORNING, MADDOX grabbed the cup of joe he'd just poured, looked at Molly, who was showered, made up, but hadn't done her hair, and was leaning against the counter, cradling her own cup of coffee, wearing her short robe.

He grinned.

She took her coffee cup from where she was holding it up to her mouth and grinned back, her eyes dancing, happy, elated . . . *thrilled.*

He knew that feeling.

Last night hadn't been good.

Last night had changed everything.

They had more than hope.

D was getting there.

D was coming to him, to *them.*

He was giving Mad—*them*—all of him.

All of him.

Mad wasn't lost in that goodness. He knew D had freaked afterward when neither Molly nor Maddox had let it slide, like they usually did when Diesel got in the zone to make love to Maddox. Not calling attention to it. Just having it. This for fear if Diesel realized what he was doing, he'd stop doing it.

Nope, last night, they'd made it clear to Diesel what he'd done.

And how much it meant to them.

So yeah, he'd freaked.

But he hadn't pulled away.

He had not pulled away.

And now Maddox had to waste no time making certain he stayed the course.

He walked the coffee back to the bedroom and went directly to the bathroom.

Like usual, on autopilot, D had gotten up, slopped himself through a shower and was now bent over the sink, wet hair slicked back with fingers, not a comb, wearing a pair of black boxer briefs, his toothbrush in his mouth.

Regardless of the shower, his blue eyes were dazed and vacant.

He had not yet been caffeinated.

This was his habit. Done by rote. If it wasn't the weekend, he got the getting ready shit done so he could focus entirely, dressed and good to go, on caffeine before he got behind the wheel of a car.

His gaze lifted groggily to Maddox as Maddox moved in with the mug.

Mad was also showered, his hair drying. He'd put on his briefs and jeans, but hadn't yet pulled on one of the branded polos he wore to work every day.

Which was probably why D's eyes dropped to his chest.

They went instantly to the mug as Maddox slid it on the counter beside the basin and it lay testimony to the depth of D's morning haze that he didn't looked shocked, seeing as Maddox had never brought him a mug of coffee after his shower their entire relationship.

He wasn't going to make a habit of it.

But that morning, he was on a mission.

He leaned the side of his hip against the counter, crossed his arms on his chest and watched as D spit, rinsed, splashed some water on his face then ran the long fingers of his big hands through his hair, slicking it back again.

When he wiped his face with a towel and started to straighten away, his attention on the mug of coffee, Maddox made his move.

He shifted in, murmuring, "Mornin', bud," his hand to D's tight abs, his intention through the trajectory of his mouth clear.

D reared back.

And Mad was ready.

He shot an arm out.

He knew he was taking advantage, D up, awake, showered, but still a total zombie.

After last night, he didn't give a fuck.

Last night, they'd jumped great bounds in their relationship, at Diesel's instigation.

D could make love to Maddox.

But in doing it, he never kissed him.

Playing the game for Diesel, Maddox could get permission from Molly to kiss D but D never asked for the same, or took it.

Last night, whatever was fucking with Diesel's head had led him there, to making love to Maddox, to climaxing with him while their mouths were connected.

And that was the right path to be on.

So if Maddox had shit to do with it, and he did, they were not straying off that path.

Not again.

This was going to become habit.

He was going to get all of Diesel, give Molly all of Diesel.

And if D didn't give it, Maddox was going to take it.

So if Maddox wanted a good morning kiss from his boy, he was going to take that too.

Catching Diesel hard at the back of his neck, he yanked his man to him and crushed his mouth down on Mad's.

He thrust his tongue inside.

Sleep, toothpaste and Diesel.

He had tasted a lot of goodness in his life, but that right there ranked with the ones at the top.

He shifted closer to him.

Diesel's tongue started to stroke his and Maddox felt warmth build in his stomach right before D went tight, putting pressure on to pull away.

Maddox put pressure on to hold him there.

So D jerked away, breaking the connection of their lips, if not the hold Maddox had on his neck.

Maddox yanked him back, face to face, eye to eye.

D froze, turning his head slightly so Mad couldn't get to his mouth, muttering, "Brother."

Maddox lifted his other hand and slid it up to his lat.

Before he could strengthen the hold, both D's hands came to Maddox's chest and he shoved, forcing Maddox back two steps.

They stood there, D breathing hard, his eyes now alert, wary, his body tense.

Maddox gave him a beat.

But just a beat.

Because he'd fucked around with this for four years.

And now there would be no . . .

Going . . .

Back.

He went at him, frontal attack, pressing Diesel against the basin, fisting a hand in his hair, pulling his mouth down to Mad's.

He was able to trace the tip of his tongue along the crease of D's lips before Diesel lurched back, arcing over the bathroom counter to get away.

Maddox was ready for him and held onto his hair at the same time he clamped an arm around his back, locking them together, chest to chest.

Diesel's eyes flared and then Maddox was pushed backward and slammed against the wall.

Right.

They were going to do this?

He'd do this.

"Don't got a good morning kiss for your man?" Maddox taunted.

"Fuck you," Diesel hissed.

"Fight it, yeah, brother, fight it," Maddox invited.

"Fuck you," Diesel bit, straining at Maddox's hold at the same time pushing him into the wall.

"You want me to win," Maddox pointed out. "You *always* want me to win."

"Fuck . . . *you,*" Diesel spat.

Maddox moved in, biting D's lower lip like he did the night before, and in Diesel's moment of stillness at the pain, Mad took advantage, thrusting his tongue inside, holding tight to that hair, crushing D's lips down on his in a bruising hold.

D jerked them both away from the wall and then back into it so forcefully it felt like the wall shook, doing this to loosen Maddox's grip on him.

It didn't work.

But still, Maddox let go the hold on Diesel's back, only to immediately go in at the front, past the elastic, grabbing hold of D's dick, which was hard as granite.

Yeah.

He wanted Maddox to win.

He coaxed Diesel's tongue in position and sucked it into his mouth.

And then . . .

The fight just left him.

Gone.

Diesel groaned, pulsing into Mad's fist and stroking into Mad's mouth.

Yeah.

Maddox pushed off the wall, taking Diesel across the room, and they hit the counter of the basin.

Fucking Mad's mouth with his tongue, D pressed into him, and Christ, the man could kiss. Always could. Maddox felt that tongue *everywhere*.

Still going at his mouth, Diesel forced his hands to Maddox's chest, pressing mightily as Mad strained to stay close, and the minute he got a wedge of space, Diesel broke the kiss.

Maddox tensed to go back at him.

But Diesel shifted his big body around, his arm brushing Maddox's chest in the limited space, doing this hooking his thumbs into his underpants.

He shoved them over his ass.

This wasn't where Maddox intended to go, the point he was trying to make.

But with his point mostly made, and Diesel's ass bared, he thought this was excellent turn of events.

Maddox went for the drawer in the vanity that held the lube.

He grabbed it, opened the tube, dropped the cap so it bounced off the vanity onto the tiled floor and he took it to D's crease, squeezing it liberally along the line. He tossed the tube aside, and using two fingers, spread it down and *in.*

A noise floated up Diesel's chest, he gripped his cock and started jacking himself.

Maddox made short work of lubing his man, opening his own pants, freeing his hard cock, positioning, and eyes moving to the mirror, locking on D's, he drove inside.

Diesel's neck muscles stood out, his body bent at the waist to take Maddox's thrust, straining into it, his free hand coming out to brace against the counter, his triceps bunching, his hand on his cock starting to work double time.

Maddox withdrew then thrust in again and watched D's head drop, the acceptance of the penetration, the submission, so fucking spectacular, Maddox went at him. Slow enough D could feel every inch take him through every stroke, hard enough it'd build quick because, regardless of how awesome it was, they didn't have a lot of time for this morning fuck, and last, as deep as he could go.

"Yeah, fuck me, Maddox, *yeah,*" Diesel groaned, spreading his long legs farther, tipping his carved ass to get more.

Christ.

"Look at me," Maddox gritted.

D's head stayed bowed.

Oh no, he was not making this about submission. He was not making that kiss about Maddox's Domination.

Fuck no.

"Look at your man," Maddox ordered.

Holding him tight at the hinge of his hip with one hand, Mad slid his other up the warm sheet of skin at D's back, wrapping his fingers around the side of Diesel's neck.

Diesel lifted his head and their eyes met in the mirror.

He drove in and Diesel clenched his teeth.

"I own this ass?" he demanded.

"Yeah," Diesel bit out.

"I own that cock your jacking?" Maddox went on, pulling out and ramming back in.

"Yeah," Diesel grunted.

"I do. And I own that mouth, D. I always have. But this isn't about that. It's about the fact you *gave* it to me last night and you aren't taking it back, brother." He slid out and thrust in again. "You aren't taking it back." Another slide and thrust. "And this is about *that*."

D stared at him through the mirror.

"Look at us," Maddox ordered, unrelentingly fucking his ass. "Look at *you*. Look how beautiful you are, takin' my cock. Look how hard you are, full of me."

Diesel's eyes swiftly wandered then came up and locked on Maddox's.

The safe place.

He probably liked what he saw.

And it terrified him.

They'd get to that last part too.

Just . . .

Later.

Maddox bent over him, forcing him to bend double, driving deep, faster, faster, shifting his hand to D's throat, his chest to D's back, breathing in his ear.

High color was spreading along D's cheekbones, his teeth sinking hard into his bottom lip as his strokes at his cock hit overdrive.

But Maddox could feel the cheeks of his ass bunching against Mad's drives in a contradictory effort to control their roll, either to slow Maddox down so it'd drive him wild, make him lose it and go at him rough or speed him up so he'd fuck D ruthless.

Two versions of the same thing.

Bottom line, he was holding back in order to push Mad where he needed him to be.

Maddox powered in faster, but not harder. He wanted Diesel to feel that cock up his ass, feel how full Maddox made him, feel every inch of the monster he loved so goddamned much, not the mindless pleasure mixed with pain of a savage fuck that drove him to orgasm.

And he wanted him to let go as he was getting that.

Just that.

He stayed bent over his boy, his gaze holding D's captive in the mirror, feeling his chest, his nipples brush D's hot skin, hearing the slap of flesh connecting, the sounds of D pumping his dick, the harsh quality of both their breathing, the muted sounds D kept swallowing every time Maddox filled him full.

Christ, if D didn't get with the fucking program, Maddox was gonna blow before he took his man there.

He rubbed his chin along D's shoulder, pulling out to the head, waiting, watching as Diesel's lips parted, feeling his legs tremble in wait, in preparation, in need.

A battle of wills that Maddox was going to lose, his balls having drawn up tight, he needed back inside so bad, his vision was getting blurry.

Thank fuck he was wrong.

A low groan rumbled in D's chest, cut off before he whispered, "Take my ass, baby. I need you. Please keep fuckin' me."

At the plea, it was a miracle Mad didn't come all over him, but instead, slowly, Maddox slid back inside, watching Diesel's eyes drift shut, Mad's own gaze dropping to see pre-cum beading the head of D's beautiful dick.

Gathering all the control he had left, he stroked in and out, slow, rhythmic, *deep*.

And then it happened.

Diesel loosened around him, shit, Jesus, relaxing into it, taking his fucking like it was meant to be.

A meeting of the bodies.

A meeting of the minds.

A meeting of the hearts.

"Come, D," he urged.

Those eyes opened and they were hot, turned on.

And embattled.

Maddox could tell he wanted to fight it. He could tell Diesel wanted to keep holding back. Do something, anything, to earn a brutal fucking. Turn this into what he needed to feel right in his head. Make it about being his warped version of a man, getting his shit jacked, his orgasm that came from loving a man's cock moving inside forced through near violence.

But instead, as Maddox affectionately squeezed his throat and glided in fully, planting his meat deep, Diesel pressed up into Maddox's chest, his chin tipped back and his eyes closed. Grunting, in pulses that corresponded to clenches around Maddox's again slowly stroking cock, his hips jerked through his climax and he blew his seed all over the basin.

And then more.

D let out a deep groan.

And more cum shot out of his cock.

Yeah. Fuck yes.

He loved that monster moving inside him.

And the man attached.

"That's it, D," Maddox whispered, only having brief moments to enjoy the view before his body forced him to let go.

He drew out and punched inside his man once. Opening his mouth, he sunk his teeth hard into the flesh of Diesel's shoulder, coming up his ass.

When he came down, he licked the marks, ran his tongue along D's neck then pulled out roughly, hearing D grunt at the loss.

He twisted his man around, went in, and with both hands fisted in his hair, pulled him down and took his mouth.

D submitted to the kiss at first, then with a low noise, he curled the fingers of one hand around the back of Mad's neck, the other hand bit into Mad's waist, and lost himself in it.

Fuck yeah.

That's where this was at.

Maddox pushed closer to his boy.

Breaking the kiss because, unfortunately, neither one of them could skip work in order to make out all day, he took his fists out of D's hair but only to cup him on either side of his head and give him a little shake, staring into his eyes.

"Yeah?" he asked quietly.

D's fingers at his neck gave him an almost hesitant squeeze.

He'd take that, even hesitant.

They were still on the right path. D was fighting it, but he wasn't veering away.

So yeah.

He'd definitely take that.

"Yeah," Diesel replied.

"As much as I can watch my two boys fucking and making out for hours, I kinda have to do my hair."

Maddox shifted away. Not much, he was still in D's space, but both their hands fell from each other as they turned to see Molly propped up in the doorway.

The bottom of her foot was planted casually on the side of her other ankle, arms wrapped around her belly like she was holding happiness close and there was a huge smile on her face like she was completely unable not to let that happiness show.

She'd been there awhile.

Diesel slid away from him, pulling up his shorts. He went to the linen cupboard, grabbed a washcloth, returned to the sink and wetted it while Maddox did up his jeans and Molly moved in to gather the multitude of equipment it took to blow out her hair.

Shoving the cloth down the back of his shorts, D cleaned his ass cursorily, a wipe. He mopped up the cum on the basin before he walked through one of the two doors to the walk-in (D and Mad had designed it so Molly could get there from bathroom and bedroom, which made it convenient since her boys could do the same), not looking at either of them, probably to take the cloth to the hamper in the closet and get dressed.

But also to escape and crawl right back into his head.

That was all right. Maddox was learning he could work with that.

He'd just pull him back out.

Both Molly and Mad watched him go, and when he was in the closet, Molly and Mad looked at each other.

"So, apparently," she said in a very quiet whisper, "fucking him into the right place in his head works."

Maddox smiled at her.

She shook her head, smiling back, but saying, "Men," like they baffled her and exasperated her at the same time, but she loved every second of it.

He went in at her back, bent and kissed her neck and then followed D into the closet.

Diesel had his jeans on and was yanking on a tee.

"It'd be good to get a rundown of the fun you had last night," he noted, reaching for one of the dozens of work polos he had that Molly cleaned in a way that was more like wringing miracles because they could get sweaty and dirty and every last one still looked brand new (and when it didn't, she threw it out and contacted George herself to get him another one).

"Tonight," D grunted. "Now I need coffee then I gotta get to work."

Maddox grinned again.

Fuck, he hadn't smiled this much since they first met Molly.

It felt good.

Really good.

"Right." Maddox pulled on his polo.

With a ball of socks in his hand, D nabbed his boots and made a move to leave, not breaking stride even as he looked right at Maddox and declared, "You're an asshole, you know that?"

Yeah, buddy, I agree. That was a fucking phenomenal session and I love you too.

Maddox smiled big at him and answered, "Yup."

"Fucker," D grumbled and walked out.

The stop and start of the hair dryer just plain stopped and Molly appeared at the door to the walk-in, still fucking smiling.

"I so, so, so, so, *sooooooo* love you guys," she announced.

Maddox looked at their beautiful girl.

And burst out laughing.

NINE

Until My Dying Breath

Molly

MOLLY WAS ON THE WAY home from work, groceries for a special meal in the back, when the radio muted and her car started ringing.

She looked to the dash, saw who it was and happily took the call.

"Hey, honey!" she cried.

"Well, hello there, sister," Rebel greeted, sounding funny.

Oh no.

Nothing could be wrong.

Not that day.

Especially not *that day*.

That day being the day after what happened last night.

And that morning.

"Is . . . uh, everything all right?" Molly asked.

"Yeah, just wondering if you guys have plans next weekend," Rebel answered.

Oh boy.

"Um, no. Not that I know of," Molly told D's sister, who was the kind of woman who was also Molly's sister, and Maddox's sister.

Bottom line, who Diesel loved, and who loved Diesel, Rebel loved too.

In fact, although Molly felt slightly ashamed to admit it (but it was true), Rebel felt more like a true sister than Holly did.

Molly loved Holly.

She was just a lot of . . . *work*.

And Rebel was totally . . . *not*.

"Cool," Rebel replied. "I got a room at the Valley Ho. I'm gonna take off Friday afternoon, Monday and Tuesday morning and head down to you guys for a long weekend. Is that all right?"

That was awesome. Amazing. Molly was delighted. Mady would be thrilled. D would be ecstatic.

Except, why did she sound funny?

And why wasn't she asking Diesel about this?

"That's totally all right," Molly said. "I'll ask the boys to make sure. But . . . I mean, I don't want to put my foot in something, but why aren't you asking Diesel this?"

Rebel, being Rebel, all out there, honest, communicative, never kept you guessing, didn't keep Molly guessing.

"I called him last night. He didn't share a lot but he seemed to be in a bad place."

Mm-hmm.

That had been right.

And then D had done what D had done with Maddox last night.

Of course, Molly felt him get tense after, when she and Mad made a thing about it.

But then he'd let Mady make love to him in the bathroom that morning, kissing after and everything.

Obviously, she couldn't share any of this with Rebel.

"I think he's been working through some things," Molly told her.

"Yeah. And that's probably not gonna get a lot better considering Mom's gonna be pushing for a family Thanksgiving with the usual tight-ass, narrow-minded view of what *family* means."

Molly felt her lips thin.

She had hate in her heart for nobody. Not a soul. People had reasons for doing just about anything. She might not like them much because of how they behaved, but hate?

No one should hate.

That said, she hated Diesel's parents.

Especially his mother.

The dad was an asshole. A lost cause. He couldn't come up with an original thought if he was offered ten million dollars to have one. He was weak of will. Weak of mind. Weak of character.

The mom, she was a different story and she had different weaknesses that were less . . .

Not understandable. Understandable wasn't the word. Molly didn't understand Mr. Stapleton.

It was just, for a woman, a woman who had a good mother, who had a good mother-in-law in Erin (that soon to be made official, she hoped), a woman who wanted to be a good mother, Mrs. Stapleton's weaknesses were just—unacceptable.

"Did you tell D about this Thanksgiving thing?" she asked Rebel.

"Yeah. Like me, he wasn't a big fan," Rebel answered.

Molly had to think on this.

Because anything that had anything to do with his parents, or that loser brother of his, always shoved Diesel right into his head.

But last night . . .

"Do you know Tommy Barnes?" she blurted.

"Tommy?" Rebel asked.

Dang.

She felt funny talking about this with Rebel because Rebel might be all about the sister stuff with Molly and Maddox, but she was D's and she had a strict code when it came to what she thought was right, and wrong, and talking behind D's back would not be right.

Though she was the one who called about this visit, going around D.

"Yeah, Tommy. Uh . . ."

Did she know about Tommy, as in *Diesel and Tommy*?

"He told me, Mol, later," Rebel shared. "After he moved to Phoenix, after he came out to me, he told me Tommy was his first guy. But yeah. They were best friends through high school. He was around a lot. I knew him. Great guy. Totally a great guy. If D hadn't found you guys, it would have sucked it didn't work out for those two, he was that great of a guy. Then again, Tommy's gay, not bi, so it probably never could have worked. But I'm still glad he was D's first. Tommy was solid. Totally down with who he was, as he should be."

There was a long, heavy, scary pause where Molly had to concentrate on driving, it was freaking her so much, before Rebel went on.

"Though, would give anything to erase what Tommy went through when he was outed so Diesel wouldn't have had to watch him go through it."

"Wh-wh . . ." Molly cleared her throat. "What did Tommy go through when he was outed?"

"Just the entire town figuratively tar and feathering him," Rebel told her. "It was ugly. Extreme. Despicable. Dad and Gunner . . ."

She let that trail but Molly could guess exactly what Mr. Stapleton and Gunner were like after Diesel's friend was outed.

"D soaked it in," Rebel said quietly.

Dang.

"That's the difference between people like Tommy, people like you and Maddox, and people like D," Rebel kept going. "Tommy looked at that as his ticket to freedom. Like the masks were torn off everyone around him so he knew who was worth his time, worth his emotion, and who wasn't. It just sucked for him that practically everyone around him wasn't. Diesel took it in and it became a kind of prison. Like the masks were off everyone else, but he had to keep his attached, solder it to his skin, so they'd never know the real him. And to make that happen in a way they'd never find out, he had to escape."

"He's sensitive, our Diesel is," Molly whispered into her car. "You'd never know it about him, the way he acts most of the time, but he cares about what people he loves think about him. People he respects."

"Yeah," Rebel agreed. "He's always been like that. He used to follow Gunner around like a puppy. Always wanting to be a part of his big brother's gang. It was kinda okay because, even if Gunner was an asshole, he had some friends who were cool. But Diesel was blind to Gunner being a dick. He wanted him to be that big brother who was worth his while, so I think, in his head, he made him that way. But Gunner is like he is because Dad's like he is. The whole 'what makes a man a man' bullshit, that making of a man being how big a dick he can be or how far he can swing his dick. It's ridiculous. And it's weird because they're all in denial at all the awesomeness that makes Diesel, and he's in that same denial at all the shit that makes them."

That sure was right.

"He . . . he told Mad about Tommy the other day. He'd never mentioned him to either of us before," Molly felt it safe to share with her.

"Maybe he's working through some things," Rebel replied distractedly.

He was definitely doing that.

"It'll be good having you here, Rebel," Molly said. "It's been too long. And I know Diesel and Maddox will be excited."

And just maybe, with the way Rebel was, how she loved D for D, that might help solidify where it seemed Diesel was going so he'd feel safer with all of them to be who he was, knowing they loved him for all that.

"Cool," Rebel responded, and at least with that sounding like she was smiling.

"But we do have a guestroom, you know," Molly reminded her. "You don't have to stay at the Valley Ho."

"Girl, you guys are fuck bunnies. When we met in Flag to ski that weekend and shared that big condo, I was all the way down the hall and I heard you going at each other. I love you guys. I love my brother. I love what you have together. But that was over a year ago and I still wonder if I should have my ears professionally cleaned."

Molly giggled, because it was funny, but she was still a little horrified.

"Oh my God, were we that loud?" she asked.

"Not you, or D, but Maddox's voice carries."

Molly giggled again because that was totally true.

"I'd say we'd refrain while you're here, but Maddox and D would probably not like that much."

"I'm there for goodness, family time and fun, not to cramp your style, or theirs. And the Valley Ho rocks."

This was true.

"Great. Make the plans," Molly said. "I'll tell the boys. And we'll do it up big. Be sure to tell us when you get in. You know Diesel would lose his mind if he wasn't at the terminal to greet you the minute you walked out."

"I'll keep you in the know, text him so he knows I'm coming and we'll do it up good."

"Awesome."

"Now I'll let you go. See you later, Mol. And love you, girl."

"Love you back and can't wait. 'Bye, Rebel."

"Later."

Molly ended the call and drove home, half excited, half weirded out.

It was without question Diesel was working through things, and it seemed he was heading in the right direction.

But that call from his mother about Thanksgiving could knock him back.

And Molly didn't know what to do.

She'd talked to her mom about it, more than once.

Molly wasn't comfortable talking trash about Diesel's family. Well, she was (because they deserved it), just not to Diesel. She felt with D she should tread cautiously. You didn't say bad things about the people someone you loved loves.

Her mother had different ideas.

"You'll learn, my sweet girl, that family priorities change as families change. You're making your own family. And that will be your only focus." At that, Helen Singer had shaken her head and amended, "No. That *should* be your only focus. What's right for the man in your life is the only thing that's right. And that's just talking surface. What's deeper is that they aren't his real family if they can't take him as God made him. So you should feel free to speak your mind if you have his well-being at heart. And I love that boy, he's a good man, but he needs to learn that love, acceptance and loyalty should be rewarded with his love, acceptance and loyalty, anything less should not."

Her mom was right.

Still, Molly couldn't bring herself to go there.

And that was her weakness.

One she needed to fight.

For Diesel.

And not so they could really have him, even though she wanted nothing more than for Maddox to have him like Molly had him, fully and truly.

What she wanted even more than that was for Diesel to feel free to be who he was with the two people in this world he was safest being just that.

She made it home on heavy thoughts, which was a bummer since she'd started home on happy ones, hit the garage door opener and coasted in (not all the way because the back hatch couldn't go up so she could get the groceries out, but as in as she could get).

She popped the hatch, went back, grabbed the handles of some bags and moved inside.

Molly saw Diesel was flat out on the couch as she walked in the back door.

He stopped being flat out on the back couch the instant he saw she had bags in her hands.

He got up, coming her way and stopping at the mouth to the great room.

"Hey," he greeted, dipping in to brush his lips against hers. He pulled back, asking, "There more?"

"Just a couple," she answered.

"Keys," he demanded, knowing her car would need to be pulled in and both of them knowing she would not be the one going out to do that.

She adjusted the bags so she could hand him the keys she still held.

He took them and moved off down the hall.

She went to the kitchen and stopped dead.

On the kitchen table, right in the center, there was a vase full of orange and red sunflowers.

Seeing them, she slowly made a turn.

Maddox had texted, saying he was hitting the gym after work.

Molly had texted, saying she was hitting the grocery store after work.

Diesel had texted that he received their texts, but he had not shared what he was doing after work.

And she was seeing that it wasn't just buying his Molly some sunflowers.

If Friday came around and Mady or Molly were doing something, like the gym, drinks with friends, grocery store runs, this was what they came home to.

Diesel had run the vacuum over the rug in the living room area.

And she could not only see it with the bright, blinking clean of the granite, she could smell that he'd wiped all kitchen counters down with that scented countertop spray she liked.

He'd also run the Swifter over the wood floors so they were gleaming.

She couldn't tell, but he probably even dusted.

Depending on time, all of this might, or might not, mean he cleaned the bathrooms. He was always careful to be stretched out on the sofa when she got home because he didn't like her making a thing about it that he cleaned so he definitely didn't let her catch him cleaning.

What he did like, if they were both gone—and sometimes he got Maddox in on the act when it was just her that was gone—was that he could clean the house so none of them had to worry about doing it over the weekend.

That was D.

That was one thing his parents (probably his mother, she had to admit) gave to him.

He was thoughtful.

He did little things that meant a lot.

Like, when she'd had that cold, he went out and bought out the entire cold and flu shelves, cough drops, sore throat lozenges, vapor rub, nighttime medicine, tissues with lotion. He did it quiet and got uncomfortable when she tried to make a thing about it.

He was just taking care of his woman, and to Diesel Stapleton, that was the nature of things and no big thing needed to be made about it.

The same with early on, after Molly had met them, when Maddox had been T-boned at an intersection. He hadn't been hurt, but his body had taken a violent jolt. She wasn't living with them yet, but she came over and Diesel made Maddox camp out, even ran him a bath with Epsom salts, brought him ibuprofen, made him drink tons of water.

Because he was taking care of his man.

Molly sometimes marveled at how it worked with the three of them. How they fit in with each other. How it was mostly Mady that did the handyman things around the house when stuff broke or wasn't working right, because he liked doing that. How it was D who did the yard, because he liked doing it, but also Mad did yards for a living so it was a break from that for him. And how Molly did the laundry and kept the cupboards stocked, because that was her thing, looking after her boys.

And in all that, Diesel was the caregiver.

Diesel went out and bought her tampons when she ran out. Diesel shook out the cocktail of pills when Maddox got one of his headaches.

And Diesel bought her sunflowers just with her mentioning she liked them.

She shook herself out of her All the Reasons to Love Diesel Stapleton stupor and moved to the island, dumping the bags. She was putting stuff away when she heard her keys hit the bowl on the table by the door and Diesel came in with the last of the groceries.

The instant she caught his eyes, she smiled big at him.

"The sunflowers are gorgeous, honey."

"Right, good," he muttered, using putting the bags on the counter as an excuse to look away.

Yeah.

So Diesel.

You did not call attention to his kindness and that wasn't about him thinking kindness was weak. It was about him thinking it was less of a kindness if he got something out of it. Even gratitude.

As he started to pull things out of the bags, Molly let that go and announced, "I'm making a special dinner tonight."

D turned her way and she sucked in breath at the look on his face.

"Sorry, baby, but you'll probably be making whatever tomorrow night, 'cause you're gonna leave the putting away to me, go back and get naked, waiting for me on your stomach in the bed."

She knew that particular look in his eye.

She loved that particular look in his eye.

But in that moment, she worried about that particular look in his eye.

They had their roles in the house. They had their roles in bed. All of them were a natural fit, what they did, who they were, what they liked.

In bed, Diesel and Maddox switched it up.

She never did.

She was their woman.

And she was their sub.

It was not rare Diesel got in the mood to dominate her.

It was just, after last night and this morning, it was the first time she wondered at *why* he was in the mood.

Did he need to center himself sexually through her?

In making love with his man (twice), to equal that out, did he have to dominate his woman?

"Okay, baby," she said softly.

That wasn't a weakness, not asking him, not pushing him to explain.

That was what Molly gave.

And she gave it to the both of them.

That being . . .

Whatever they needed.

MOLLY WAS FLAT ON HER belly, legs straight, thighs pressed tight together, head turned, cheek to the bed.

And her arms were tied at the wrists behind her back with a wide, strong, pink satin ribbon.

All the toys and bindings her men used on her were feminine because they let her pick them, but also because they liked her dressed up, trussed up or worked over with the things they felt defined her, not what defined them as her Doms.

They didn't want their Molly in leather.

They wanted her in lace (and the like).

So pink satin it was.

She was biting her lip but the moans still came considering D was straddling her, his thighs splayed wide, a good amount of his power braced into his hands at her ass, his cock pounding hard inside her.

He wasn't going to let her come, not like this, she knew it. But the tight fit of her legs trapping her clit and his thick cock driving inside was torture.

Molly loved it.

It was hot.

Beautiful pain.

Awesome.

"Fuck me harder, big daddy," she breathed.

"Hmm?" D hummed.

"*Please*," she begged.

The pads of his fingers dug into her flesh as he stroked deeper, but not harder.

That worked for Molly.

If he went harder, she'd come and that would be good, but it could also be bad.

Though bad wasn't ever *bad*, as such.

Not with her boys.

But now, she focused on her role as a sub (and as his woman). Giving him what he needed, clenching the walls of her pussy around his cock, keeping her legs tight together, holding back her excitement so he could ramp it up further, and get off doing it.

Not her noises. She didn't hold back her noises, knowing he liked them, knowing he enjoyed hearing what he did to her.

She was trying not to let it penetrate how good his cock felt driving inside, his weight pressed into her ass, her arms bound at her back, her vulnerability, the fact she was his however he needed to use her and how much *she* got off on *that*.

And Molly was so into all of this, the thump took her by surprise.

She whipped her head around and saw Maddox standing by the side of the bed.

If D went to the gym, he showered before he came home and left his gym bag in the laundry room, as Molly wished it.

If Mad went to the gym, he came home immediately, sweaty and in workout clothes, usually because he was then ready for another workout and he didn't want the delay.

And right then, he left them in no question that he was ready for his second workout.

Molly whimpered when he pulled his loose muscle shirt off, exposing his chest, and yanked the elastic waistband of his long, loose workout shorts down to his thighs, exposing his huge, beautiful cock.

A huge, beautiful cock which was fully erect.

Molly's mouth started watering.

Maddox started stroking his cock, his dark eyes heated and roaming all over his man and woman and what they were doing in the bed.

"Don't let her come," Mad's voice growled out.

A voice that Molly thought always sounded ferocious, which she also thought was cute because there was nothing ferocious about Maddox Vega, and she shivered full body at hearing it.

Okay, there was nothing ferocious about him.

Unless he was in the mood to seriously fuck.

And she had the feeling he was in that mood.

Yay.

"I'm not gonna," Diesel replied as Maddox shoved his shorts all the way down, still stroking his cock.

He stepped out of them, moved like he was flipping off his shoes, and then he let his shaft go to crawl into bed.

Molly watched, still getting fucked by Diesel, still loving being fucked by Diesel, and now the full-body shivers were coming strong and not stopping as she took in that big, powerful, furred body coming their way, the look on Mady's face that made him appear villainous even though he was anything but, his big cock swaying like a huge tease as he moved.

God, she hoped he made her suck it.

And she had to bite her lip harder because just the thought of taking Maddox's cock in her mouth could drive her over the brink.

Mad came up, straddling Molly's head and she cranked her eyeballs as far sideways as she could when she heard Diesel make a noise, felt his hands leave her ass and land hard in the bed at her sides.

And then, out of the corner of her eye, she saw Maddox feed his cock into Diesel's mouth and start pumping inside in tandem with D's cock moving in her pussy.

How hot was *that*?

Almost better than getting to suck him, getting to watch him make D suck him.

Oh God, she was going to come.

"Babies," she whispered desperately.

"Don't you fuckin' come, Molly," Maddox ordered, shifting in a way she knew (because he'd done it to her, a lot), he was rubbing the head of his cock against the top of D's mouth.

She fisted her hands, digging her nails in, doing her best to ignore her quivering clit, her spasming pussy as she took her fucking, watched Maddox take Diesel's face and saw through D's expression how much he loved sucking Mady's cock.

Boy, she loved . . .

Them.

The three of them.

She so *fucking* loved *them*.

Right when Molly knew she could take no more, thankfully Maddox pulled out of Diesel's mouth, murmured, "You're out, I'm in," and Diesel slid out of her pussy

They switched, but as Maddox drove his huge dick inside her and Molly cried out in pleasure at the delicious stretch of taking it, Diesel lifted up her head and shoulders, positioning under her with his legs open, knees cocked.

"Balls, baby," he murmured gently when he had her cheek against his inner thigh.

She sucked his balls in her mouth.

"Yeah," he groaned, stroking her hair and she watched as he wrapped his other fist around his dick and lazily pumped. "So pretty, takin' Maddox like that," he cooed, and her eyes drifted from his work at his cock up to his face to see his gaze was glued to her taking Maddox.

He liked what he saw.

She liked what she saw.

Molly trembled.

"Fuck this girl, our girl, she's goddamned, fuckin' *everything*," Maddox murmured, pulled out to the head then thrust hard, like a stab, and she moaned as he grunted, "So," he repeated the move, "*hot*."

And with that, Mad planted his hands in her ass like D had done and used her cunt hard, like it was his to do just that whenever he wanted.

Because it was.

Oh yes, she loved *them*.

She sucked desperately at D's balls, her eyes closing, fighting her orgasm at every beautiful stroke.

"Brother, you need to finish up or our baby is gonna blow and she might take my balls with her when she does," D warned.

Maddox's rhythm immediately increased in strength and velocity until he groaned, "You want my cum, Molly baby?"

His fingers gently curling in her hair, Diesel pulled her mouth free of his balls so she could answer, "Yes, Mady. Please give me your cum, honey."

"You got it," he grunted and then blew as she shuddered under him, taking his seed, panting through it, tightening around him to milk him and give him more, hearing his noises change as he felt it and showed her he liked it.

He buried himself to the root, stretching her, filling her, and stilled his thrusts, but massaged her ass affectionately to share she'd performed well.

"My cock was made for this cunt," Maddox murmured tenderly, pulsing gently inside.

"Yes," she whispered.

"Time to get what you earned, Molly," Maddox told her.

"*Yes,*" she breathed.

"Back, bud, she's on your face, reverse."

Maddox pulled out.

D moved.

They moved Molly.

And then, hands still tied behind her back, she was sitting on Diesel's face aimed toward his lower half. One of his hands was at her waist, one arm slanted strong across her belly and chest, fingers curled around her breast. Both were positioned to hold her steady as he drew her down and commenced eating her and Maddox's cum out of her.

"D," she whimpered, rolling on his mouth.

He went at her, her Diesel loved eating her pussy, when it was just her, after he'd come inside, after Maddox had come inside, after they'd both done it, it didn't matter.

And he was oh so good at it.

She rode his mouth as she watched Maddox arranging Diesel down below. Knees up and bent. Legs spread wide.

"Hold that position," he ordered, then with no further hesitation, bent in and swallowed D whole.

D groaned up her pussy.

She could take no more.

Without asking permission, Molly came.

Popping D out, Maddox tipped his chin back, lifting just his eyes to her face, encouraging, "That's it, baby."

Then he went back to blowing Diesel.

And she watched.

Apparently she'd earned a really, *really* good reward.

Diesel ate and grunted and ate and tongue fucked and ate and growled and ate and pulsed into Maddox's mouth and Molly came, and came and came and *came*. Crying out at first then moaning, whimpering and finally riding D's face with her head practically lolling on her shoulders, held up only by Diesel's arm, actually thankful when the noises Diesel was making made Maddox slip a finger up his ass, cup his balls with his other hand, and squeeze and finger fuck him while Diesel shot down Maddox's throat.

Maddox stroked him and massaged him as he licked his cock all over while D came down.

He kept doing it after Diesel came down, and with a few tugs, she felt Diesel untie the satin ribbon at her wrists, freeing her.

Then he slowly let Molly go at her front.

She listed toward Maddox and he caught her, not wasting time connecting, taking her mouth and kissing her deeply.

She tasted Maddox and D, and since that was her whole world right there on her tongue, she smiled languidly through the kiss.

When Maddox ended it, his eyes were warm, his lips tipped up. He brushed his mouth on her forehead as she floated down to nuzzle and kiss Diesel's cock.

Through this, D lapped gently at her pussy and Maddox let this go on for a few more moments before he pulled her off and arranged them how he wanted them.

Molly was sexed up and sexed out but she still held her breath as Maddox pressed her back to Diesel's front, both on their sides. Then he pressed his front to her front, trapping her hands upturned against his pecs, Diesel's hand curled around her breast, when he wrapped his arm around both of them and tangled his legs with both of theirs.

She had a view to Maddox's throat.

Maddox had a view to Diesel's face.

And at her back, Molly felt Diesel not as loose as he should be after that beautiful session.

She licked her lips nervously.

They cuddled after a threesome, definitely. But not this close. Not as close as Maddox made them last night.

Leading up to and during a session, Maddox and Diesel would tangle up without thought.

After, they usually didn't get close enough to touch, or at least not too much.

They were touching now.

A lot.

"Mouth," Maddox demanded.

She closed her eyes tight, refusing to tip her head back in order to make her point to Diesel.

He means you, D, he means you, he means you, hemeansyou. Kiss him. Kiss him. Kisshimkisshimkisshim.

Throughout her mental chanting, D didn't move.

Her heart jumped when he did.

Pressing into her back, his hand at her breast squeezing, he leaned into Maddox.

Maddox took his arm from around them and she felt the inside of his forearm brush her cheek as he caught hold of D's neck.

She listened to the gorgeous, soft, wet sound of their kiss and felt like crying with happiness.

Mad's arm moved and his fingers curled round her neck as he whispered, "Now you, my Molly."

She tipped her head back then and he took her mouth.

When he was done with her, he let her go and wrapped his arm around both of them again.

She heard and felt Diesel let out a huge sigh and Molly couldn't read that. Couldn't read if that was good, relief, settling in to the beauty they just had, coming to terms with it, understanding it was right, it was safe, it was as it was meant to be.

Or if it was giving in.

Which still worked (for now), but it wasn't ideal.

"How many times did you come?" Maddox asked a question she knew, due to the unfortunate limitations of the male body, was for her.

She snuggled into both her men and answered, "I don't know. A hundred?"

Maddox chuckled.

Diesel gave her breast another squeeze.

"So, D eat the ability for you to cook dinner outta you?" Maddox went on.

"It's a wonder I'm conscious," Molly told him.

Maddox's eyes danced at her.

Happy.

God.

He was so happy.

Please, let us keep this, she prayed. *Please let this be real.*

"Then I'll feed my babies," Maddox muttered.

"Special dinner tomorrow night," she told him. "I have it all planned. It was supposed to be tonight but D had other ideas."

Maddox looked over her head at D. "They were good ideas."

"Mm," D mumbled.

"Sunflowers rock, brother," Maddox told him on a grin.

"Whatever," D kept mumbling.

"Can I ask why it's so hard for you to take us tellin' you you're pretty fuckin' awesome?" Maddox inquired, not angry, or annoyed, but curious.

Diesel's body totally tensed.

Molly's body totally tensed.

Maddox's arm around them went iron tight and his legs tangled in theirs curled like claws.

"Don't pull back," Maddox growled his warning.

Okay, that was annoyed.

"Mady," Molly whispered anxiously.

"I'm not pullin' back," Diesel lied.

"You're awesome," Maddox bit off like it was an insult.

Molly actually wanted to laugh at that.

Instead, she kept quiet and tense.

Diesel went with the cocky. "Yeah. You're right. I'm awesome. I'm the shit."

"You are and that's no joke," Maddox stated firmly.

"You are, DD," Molly said carefully. "No joke."

"Can we shift convo from the Diesel Admiration Society to what's for dinner 'cause I just fucked hard, sucked hard and blew hard and I need food," Diesel requested.

He was being funny.

Molly relaxed.

Diesel relaxed.

And only then did Maddox relax.

"We got any steak that's not frozen, Mol?" Maddox asked.

She tipped her head back again. "No. Just chicken."

He looked to D. "Barbeque chicken work for you?"

Molly's stomach rumbled.

"Works for Mol," D muttered amusedly.

Maddox smiled at Diesel then at her. "Then I best feed you, right, baby?"

She nodded.

He dipped in and kissed her and she loved it as usual.

Then, before D could read him, he lifted up and kissed Diesel and she loved that almost better.

After that, before Diesel could stiffen, Mad broke away and was on his ass on the bed before he twisted back, gaze to D.

"Watchin' you go at Molly tied, I'm in the mood for you to work me. Get creative. You're goin' at me tomorrow. Workout room. Think big 'cause I already got plans for retribution and you'll feel cheated, you don't earn them."

She felt D press his cock into a cheek of her ass, and it was not totally hard, but it also was not soft, as Maddox spoke and she knew how much he wanted that.

But he said nothing and Maddox took it no further.

He just got out of bed, snatched up his gym clothes, shoes, socks and bag and walked to the bathroom, stating, "Quick shower then I'm on dinner."

When he disappeared, Diesel turned Molly in his arms to facing him.

"You okay, sweetheart?" he asked.

"Yeah, honey," she answered, gliding her hands up his chest.

He curled his fingers just under her wrists and pulled them up farther.

"These good?" he asked, studying them.

Both men did this, but particularly D. Always about the aftercare, making sure her orgasms didn't mask any hurts, inattention to important physical details, or getting so into the session, unconsciously taking things too far.

"The satin never makes marks," she reminded him. "And you know I like it like that, DD."

He pressed her hands to his chest at the same time he massaged her wrists, regardless of her answer.

They heard the shower go on.

"You okay, D?" she asked when his attention wandered to the side of her head which meant it really was in the bathroom.

He looked at her.

"Yeah, baby." He gave her his cocky grin, and yeah, for her with him, the first time she saw him, it was that grin that made her want him to tie her up. That and the fact he was beautiful to look at and had a beast of a body that could dominate at rest. "Great. Should film you tied like that, between my legs, takin' my cock, your ass in my hands. Have that shit painted. Prettiest thing I've ever seen."

She felt a blush of pleasure stain her cheeks as she pressed closer.

"I know what you mean. That's how I feel when Mady goes down on you with you spread for him like that."

His eyes shifted away.

Dang.

She needed to be stronger, for Maddox, for her.

For D.

Which meant she needed to push him harder.

In order to pull him closer.

She cuddled deeper into him.

"You do know it's beautiful, yeah?" she asked.

"Mm-hmm," he mumbled then looked again to her. "You're callin' me DD."

She slid a bit back. "Sorry. I . . ." She shook her head, feeling the impossible. Weirdly awkward. With Diesel. "Sorry," she mumbled.

"Why?" he asked.

"Why am I calling you that?"

"Why are you sorry?"

"I don't know . . . you don't like it. But sometimes it just slips—"

"I like it," he told her, suddenly looking confused. "Why do you think I don't like it?"

"I thought . . . you're . . ." Molly felt her brows draw together before she felt her lips lift up. "I don't know why I thought you didn't like it."

He wrapped his arms around her and gathered her closer. "I do like it."

"Cool."

"It's sweet."

She grinned at him. "Yay."

Wow, it was weird, how carefully she handled him not even realizing it.

Weirder to know that maybe she didn't have to do that.

That last being weird in a good way.

His gaze moved over her face with obvious indulgence before his expression got serious and he looked into her eyes.

"I love you, Mol, you know that, right?"

She melted into him.

"Of course I do, Diesel," she whispered.

"I'll always love you. Until my dying breath."

The melting stopped.

Oh no.

What was this?

"Me too, honey," she replied. "But—"

"Just that," he cut her off. "Just wanted you to know . . ." His head did a strange jerk on the mattress before he finished, "that."

"Is there something you wanna talk about?"

"No, just want you to know. Just want you never to forget that."

Oh no.

What was *this*?

"I won't. Not ever," she promised.

"Good," he murmured.

"D?" she called.

"What?"

"I love you too, until my dying breath."

He shifted into her, still holding her in his arms, but taking her slightly to her back, giving her some of his weight and a lot of his warmth, not just his body, in his face, from his beautiful blue eyes.

"I know, sweetheart."

"And there's nothing that will make me stop," she vowed.

"I know," he repeated.

"And I'm always there for you," she kept at him.

He touched his mouth to hers, lifted only a bit away, and whispered, "I know, Molly."

She pushed her hand from his chest up to cup his jaw, taking a chance, needing him to know she knew him, read him, worried for him, was there for him.

"I know you're struggling with something," she said quietly.

His eyes closed down.

But she didn't stop.

"And I'll be there, Maddox will be there, we'll *always* be there, so we'll definitely be there when you get to the other side," she said.

He looked her over, muttering like he wasn't actually talking to her, "What did I do to deserve you?"

Sunflowers, she thought.

"You're the shit, remember?" she teased.

He tried to hide the relief he felt that she was lightening the conversation, failed, but grinned at her through it and said, "Right. For a second I forgot how totally fucking awesome I am."

She snuggled into him, taking her hand from his jaw and wrapping her arm around him, asking conspiratorially, "So what are you gonna do to Mad tomorrow?"

"I haven't weighed his balls down in a while."

Nice.

She wriggled underneath him.

He grinned at her. "Wanna suck him off while he's wearing his weight ring around his balls and he's got his belt on?"

"The big plug attached to the belt?" she asked.

"You pick," he offered.

"The big plug," she decided.

"You got it," he agreed.

"The one that vibrates," she clarified.

His grin got wicked. "Like the way my girl thinks. Gonna ring his balls too."

"No coming?" she queried.

He shook his head. "Not for a good while."

She suspected her grin was a form of wicked, or the best she could do, she didn't have a lot of that in her. She let her boys take care of that goodness.

He rolled fully over her, saying, "Make him squat straddling the bench, tie his hands to the weight supports, ass tipped, back arched, balls pulled down, hanging in the breeze. Fifteen minutes of that will feel like five hours."

She opened her legs, his hips fell through and she felt his cock hard against her thigh.

"Paddle?" she whispered.

She sighed as Diesel read her invitation, shifted his hips and slid inside.

"You're devious, sweetheart," he whispered back, beginning to stroke. "A paddle might kill him. But that ass'll be spanked good and red."

She wrapped her legs around his thighs and met his thrusts.

He kissed her.

She kissed him back.

"Are you serious?"

At Maddox's question, they broke the kiss and turned their heads to the side to where Maddox was standing.

"Fuck off and go cook food," Diesel ordered.

Maddox's brows were downright terrifyingly knit (if you didn't know him) as he asked Diesel, "How the fuck are you hard?"

"I just told Molly what I was doin' to you tomorrow."

The brows unknit, the chin lifted and those handsome lips embedded in that awesome beard muttered, "Ah,"

"Food," Diesel grunted on an inward slide.

"Have a fun fuck," Maddox replied, giving Molly a wink before he turned and left the room.

Diesel's hand curved around her jaw and righted her head.

He kissed her.

He fucked her.

And all was good in the world.

"REB'S COMING OUT NEXT WEEKEND," Diesel announced as he walked back out on the patio where they'd been enjoying after dinner beers before D heard his cell go with a text, then another one, so he'd gone in to check and then he got on the phone.

"I know, she called me earlier," Molly told him.

"She told me," D said, easing into the slider he left behind. He looked watchful and maybe a little ticked as he asked, "Why didn't you say something?"

"Someone told me to get naked and wait for them on my belly in the bed," she reminded him. "So it kinda slipped my mind."

Molly saw his face clear and he nodded, beginning to grin. "Right. That did happen."

"I know, I was there. PS, Rebel's coming for a long weekend next weekend," she declared.

Diesel chuckled.

Maddox, who she was cuddled into on the loveseat glider, tucked her closer and chuckled with him.

"Visit from Rebel will work. Your sister should move down here. We could use a little of her brand of the good kind of crazy. It'd balance out Holly," Maddox said.

Molly pushed away but did it slapping his abs.

"Maddox!" she snapped.

He grinned down at her. "Tell me you don't agree."

"I'm not saying the words out loud," she returned, on a flop, going back to lounging against him.

"Right," he muttered, sounding entertained.

"How'd Minnie get to be so normal?" Diesel asked. "I mean, under that blue hair and those piercings, she's practically a choirgirl."

"Fate handing us the spectrum, brother," Maddox answered. "The high maintenance princess sister we gotta put up with. The straight and narrow sister with blue hair we gotta wonder at. And the spitfire with a heart of gold we thank God rounds out the lot."

"I love Minnie. She's quiet but she's sweet," Molly put in.

"She scares the shit outta me. No woman is *that* quiet," Maddox shared, and Molly got up and slapped his abs, harder this time.

"Brother, I cannot believe that shit just came outta your mouth," Diesel muttered, sounding like he was trying not to laugh.

"I can't either," Molly hissed.

Maddox reached out and twirled a lock of her hair. "Baby, when you babble on, it's all kinds a' cute. But I'm *fuckin'* you, so it would be."

Molly looked to D. "Can I cuddle with you?"

He threw out a long arm. "Always, sweetheart."

She got up, taking her beer with her, and stomped to D.

He wasn't in the loveseat and it was still hot outside but he also didn't blink at her curling up in his lap to the point he wrapped both arms around her.

"Keep bein' a chauvinist, my man, and I'll get all the lovin'," Diesel joked.

When Molly looked at him, Maddox didn't appear broken up that he lost her.

And that didn't break her up because he looked content to the point of serene, gazing at his man and woman curled up together.

His expression shifted and his focus did the same, all of it on Diesel.

"So, this work with Sixx gonna become a regular thing?" Maddox asked.

Molly looked up at D to see him shrug.

"Regular. No. But I made it clear if she needed me again, I'm there," Diesel answered.

They'd heard about the earbuds and transmitters over barbeque chicken and pasta salad.

And when they did, it was not lost on either of them that Diesel really enjoyed hanging with Sixx last night.

Now, they were here.

And Molly took a sip of her beer, mostly because she didn't know what to think about this turn of events.

"You got off on it," Maddox noted.

"Yeah," D replied. "Hard not to. It was the shit."

"You know, after that clearout they had, Barclay and Josh are still lookin' for people they can trust who know what they're doin' to be Dungeon Masters at the Bolt," Maddox announced.

"Really?" Molly asked.

"Yeah?" Diesel asked.

"You'd be good with that," Mad told D.

He would.

But Molly didn't like it.

"Yes, and he'd be on a different schedule than us," she pointed out.

"I wouldn't quit my day job, sweetheart," Diesel told her.

She looked up at him. "So you'd be away a lot and not getting enough sleep."

"Okay, before this discussion runs away from us," Maddox put in, "I'm just sayin', D, if you're not diggin' what you're doing, you should find something you dig doing. Do this work with Sixx. Maybe check things out at the Bolt," his eyes dropped to Molly, "if he wants to give it a shot. Barclay and Josh could use someone decent who gives a shit about the players, not to mention someone who's in the scene, as head of security, not someone who looks at it as just a job. I don't even think they got a head of security, but after that shit went down there, they need one. And maybe D, if he got into it, could share that with them."

"And if he did, he'd be a different schedule than us, Maddox," Molly reiterated.

"And he might be happier with what he's doin' and we'd work it, darlin'," Maddox returned gently.

"And, uh, just to say, that *he* you're talkin' about is sittin' right here," Diesel butted into the conversation about him that was happening without him. "And yeah, I dug workin' with Sixx. And yeah, I'm totally gonna do it again. And yeah, I'd rock being a DM so I'll contact Barclay. But no, there's no reason to get uptight about anything because it's nothing now but talk and some fun with Sixx every once in a while. We'll hash out a change if there's actually a change to hash out. You both with me?"

"Sure," Maddox said before taking a tug on his beer.

Molly looked again at D. "If the work with Sixx isn't dangerous, then . . . sure too. If it is, you shouldn't keep that from us."

"It wasn't last night, but if it is, I won't keep it from you, Mol," D said softly.

She stared into his eyes.

Then she nodded.

He gave her a grin and a squeeze of his arm.

Then he took a swig of beer.

She took one too and settled back into him.

Maddox spread his arm across the back of the loveseat and stared at the two people across from him like he'd be happy watching them for years.

God, she really loved that man.

He knew it.

But it didn't hurt to remind him.

So when his eyes rested on her, Molly mouthed, "Love you."

"You too," he said out loud.

"Jesus, you two are a pain in my ass," Diesel grumbled.

Maddox smiled.

Molly looked again to him. "What? Why?"

"You're gooey. It's disgusting," he replied.

She pulled away and slapped his abs, exclaiming, "It is not."

"It totally is," he returned, a teasing twinkle in his eyes.

"You're both annoying," she declared.

"And you love it," Diesel returned.

"Only when you're annoying while you're fucking me," she shot back.

D aimed his cocky grin at Maddox, lifting his bottle to his mouth and saying before taking a tug, "She does love that."

Molly transferred her gaze to Maddox as he replied, "She fuckin' does, thank fuck."

She pushed off Diesel and got to her feet, declaring, "I'm watching TV.

"Don't be like that, baby," Maddox called.

She fired a glare over her shoulder at him and flounced away.

It was all show.

Maddox might read it.

D might not.

But Molly wanted them to have time alone and would clutch at anything to give them that time to be normal, sit, relax, unwind, be together—not fucking, not in a scene, not even making love—just two men who loved each other being together.

"It's good she's gone. Now we can talk about how sweet her ass looks when she's trussed up, her pussy stuffed with one of our cocks," Diesel remarked.

"I don't know, brother, my show mighta been better, her bound and ridin' your face," Maddox replied.

"I see that," Diesel agreed.

"You're both pigs," Molly decreed as she yanked open the door.

"Unh-hunh, how many times you come again, baby? A hundred?" Diesel called.

She whirled at the door and stuck her tongue out at him.

They both busted out laughing.

She pranced into the house, giving the door a little slam behind her.

And she did it smiling.

BUT HOURS LATER, TANGLED IN her men, mostly asleep, Molly's eyes shot wide.

Until my dying breath.

Why would he say that?

Why didn't he just tell her he loved her like he usually did?

Until my dying breath.

She listened to the deep male breathing around her, felt the somnolent, hard bodies caging her in.

Both her boys were asleep.

"He's leaving," she whispered to no one.

Molly was not fooled by sunflowers and joking on the patio.

Rebel had a phone conversation with him and was coming down, for goodness sakes.

Something was wrong.

And she wasn't sure with the changes that were happening that it was actually coming right.

Maybe it was more like a prolonged goodbye.

As tears filled her eyes, determinedly, she shifted so both men would shift with her, pulling closer, snuggling deeper, into her . . .

And each other.

"'Kay?" D asked drowsily.

So Diesel, even asleep, all she had to do was move, and he'd ask her if she was okay.

"Yeah," she lied.

"'Kay," Mad muttered vaguely.

So Maddox, ascertaining she was okay and only then was he okay.

Their breathing eased back to sleep.

Molly stared at the ceiling.

She couldn't lie there and cry.

She couldn't make her point by making them cuddle when they were mostly asleep.

She had to do something.

Because most important of all . . .

She could not, *would not*, let them lose Diesel.

TEN

Stop Being Stupid

Diesel

"NO, REALLY, PRIME RIB SLIDERS are *not* necessary, Holly. I thought we made this decision when I was down in Tucson," Molly said into the phone as D put his knee to the bed and leaned into her.

She was back to the bed, ass facing the pillows, legs raised up straight, ankles crossed, heels resting on the wall over the headboard, phone to her ear.

This was her Take a Load off While Holly Attempted to Drive Her Nuts position.

It was also her Take a Load off While Gabbing with Her Mother for Two Hours position.

When he got in her face, she rolled her eyes at him.

He memorized that second. That heartbeat of life. That overload of cuteness. That beautiful piece of Molly.

And he did it as he grinned at her in an effort to hide where his thoughts were really at, then bent in and touched his mouth to hers.

He pulled back.

She gave him her own grin then her eyes unfocused as they narrowed.

"Holly, no," she said into the phone. "No backtracking. That's eight hundred dollars-worth of food and you're having a banquet. You don't need people stuffed full of hors d'oeuvres right before they have dinner. It's a total waste of money."

Seeing as he had something pressing to do, and sadly no hope of saving her from her situation, Diesel left her to it, pushed off the bed and moved down the hall, through the great room, to the back hall and into the workout room.

He stopped in the door and took in the view.

Maddox was in full quiver where D had left him, squatting over the weight bench he was straddling, bare plugged ass tipped, back arched, head back, wrists tied to the bar supports. He had his black leather belt tight around his waist. Buckled at the small of his back was a strap going down between his ass checks, holding in the vibrating plug. The end of it looped around a ring that was banding his balls.

Topping that, his balls were weighted down with his heavy, thick, steel weight band.

He had to be in agony, his balls weighted like that, his quads burning in the squat, not to mention his ass red from the spanking he'd taken earlier.

D had left him like that for ten minutes. Any more would not only be torture, it'd be uncool.

But he was holding.

That was Maddox. He'd endure anything because he liked it like that.

And because D liked dishing it out.

Diesel moved into the room, right to the bench and enjoyed watching Maddox's entire body jump powerfully when D touched his ass lightly. Enjoyed the groan of pained pleasure that accompanied it when those weighted balls swayed.

D ran his hand up his back, his shoulder, his arm as he walked around to his front.

Mad's head tipped back, agony and ecstasy carved in that harsh, handsome face.

Diesel could stare at that face looking like that for ages.

He could stare at it in sleep, while he was watching TV, while he was smiling at Molly, while Mad was driving his truck.

He'd never get sick of that face.

"All right, brother?" he asked.

"Gotta come, D," Maddox gritted.

That'd be the pain Mad so got off on, accompanied by the position. He liked being physically challenged. Not to mention that big plug thumping relentless up his ass.

"Mm," D murmured and slid his fingers through Mad's thick beard, watching his hand move, feeling the soft bristles against his skin.

He cupped the underside of Mad's jaw, put a knee to the bench and yanked his workout shorts down to expose his cock.

"Open up, buddy," he whispered.

Maddox immediately opened his mouth.

D fed his cock in and watched Maddox's cheeks under that beard hollow as he sucked hard.

Fuck, his man had a mean draw.

Goddamned heaven.

It was Diesel's turn to groan, his head falling back.

He started to face fuck his boy, tipping his chin back down, watching Maddox's mouth take him, the focus in his expression.

The pain was gone.

His position didn't factor.

He was all about sucking Diesel's cock.

D ran his hand gently over Maddox's hair and those black eyes opened, shifted up, and what Diesel saw shining there . . .

He slipped his dick out, bent in and took Maddox's mouth with his own. He drank deep, taking his time, and Maddox gave it all up.

All of it.

Everything.

D broke the kiss, opened his eyes and saw Maddox gazing at him, not hiding the need that lay stark right there.

"Fuck me, baby," Mad whispered.

Diesel didn't mess around with unfastening the ball weight and letting it drop. Removing the belt, plug and ring.

But Maddox held position, squatted over the bench, as D lubed, moved in, and took his ass.

The minute he drove home, Maddox's body jerked spasmodically, head shafting back, his cum jetting all over the bench.

Oh yeah, he got off on the pain.

And D's cock hitting home.

It didn't take long for D to shoot inside him.

Still coming down, Diesel sat on the bench, pulling Maddox down to sit on his cock, and he rested his forehead at the back of Mad's neck.

"Love you, buddy," D whispered.

Mad went entirely still, his ass clenching so tight around D's still hard dick, it milked an aftershock of cum out along with a grunt.

"Untie me," Maddox ordered, his rough voice thick and throaty.

"We're done," Diesel told him.

"Untie me, D," Maddox commanded.

Diesel pushed him up and off his cock. Reaching out, he untied one wrist.

"Last part of your service is to clean up," Diesel told him.

Then he moved away, left Maddox to untie himself from the other support, and walked out of the room, straightening his shorts.

He went back to the bedroom and hit it in time to see Molly rolling off the bed.

She looked to him.

"I'm going for a run," he announced.

She blinked then looked concerned. "Did I miss it? I mean, you're not leaving Mad like that—"

"I finished him off," Diesel told her, ignoring the surprise he felt from her as he walked into the closet.

He grabbed his running shoes, socks and a tee. He pulled the tee on and went out to sit on the edge of the bed to put on his socks and shoes.

Molly was still there but D didn't look at her.

"So you guys are done?" she asked hesitantly.

"Yeah."

"Stupid Holly," she muttered, and he felt her attention remain on him. "Now you're running? In the heat of the day?"

He glanced at her to see she didn't look any less concerned but now also looked perplexed.

He went back to his shoes. "Yeah."

"After doing Mady?" she pushed.

"Yeah."

He finished tying his shoes and straightened, beginning to move to the door as Mad walked in wearing a pair of cutoff sweats, his eyes on D.

He looked concerned too.

His gaze swept Diesel top to toe.

"Goin' for a run," Diesel told him before he could ask.

"You're . . . what?" Maddox asked anyway.

D walked to him and stopped.

"A run, buddy," he said quietly, lifted a hand and wrapped it around the side of Mad's neck. "You good?" he queried, running his thumb through the beard at Mad's jaw.

"Yeah," Maddox answered, brows drawn, eyes studying Diesel. "Are you?"

D nodded, his gaze dropping to Mad's mouth as he pulled his man to him.

He took his mouth, quicker this time than when he had him positioned for him, but he still got a good taste in with his tongue.

He let him go, ignored the surprise on Maddox's face and didn't look at Molly altogether as he muttered, "Later."

With that, he walked down the hall, out the front door, down the walk, to the road.

He let himself feel the heat as he pounded out the miles, focused on it entirely, the oppression, the discomfort, the sweat pouring off his body.

But even the Phoenician sun in summer couldn't take Diesel's mind off where he was at and what he was intent on doing.

A good hunk of time. Giving it all. Getting it all.

Having Rebel there with them that weekend.

And then, after she was gone, the weekend after that . . .

This had to end. He had to stop wasting their time. He had to make the cut so they could heal and move on.

So he was going to give it all to them.

He was going to get it all while doing that.

And then he was taking all his baggage, all his damage, all his bullshit . . .

And he was leaving.

Maddox

MOLLY WAS IN THE KITCHEN cooking their "special dinner."

Diesel was flat out on the couch watching TV.

Maddox was in their bedroom, his phone in his hand, trying to decide if he should make a call, and if he made it, who he should call.

Rebel?

Or Sixx.

He had not made up his mind when movement at the door caught his eye and he saw D walk through.

"Hey," he said.

"Yo," Diesel greeted, his hand in his front jeans pocket.

He walked up to where Maddox was standing in the middle of the room, stopped, opened his mouth, shut it and looked around.

Then he looked at Mad.

"What're you doin' standin' in the bedroom?"

Fuck.

Maddox didn't have an answer for that.

He couldn't say, *With this new zone you're in, you're freaking me and Mol way the fuck out so I wanna know why all of a sudden Rebel's coming down. I also wanna know if Sixx has some insight into your shit and/or has some idea how to help out. Because I'm too fuckin' terrified of asking you to your face seeing as I thought we were getting somewhere and now I'm scared as fuck we are not.*

"Got distracted," Maddox answered vaguely.

"By what?" Diesel pushed.

With no choice, Mad had to give it to him.

Maddox looked him in the eye. "Not usual, you got a good thing goin', workin' me over. You fuck me quick, let me come, then take off for a run. Wonderin' where your head is at. Strike that, worried where it's at."

D blew it off. "It's all good."

Mad stared at him. "You sure?"

"Yup," Diesel told him and pulled his hand out of his jeans. "The money. From the job with Sixx."

Maddox looked down to see in D's hand several bills folded in half. They were hundreds.

He looked back up to D.

"Why are you givin' it to me?"

"For the ring. Add it to what your folks give you."

That seemed plausible.

Except for the part it was a lie.

"So we're goin' ahead with the ring?" Maddox asked.

"I think we should hang tight for a while," Diesel answered.

Yeah.

It was a lie.

"We need to—" Mad began.

"Sixx is gonna use me again. She told me so. It might not be five hundred bucks for a couple hours of work every time, but I get the sense the pay's gonna be good. And I'm totally going to Barclay and Josh at the Bolt, see if I can take on some shifts as DM at nights, on weekends. It might take a while, but it'll close the gap from what we have and what we need."

That was plausible too.

It was also a lie.

"Diesel—"

D didn't let him finish. "You down with that plan?"

"I think she's expecting us to move forward with the commitment," Maddox stated. "And we can't let her expect that too long or it's gonna upset her nothing is happening with it."

Diesel nodded. "I agree. And we can get the ring, if Clay and Josh take me on, in a month, maybe six weeks. We can borrow from your parents, give her the ring, use what we got to pay them back when she has the ring, so she'll expect that money in our savings to be gone. She gets her surprise. We start paying it off. But that way, we'll owe them less, and with me workin' a second job, we'll be able to pay them back faster."

That was plausible as well.

It still felt like a lie.

"You're bearing the brunt of that, brother, workin' two jobs," Mad pointed out.

There was a tightening around his cheekbones Maddox caught as D replied, "I don't bring in as much as you do and this isn't a discussion. I know you get me. It's gotta be fifty, fifty. Right down the middle. So that's somethin' I gotta do."

Maddox again stared right into Diesel's eyes.

D stared back, unblinking.

When Maddox said nothing, sounding slightly impatient, D pressed, "Sound like a plan?"

"Yeah, man."

Diesel nodded again and pushed the bills toward Maddox.

For reasons he didn't totally understand, not liking it, Maddox took them.

The second the money exchanged hands, D turned on his bare foot and walked out of the room.

Maddox watched him go.

Then he looked down at the cash in his hand.

He had a feeling that Diesel wanted Maddox to use that money to buy Molly a ring.

The problem was, he also had a feeling that wasn't going to be fifty, fifty for shit.

Because one of those fifties wasn't going to stick around.

THE NEXT MORNING, SUNDAY, MOLLY was in her nightie, on her back in the loveseat glider out on the patio, mug of coffee on the table over her head by the arm of the seat. She had a section of the newspaper (entertainment) open, reading it with it practically obscuring her face (and entire torso).

Maddox was opposite her, in the slider facing the French doors, feet up on the ottoman, the sports section folded halfway and laying along the tops of his thighs.

They were both in the position to see Diesel lurch out the doors holding a mug of coffee in his hand.

He moved to the open slider, collapsed into it, lifted a heavy leg and dumped it on the ottoman next to Mad's feet and mumbled, "Yo," before taking a sip from his mug.

"Mornin', DD," Molly said through a grin.

"Mornin', man," Maddox said, also smiling, but not entirely committed to it.

D made a distracted move with his mug in the air before he sucked more back and stared unseeing at the sun beyond the covered patio.

Molly gave it time.

Maddox gave it time.

Diesel drank coffee (so he took the time).

When Maddox finished the sports section, he shoved up out of his seat, grabbed his mug, reached over, grabbed Molly's and bent deeper, touching his mouth to hers, before he straightened.

He then moved around the ottoman, dumped the sports in D's lap and took his empty mug from his unresisting hand.

"Warm up?" he asked unnecessarily.

"Duh," D mumbled.

Maddox chuckled, linked the handle of Diesel's mug with the other two he had hooked in his finger and used his free hand to give the hair at the back of D's head a tug.

D tipped that head back.

Half alert, half still hazed, all so good looking, Maddox's cock took notice and his mind took that opportunity to run over what he intended to do to his boy later.

But right then, he just bent in and touched his mouth to D's.

D accepted it and his blue eyes were still half hazed, but now warm when Maddox pulled away.

Easy as that.

One day, none of that shit.

A few days later, he was offering up his mouth without hesitation, and taking Mad's at every opportunity.

And telling him he loved him.

Connected, post-scene, telling Mad he loved him.

Maddox didn't make a deal of it.

Any of it.

Then.

Or now.

He took the mugs into the kitchen and did the refills.

As he was walking back out, he did it looking at the back of D's head.

Love you, buddy.

It just came out of him like he said it all the time when he fucking didn't.

Maddox should be thrilled.

But it was carving him up.

Because that *love you, buddy*, felt a lot like *goodbye*.

Mad handed Diesel his cup. Gave Molly hers.

And settled in his slider with his.

Ten minutes later, D arranged the sports so he could read it.

Sunday morning it was together time but quiet time. There was eye contact. Smiles. Kisses (or, at least there were between Mad and Mol, or D and Mol, but now it seemed there were between Mad and D). Touches. But not a lot of talk.

Sunday mornings with his man and woman were Maddox's favorite times with them.

Not that day.

The sun was shining.

But he couldn't get it out of his head that a cloud was on the horizon. It was huge. And it brought doom.

Molly shifted and Maddox looked to her, seeing she threw her feet over the back of the glider, the seat rocking with her movement.

Her pretty face was relaxed but there was tension around her eyes as she lay there, not reading, not doing anything, her mug of coffee sitting forgotten in her hand resting on her belly, her eyes aimed at her feet.

"Baby," he called.

She turned her head his way.

"In a little bit, I'm takin' D back and fuckin' him. Just him and me. You cool with that?"

He felt heat coming his way from Diesel's direction, but Molly got him.

Totally.

"Take care of me later, Mady?" she asked.

"Absolutely, darlin'," he promised.

She nodded. "I'm cool."

Only then did he look to Diesel to see he'd lost interest in the paper and his gaze was glued to Maddox.

"When you're ready, go. Naked. Get out your ropes, bud. And wait for me," he ordered.

D nodded too, his eyes hot, but there was a tightness around his jaw like the tightness around Molly's eyes.

This wasn't right.

None of it was right.

Somehow, after a ray of light broke through, brightening their world, they'd all slid into a zone where they seemed to be stumbling through the dark, going through the motions.

D finished his coffee, got up, and without a word, but more unusually, without even a look at Molly, he walked into the house.

Maddox watched the door close behind him and turned right to their girl.

She didn't hesitate.

"I'm scared, Mady. He's so deep in his head, he's like a zombie. Last night at dinner, his favorite, crab and lobster mac 'n' cheese, the only thing he said was, 'This is great, Mol.'"

"What did Rebel say when you talked to her?" Maddox asked.

She shook her head. "Not much. She told me she had called him the night before and she thought he sounded like he was in a bad place. But that wasn't news, since he was. And then he wasn't. But now there's this."

"She didn't say anything else?"

She shook her head then her eyes lit and she sat up abruptly.

"She told me about what happened when D's friend was outed."

"D told me that too," Maddox shared. "It didn't go down too good, but it worked out for him. An excuse for him to get away from somewhere that was toxic."

"It might have worked for Tommy, but Diesel having to watch him go through it didn't work for D."

Maddox felt something move in his chest. It was huge. Colossal. Titanic.

Of course.

Fuck.

Christ.

Of course.

That was why D told him about Tommy. With them getting closer to making the moves to declare to the people in their lives what they had and their commitment to it, which meant D would need to let it all hang out, Diesel was thinking about what happened to his friend.

Maddox stared at Molly hard.

So hard, her voice was trembling when she called, "Mady?"

"He doesn't care," he announced.

"What?"

"About what they'll say. What they'll do. About losing them. He doesn't care."

Her voice was gentle when she disagreed. "You're wrong, Maddox. He totally does."

"No he doesn't. What he cares about is what *we'll* go through when they hit him with the ugly, because he knows exactly how that feels because he watched Tommy go through the same thing."

Molly sucked in a breath so sharp, he heard the hiss.

"Oh my God," she breathed. "You're right."

"And Rebel," he went on. "It's all on him, not that he's going to lose them, but when they make that play, she's going to lose them too."

Tears brightened her eyes. "Yeah . . . yes, he . . . that'd kill him."

"He's got issues about money," Maddox told her and watched her head twitch.

"Sorry, what?"

"He's got issues that he doesn't make as much money as us. He's gonna take a second job at the Bolt."

Molly started to look angry. "That's . . . it doesn't matter to me. Or you. He has to know that."

Maddox shook his head. "This, baby, I see. If it was me where he's at, that'd eat at me too."

She studied him a beat before muttering, "Men."

"It is what it is."

"What it is, is not a discussion for now. I took on this amount of testosterone. It's not like I can play dumb about not knowing there'd be times when you two would do stuff or think stuff that was completely annoying and totally frustrating. And just FYI, this isn't the first instance that kind of thing has happened."

At least that made him grin. "Like you said, darlin', you went in, eyes open."

Those eyes rolled.

It was cute.

But he couldn't get caught up in her cute.

"D's gonna try to save us from all that," he declared.

"Rebel doesn't care. *We* don't care," Molly pointed out.

"He does."

Molly sat straight in her seat, lifting both hands to wrap her fingers around the base of her throat because she knew he was right.

She crossed her legs under her and dropped her hands in her lap.

"How do we get him around all this?" she asked.

"I don't know. But maybe Rebel will."

She nodded.

Then her pretty face grew hard with determination, her green eyes glittering with it.

"Fuck him good, Maddox," she said in a voice he'd never heard from her. "Give it to him hard and sweet like you can do. Give it to him in a way, when you're through with him, he'll know he'll never have better."

"I can't do that without you there," he reminded her.

She lifted a hand and waved it at her side. "Don't you worry. I'll give him my goodness later." She jerked her head to the door. "It's your turn now."

He loved all things about Molly.

This new goodness was just added to all the rest.

He pushed himself from his chair, went to his woman, wrapped a hand behind her head, bunching her hair as he leaned in and took her mouth.

"Love you, baby," he whispered.

"Love you too, Maddox," she replied.

He touched his lips to hers, let her go and moved to the French doors to get to D.

WITH DIESEL TRUSSED ANKLES TO wrists, both to the headboard, open and spread wide, watching his thick, hard cock bob, listening to his clenched grunts, with a short paddle, Maddox spanked his ass red and raw.

Always a sight to see no matter how he saw it, D's ass after a thrashing.

Phenomenal.

"Jesus, brother," D bit out as Maddox covered a spot he'd hit again and again.

Maddox looked at him. "Enough?"

"Take it until you're done givin' it," D returned.

Yeah, but not to prove you're a man anymore. No. Now so you can give me whatever I want before you take it away.

"Enough," Maddox muttered, tossed the paddle aside, positioned facing D, bent to his boy and sucked his cock deep.

D's hips jerked up as he ground out, "Christ."

Maddox sucked him, hard, fast, added a hand to pump, and snaked the other one up his chest to tweak a nipple.

"*Christ,*" D gritted, his limbs jerking.

He liked the feel of that so Maddox latched onto Diesel's nipple, squeezing and twisting as he fisted his dick and sucked him off.

"Gonna have no choice but to blow, brother," Diesel shared thickly.

Maddox knew that, considering his man's entire body was straining to hold back the load.

Maddox slipped him out, came up to his knees, and jacked him off, still twisting his nipple.

He did this as he took Diesel in, that big, muscled body of his bound like that.

It was how he did him when he shaved him.

Totally on offer. The only movement was reactionary.

No control.

Giving that up to Maddox.

Even when he worked Maddox, D gave the power to Mad. Maddox didn't even know if D knew he was doing it.

Then again, that went both ways like it always did in kink.

In relationships.

You gave your power.

And that gave you power.

"String you up like this an entire weekend," he murmured, letting his eyes move over the meat on display in front of him, stroking up to the tip, running his thumb hard along the soft, distended skin there, watching Diesel swallow, his hands clench into fists. "Let Molly strap in, come use you, watch her take you 'til she comes, move in behind her, fuck you 'til I come and you blow for me. Cover you in your cum. Fill you with mine. All weekend long."

"Maddox," D whispered.

Mad looked in his hot eyes, pumping his dick again, harder, pulling at his nipple, and he watched D clench his teeth.

"Do you have any fuckin' clue how beautiful you are?" Mad asked.

A flash in those blue eyes before they closed down.

Nope.

He still couldn't handle shit like that.

"Fuck me," Diesel grunted, rolling up into Maddox's strokes, trying to gain some control over the situation, Maddox, where they were at.

"I will, baby," Maddox replied. "Now I'm gonna spend time lookin' at you."

"Just fuck me, Mad."

Maddox bent and licked the head of D's cock.

"Fuckin' love this dick," he muttered.

"Suck it," D encouraged.

He straightened and kept pumping him, slowing it down, but deepening the strokes and letting go of his nipple to allow his hand to roam that warm skin, his gaze again capturing D's.

Maddox's voice dipped way low when he said, "You'll never taste better pussy than Molly's."

Another flare in those eyes, anger, maybe fear, or sadness, before he bit out, "I know that."

"You'll never love the meat up your ass like you love takin' mine."

"I know that, asshole. So give it to me," D clipped.

Maddox let his cock go and reached to the drawer in the bedside table.

He then knelt in front of Diesel and made a show of lubing his dick.

D watched his hand move on his cock, hunger filling his features, and muttered, "Jesus, fuck, you're a motherfucker."

With that, Maddox moved in, positioned the head, then he *moved in*, sliding inside Diesel slowly, his chest brushing against his boy's, his face an inch away.

"How much you love your monster, baby?" Mad asked after he'd filled him.

"Love it, Mad," D whispered.

"Yeah," Maddox replied, taking long, deep thrusts. "Now I'm gonna fuck you hard, D."

"Yeah," Diesel grunted.

That was when Maddox kissed him, wet, long, taking his ass faster, both men grunting against each other's tongues.

And then Mad broke the kiss, positioned for leverage and power, and fucked his boy hard.

And his boy took it hard, not hiding how much he liked it.

So that bought Maddox fucking him harder.

"Need your hand," D groaned.

Maddox wrapped a fist around D's cock and jacked.

"Gotta come," D huffed out.

Maddox kept driving in. "Not without me."

D's ass clamped around him and his dazed eyes semi-focused on Mad's.

"Get there," he growled.

"You ever gonna take another cock but your monster?" Maddox asked.

Diesel's head jerked.

"Mad—"

Jacking his cock, fucking his ass, Maddox dropped his forehead to D's.

"Is any cock but mine ever gonna be up this ass?" he demanded.

"Baby—"

"Answer me," Maddox bit.

"No," D bit back.

"Ever?"

"Never."

"Your dick gonna take any other pussy but Molly's?"

"No."

"Never?"

"Never."

"Vow it, D."

"Let me come."

Maddox punished that red ass with his meat and commanded, "Vow it, Diesel."

All his limbs straining to hold back his orgasm, or break free in order to get away to escape the words, Diesel looked into Mad's eyes.

"It's only you. It's only her. Always," he growled.

"Go," Maddox ordered.

"*Fuck*," D hissed, pissed he was there, pissed it was Maddox that took him there because he was pissed at Maddox, and pissed he couldn't stop it, his head shot back, slamming into the headboard as he flooded up his chest and stomach and Maddox let go and shot his load up D's ass.

Maddox came down, resting inside, D's dick to his stomach, chest to chest, but on a forearm to hold himself up so he could catch Diesel's eyes when he stopped pulsing under him and came down to the Land of the Not Orgasming.

But Diesel pushed his recovery, his eyes still vague when he righted his head and clipped, "Untie me."

"Diesel—"

"Fuckin' untie me, asshole."

"I'm not done with you."

"Yes, you are."

"That's my call," Maddox reminded him.

"Not right now. Right now I'm tellin' you I'm done. So fuckin'" he jerked at his bounds, "*untie me*."

"Baby, I'm gonna eat me outta your ass and get you primed again and then Molly's gonna come in and let you do your thing."

"Untie me."

"D—"

"What game you playin', Mad?"

Wait a fucking second.

That . . .

Now *that* pissed him off.

Enough to slide out and reach to undo the ropes.

When he was done with both sides, Diesel, just like the motherfucker, totally able to hold back shit that was important, but had no problem with confrontation, simply sat up on his ass, planted his feet in the bed, knees cocked, spread open, fucking gorgeous, every goddamned inch.

Even his face, which was ticked.

"I got no game," Maddox finally replied. "I'm just reacting and you know it."

"Reacting to what?" D asked.

"You're not leaving."

Diesel's mouth clamped shut.

Yeah.

"She's terrified you're gonna go," Mad told him.

D's eyes slid to the door.

"And so am I," Maddox carried on.

His eyes slid back to Mad.

"It's time to commit and that's what's terrifying you because it's gonna all be out there. She loves you. I love you. We'll fall apart without you," Maddox told him.

"You'd be fine," Diesel said quietly.

Maddox could not believe what he was hearing.

Had he lost his fucking *mind*?

"We'd be destroyed."

Diesel stared at him.

Jesus Christ.

"I'm done trying to fuck some sense in you, brother," Maddox shared. "You are our world. We can endure anything, as long as we do it as our three. Take one part away from that, the rest vanishes. She's not the same to me, without you. I'm not the same to her, without you. We're just not right, at all, in any way, *without you*. And you know it. You *know it*. Talk to me. Talk to Mol. Talk to your sister. Talk to Sixx. Talk to *somebody*. But you are not fucking *leaving*."

With that, Maddox pushed off the bed and stalked to the walk-in.

He was yanking on some boxer briefs when Diesel's long, naked body filled the doorway.

Leaning against the jamb, he asked, still going quiet, gentle, "When are you gonna be done dealing with my shit?"

Maddox shoved one leg into his jeans, the other, hauled them up, straightened, and looked right at D.

"Never?" he asked as answer. "How's that work, D? I'm never gonna be done with your shit."

"And I'm supposed to believe that?" D asked back, not confrontational, again with the gentle.

"That's commitment," Maddox educated him, doing his fly. "That's a relationship. Until death do you part through the crab and lobster mac 'n' cheese, rockin' sex, being accosted at the mall about male skincare, annoying sisters-in-law, and all your partner's shit."

"I got more shit than both of you," Diesel pointed out.

"So?" Maddox asked.

"You're gonna get sick of it."

"Don't tell me what I'm gonna get sick of, D."

"Mad—"

"Fuck, man, *I'm in love with you!*" he shouted.

D went visibly solid.

"Is that too tough for you to take?" Maddox demanded. "I got a cock, you got a cock, and this man with his cock is telling you he's in love with you."

"I know that, Maddox. I'm in love with you too," Diesel whispered.

Maddox threw out both arms. "So what's the fuckin' problem?"

"What about me?" Diesel asked preposterously.

"What about you?"

"I just got years of watchin' you two deal with my shit?"

Maddox's spine snapped straight.

"Babies," Molly whispered, squeezing in beside Diesel's naked frame, her arm around his waist at the back, her other hand at his abs, her eyes locked to Maddox. "Is everything okay?"

Diesel pushed away from the jamb to wrap both arms around her and pull her to his body.

Maddox watched, keeping his mouth shut, wondering what Diesel would say.

Would he lie, even though Maddox was shouting and you could cut the air only using a hacksaw?

Or were they finally going to have this shit out?

"I've pissed Maddox off," Diesel admitted, and the fact he did made Maddox feel so much relief, his fucking legs actually got weak.

"How did that . . . uh, happen?" she asked, glancing at Diesel but turning to Maddox.

"I told him we're worried about him leaving," Maddox shared.

"Oh boy," she murmured.

"He thinks we're gonna get sick of his shit," Maddox continued.

She looked up at D, her head tipped to the side. "What shit?"

Diesel stared down at her, face blank, totally thrown, for long beats before his expression softened and he whispered, "Fuckin' fuck, but I love you."

"I love you too, but what shit?" Molly replied.

That was when Diesel stopped holding her and started trying to absorb her in his body, his face shoved in her neck, his embrace so tight, Maddox could see the muscles flexing and the veins standing out in his forearms.

Jesus.

Were they getting through?

Maddox moved their way and caught Diesel's attention by curling a hand around his neck.

He didn't remove his hand when D's grip on Molly loosened (but he didn't let her go) and his head came up.

"Just to say, I kinda like how you try to fuck sense into me," he joked.

"It sucks you're so fuckin' hot 'cause now is no time to joke and I still wanna tie you back to the bed," Maddox returned.

What he said next, the tone, the sudden look on his face, Maddox braced at the same time he felt Molly do it too.

"I've got it good," Diesel whispered, his voice pained. "So good. I hope like fuck you both know that I know that. So I hope you get how it's not easy bein' the one who doesn't give the good back."

"What on earth are you talking about?" Molly asked, also sounding pained.

Diesel looked down at her. "It's always all about me. That's gonna get tired, baby. And if it hasn't already, I know it will."

"Shit, shit, fuck," Maddox clipped, swaying D's neck, and in doing so swaying D (and Molly) with each word.

Therefore, both turned their eyes to him.

"I said that pissed," Maddox explained.

"You said what pissed?" Molly asked.

He looked to her. "Diesel and me fought when you were in Tucson and I told him it was always all about him."

"Oh, Mady," she muttered, sounding and looking disappointed.

Yeah, he'd fucked up.

He knew it back then, when he'd said it.

But apparently it was huge.

"It's true," Diesel said.

Both of them looked back to him.

"I was pissed and my mouth was running," Maddox replied.

"It's still true," Diesel pushed.

"Brother, it isn't. I was pissed you were holding back and I was letting off steam."

"I got that steam jacked up my ass, so that isn't news," Diesel returned.

"And yeah, there was also that. I fucked you angry and I was pissed at myself for doing it and taking that out on you too," Maddox told him.

"So it's all your bad?" D asked.

"Uh . . . yeah," Maddox answered.

"That's bullshit, Mad."

"Diesel, you a part of us hanging in the balance here, I'm not gonna bullshit you. It's too important. *You're* too important. I fucked up. You were pulling away after that scene with Sixx observing and I'm an asshole who doesn't know how to talk shit out so I fuck shit out and I fucked you over doing that and our shit just got more jacked, apparently worse than I expected, and I knew it was bad. Now we're here."

"We're talking commitment," D reminded him.

"I know that," Maddox confirmed.

"And that means we're headed for a shitstorm with my family. I've been putting you through my mindfuck about where I am with you in my heart, knowin' where you are with me in yours, and what's your reward I find my way to the other side of that? You gotta put up with my folks' shit."

"It's their shit, not yours," Maddox pointed out.

"They're mine and I'm forcing that shit on you," Diesel retorted.

"Oh for fuck's sake!" Molly shouted, yanking out of D's arms, taking three big steps into the closet, and both men turned slowly to her at her uncharacteristic outburst. "Who cares?" she yelled at Diesel. "You're so totally worth it! My God, Diesel, *we love you*. *You*. And because we do, we're there for you, always, *through anything*. I have breasts. I can get breast cancer. Breast cancer is bad. Do you think for a second that *I* think that if I got breast cancer, either one of you wouldn't be by my side every step of the way?"

"I hope the fuck not," Diesel growled.

And at that, Molly moved right back in and shoved his chest with one hand in sheer frustration.

"Of course not!" she snapped then shook a finger in his face. "So stop being stupid! I'll put up with my men doing stupid men shit like, Mad," she turned to Maddox, "could you *please* take your fucking *workout clothes* to the fucking *laundry room* and not dump that sweaty crap *in the closet hamper* so it stinks up our *closet*?"

"Yeah, baby, absolutely," Maddox murmured soothingly.

She nodded sharply at Mad, looked back to D and kept raving.

"What I won't put up with is either of you being stupid. I'm done with it. And now you're being stupid. I'm sorry, D. But you're just being stupid. Get over it. You don't get to look after us and buy my tampons and clean the house so we don't have to bother and mow the yard so Mad doesn't have to contemplate yet *another* blade of grass and give me rubdowns when those doctors work my *last nerve* and I get all tensed up without us getting to look after *you too*!"

And with that, she shoved past Diesel and stomped out of the room so hard, they heard her bare feet on the wood stomping down the hall.

Diesel had shifted out of the door and Maddox had moved into it to watch the bedroom doorway until they heard the back door slam shut behind her.

They turned to each other.

"Okay, well I guess Molly's over my shit," Diesel joked.

And Maddox couldn't hold it back.

He burst out laughing.

When it was dying down, he couldn't begin to describe the relief at seeing D grinning at him like the old D, pre-scene with Sixx, open, easy and cocky.

"How big a load did you shoot up me, asshole?" he asked when Maddox's laughter stopped being verbal. "Feels like a river of cum is sliding outta my ass."

"Got a big dick, comes with big balls, brother. Not like you don't know I shoot a big load," Maddox replied.

"Serious as fuck, it was not easy to have a world-rocking conversation with my people with an irritating trickle of cum running down my leg," D told him.

Maddox bit back laughter and shared, "You shoulda cleaned up before you got into it with me."

"Was worried there wasn't time."

Maddox nodded. "Probably wasn't."

D looked to the door Molly just flounced out of then back to Mad. "You think we should try to fuck some sense into Molly now?"

Maddox grinned at him. "Not sure she's in the mood."

"Yeah, we'll let her burn out a bit before we attempt more dealing with our shit through orgasms."

Maddox started chuckling.

D smiled at him when he did it.

He wasn't done doing it when D's smile died.

So Mad's laughter died.

"Straight-up truth, minute I clapped eyes on you, man, I wanted to suck your cock and I had no idea what kind of meat you were packing," D said quietly. "And that's what was in my head. But the next morning after we fucked the first time, I walked in to see you sitting at the kitchen table and I knew there'd never be another man for me. And that had not one thing to do with the meat you were packing."

Maddox's throat felt tight when he forced out of it, "Jesus, D."

Diesel reached out with his big mitts and grabbed Maddox on either side of his head, dipping his face to Mad's.

"Don't deserve you," he whispered.

"Shut it," Maddox growled.

"No. It's cool." His lips twitched. "Because you don't deserve me either, seein' as I'm so awesome."

Maddox shook his head in Diesel's hold, his lips not twitching seeing as he was smiling.

D kissed him and he stopped shaking his head.

And smiling.

Diesel broke it and let him go, muttering, "Now I really need to clean up this cum. Can't even stick my tongue down my man's throat without it irritating the shit outta me, breaking my concentration."

With that, he walked into the closet to get to the bathroom.

Mad watched him go.

Then he closed his eyes.

After that, he took a deep breath.

When he opened his eyes he was smiling again.

And for the first time in weeks, maybe months, possibly years, he was breathing free.

"How close to the rag is she?" he called to D.

"Brother, *do not* go there," Diesel called back. "Christ, she might cut you off from her pussy and transfer that to me just 'cause I got a dick."

"Maybe next time you go get Molly's tampons, you buy her some Midol," Maddox suggested.

"Fuck off," Diesel returned.

Never.

He was about to go do what he could to smooth things out with Molly when he realized he had D's dried cum on his chest.

So he headed to the bathroom first.

He cleaned up while D pulled on some jeans and a tee and Mad took that opportunity to throw on his own tee.

And then her men went out together to smooth things over with Molly.

ELEVEN

Having It All

Diesel

DIESEL WALKED OUT THE FRENCH doors toward the pool that Maddox was sitting in, and Molly was sitting on the edge opposite him, turned to the side, one leg bent, foot to the deck, the other leg down and dangling in the pool, her weight held in her hands behind her, her face tipped to the sun.

She was in a little polka-dot bikini with ruffles on it.

It was cute.

It was Molly.

It was also late Sunday afternoon. They'd sorted things out with Mol. Then they'd had a good, long session of fucking so they were all loosened up and on the same page.

And now they were hanging at the pool, drinking beer, chilling out.

D dropped Mol's fresh beer in its koozie by her hip and put Mad's in the hand he'd reached out before he slipped in the pool to sit on the shelf bench between Mad and Molly.

"Sixx texted while we were fucking. Wants us to go to dinner at her and Stellan's on Saturday," he announced. "Think that'd be cool. Rebel would love Sixx. Sixx will dig Rebel. And according to Sixx, her man's got some chops in the kitchen and their crib is tight."

"Works for me," Maddox muttered.

Molly didn't say anything so D looked to her.

"Sweetheart?" he prompted.

She didn't give either of them her gaze when she said softly, "I love it. All in the family."

Her tone, her words, hit D right in the gut and his eyes moved immediately to Maddox.

Maddox was giving Molly a sharp look, eyes narrowed, face sinister, which meant he was concerned.

"Mol," Mad called.

"You know, I wanted a white picket fence," she said wistfully.

That was when D's gut got straight-up tight, so much, he thought he'd puke, and Maddox's eyes shot to him.

"A husband," she said. "Babies."

"Molly." Her name out of D's mouth came strangled.

"Birthday parties and high school graduations and finding the perfect mother of the bride, or groom, or whatever outfit for their weddings," she went on.

D and Mad stared at her and didn't say a word.

She reached to the beer Diesel set beside her and they watched as she lifted it to her mouth, took a pull, set it back down to the deck and kept her eyes aimed away, face tipped to the sun.

"I had a boyfriend who tied me up, and I liked it," she shared.

D felt the growl roll up his throat and realized it wasn't just his own sound he was hearing. The same was coming from Maddox.

They, neither one of them, were fans of anyone touching their Molly, even if it was in the past. It was just how they were, who they were, and who she was to them.

"I started, you know, looking into it, I liked it so much," she continued. "Got some porn. Erotic comic books. Regular books. Erotica. Found out about the Bolt, went there, didn't know what I was doing."

"Baby," Maddox whispered.

She kept her gaze aimed away and took another drag from her beer.

"I was too scared," she carried on after she'd sucked back her brew. "Doms would approach. I was just . . . scared. I never let any of them work me. But I hung out. I watched. I talked to other subs. And everyone, all the female subs, all of them . . . all they could talk about was the mother lode. Getting chosen by Mad and D. And then, the first time I saw you two, I knew why you were the ones everyone wanted."

"Fuck," Diesel muttered.

She turned her head then, caught both of them with a glance of her eyes. "I watched you work a girl."

"Sweetheart," Diesel said gently.

"I wanted her to be me."

Diesel swallowed.

"You were so beautiful, working her, but just being you." Her gaze lighted on D. "Your grin, DD. So cocky. So cute. I wanted so bad for you to tie me up. Tie me up and do dirty things to me, smiling that smile." She turned her attention to Maddox. "You were so dark and scary and handsome. I'd get the shivers, just thinking about you touching me. And you know, I counted. You came to the Bolt nine times before either of you even looked at me. But it was on the twelfth time you were there when I was there that you asked me back to the playrooms."

"Darlin'," Maddox murmured.

"The first Doms I took were you two," she shared.

"We know, baby," Maddox rumbled quietly.

And they did know. They'd had a long conversation before they took her back, starting with safe words and hard limits and finding out they were her firsts.

They'd broken her in gently.

It was the best m/m/f play they'd ever had.

But that was only a small part of the reason why Molly Singer was sitting right there at the edge of the pool her two men had built for her.

She nodded and kept going.

"The first time you worked me, it was so beautiful. I couldn't believe it. I couldn't believe how easy it was with you two, the way you were with me, to fall into it. I felt totally safe with you. You were all about me. All about each other. We were the only three people in the whole, wide world. Just us. It was the most amazing thing I'd ever experienced. So I went home and I prayed. I actually *prayed* you'd pick me again."

Her gaze honed in on Maddox and she carried on.

"And then you called, Maddox. The very next morning. You called and asked if I wanted to go to dinner with you guys. You didn't call and ask me to meet you at the Bolt. You asked me out for a date. After that it wasn't about white picket fences. Then I had dreams no girl ever dreams because no girl could ever think in reality she'd be that lucky. I dreamed you'd make me a part of you two forever and ever."

"And we got that, Molly," Diesel reminded her, now feeling his stomach sink, pissed as shit at himself with what he put his girl, his man, through. "It's all good."

"Rebel told me your mother is gonna call and ask you and me to Thanksgiving," she announced.

D felt his mouth get tight.

He also felt Maddox's eyes cut to him.

"I'll take care of it when she does," Diesel promised.

She sat up, twisted, put both her feet and calves in the water, and looked right in his eyes.

"I do not like them," she declared.

D stared at her because that was so *not* Molly.

She liked everybody.

She was not done shocking the shit out of him.

"I talked to my mother about it and she said that you need to learn that love and loyalty should be rewarded with love and loyalty. If you don't get it, you shouldn't give it. They may think they love you, but they are not loyal to you, so they really don't. Until they can love you as you, I don't want them in my life. I don't want them interfering with my family. I don't want them getting the opportunity to harm you."

"You don't want that, Molly, then I'll make that happen," Diesel replied.

It was then, Molly stared at him.

Neither man broke the silence.

Eventually, Molly did.

"There will always be people in our lives who don't get us, what we have, and they never will. If you told me this was what I'd have, what I'd want, what I'd work to keep strong and good and happy, what I'd cherish, just three years ago, I would have told you you were crazy. What a mess, two men, one woman. How do you raise kids with that? How do you balance it out so there's no jealousy? Where one doesn't feel left out? How do you make love split into three and make it equal? And then we happened and we're a *miracle*. We're so beautiful, we're a *miracle*. We're everything. We have so much to give to each other, it spills over, so our children are going to be so lucky. Just like us. So . . . *fucking* . . . lucky."

Her voice broke on the word "fucking" which meant Maddox called out, soft but firm, "Come here now, baby."

She slid into the water and did a stroke to make it to him, but he'd reached out an arm and hooked it around her waist, gliding her through the water as Diesel shifted positions from his bench to the one Maddox was sitting on.

Mad arranged her in his arms in his lap and Diesel leaned into her, wrapping her legs around his middle.

Diesel laid his hand on her chest. "My shit's done, baby. I'm here with you. I'm not goin' anywhere. I promise that. Promise it, Mol. I know how lucky we are. I know how lucky *I* am and I'm not gonna do anything to fuck that up. Swear it, sweetheart."

"Th-they mess with your head," Molly said.

"Yeah, they did," D admitted. "But if you guys can ride that with me, then I can ride it too."

"Promise that as well, DD," she demanded brokenly, and fuck him. He put her through the wringer. "Promise that to both of us too."

"Shit, I put you through too much," Diesel bit off.

"Stop it, D, and just promise her, yeah?" Maddox rumbled.

Diesel looked at him, nodded. He looked at their Molly, and nodded.

"Promise, baby," he said, eyes back to Mad. "Promise, bud. I'm with you. I'm here, with you. And I'm not going anywhere."

"I love you, DD," Molly blubbered.

He grinned at her, leaning deeper into her and sliding his hand up to curl it around the side of her neck. "I know, and that's good since I love you too."

She bent forward and kissed him, going hard, tangling her tongue to his.

She broke the kiss and turned her head, taking Mad's mouth, giving him the same.

When she broke it off, she whispered, "Now you two."

Their girl, testing him.

Diesel didn't hesitate.

He moved into Mad, who met him halfway. Connection, a stroke of the tongue, but when it ended, Diesel pressed his forehead hard into Mad's before he broke away.

"Happy?" he asked Molly.

She still had bright in her eyes and her smile was kinda wobbly, but it was there.

"Yeah," she answered.

"Anything else you wanna let out after that?" D invited. "And, of course, you reaming Mad about his workout clothes. We leaving the toilet seat up? Does Mad drinking straight out of the juice carton piss you off?"

Her eyes got big and she looked at Maddox. "You drink out of the juice carton?"

"Motherfucker," Mad growled, scowling at Diesel.

D grinned, sat back and massaged Molly's calf. "It's sick, Mad. No one wants your backwash."

"You don't even drink juice," Maddox returned.

"I do," Molly declared.

Maddox looked to her. "Baby, you suck my dick, take my tongue and swallow my cum."

"Backwash is still gross," she replied, and his brows hiked up.

"How?" he asked.

"It just is," she mumbled and gave Diesel big eyes.

D chuckled.

Maddox scowled at him again. "And you're perfect."

"I didn't think so. I thought I was a pain in your asses. But apparently, I'm amazing," D retorted.

"Just to say, you're not amazing right now. Right now you're a pain in my ass," Maddox shot back.

"Let's not fight," Molly put in.

"We're not fighting, sweetheart," Diesel told her. "We're busting Maddox's chops."

"Let's not do that either," Maddox suggested.

Diesel shrugged.

"Text Sixx, tell her Rebel's in town and if she'd down with that, we're all coming for dinner," Molly ordered.

"Will do, Mol," D muttered, reaching a long arm out to nab his beer.

"Get Mol's beer while you're reaching, asshole," Maddox commanded.

"He's so bossy," Molly murmured in a tease as D disengaged from her legs to do that.

"Don't complain, darlin', or I might stop being bossy when you like me bossy," Mad warned.

"Forget I said anything," Molly replied quickly.

Maddox chuckled.

D grabbed her beer and went back to his people.

They wound up in each other again, sitting in their pool, drinking beer, shooting the shit, being together.

Diesel did not look forward to the time his mother drew up her courage to make her phone call.

But for the first time since . . . well, fuck—since forever, he wasn't beat down by the idea of what he'd have to face, and worse, what *they* would, his man and his woman, when he made shit clear.

It wouldn't be fun.

It would be ugly.

But they'd make it through to the other side.

Together.

And it would never just be this, the three of them, knowing it was right, getting why it was right, having it all. Other people's shit would always try to press in.

But now Diesel understood.

For them, the ones who mattered, it would always only be just this.

Their three, knowing what they had was right.

Getting why.

And having it all.

UNFORTUNATELY, DIESEL DIDN'T HAVE TO wait a lot longer for his mother to draw up the courage to make her call.

It was late the next afternoon, twenty minutes after he got home, when he was out of the shower, washing the day's dirt, road, and sweat off him. He was in cutoff sweats, a loose tee, hitting the kitchen, about to pop a beer and wait for Mad and Mol to get home, which would be imminently.

The jacked-up coward in him saw the name Mom on his phone and he honest to Christ wanted to let it go to voicemail.

He didn't.

He had no idea how this was going to go. He'd never let his mind wander to that place of how he would want to do this. Not the dream of sitting his parents down, sharing a few truths, working them through their issues and accepting their hugs and declarations of, "We love you no matter what." Not the nightmare of sitting them down, giving it to them straight, and eating their shit.

But it was going to happen. He knew it even before Tommy was outed. And he'd dreaded it after Tommy was outed.

It had always just been a matter of time.

He couldn't run from it anymore.

He had a ring to buy.

(Or, half of one.)

"Yo, Ma," he answered.

"Hey, sweetie, uh . . . how are you?"

She was always hesitant when she asked that question, and a lot of other times besides, which drove him up the wall.

He was her son, for fuck's sake. He wasn't going to say, "I'm great, Mom, the bi-life is awesome. Maddox jacked me off in the shower this morning, fingering Molly until she came with me. I returned the favor by dropping to my knees on the tile and sucking him off while Mol made out with him. It was spectacular. Wassup with you?"

"Good, Mom. Great. Everything's awesome. How are you?"

"Your dad and I are doing well. Your dad's looking forward to retirement. Only eight months to go now," she answered.

"Cool," D muttered, opening the fridge and grabbing a beer.

"And, uh, well, Gunner's not doing too good. He lost another job," she shared.

Not a surprise.

Gunner got canned on a regular basis, mostly because he hadn't learned yet that not everyone was going to put up with him running his mouth.

The man was thirty-four years old.

And Diesel was realizing he'd never learn.

"He'll find something, though," his mom said hurriedly. "He always does."

"Yeah," D replied, popping the cap just as he heard the back door open.

The garage door hadn't gone up.

That meant Maddox.

His eyes went to the mouth of the hall as he put his beer to his lips.

"So, you and Molly haven't been out to visit in a while," she noted carefully.

Maddox rounded the corner and the instant he saw D, he grinned and jerked his chin up.

"Mom," he said into the phone, and Maddox stopped dead, his brows popping before they dropped and his eyes narrowed.

Fuck, just that, he looked capable of killing somebody.

It was insanely hot.

"Molly's never been out there," Diesel went on.

And she hadn't. The only times Molly had met his parents were when they'd come out to Phoenix for a bike rally and Molly, Mad and him had been dating and another time after they'd moved in together and his folks had come out for the same rally.

His dad was a biker.

Gunner was a biker.

Maddox and Diesel would both have bikes if, first, they weren't all in to fix up the house, and second, if Molly didn't lose her mind at the mention of them buying "death on two wheels" (her words).

"Well then," he could actually hear her pulling herself together, forcing her voice stronger, "it's high time she came out. You two have been living together for a while so it's clear where this is going. And Thanksgiving is the only day of the year dedicated to family so that's the perfect opportunity for us all to get together and have the chance to get to know her better."

He could argue about Thanksgiving being the only day of the year dedicated to family, but he didn't get into that. He watched Mad get close and lean a hip against the counter by D.

"Mom—" D started.

"No excuses, Diesel," she cut in. "There's plenty of time for you both to ask for vacation and buy tickets. And you should have a word with your sister. She's hemming and hawing and I want her at my table too. All my babies all together. It'll be the first time in years."

Diesel looked in Maddox's eyes.

"Mom—" he said low, trying again, but that was as far as she got.

"You can do that for me. You can do that for your father. And Diesel, you *should*."

Diesel lifted a hand, curled it around the front of Maddox's throat, watched Mad's eyes flare, go warm, a muscle flex up his jaw, a crush of feeling pour out of him.

He'd take this for me. He'd do this for me. If it was at all in his power, he'd save me from this.

Diesel dropped his hand.

"Molly and I aren't coming without Maddox," he announced.

Maddox fisted his hand in D's tee at his stomach and murmured, "Buddy."

Diesel kept staring in his eyes.

Verna Stapleton was deathly silent.

"Do you get me, Ma?" Diesel asked.

"I cannot understand why you'd want your roommate to—"

"He's not our roommate, Mom, and you know it," Diesel said gently.

"He's—"

Before she could say shit that might make his head explode or take this to a place neither of them could pull back from, he interrupted her. "I come with Molly and Maddox or I'm not there at all. You think on that, Mom. You talk to Dad. Unless they're both invited, and *welcome*, with no bullshit, no asshole remarks, none of that crap, we're not there. Are you understanding what I'm saying?"

"I absolutely am not, Diesel Joshua," she snapped.

"Then I'll share this. Maddox and I are buying a ring for Molly. We'll be having a commitment ceremony in front of our family and our friends.

And we'll be together, building a family together, the three of us, until we die," he stated, then gentled his tone. "I'm sorry to do this over the phone, Ma, but you're most a continent away and it shoulda been said four years ago. Even earlier. There's never gonna be a good time to—"

"That's not even *legal*," she spat.

"No, it isn't. And that doesn't matter."

"It does in the eyes of God."

"Maybe your God. Mine digs what He gave us and it's all cool."

"All cool with what? What is *He* all cool with, Diesel?" she demanded.

"You know, Mom."

"I do not."

"Ma, I'm bi. Maddox is not my roommate. He's my man like Molly's my woman. We're together, all of us, together. All three. We're in love, living together, building a life together, committing to each other and making a family together."

A hissing whisper of a reply, "I cannot believe my son is saying these things to me."

Diesel didn't have a reply to that.

At the pause, Maddox tugged on his shirt, bringing him closer.

D lifted a hand again, squeezed the side of his neck, left his hand there, and nodded to share he was good.

Mad didn't move away.

His mother broke the silence.

"Well, you can rest assured that man will not be invited *or* welcome at your father's and my table."

"Yeah," Diesel muttered, "I figured that."

Her voice was rising, hysteria sliding in. "You've just *destroyed* your mother. You've just *destroyed me*! And all you can say is, 'Yeah, I figured that'?"

"Ma, how does this destroy you?" he asked quietly. "I'm still me. Molly's still Molly. And Maddox is—"

"Don't say that man's name to me!" she shouted.

Oh hell no.

Diesel broke away from Mad, turning. "Then we're done."

"*We're not done!*" she shrieked, the sound so piercing he had to take the phone from his ear. "*You're my son!*"

"Think on that, Ma," he replied softly. "Think on those words. Please."

"What's that supposed to mean?" she demanded.

"Think on it. Calm down. I'll talk to you later."

"Your father is going to lose his mind, Diesel. He's going to come undone. I *knew* it. I *knew* we should have never let you be friends with that Tommy Barnes. He *stained* you. He *polluted* you."

Oh *hell no*.

"Stop. Fucking. Talking," Diesel snarled.

His mother shut up and the silence was deafening.

Diesel didn't give a shit.

"Think on this. Calm down. And when you're calm, I'll talk to you. But I'm not listening to any more of this. I love you. I hate this is hurting you. But you don't understand *why* I hate it. And the why of that kills me and has for years. Think on that too, Ma. I'll talk to you later."

He said that and then he disconnected.

He also turned off his ringer and tossed his phone on the counter.

He then dropped his head to look at his feet.

He barely got in that position before Maddox's hand curled warm on the back of his neck.

He said nothing, didn't force D to look at him, just held on.

But Diesel sensed him moving and he'd know how when he heard Maddox say, "Mol? Yeah, baby, you on your way home?" Pause. "Okay, D's mom called and it went as expected." Pause. "Quiet night. Just giving you a heads up. We gotta look after D."

Diesel lifted his head to look at Mad, but Maddox's hand at his neck didn't go anywhere.

"See you soon. Love you too," he finished and then he disconnected. "You wanna talk about it?" Maddox asked.

"Absolutely not," D answered.

"You wanna get drunk?" Mad asked.

"Absolutely," D answered.

Maddox let him go, muttering, "I'll get the bourbon."

D watched him head to the cupboard where they kept their liquor.

"Mad?" he called.

Hand to the handle on the cabinet, Maddox twisted around to look at him.

"I don't want you to feel what you're feeling," Diesel told him.

Mad dropped his hand from the handle and turned fully to Diesel.

"What am I feeling, bud?" he asked quietly.

"Pissed. Upset. Worried about me. Concerned you're the reason I'm losing my family."

Maddox nodded. "Yeah, I'm feelin' all that."

D clenched his teeth, his fists, and looked away.

"D," Maddox called.

Diesel looked back.

"It'll pass."

"I'm the reason I'm losing my family, Maddox," he pointed out. "I fell in love with you because you're you. You didn't make me fall in love with you, outside of the fact you were just you and that shit happened. But I'm the man I am so it *could* happen."

"Brother, your *family* is the reason you're losing your family. It has dick to do with you. Or me. Or anyone, but them. Honest to Christ, there could be no me, just Mol, and Molly could be Catholic, or a Jew, and your mother would behave like that. That's who she is. That's how she thinks. I just thank fuck she made you and you turned out different."

His phone vibrated on the counter, both men looked to it, and D read his father was calling.

"I forget, is the iPhone waterproof yet? 'Cause for tonight, that piece of shit needs to be at the bottom of the pool," Diesel grumbled.

"Baby," Maddox called, sounding amused.

D turned again to him.

"We will get through this," he stated firmly, no longer sounding amused.

Diesel looked him in the eye for a beat, two, then three.

"Yeah," he said, but the word was drowned out with the back door being thrown open loudly, racing feet heard on wood floors and Molly appeared in the room, hair flying.

She skidded to a stop, looked to D, Mad, D, Mad and back to D.

"You okay, baby?" she asked on a rush, breathless.

"I am now, you bein' all cute and everything," he replied.

She stared hard at him and looked to Maddox. "Is he okay?"

"He said he was, darlin'," Maddox answered, back to sounding amused.

"You called me, like, five minutes ago saying we had to look after D," she reminded him.

"Well, we're dudes. We talked shit out. It's all cool now," Maddox told her.

"That's impossible," she returned. "It was *five minutes ago*."

"You want me to be all busted up my ma's messed up in the head?" Diesel asked.

Molly shifted her attention to him, her face softening. "No, honey, of course not."

D grinned at her. "Come here, sweetheart. I'm teasing you. I'm all torn up. I need some Molly love."

She tossed her purse on the kitchen table and moved to him.

He wrapped his arms around her.

She wrapped hers around him.

"There, all better," he murmured to the top of her head.

"You're a jerk, D," she mumbled into his chest.

"Yup, an *awesome* jerk," he agreed.

Her arms gave him a squeeze.

Diesel looked over her head to Maddox.

"You were getting bourbon?" he prompted.

"On it," Maddox muttered.

D watched him then dropped his face back into Molly's hair, closed his eyes and breathed deep.

"You sure you're okay?" she asked his chest.

No.

But he was sure he would be.

"Just keep holding on, Molly, and I will be."

She kept holding on.

It didn't take long for him to be proved right.

Molly love, a shot of Jack from Maddox, and it was all good.

Mostly.

"HEY. THIS IS A SURPRISE."

"Hey, yeah. Sorry, is it too late?"

"Nope, the princesses from hell are asleep and I'm out on the back deck with a Jack and Coke so it's all good. What's up?" Tommy asked.

D sat in Mad's slider, staring at the light glowing up from their pool, shining on the big pots around it, the squat stand of short palms off to the side, up into the night sky.

They'd rocked that pool.

"Just callin' to give you a heads up, Maddox and I are buying Molly a ring. We'll probably have our ceremony sometime next year. That's up to Molly and whatever planning she's gotta do. But I'd dig it if you and Harvey and the kids would think about making the trek. It'd be cool, you were here for that."

"You . . . whoa . . . so you . . . wow. Uh. You guys are making it official?"

"The only ring that we think works for Molly cost thirteen K so as soon as we can swing that fucker, yeah."

"Your folks know?"

"Told Mom today."

"Ah. Right," he whispered.

"So, think about comin' out, yeah? I want you to meet them," Diesel said.

"Diesel," Tommy replied low.

Hearing his tone, Diesel bent over, closing his eyes, lifting his hand and rubbing the back of his head.

But he didn't say anything.

"Let me guess, words with your mother didn't go well," Tommy surmised.

"Ma called Maddox 'that man,' and that was far from the worst of it," D shared.

"Yeah, Harvey got a lot of 'that mans' from my mom too after she semi-let me back into her life, but before the kids started coming. Now I'm trying to break her of asking him about every fucking handbag she wants to try to convince Dad she can buy, like every gay on the planet knows how a woman should accessorize. She can't wrap her mind around the fact that he wouldn't know Louis Vuitton from a Kmart special even though she'd never ask me that shit and I *do* know LV from Kmart because LV is life."

D lifted his head, dropped his hand, looked at the pool and grinned.

"If they don't get there," Tommy said quietly, "fuck 'em. But they might get there, Diesel. When it all came out, my father told me the sight of me made him sick. And now he golfs with Harvey and his two granddaughters are the light of his life."

"Harvey golfs?" D asked.

"Took it up for something to do with Dad, likes it. What can I say? Tell him all the time golf is total pussy. He gets in my face about calling shit 'pussy' and how I gotta watch that or we'll unconsciously share with our daughters that 'pussy' is weak and I'm being a chauvinist. Serves me right for marrying an east coast liberal. He won't even let me have guns. It's a nightmare."

"Feel bad for you, bro," D said through a chuckle.

"Don't feel too bad. He might be an east coast liberal but he fucks like a redneck and is built like a pro wrestler so I might not have a handgun in the house to protect my family and defend my property but there are tradeoffs where I'm not complaining."

"That puts an end to that pity party," D joked, but drew in breath and got serious. "I hated what you went through."

"I know you did," Tommy replied.

"I wish that I'd—"

"Man, there was nothin' for you to do. That wasn't your deal. It was mine. And you stood beside me the only way you could. It meant a lot to me, Diesel. You could have turned your back. And coming from you, that would have been worse than all the other assholes who turned their backs, because you were you and you were who you were to me."

"Yeah," Diesel muttered.

"Also," Tommy continued, "seein' as it would be you gettin' where I was at, walking right into the closet and shutting the door, shutting me out. You might not have shouted from the rooftops we were fucking each other stupid any chance we got, but I don't give a shit you didn't. What purpose would it have served? It wasn't your time and now I know how you felt back then because I hear the shit comin' at me from whatever you took from your mom and I wish I could do something about it. But I can't. Except to let you know that love always wins, Diesel. In the end, and it took time, and it wasn't without pain, my parents pulled their heads out of their asses and it wasn't because they wanted to be a part of their granddaughters' lives. It was because they missed their son. And your folks might get there. I don't know. The only thing I *do* know is, if they don't, there's no love in that, so there's no love lost, so you really haven't lost anything but shit that weighs down your mind and heart and your soul. Just let that weight go. Live the light. It's not easy to get to that point, but when you do, it's all good."

Halfway through this, the back door opened and Mad came through.

He was on his phone, speaking quietly, but walking Diesel's way.

"Now that you've laid the wisdom on me, and no fuckin' with you, Tommy, I heard you and I appreciate it, but are you gonna answer my question?" D asked as Maddox sat in the slider D usually used.

"What question?"

"You haulin' ass out here for our commitment ceremony?"

"Oh. Right. Yeah. I'd be down with that. You could meet Harvey and the girls. Harvey could golf. I could have a variety of opportunities to give him shit about golfing. Total win. But do me a favor, have it when it's not a million degrees. It gets cold as fuck in Boston in the winter. It'd sweeten the deal we could vacation in the desert when everyone here is freezing their tits off."

"I'll put that to Molly," D replied, holding Maddox's gaze. "But Mad came out and I think something's up. Sorry, but gotta let you go."

"No worries. Glad you called. See you for your Valentine's Day or Halloween or Thanksgiving commitment ceremony next year."

"Fuck off, and yeah, I hope you do. Later, brother."

"Later, Diesel."

They disconnected and Diesel raised his brows when he heard Maddox say, "Yeah, okay . . . but D's off the phone. Yeah?"

He listened for a second then held his phone out to Diesel.

Diesel saw on the screen it said Mom.

He looked straight at Mad but took the phone and put it to his ear.

"Hey, Erin, everything cool?"

"You are loved," she stated clearly, forcefully and more than a little pissed off.

"Erin," he said quietly.

"And they're jackasses," she snapped.

"Honey," he murmured.

"So . . . so . . . so . . ." she stammered, "*fuck them*," she bit out.

D pressed his lips together so he wouldn't burst out laughing.

Erin wasn't immune to a swear word but he didn't think he'd ever heard her drop the f-bomb.

"I'd adopt you but that might get a bit weird, me adopting you when you're going to be my son's husband," she declared.

"Yeah, that might get a bit weird," he agreed.

"But whatever, you're my son anyway."

Diesel shut his eyes tight and dropped his head again.

Shit, that felt good.

"You hear that, Diesel?" she asked irately.

"I heard it, Erin."

"Love you, boy. Bob sends his love too, I'm sure, but right now he's building a ship in a bottle or putting together some model airplane or I don't know what the heck he's doing in his man cave. I'm worried he's addicted to sniffing glue. Everything he does is all about the glue. But at least it frees me from having to fight to watch my programs so I let him. Tell Molly I send her my love and Maddox too. I'll make my Mexican lasagna for you soon. Love you. Bye."

And with that, as was Erin's way when she was done saying what she had to say, she was gone.

He opened his eyes, watched the screen blank out, lifted his head and handed the phone to Maddox.

"Mexican lasagna soon, brother," he told him.

"Excellent," Maddox replied, then immediately asked, "Who'd you call?"

"Tommy."

Maddox nodded like he totally understood, and D had a feeling he did.

"He good?" Mad queried.

Diesel nodded. "Yeah. And thinking about bringing his brood out here for our ceremony, if we have it when it's cold in Boston."

"We totally have to have it in the summer. No one will show but locals. Less people we gotta feed, more money for the honeymoon."

Diesel grinned at him but felt the grin fade.

"Your mom rocks, bud," he told Mad something he definitely knew.

"Yeah," Mad agreed.

The door opened, Molly came out with a look on her face that D wasn't sure how to read and she came right to him, collapsing in his lap in another way he wasn't sure how to read.

He still wrapped his arms around her.

She didn't keep him guessing.

She grabbed his face on either side and said, "Right, okay, she's mad and I don't know your mother's number, so I couldn't give it to her when she demanded it, but Mom wants her number and she's pretty ticked. In other words, if your mom is listed, shit might happen, and I'll apologize in advance for Mom calling her and telling her to go fuck herself."

Diesel stared down at her pretty face.

But whatever, you're my son anyway.

I'll apologize in advance for Mom calling her and telling her to go fuck herself.

He burst out laughing.

Molly was smiling tentatively at him when he quit.

He gathered her closer and she let his face go and snuggled in when he did.

"So, babe, this commitment ceremony we're doing, is it gonna be a summer thing or a winter thing?" Diesel asked.

"Totally winter. That way everyone will want to come to escape the snow and it'll be a huge party," Molly answered.

D looked to Mad.

Mad sat back, shaking his head but smiling.

D sat back, holding Molly close and smiling.

And yeah.

What happened with his mother happened.

And now it was just this.

Their three, knowing what they had was right.
Getting why.
And having it all.

TWELVE

Freedom, Love and Family of the Heart

Maddox

B&J JUMPED AT ME AS *DM. Start at the Bolt weekend after Rebel leaves. Get the money. Get the ring. We'll give it to her this weekend while Reb's here. Reb'll get off on that.*

D's bossy-as-fuck text came while Maddox was leaving the gym to head home the day after the shit hit with D's mom.

He beeped the locks on his truck, opened it up, tossed his workout bag across to the passenger seat, and before he hauled himself up, he leaned a shoulder against the side of the cab and texted back, *Not asking Mol while Reb's here.*

He pulled himself into the cab and had the truck on, AC cranking, when he got back, *Why not?*

Celebration, D, as in no holds barred. Not hours. DAYS, Mad replied.

He'd put the truck into gear and was about to pull out of his parking spot when he got, *Gotcha.*

He grinned, drove out of the spot and was waiting for the road to clear in order to turn into it when his cab rang.

He looked to the dash.

The number was not programmed into his phone.

But it had a 317 area code.

"Shit, fuck," he bit off, taking the turn.

Which one was it and how did they get his number?

He should blow it off. Not answer. Block the caller.

But maybe this could lead to something.

Something for Diesel.

He took the call.

"Maddox," he said as answer.

There was nothing.

Good, maybe they'd lose courage, hang up.

"Maddox?"

Shit.

They didn't hang up.

And it was D's dad.

"Yeah?" he faked not knowing who it was in hopes the man would chicken out.

"This is Gene Stapleton. Diesel's father."

"Yeah, Gene. I know who you are," Maddox said on a sigh.

"Are you . . . away from my son?" Gene asked.

"For the next ten minutes. I'm heading home."

"We need to talk."

The man said no more.

Maddox pulled his shit together to be cool and prompted, "I'm right here, Gene. What do you have to say?"

"You need to leave our son alone."

Fuck.

"Gene—"

"You've got some kinda hold on him I don't get. But for him, you need to let go. You need to move out. Let him and his girl be. Let him be who he—"

"First, Gene, the house is mine. I own it."

It took a second for him to recover from that before he said, "Then you need to let them move out."

"Right, I own it but we all live there, it's a home we share and will continue to share until we have children. Then we'll probably need a bigger place."

"You . . . you're gonna . . . *have kids*?"

He sounded like he was choking.

Shit, this was actually kinda fun.

"At least two, maybe four," Mad shared cheerfully.

"Jesus, that's . . . Jesus, it's—"

"Second," Maddox interrupted, "I don't have to tell you that your son is thirty-two years old. He's mature, intelligent, quick as a whip. He's also strong-willed and knows his own mind. There is no way anyone could make him do something he doesn't want to do."

"It is not *my* boy who spoke to his mother the way Diesel did yesterday, saying the things he said," Gene retorted.

That's funny, I watched your *boy do just that*, Maddox thought.

But he said, "I'm not sure we're gonna get anywhere with this conversation, Gene, so maybe we should just leave this here, you and Verna think on things a little further, and when you come to terms with how it is, you give Diesel a call."

"Diesel's confused," he decreed.

"Diesel isn't confused."

"My son is not one of those . . ." Gene trailed off.

"What?" Maddox asked.

Gene didn't answer.

"One of those what, Gene?" Maddox pushed.

"He's not one of your kind," Gene spat.

Right.

He was wrong.

This was not fun.

"And I thank God every day you're wrong," Maddox returned. "Now I got a feeling this is just going to deteriorate so we should end it here."

"This is tearing his mother apart," Gene announced.

"This is gonna make me sound all kinds of asshole to a man like you, Gene, but I have to tell you I have little compassion for that. There is no reason why this should mean anything to you or Verna outside making you both thrilled your son is happy and he's found two people who love him very much. But I have a feeling that's not gonna get through to you. Maybe someday it will. Until that happens, let's all live our own lives, yeah?"

"It took a lot for me to stop Diesel's brother from drivin' right out there and showin' you exactly what we think about this . . . fuckin' . . . *shit*."

"Glad you stopped him, Gene, 'cause once Gunner got here, that wouldn't have gone too good for him."

"Diesel's close to his older brother. Looks up to him. Always wanted to be like him. Gunner'd be able to talk some sense into my boy, so I think you're wrong. I think if Gunner made it there, it wouldn't go too good for *you*."

"Trust me on this, you don't want to find out the way that'd go."

"Feel like lettin' him head on out there now," Gene sniped.

"Again, I'd advise you not do that."

"And what you gonna do, a fuckin' pansy faggot? My Gunner'd wipe the—"

Maddox had never . . .

Not once . . .

Not in his life . . .

Been called that word.

"We're done," Maddox growled. "I'm hanging up and I'm blocking you so don't waste the time calling back. And I swear to *fuck*, Gene, you call D and feed him any of this shit, it's another Stapleton who's gonna have to pull back a man in his life from going fucking *apeshit*. I don't give a fuck you're an old, tired, bigoted asshole. You've met me. So you've seen me. You think about that. I'd break you in two. And I'd have decency on my side and I'd be fighting for my family. Never met Gunner, but with both those at my back, he thinks to fuck with Diesel, he wouldn't stand a fucking chance."

He landed that, ended the call on his steering wheel, snatched up his phone, and did something Molly would have fits over. He drove while he engaged his phone to find that number and block it.

Only then did he toss the phone on his workout bag in the passenger seat and fully concentrate on driving.

He had five minutes to get his head together so he didn't bring that shit home to Diesel and Molly.

Because he had absolutely no intention of saying dick to either of them about that call. If by some slim chance Gene, Verna or Gunner shared about it, it wouldn't take much to explain why he didn't.

But right now, they were in the best place they'd ever been. With Barclay and Josh taking him on at the Bolt, D was feeling in the zone he could do his part to get Molly's ring and texting Mad to get the money and pick it up.

That bullshit didn't factor in their lives until it shoved its way in in a way that Maddox couldn't keep it out.

He made it home, parked, let himself inside and saw D and Molly camped out on the couch, eating chips and salsa, watching TV.

"Hey, honey!" Molly chirped.

"Yo, bro," D called.

"Hey," Maddox called back, hooked a right, hit the laundry room, dumped his bag and then retraced his steps to the hall. When he was about to pass the couch, he pointed to D, "You, bedroom."

Molly rolled her eyes. "I suppose the little woman stays out here and makes dinner."

"Doin' him fast, later doin' you slow, that later being after D orders us Thai," Maddox told her.

She clapped and her face lit up. "I love Thai."

Like he didn't know that.

He grinned over his shoulder at her as he moved down the hall to the bedroom.

He went right to the bathroom.

D came in slowly, looking around the room before he caught Mad's eye.

"Am I coming in the sink again?" he asked.

Maddox smiled at him and ordered, "Shut the door."

D gave him a look but twisted at the waist, reached out a long arm and shut the door.

When he turned back, Maddox announced, "The Phoenician, long weekend. We'll take a Monday off. Room service with champagne when we ask her. Marathon fuck session. We'll set up some spa shit for her on Saturday. She gets back, more marathon fucking all weekend long. When you and I got our days off cleared, I'll call her boss to sort her day off. I'll get the ring. You handle flowers and chocolate and shit like that. And ask Sixx what spa shit we should do for her."

"I'm not sure Sixx is a spa chick. Holly might be better for that," Diesel noted.

"Find some other chick. Holly'll totally let it slip just so she can be the one to share the news and be in on something in order to make it partially about her when it's not about her at all. And not either of the moms. They'll be so excited, who knows what they'll fuckin' do."

"Yeah, didn't think about that. Maybe if Sixx doesn't know spa shit, she knows some other chick who knows spa shit."

Something surprising occurred to Maddox.

"Other than Sixx, do we know any other women?" he asked.

"Not ones we haven't fucked," Diesel answered.

"We're not asking some chick we fucked for spa recos for Molly."

"Word."

"So it's Sixx," Maddox decided.

Diesel nodded.

"We sorted with that?" Maddox asked.

Slowly, Diesel grinned. "Sounds like a plan."

"Right."

D tipped his head to the side. "Now you fuckin' me, or what?"

"I asked you in here to talk about how we're gonna give Molly her ring."

"And we talked about that, so you gonna fuck me or what? Alternate, am I fuckin' you or what?"

Slowly, Maddox grinned. "You want me to bend over the sink or the bed?"

"I don't give a shit about locale. I just give a shit about getting a fast, hot fuck."

Maddox dipped his voice low. "Then show me your cock, baby."

Diesel started to do just that, the problem was, when Maddox pulled his jeans down, his big, hard dick sprang free and Diesel caught sight of it.

So apparently, Diesel felt he was forced to push Mad up on the counter, face to face, so he could be face to something else and go down on him a while before he fucked him with Mad's ass to the edge of the counter, knees up and cocked, his legs spread wide. Maddox's hands were pressed to the counter, holding himself steady. D had one hand jacking Mad's cock, the other flat against the mirror over Mad's shoulder, bracing.

They were both close, to each other and to orgasm, Diesel jacking him hard and fucking him harder, their lips locked, when the door opened.

They broke the kiss and turned their heads to look at the door to see

Molly there, hands on her hips.

"Jeez, you guys are taking forever," Molly complained.

"Five minutes," Maddox grunted.

Her eyes moved over them, ending on D's hand on the mirror.

"You're gonna leave a handprint," she declared.

"Baby, stop being cute, I'm losing my concentration," Diesel growled.

Maddox started laughing.

He stopped when he groaned as he started coming.

Diesel turned to his man, fucked his ass, milked his dick and kissed the orgasm rolling from his lips.

Within seconds, with that last, Maddox returned the favor.

They were breathing in each other's faces, foreheads touching, Maddox looking close into D's blue eyes, thinking about Molly's speech by the pool about how lucky they were.

Just weeks ago, he was worried they were falling apart.

And now they were closer than ever.

"Good?" Diesel asked quietly.

"Yeah, man," Maddox answered.

In unison, they turned their heads to see Molly still there.

"We're done. Happy now?" Diesel inquired.

"No. Because you both just came hard. You better have saved some up because if I don't get it good later, *from both of you*, I'll be peeved."

And with that, she flounced off.

Maddox wondered if she knew that they knew her bullshit drama was all show.

Seriously, the woman didn't even try to hide her smile as she turned away.

Mad wasn't sure, he didn't remember, but he didn't think he'd ever had D slip out of him while Mad's body was shaking with laughter.

Or feeling D slip free with D's body shaking with it.

But he'd never forget that moment, that time, all that goodness, making plans with D on how to give Molly her ring, a quick fuck with his boy, a dose of cute from their girl.

Never.

Diesel

THAT FRIDAY AFTERNOON, D STOOD at the opening of Gate B, Terminal 4, Sky Harbor Airport, scanning the groups of people the hall coughed up until her red head came his way.

No one in the family knew where Rebel got her thick, waving, dark red hair, but her light blue eyes were the same as D's, which were the same as their father's, so their mom stepping out was probably off the table.

She was grinning at him as she was practically skipping to him, her pretty face prettier than he remembered.

Then again, after they were apart for a while, when he saw her again, he always thought that shit.

But even with the grin, she couldn't quite hide she was taking him in with a focus that was a lot more than Rebel being happy to see her big brother.

"God, you're good-lookin'," she declared when she was three feet away.

Then she threw herself in his arms.

Those arms closed around her, holding her tight.

"Hey, babe," he muttered into the hair above her ear.

They moved apart, but held on, Rebel pressing her hands against his shoulders affectionately, then clasping onto the sides of his neck, up to his cheeks, then to his shoulders again where she squeezed.

All this while her eyes did a scan of his face, taking in every inch.

"Mom called about seventeen thousand times," she declared.

Yup.

Not a surprise.

No beating around the bush for Rebel Eugenie Stapleton.

"Mm-hmm," he muttered.

"I wanted to call *you* about seven million times, but I figured I'd be down here so we could talk in person."

Two could not beat around the bush.

"They know I'm bi. They know I'm committing to Molly and Maddox.

And they're not super hip on these ideas," he announced.

"So you went with ye ole 'tell the mom unit over the phone' route rather than having a sit down," she remarked, and D got tense.

"Molly's ring costs almost as much as a car. I'm not wasting money and vacation time on a plane ticket just to have them be assholes to my face."

"D," she said softly, "not givin' you shit. But just to say, of the thousand of those seventeen thousand phone calls that I took from Mom, she's degenerated from bein' pissed on the whole about this sitch to being pissed on the whole about this sitch *and* the lack of respect that you threw that out over the phone."

"Not surprised she's finding new ways to work herself up," he replied. "As for me, I'm still just pissed on the whole they haven't sent a fruit basket to share how thrilled they are I've set up house with the people I love."

She grinned up at him. "A fruit basket?"

He burst out laughing.

He also let her go but tossed an arm around her shoulders, feeling hers slide along his waist, and he directed her to the escalators that led to baggage claim.

"So this ring?" she asked when they were on the escalator.

D dug out his phone, went to Mad's text string and scrolled up.

By the time he got through all the stuff in between, they'd located her carousel and were standing by it.

He showed the picture of the ring to his sister.

Rebel took the phone, her brows went up, her eyes got wide, and her smile was huge before she said, "Holy crap, that's sheer perfection."

"I know," he agreed.

She handed him back his phone, still smiling, and again scanning his face.

"You seem good."

"I am good," he confirmed.

"Last time we talked . . ." She didn't finish that.

"Last time we talked I was workin' through some shit. I worked through it. Now I'm tight."

"Yeah?" she asked softly.

He looked in her eyes. "I'm happy as fuck. I get it now."

She moved closer to him. "Get what?"

"How Tommy was when it all came out all those years ago. How it was this huge, nasty drama to everyone but him. How to him it was like, 'Right, that's your damage, I'm not gonna let it damage me.' How that was a relief. Like lifting off a weight. Talked to him after I told Ma and that's what he called it. A weight. You live with it, you don't realize how much it's holding you down. Until it's gone. And it's gone. And that feels fuckin' great."

"That's awesome," Rebel said quietly, still working her scan.

"It's more, Reb," he shared. "The weight is about me, yeah. It was bringing me down. But that wasn't the important part. It was weighing on Mol and Mad too. The longer I hid who they were to me, the heavier it got for all of us, and that was what was draggin' my shit so low. Freeing myself was freeing them. And that's the best part, not that I'm happy without anything dragging at it. That we all are."

His sister's face finally cleared.

"Then that's super, freaking, crazy awesome," Rebel replied.

He hooked an arm around her shoulders, brought her in, kissed her forehead, then shoved her face in his chest.

"Glad I worked my shit out before you got down here, so it could just be good," he said in her hair.

She tipped her head back. "I am too, even though I would have been good helpin' you get to where you needed to be."

"I know, honey," he murmured.

She gave him a squeeze. They let each other go. And not long later, the carousel started rolling.

When she went for a bag, D muscled her out of the way, nabbed it, tossed the strap over his shoulder, his arm over hers, and guided her to his truck.

The airport was barely fifteen minutes from their house and they gabbed about nothing all the way there.

And like she was watching (which she probably was), Molly shot out the side door of the garage before he had his truck fully stopped.

She was in Rebel's space, barely enough room for his sister to get out of the door she'd opened, jumping up and down, clapping and shouting,

"You're here!"

"In the flesh, sister," Rebel replied, sliding out and into Molly's arms.

They hugged. They did that swaying side to side thing chicks did. They laughed at nothing.

"Jesus, Mol, let a man stand a chance," Maddox growled from behind them.

And only then did Molly let Rebel step out from the opened door to Diesel's truck.

Maddox enveloped D's sister in his arms, kissing the side of her head, then saying, "Fuck, good to see you, Rebel."

Rebel held tight and replied, "You too, Mad. Totally."

Molly shut Rebel's door. Diesel grabbed his sister's bag. And they all moved into the house, Molly babbling a mile a minute, Rebel attached to Maddox like D held her, his arm around her shoulders, hers around his waist.

"Not to be rude, but I hope you're gonna feed me because I'm starved," Rebel declared.

"*Chile queso* coming right up!" Molly announced, hustling to the kitchen.

"We'll get some food in you, get you to the Valley Ho to check in, then we're going to dinner," Diesel told her.

"You can have my car while you're here, if you want," Molly put in, dumping things from the fridge onto the counter.

"We can also play chauffer if you're not down with that," Maddox put in.

"I'll Uber it when we meet up so I won't put you guys out," Rebel said, having pulled her purse off her shoulder, her phone out of her purse, her head tipped down, her brows drawn as she stared at the screen.

"Everything good?" D asked, coming out of the fridge himself with a couple of beers, seeing her expression and thinking that took precedence over telling her she wasn't gonna Uber shit.

"Yeah," Rebel answered distractedly. "Got the text dumps after I turned on my phone when we landed." She looked up, pinned a smile on her face and went on, "Was too excited to see my bro to pay attention."

He wasn't a fan of the way she'd pinned that smile on her face.

"And it's all good?" he pushed.

She tipped her head to the beer bottles in his hand. "It will be, if one of those is for me."

D gave her a look, transferred that look to Maddox who was studying Rebel. He felt Diesel's gaze and turned his attention to D, dipping his chin meaningfully.

He didn't like Rebel's pinned smile either.

"Just to confirm, Rebel, you like it hot like we like it hot, right?" Molly said to a bowl she was dumping shit into.

"Girl, I totally like it hot," Rebel replied.

Diesel handed her the beer and let shit go.

He knew what was happening.

His family knew Rebel was down for the weekend and she was getting fed all the shit.

But now it was time for beers, *queso* dip, family time and winding down, taking her mind off of it.

Saving his sister from that shit would come later.

"THEY'RE UP IN HER SHIT," Maddox declared.

"Mm-hmm," Molly agreed.

"I know," Diesel muttered.

They were all naked. In bed. It was dark. Rebel was at the Valley Ho. They'd just finished fucking, cleaning Molly up. Now Mol was tucked up, back to front, with Maddox, tangled up with D at her front, Mad's arm draped over both of them, D's arm draped over Maddox's, palming his man's ass.

"I asked, she wouldn't give," Diesel told them.

"I asked, and she wouldn't give it to me either," Molly said quietly.

"That means not only are they ranting all their bullshit hurt and anger to her, they're probably trying to push her to talk some sense into me or get me to come home so they can do it," D surmised. "And she's trying to shield me from all that."

Maddox ran his hand over the side of Diesel's hip. "Brother, don't let their bullshit sink under your skin. Rebel's tough. She's got your back. She'll be good and we've got her all weekend. We'll get in there."

"We all knew this would happen. Rebel knew it better than any of us, except you, DD," Molly put in.

"Yeah," D mumbled.

Molly pressed into him. "We'll all get through this, Rebel too."

"They're gonna push her until they lose her," D replied.

"Their choice. Rebel's too," Maddox said carefully.

"I know, still sucks."

"Honey, it isn't you that's tearing your family apart. It's them," Molly pointed out.

"I know, baby," Diesel said gently. "It still sucks."

"Yeah," she whispered.

D took in and then let out a huge breath.

After that, he shared, "Loved watchin' her walk off that plane. Loved rappin' with her in my truck on the way home. Loved watchin' you two welcome her like she's your own sister. It's what I can give to this. What I can give to us."

"*Part* of what you can give, D," Maddox rumbled.

"Yeah, but a good part," D returned. "And their shit is fucking with a good thing."

"You need to let it go, honey," Molly advised.

"No, darlin', D needs to let it out," Maddox revised. "This is big shit. Not good shit. And just gonna say, man," Maddox slid his hand back and gave D's ass a squeeze, "I'm glad you're talkin' it out."

"Yeah, me too," Molly added. "Forget about me saying you need to let it go. Unless you let it go all over us."

Her words made Diesel's body start shaking with laughter.

And that made Molly slap at his chest. "And no, you can't make a comment about letting it go all over me."

That was when D felt Maddox's body add to shaking the bed.

"You can't either, Mad," she snapped, twisting her head to look at her man behind her through the shadows.

Mad's voice was also shaking when he reminded her, "Wasn't me he shot all over fifteen minutes ago."

"Does everything have to be about sex with you two?" she asked snippily.

"Yes," Diesel answered.

"Totally," Maddox said at the same time.

"Jeez," Molly muttered.

Her men kept laughing.

Maddox used his arm around them to pull them in tighter.

Diesel did the same with his arm until Molly was practically crunched between them.

Molly let out a big sigh and whispered, "I love my guys, even when they're completely annoying."

"Back at you," Diesel replied.

"Same," Maddox said.

"When am I annoying?" Molly asked.

Neither man was going to field that one.

Molly snuggled in, murmuring, "Yeah, even when you're *completely* annoying."

Diesel grinned in the dark.

Maddox gave his ass another squeeze.

He returned the gesture.

Then D closed his eyes, settled into the warm tangle of bodies, and he fell asleep.

Maddox

"YOU FIND YOU LIKE IT, D, I'll talk to Branch at the Honey. He's their operating manager. I think they have their security tight, but I'm sure he always needs good people on his radar. They get an opening, he might want to talk to you," Sixx said.

It was Saturday night.

They were talking about D's taking extra work at the Bolt as a Dungeon Master while sitting around Sixx and Stellan's huge-ass, kickass dining room table that spread out along a row of arched French doors with a view to a pool deck. All of this was in a massive great room that was in a gigantic mansion in Paradise Valley.

The place was fucking amazing.

It also wasn't surprising.

Sixx was a badass but she was a stylish one. She dressed like a model, was graceful, confident, sharp and she made edgy, which was not Maddox's thing, hot.

Stellan, her man, on the other hand, was pure class, including classically handsome. His woman dressed like a model, he just looked like one (though he dressed like one as well, his clothes were just as sophisticated as he was, and he was off-the-charts with the urbane).

The dude was obviously dripping in money.

He was also straight-up good people.

He didn't act like he'd welcomed them for some amazing dish of salmon covered in some sauce that was like heaven on your tongue and an open, stocked, top-shelf liquor cabinet, his backyard landscaping, to Mad's professional eye, exceptionally designed and maintained, his big pool lighting the area, including clean-lined deck furniture, like it was a resort.

When they'd arrived, Stellan and Sixx made it clear they'd entered a home, not a showplace.

They also made it clear they were not only welcome there, but wanted there.

Like family.

Stellan Lange was interested, interesting, and even though he did not hide even a little bit he was a total snob, that shit wasn't about being elitist. It was just a part of who he was.

He could afford the good stuff that allowed him to be a snob about having good stuff.

But he wasn't a snob about people.

The entire time—from arriving, getting drinks, chatting over some cheese melted with some jelly in puff pastry spread over crackers that was unbelievably delicious, then sitting down where they were to a dinner Stellan and Sixx let them all help carry to the table—had been great.

Except, as the night progressed, and Rebel's purse chimed, then vibrated, it was also coming clear that Stellan was not wealthy as fuck because he was born with a silver spoon in his mouth (though Mad had a feeling he was).

He was entirely clued in.

To everything.

Including Rebel's increasingly tense manner that got increasingly tense as her phone kept going and she was running out of ways to hide she kept checking it.

The table could sit twice their party, and then some, but they only occupied one end, with Stellan at the head, Sixx to his left, D next to her. Rebel was to Stellan's right, and Maddox had made Molly sit next to Rebel and took the odd man out seat at the end of their side.

He still heard Rebel's phone buzz in her purse hanging on the back of her seat, something Stellan's gaze wandering to her chair told Mad he heard too, as Molly answered, "That'd be cool, Diesel. Working security at the Honey. Wow. I've always wanted to see what it looked like inside there."

"A tour can be arranged, I'm sure," Sixx replied.

"Just turn it off," Diesel bit out.

On his trek to look that way, Mad caught Stellan's gaze cutting to Diesel.

Sixx's did too.

But Maddox felt Molly's eyes on him.

It didn't have to be said, throughout the day, they hadn't gotten Rebel to share how much crap she was taking from D's family.

But the texts, calls, and vibrations when she turned the ringer off were not lost on any of them.

"I actually kinda can't, D," Rebel said quietly. "I have this work situation that means I need to keep my mind in that game."

This made Maddox wonder.

Rebel was a filmmaker. She did band videos and corporate videos and wedding videos. As far as he knew, for the most part, she worked on her own.

What was she working on that she was away for the weekend but had to keep her mind in that game?

With all that was going on, Maddox didn't have his shot to ask after that.

Primarily because, at that exact moment, Diesel indicated he was done.

"Right," D spat, scraped his chair back, his hand going to his back pocket, his eyes going to Stellan. "Mind if I use your deck?"

"By all means," Stellan murmured.

Yeah.

The dude was pure class.

"Sorry. It's rude. But excuse me," Diesel muttered,

And with that, he prowled to a pair of the French doors behind him, pulling his phone out of his pocket as Maddox called, "D."

D ignored him, opened the door and stepped outside.

"I think maybe I should—" Rebel started, pushing her chair back.

"No," Molly interrupted her, putting a hand on her arm to stop her. "He needs to do this for you."

"Okay, none of our business, but, uh . . . do you want to make it our business?" Sixx asked.

"Darling," Stellan tried to shut her up the classy way.

"Diesel came out to his family this week," Molly announced.

Stellan turned his gaze to Molly like he was aiming a laser beam and stated firmly, "Excellent."

"They're not super thrilled about it," Molly told him.

Maddox watched Stellan's jaw go hard.

Yep.

Maddox totally liked this guy.

"He should just let me deal with their bullshit," Rebel muttered.

"That's not in him, Rebel," Maddox told her something she knew.

"It's not in *me* to let him go this alone," Rebel returned heatedly, her attention directed at the door Diesel had used.

"I'm so sorry this is ruining our dinner," Molly said to Sixx. She indicated her cleaned plate. "It was delicious. It really was. As you can see since we all practically licked our plates. But D's D and—"

Sixx cut her off gently. "I'm not sorry, Molly. Although I hate that

D's going through this right now," her gaze strayed to Maddox, "I'm very glad he's gotten to this place."

She hadn't quite finished that when the door swung open and D came in.

Nope.

He didn't come in.

He *stormed* in.

Eyes on Maddox.

Everyone looked to him, Sixx twisting in her seat to do it.

"Dad call you?" Diesel asked.

Fuck.

"Brother—"

"*Did my father call you?*" Diesel roared.

"Yeah, buddy," Maddox said quietly.

"He call you names?" Diesel asked.

Fuck!

He felt Molly's gaze come to him and he also felt the anger that began to beat off her.

"Diesel—" Maddox tried

"What did he call you?"

"D—"

"*What'd he fuckin' call you?*" Diesel barked.

"I'm not gonna say it, baby," Maddox answered.

"Right," D bit, put the phone in his hand back to his ear and said, "Dad? Yeah. *Fuck you.* Just . . . *fuck* . . . *you* and your lunatic fuckin' bullshit. I cannot believe you called Maddox and laid that shit on him."

There was a pause.

Then an explosion where Molly and Rebel jumped, Molly letting out a muted mew, Rebel making a sound like a growling purr, but Stellan, Sixx and Maddox all grew tense like they were about to spring into action.

"*No! You don't get that!* For fuck's sake, what's the matter with you? That time has passed and it *never should have happened in the first place.* In *these* times, you don't get the excuse of righteousness. That's bullshit. You don't get the excuse of ignorance. That's bullshit too. It's not my place to explain *dick* to you. You don't ask me to explain why I breathe. It's what

I need to do. You don't get an explanation for *this*. And you don't get to be the injured party here, Dad. *You made me and there's not one goddamned thing wrong with me*. But there's something wrong *with you*. And that's about riding Rebel's ass about something that has shit to do with her, and everything to do *with you*. And it's about you handing me this shit, when there should be no shit *at all*, and making it about you. But mostly, it's about phoning *my man* and laying *your shit on him*. I will not tolerate that, Dad. And you know why? Because that's the man you made. That's the man you raised. He's *mine* and *nothing harms him*. Not even *you*. Actually *especially* not *you*."

The entire room was frozen.

But for Maddox it was more.

It felt like his heart had stopped beating.

D gave that to Molly.

Nothing hurt Molly.

Ever.

But now . . .

"Hear me," Diesel growled in a rumbling thunder of a tone Maddox had never heard in his life, "there is no coming back from this. Never. We'll have our commitment ceremony, and you will not be welcome. We'll have our children, and they will not have their grandfather. You just lost your son because your son has just erased his father from his life in a way you won't *ever* be written back in."

Another pause and . . .

"Then that goes for Gunner and Mom too. I'll let you to share that news. Goodbye, Dad. Have a good life. What's left of it."

And with that, he took the phone from his ear and started moving his thumb over it, staring so hard at it, it was a wonder the thing didn't combust in his hand.

Maddox pushed up to his feet. "D."

D's head shot up.

"I love you," he said to Maddox.

Right in front of everyone.

"And no one fucks with you," D finished.

"Okay, buddy," Maddox whispered.

"You know, darling," Stellan drawled, shoving his chair back and getting up. "I was in little question before, but I see how right you are now. Your friends are quite incredible people."

Everyone then watched as he sauntered from the dining room table to the kitchen, the women sitting, Diesel and Maddox still standing.

Stellan then walked down a back hall and disappeared.

Molly sniffed.

Maddox looked down to her and it was like she felt his attention because she waved her hand and announced, "I love you. But if you touch me in this moment, I'll fly apart."

"Right, baby," Maddox muttered.

"And *you*," she snapped toward Diesel then finished fiercely, "are the most beautiful man I've ever known."

Mad grinned at her then turned his grin to D.

"Except him," she went on and in his peripheral vision Mad caught her jerking her thumb his way, "it's a tie."

Maddox started chuckling.

Diesel asked tightly, "Why didn't you tell me he called?"

Maddox stopped chuckling.

"Because that would have fucked with you," he explained. "And nobody fucks with you. Especially not through me."

D's eyes flashed and his face warmed.

But his mouth asked, "You're an asshole, you know that?"

"Totally," Maddox answered.

"Oh my God, you guys are such dorks," Rebel groaned.

"Uh, Sixx, where did your man take off to?" Molly inquired.

"He's right there," Sixx said, tipping her head to the side, a smile on her face that shocked the shit out of Maddox because it was downright goofy in its happiness and Sixx was about as goofy as a switchblade.

Everyone looked back to the hall to see Stellan walking in carrying two bottles.

And Maddox might be solid middle-middleclass. But even he knew the labels of that brand of champagne.

Fucking hell.

"We have a wine cellar in the basement," Sixx shared, pushing back from the table.

"Darling, if you'd get the glasses," Stellan called to her.

"My pleasure," Sixx replied, hustling on her high heels toward a killer, built-in wet bar that was in the family room area.

"Will you do the honors with this one?" Stellan asked, handing Diesel one of two bottles of Dom Perignon.

"Sure," Diesel said casually, moving to Stellan and taking the bottle.

Sixx got the glasses.

D and Stellan popped the corks and poured.

Glasses were passed around.

Everyone standing resumed their seats.

But Stellan lifted his glass before anyone took a sip.

"To freedom," he toasted.

They all hiked up their champagne, but he wasn't finished.

"To love," he continued.

Maddox probably wasn't the only one about to open his mouth to lay a cheers on that.

But Stellan wasn't done.

"And not least," he raised his glass farther, "to family of the heart."

Molly sniffed again.

"Hear, hear," Rebel hooted.

Sixx kept smiling goofily at her man.

Maddox slid an arm around Molly's shoulders, kissed the side of her head and looked to D.

Diesel was watching them.

He tipped his glass their way.

Mol and Mad tipped theirs toward their man.

And then they all drank.

EPILOGUE

The Three Kisses

Molly

MOLLY SLID FROM BETWEEN HER two sleeping men in the big bed.

"Baby?" Maddox mumbled in a rumble, making a drowsy grab at her that missed.

"Mol?" D murmured, his hold on her hip slipping even if he tried to catch on.

"Shh," she shushed. "Gotta hit the loo," she whispered.

They made sleepy noises and adjusted their bodies without her being there as she climbed over Diesel to get out of bed.

Then she stood at the side as D shifted Maddox so Mad's back was to Diesel's front. He curled into him, resting his nose in the back of Mad's hair, his arm around him, cupping Mad's junk like he would cup Molly's breast in sleep.

Mad had an arm flung out.

The other hand he slid down Diesel's forearm and curled it over D's holding his package.

They stopped moving and started breathing steady.

Molly felt her lips tip up.

This happened now and had been happening for months.

She wasn't always in the middle.

Sometimes she was tucked at a back (that was tucked at another back, or wrapped around a front).

Draped across a pair of bodies.

Full on top one but with her other pressed down their sides.

Whatever it was, it was always a tangle. It was always maximum contact. It was always like they wove themselves together to draw in as much of the beauty they shared as they could, even when unconscious, because it sustained them for whatever they'd face out there in the world that might not be so hot.

As it should be.

As she hoped it always would be.

Molly let herself take her boys in.

Then she hit the loo.

When she came out, she didn't go back to bed.

She went to the wispy, short white nightie on the floor.

She picked it up, tugged it on, tiptoed across the room and rescued her phone from the mess of charge cords attached to her and her husbands' phones.

She walked to the French doors and opened them, the breeze drifting in, blowing the delicate white curtain lazily back, the soft, steady, soothing crash of the waves hitting the beach beyond drifting into the room.

Molly had no idea how her men had scored such an awesome, swank, exclusive vacation property for their honeymoon.

And she didn't ask.

It wasn't important to her. She could have a honeymoon in a motel in the dusty middle of nowhere.

But it was important to them. They'd found a way to give it to her.

And since it was important to them, there they were.

Her feet felt the sandy grit that dusted the wooden deck boards as she walked to the wicker chair five feet away.

She sat her ass on the pad, lifting her feet up to rest the soles against the chair opposite where, not but a few hours ago, she'd been in the same position, except her feet were in Mady's lap and he was giving her a foot massage while shooting the shit with Diesel.

She lifted her phone up to her face and had to blink a little when the light came on in the dark as she engaged it.

Molly went right to the photos.

There was a lot you could say about her sister, Holly. Some of it bad. Some of it good.

But her big sister had done her right on Molly's wedding day.

That being, unbeknownst to Molly, Holly had confiscated her phone and took tons of pictures so Molly would have them on her honeymoon.

Since they'd arrived two days ago at that remote beach house that Diesel had found and Maddox had booked, she'd lost track of how many times she'd flipped through them.

It didn't matter, that number would ever increase.

Like the times she was adding now.

She'd gotten her sunflowers and her arch and she'd gotten them in their backyard.

Diesel and Maddox had built it permanently over the pool, D planting wisteria around it so next spring it would be *amazing*.

But for their wedding, it had been laced with sunflowers and red roses and that's where they'd been married.

Diesel had worn a smart, khaki colored suit, white shirt, no tie, red rose in his lapel.

Maddox had worn a sharp black suit, black shirt, and a red rose in his lapel.

Molly had worn white. A simple gown made of delicate lace with gathers of fine tulle holding the bodice up, coasting over her shoulders and down to a V at the small of her back, off which lace hung cut like fairy wings at the sides.

It was perfect.

She could tell when she walked out on the patio and then to them that her boys had felt the same.

But she didn't have to try to recall.

Holly had taken a picture of them standing together under the arch the instant their eyes caught sight of her.

God, they were so handsome.

She looked at the picture, grinning to herself, then slid back one.

It was a photo from before she'd walked out. Diesel had his hands to Maddox's rose, his head bent to it, and Molly knew he'd just said something smart because Maddox's head was tipped back and he was laughing.

"God, I love my boys," she whispered.

She scrolled through. Past the three of them standing together listening to the lady preacher, Molly between Maddox and Diesel. Mad and D putting the ring on Molly's finger. Molly and Mad putting the ring on D's finger. D and Molly putting the ring on Mad's.

The three kisses.

Oh, those *three kisses*.

Molly traced a finger on her phone.

And there she was walking back into the house with a hand through each of their arms, her bouquet of sunflowers and red roses and green hypericum berries tucked in the crook of Mad's elbow.

Mad's head was turned to the side. He was smiling at Rebel sitting next to her man, Rush, in their white chairs festooned with sunflowers, roses, berries and red and yellow netting in the front row in their backyard.

D's head was turned the other way, his free arm out, touching Erin's shoulder as he walked by her, tears still streaming down Erin's cheeks.

Molly was looking forward, absolutely beaming.

She flipped through photos.

Her hugging Rebel.

Mad hugging Molly's mom.

Diesel shaking hands with Bob.

Both her men laughing with Rush.

Minnie, with her now purple-haired head resting on her brother's chest, her arms around his middle, as they talked to Dylan.

Stellan sitting in a white chair with a poof of netting at the back at one of the tables that was brought in after the ceremony so they could have their buffet. Sixx was on his lap. Her arm was wrapped loose around his shoulders, both his were loose around her waist, but their faces were so close, they were almost kissing, though they were smiling at each other so big, a kiss would be hard to achieve with all those white teeth.

Sixx's engagement ring could be seen on the hand she had at his jaw and Molly was stunned, moved, thrown, and freaking *thrilled* with the gorgeous ring D and Mad gave to her.

But the rock Stellan laid on Sixx?

Whoa.

She flipped and saw Diesel with Tommy, their arms around each other's backs, hands in front of them clasped, bodies slightly bent forward because they were supposed to be posing but Tommy had more of a smart mouth than Diesel did, so they were both lost in laughter.

Another slide of the screen and there was Maddox and Harvey, Mad holding one of Tommy and Harvey's daughters to his hip. Britta had a fascination with Mad's beard and even if the three year old was stroking it like Mady was a puppy, Maddox expression was intent, listening to what Tommy's husband had to say.

Another slide, and there she was arching over Gavin's arm, Maddox's ex-boyfriend, their good friend. He was smiling wolfishly at her while his lover stood close and rolled his eyes because Gavin had just said something incredibly forward, but Molly's face was awash with laughter because it was also hilarious.

And she slid her finger on the screen and there she was again, sitting close to Rebel. Both of them were turned to each other, bent nearly double, heads nearly touching, knees definitely touching, holding each other's hands, looking like they were plotting. But they weren't. They were talking and trying not to cry.

They were trying not to cry because it was a beautiful day and everyone was so happy.

They were not thinking or talking about the fact that none of the rest of Diesel's family was there.

Apparently, Gene Stapleton had said unforgiveable things to Maddox *and* Diesel. Since that night at Stellan and Sixx's, Diesel had refused to talk about it, or them. They were cut out of his life, *their* lives, and that was that.

Rebel had, not surprisingly—her loyalty was stalwart with D and Molly fucking loved her for it—not long after, followed suit.

Both Maddox and Molly (and Maddox *with* Molly, though, if she was honest, she didn't try *too* hard and she felt absolutely no guilt about that, but Maddox was a big believer in family, forgiveness and being the better person, so he gave it his best shot) had tried to talk to him about it, get him to a place where he'd be open to an approach should they make one.

D adamantly refused.

It was, as Maddox said, his call.

It didn't matter.

They didn't approach.

They were also not missed.

And that was their loss.

It had been a beautiful day of love, laughter, food, drink, good people, and happy tears, and they'd had no part in it.

She refused to think of that, not ever, but definitely not on her honeymoon.

She kept gliding through her wedding photos.

Barclay with his girl. Josh stuffing his face. George and his wife sipping champagne and laughing with Molly's parents. Some of Maddox's landscape team messing around at the big tins filled with ice and bottles of beer, their wives and girlfriends looking on with expressions varying from indulgent to indignant.

Molly with her dad. Maddox with her dad. Diesel with her dad.

And Molly with all of them.

Then there was Molly with Maddox. Molly with Diesel. D with Mad.

The three of them together.

They all now had the last name Vega. Even D. He had no hold on Stapleton, he said, outside Rebel, who was engaged to Rush anyway (and she wasn't a big fan of the name by that time either) and he wanted their children not to be confused.

So, weeks before the wedding, Maddox had gone with them as they appeared before the judge, Molly first, then Diesel, to have their names legally changed.

That had just been the three of them.

Maddox had been . . . well, there was no other way to put it.

He'd been beside himself with happiness that day.

Utterly beside himself.

She'd never seen him smile so big or so much, not in her life.

And he was a relatively happy guy.

They'd gone for a fancy steak dinner after.

And the celebration after that at home was one she'd never forget.

She sighed and slid a finger on the screen.

It went on.

And on.

Another finger glide.

And on.

The best day of her life.

Bar none.

On that thought, the phone was gently taken from her fingers by a hand that had come over her shoulder.

She looked up and saw Mady.

He smiled down at her in the moonlight reflected on the sea and sand, turned and walked back to the doors only to expose Diesel who moved in and plucked her out of the chair, carrying her like a groom carried his bride.

Which they were.

"Baby—" she started.

"Enough with the trip down memory lane," he said, walking her to the bed.

He put a knee in, put her in, covered her but rolled to her side as Maddox moved in at the other.

"Time to make more memories," Maddox murmured before his mouth hit her neck.

That neck arched, her hand sliding into his hair.

Diesel's mouth hit her belly.

She slid her hand in his hair too.

Both of them moved down with two different destinations.

Molly's eyes drifted closed and another smile curved her lips.

She didn't have to be in a quaint, remote cottage on the beach on her honeymoon.

Anytime she was with her boys, it was everything.

More than everything.

Heaven.

The End

"Tell Me What You Want"

This short is a little bonus for this Loose Ends anthology and was originally written for The Ripped Bodice's Patreon program, with the gals from that lovely bookstore giving me the prompt . . .

At a Spice Girls concert, a teenage fairy makes a life altering decision . . .

"TELL ME WHAT YOU WANT, what you really, really want . . ."

Maurelle was floating at the rafters. Floating and dancing.

It wasn't the best seat in the house for the Spice Girls concert, but it was a good view and luckily, being a fairy, she had really good eyesight.

She didn't have to have really good hearing (even though she did). The sound system was *rad*.

But rafters it had to be. She couldn't be seen.

Though it wasn't like it was easy to see her. She was two inches tall, had dark coloring—hair and skin—so she could blend into the shadows.

If it wasn't for her glimmer.

Maurelle had a lot of glimmer (more than most fairies, and she liked it like that). It drifted from her translucent wings with their soft purple and pink highlights, it sparkled from her eyes and it glittered from her clothes (jazzy, hipster purple disco pants with an adorable white cropped babydoll tee, both adorned with copious stars).

She wasn't supposed to be there. She hadn't hit her quota of matches this month, and she wasn't going to help make that number at a Spice Girls concert. No one was looking for love at a Spice Girls concert.

But that was what Maurelle wanted to make her specialty.

Helping people find love when they least expected it.

(Not to mention, Maurelle *loved* the Spice Girls, and was slamming it to the left and shaking it to the right, spicing up her life right that very moment as proof.)

She was still in match training. Though recently she'd been let off on her own. But she still had to give a full report on her activities after each match she made, unlike the fairies who had hit age eighteen, graduated from Match Academy, and were *really* off on their own, given Free Wing, making matches willy-nilly.

At sixteen (in fairy years, which was eighty in human years), she had ambitions.

Maurelle was going to be the best there was at helping folks find love in the unlikeliest of places.

Like at a Spice Girl concert.

The Elder Fairies were fans of this.

What they weren't fans of were some of Maurelle's tactics. She'd had to go in front of a Gathering to explain herself on more than one occasion (like . . . nineteen of them, okay, maybe twenty, or . . . ahem, twenty-four).

But it was easy to do the meet-cute. Cause the girl to trip and fall into the guy. Send the guy's new puppy running off in the girl's direction. A wayward Frisbee. The perfect placement of the splat of a scoop of ice cream from a cone. Sending a gust of wind to hit *just right* on a floppy hat.

Maurelle liked a challenge.

Maurelle liked to spark love in unlikely places . . .

To unlikely people.

So she was floating and dancing (and singing).

She was also keeping an eye out.

And because she was, she saw him.

No, she saw *her* first.

But that *her* was staring straight at him.

And really, Maurelle thought, she couldn't blame her.

There was a lot of him to look at and all of it was good.

He was close to the front, his arm slung around a pretty girl who he barely could keep hold on, she was bouncing and dancing so much.

He was tall.

He was broad.

He was handsome.

And the woman watching . . .

Maurelle stopped dancing and honed in on the woman gazing at the man.

Specifically, the look of longing on her face.

"Tell me what you want," Maurelle whispered into the air, "what you really, really want."

Just as she did, the woman's face fell and Maurelle looked back to the man.

He'd dipped his head and was talking into the ear of the girl he was holding. Maurelle could see from his profile he had a smile on his face.

He was not happy to be at a Spice Girls concert (this Maurelle knew by pure instinct, and this instinct had a lot to do with the fact he was more than a little rugged and he was wearing faded jeans and a plaid shirt that was very nice, but it wasn't tailored or designer to the point if she caught it, it might make Posh swoon).

He was just happy that she was happy.

Maurelle looked back to the woman across the way in time to see her rush from her row of dancing, sing-shouting Spice Girls fans to the aisle.

And then she lumbered down the aisle.

Yes, *lumbered*.

There was something wrong with her leg.

Like . . . *really wrong*.

"Oh dear," Maurelle murmured into Sporty Spice belting it out.

She didn't know what Maurelle knew from just looking at the man's demeanor and the kind of hold he had on the lady at his side, knowing this from having been discerning this kind of thing for a long time (in human years).

The lady the man was with was his sister.

At this point Maurelle knew the drill (she'd taken two whole classes on it, not to mention two fairy years of practical).

She should spend some time observing the both of them. Use some of her magic to become invisible and get closer to listen and learn about these two people before she made any moves.

But Maurelle saw the look on that woman's face (actually, she'd seen *both* looks).

And she saw the man had let his sister go in order to let her fully get into the song, but he still had a dashingly handsome smile on his face, happy his sister was having a good time even though his top choice would not be entering Spice World . . .

And Maurelle turned her gaze to the woman making her awkward way down the aisle and Maurelle knew, *she just knew* in her head that woman had convinced herself a tall, broad, handsome man, who was the kind of man who didn't have a problem showing how much he loved his sister (even though she didn't know she was his sister), would never be for her.

Maybe, with that limp, she wasn't sure she'd ever find a man who would be for her.

"That does it," Maurelle decided as she wound her arm up high, kicked out a hip, did her patented disco stance (well, it wasn't patented yet, but she was going to patent it with the Fairy Patent Board after she was given Free Wing) and she let fly.

An aqua, hot-pink and violet stream of twinkling fairy dust shot down and slammed right between the shoulder blades of the man.

Those around him who caught it oo'd and ah'd, thinking it was a part of the show, looking around to see if they could spot more such displays of bodaciousness, and Maurelle bit her lip.

Doing things like that, the Elder Fairies didn't like all that much.

Maurelle drifted deeper into the rafters, waited and watched as the man suddenly leaned into his sister and spoke in her ear.

She looked up at him, nodded, and he moved, causing quite a sensation and taking some attention from the show so the women he squeezed in front of could watch him go.

He started down the aisle and Maurelle moved with him overhead, out of eyesight, and only dipped down to buzz the top of the entrance out into the concourse at the last minute.

He thought he was heading to the bathroom, she knew.

And he started heading that way, she saw.

But his eyes caught on the woman leaning a shoulder to the wall, her back to him, her head bent.

Her shoulders were lightly shaking.

And it was clear she wasn't laughing.

Oh boy.

It was worse than Maurelle thought.

He hesitated (Maurelle just *knew* he would).

Then he started heading her way (something else Maurelle just *knew he would do*).

When he did, she started to smile.

This was going to be easy!

Just one of Maurelle's Patented (soon) Disco Fairy Blasts and . . .

Boom!

"*Maurelle*," she heard hissed, and her head flashed to the side, glimmer flying everywhere, to see Nissa there.

Nissa was her friend. Before they let her out on her own, Nissa had been her hands-on mentor and Nissa had always been at her side when she'd made her first matches, guiding her through amusing misunderstandings when a hostess called names of parties waiting for tables at a restaurant, or two people reached for the same carton of eggs at the exact same time at a grocery store.

Nissa was still her mentor, always there when Maurelle gave her reports.

Nissa was a whole twenty-six fairy years old (her birthday was just five fairy days before (that would be fifteen human days)), had graduated Salutatorian at the Match Academy, and thus had had Free Wing for eight years.

Nissa always hit her quotas, and then some, doing it right smack in the rules.

Ice cream scoops falling.

Wayward Frisbees.

Tumbling floppy hats.

Kites stuck in trees.

Puppies *galore*.

And rambunctious kittens who somehow got loose at rescue centers?

Forget about it.

That was Nissa's *thing*.

"What are you doing?" Nissa (who had a kitten with a crown on its head on the T-shirt she was wearing, unsurprisingly) was still hissing.

"I—" Maurelle started.

"You don't even know *their names*," Nissa pointed out irritably.

"Hey. Is everything okay?"

The deep voice stopped their fairy conversation (which, by the by, was below human hearing level—dogs could hear them, and cats, and horses, and such (no, your cat or dog was not staring at nothing with perked ears just for the sake of making you think they were weird or dotty, they were listening to a fairy conversation)—they'd have to shout really loud to be heard by a human, though that was strictly verboten).

Maurelle felt Nissa touch her arm and then she felt herself go invisible just as they both watched the woman look up at the man.

This is the good part, Maurelle thought as she watched the woman pale, her lips parting, and then the becoming pink started to creep up her cheeks. *Yep, this is the good part.*

Maurelle smiled.

"You're not okay," the man murmured, his gaze falling to the woman's wet, flushed cheeks.

"Yes . . . I . . . no, really . . ." the woman stammered, straightening and pushing back into the wall at the same time lifting a hand to her face to rub some wet away. "I'm fine."

"You're crying in the hallway of an arena at a Spice Girls reunion concert," he pointed out bluntly.

Maurelle winced.

It might not be good if he wasn't the kind of guy who could go gently.

"You . . . are . . . gonna . . . get . . . into . . . *so much trouble* for this," Nissa whispered. "They told you last time you did something like this, and it didn't go that well, that you might be pulled out of the field so you can re-take the entire Appropriate Match Scenario course. And that's a *whole year*!"

Maurelle had forgotten to mention that sometimes her maverick ways didn't work out as she'd hoped.

"It's gonna be okay," Maurelle whispered back.

"And what if it isn't, Maurelle?" Nissa asked. "What if this goes *really* bad and they get *really* mad and they don't make you retake Appropriate Matches. They take you off Match Duty *altogether* and reassign you to Woodlands. I mean, you'd be sitting on toadstools or guarding four leaf clovers *forever*."

Maurelle liked the Woodlands (toadstools were super cushy).

But only for a visit.

Her fairy heart started pounding.

"Well, it's kind of an emotional song," the woman stated lamely, and Maurelle and Nissa's conversation was halted.

"'If You Wanna Be My Lover?'" he asked incredulously.

Boy, he had very pretty green eyes (though, with his erroneous titling of the song, she found she was correct, he was *no* Spice Girls fan).

Goodness, Maurelle hoped he wasn't a dud.

And not just because her future actually did have Woodlands Duty complete with toadstool lounging on the horizon if this went bad.

"That song is called 'Wannabe,'" the woman corrected.

"Whatever," he muttered, his lips twitching once before he got serious again. "It's obvious you're not fine. Do you need something?"

The woman blinked up at him.

"I . . ." she began but stopped.

Gracious, but she had very pretty blonde hair. It was straight, though there were some flips at the ends, and it was really shiny.

"What would I need?" she asked curiously.

"I don't know," he answered. "Seeing as you're all by yourself, leaning against a wall crying at a concert, maybe someone to talk to," he suggested.

"I don't know you," she stated the obvious.

"Best person to talk to when things are going down that make you cry," he returned.

"I don't know if that's true," the woman refuted.

"Are you crying now?" he asked.

She was not.

For a second she just stared up at him. Then she curled her lips in between her teeth, but that move didn't hide her smile since her pretty brown eyes were sparkling.

And not from tears.

He blinked.

Good.

He was observant.

He absolutely did not miss that sparkle.

No, I was wrong, this *is the good part*, Maurelle thought.

The woman uncurled her lips to answer, "No."

"So one thing down," he replied. "Now, hit me."

"With what?" she asked.

"With what made you cry," he explained.

It was then her cheeks got *very* pink, it was *very* pretty, and Maurelle bit back a giggle because she knew what made the woman cry and it wasn't something she could share with him.

Namely, it was that she found him attractive and never thought in a million years he'd be right there, standing close to her, asking (okay, maybe kinda demanding) she bare her soul to him.

His eyes narrowed on her face.

Hmm.

How did that ominous look make him even *more* handsome?

"Shit, is it a guy?" he demanded to know.

"I—" she began.

His shoulders straightened and his face got hard.

And he was even more handsome.

For real, that square jaw looked made from granite!

"Is some guy being a dick to you?"

The woman immediately waved her hand between them. "No, no . . . it's not a guy."

"You sure?" he pushed.

She nodded.

He studied her a moment before looking over his shoulder at the concession stand then back to her. "Let's go get a beer, find someplace to sit down and then hash it out. Or . . . do they sell beer at Spice Girls concerts?"

Panic hit her as she glanced at the concession stand across the wide walkway, and her voice was a lot louder when she cried, "No! No beer."

"Oh man, damn. Sorry," he muttered. "You don't drink."

"No," she stated hurriedly. "I drink. Wine and cocktails and beer. Wine mainly. And cocktails. Okay, maybe cocktails mainly, if I'm not at home. But I like beer. Beer is good. I like the darker beers, and craft ones, though IPAs are kinda bitter, I think. But I've had some good ones and . . ." she trailed off from her blabbering when he started chuckling.

"Okay, so you drink beer, and apparently you're down with alcohol on the whole. Are you driving tonight or something?" he asked.

She shook her head then apparently changed her mind and nodded it.

Another deep chuckle.

He had a nice laugh.

"Is that a yes or a no?" he queried.

"I . . . no, my friend is driving," she admitted like she didn't want to say the words, which she didn't since saying them gave her no reason to refuse a beer.

"Okay, then you just want a pop?" he offered.

What she didn't want to do was limp to the concession stand.

This was where it might go bad.

Maurelle's teeth caught her bottom lip.

"Listen—" the woman began.

But he reached in and grabbed her hand.

Tugging on it gently, he said, "Let's go."

Maurelle got stiff.

Nissa murmured, "Oh dear."

He tugged her from the wall and she took one step with him before she ripped her hand from his.

He'd turned toward the concession stand, but when she pulled away, he twisted back to look down at her.

The instant he caught sight of her stricken face, he mistook the reason behind it and whispered, "God, I'm sorry. That was . . . I shouldn't have touched you."

"I'm lame," she declared.

He stared at her, obviously thrown.

"You're—?" he started.

"Lame," she said decisively.

He shifted to face her fully, stating deliberately, "You're not lame."

She looked into his eyes, lifted her chin, Maurelle held her breath and heard Nissa pull in hers and she and her friend watched the woman walk a small, ungainly circle before coming again to stand still in front of the man.

He'd watched.

And he'd seen.

And now a muscle was jumping up his cheek.

With her chin still up, but her hands in fists, she repeated, "Like I said, I'm lame."

"You're not lame," he growled.

Her eyes got big.

Maurelle nearly let out a fairy burst of twinkle dust for joy.

"Oh my," Nissa breathed.

"What happened?" he asked low.

"A . . . a . . . car wreck. When I was fourteen," she answered.

"How old are you now?"

"Twenty-eight."

"Christ," he bit off. "You still have pain?"

"Oh dear," Nissa mumbled.

She could say that again.

It was rather known in fairy circles that some men had difficulty taking on issues, like chronic pain due to a car accident, especially at the very beginning.

It was rather known in fairy circles that some women had that same hesitation.

Maurelle had a feeling this particular woman knew this all too well.

And this was one of the reasons most fairies (read: nearly all but the most adept or experienced) steered clear of this kind of matchmaking just because (but also at the strict decree of the Elders, a major reason why Maurelle was always getting into trouble, because she didn't steer clear, as was currently apparent).

Maurelle was holding her breath again.

"Sometimes," the woman said.

"Shit," the man muttered. "You in pain tonight?"

"Not my leg," she told him.

"So it's not dancing or something that made you come out here?" he asked.

She shook her head.

"You shouldn't call yourself lame," he told her.

"That's what my mom says," she told him.

"Your mom is right," he returned.

"And my dad," she went on.

"He's right too."

"And all my friends," she kept at it.

He made no reply, just scowled down at her.

Really, he was just . . . *everything.*

"But . . . I *am* lame," she pointed out.

"You got a bum leg as a result of a car wreck. That makes you a woman with a bum leg. Not lame," he retorted.

Maurelle let out her breath in a gust.

She just *knew it.*

That man. Spice Girls. With his sister.

Yes.

She *knew it.*

Maurelle grinned.

"A *pretty* woman with a bum leg," he amended.

Maurelle's grin grew into a smile.

"A pretty woman with great hair and a bum leg," he added.

Maurelle let out a fairy burst of twinkle dust for joy.

Nissa immediately swung out an invisibility web to shroud it.

A new blush had crept up the woman's cheeks, and she was opening and closing her mouth, but no words were coming out.

"Not to make myself seem less of a concerned citizen, but if you weren't as pretty as you are and you didn't have that head of hair, I might have asked if you were okay but I wouldn't have pushed the beer," he explained.

"Oh," she whispered.

"But just to make things clear, at this point, I'm still pushing the beer," he went on.

"Oh," she breathed.

Maurelle giggled.

"And just to say, I don't give that first shit about a bum leg," he finished.

"Oh," she mumbled, looking nervous, cautiously happy, but still troubled.

"So, can we get a beer and find somewhere to sit so I can make sure you're all right before I ask you out on a date, this being after I ask your name, which I'll do while we're waiting in line for a beer?" he requested.

"I . . . you should know, I saw you in there with a girl," she admitted. "You're hard to miss, being tall and all," she quickly added.

He certainly was tall.

And all.

Maurelle giggled again.

"Yeah, you were hard to miss in there too," he returned.

"Nice," Nissa whispered.

"Not because you're tall," he carried on. "Because of other things."

"*Nice,*" Maurelle whispered.

"Though I didn't see you walking," he went on. "But even if I did, it wouldn't have mattered, like it doesn't now."

"*Niiiiiice,*" Maurelle and Nissa drawled in unison.

He continued, "And that girl is my sister. She grew up on the Spice Girls. Tickets were my birthday present for her. She was supposed to bring a friend. She wanted me to come with her instead, mostly because she's my baby sister and it's her job to torture me, but partly because she kinda likes spending time with me. I didn't grow up on the Spice Girls, except having to endure it when she blasted it. I grew up on Green Day." He gave a one-shouldered shrug. "But she's my sister. I love her. She wanted me with her. What was I supposed to do?"

"Take her to see the Spice Girls," she replied.

He grinned. "Yeah."

Maurelle and Nissa watched as the woman took her time taking in his attractive grin before she pulled in a visibly large breath.

She let it out saying, "I . . . think I'd like a beer."

Maurelle fought another fairy dust burst of joy.

His smile widened. "Good."

"So, um . . . what's your name?" she asked, and he shook his head, but he did it reaching out to wrap his fingers around hers again.

"Oh no," he began. "We don't want to jump ahead. That's for our wait in line."

It was then, eyes sparkling once more, head tipped back, the nerves were gone as was the concern, and so was the cautious in her happy.

He drew her closer then he drew her toward the end of the line at the concession stand.

And Maurelle and Nissa blipped out of the arena smack dab into the front of a Gathering.

Oh boy.

Maurelle looked over her shoulder.

A lot of fairies had been called to order.

Oh boy.

"Maurelle," Aelfric, Elder of the Elders, the head honcho, the big cheese, the one who was sitting on the biggest throne made of twisting branches and twigs with leaves growing from them, plus flowers, with the occasional spread of attractive moss, droned loudly.

"It worked out!" Maurelle exclaimed in her defense.

"It could have been a disaster," Suzette, the Elder Crone sitting at Aelfric's side, snapped.

"It wasn't," Maurelle pointed out.

"And what would become of that young woman if he'd watched her make her circle and then shut down?" Aelfric asked.

"She survived a car crash. She's out with a friend at a Spice Girls concert," Maurelle retorted. "She'd pick herself up and get on with it."

"You can't know that," Orla, the Noble Elder, said softly.

She couldn't.

She still did.

"You've been warned. *Repeatedly*. We really cannot have you continue to—" Aelfric started grandly, clearly about to make a statement, and by the look on his face, not a good one for Maurelle.

So what she was going to do next might buy her Woodlands Duty and an eternity of toadstools, four leaf clovers and gathering dew drops from the bells of lily of the valley (or whatever those Woodlands fairies did).

So what?

Her ambition had reason.

It had purpose.

It was important.

And even if this meant toadstools forever, she was going to have her say.

"And what is love?" Maurelle asked heatedly, interrupting him. "But risk?" she answered herself. "What is risk, without reward? Would you sentence that woman to dash out of every concert and every tavern and every celebration to cry alone, thinking she'll never find love?"

"She would find love," Meeric, the Gentle Elder, stated.

"Who? When? Where? *How*?" Maurelle demanded. She threw out both her arms. "Should she settle for someone she *thinks* she deserves, who might be less than what she should have, rather than take a risk on finding something that will make her deliriously happy?"

"Just because he's handsome, you think he'll make her happy?" Orla queried.

"No," Maurelle answered firmly, but before she could go on, Suzette spoke up.

To scoff.

"And you can't possibly know he'll make her deliriously happy."

"To answer both of you, he took his *sister* to a *Spice Girls* concert when he likes *Green Day*," Maurelle reminded them. "I mean, seriously?"

The Elders shifted in their thrones and glanced at each other.

Spice Girls and Green Day did not compute for most males.

Unless they loved their sisters, their daughters . . .

Or their lovers.

"She went to a Spice Girls concert," Maurelle whispered, her sudden shift in tone getting the full attention of the Elders again, and she felt the same from the gathering of fairies at her back. "She went there thinking she'd listen to an act she enjoys and have a good night with a friend. Then the night turned, she thought in a bad way. She saw a man she found beautiful. A man in a perfect world she'd want to meet. But at fourteen, she'd come to think any chance for a perfect world was stripped from her. She ran from that concert like she undoubtedly shied from hundreds of situations, thinking he was out of her league, taken by a pretty woman she thought was his match, but even if he wasn't, he wouldn't want her. And she ended up with her hand held in his, about to be bought a drink and asked out on a date. Her perception of the world changed tonight. Her perception of herself changed tonight. He did that. *I* did that. But mostly, she let herself take the risk, believed in herself, agreed to a drink and took his hand. So *she* did that. But just to get this point home, it was *me* who made it so she had a risk to take."

Suzette stared crossly at her knees. Orla bit her lip to hide her smile and glanced to her side. Meeric sighed.

Aelfric held Maurelle's eyes.

"This is what I do," Maurelle told Aelfric. "And frankly, Lord Elder, this is what we *all* should be doing. We shouldn't just leave it to the most experienced, the most skilled. There aren't enough of them and there's *millions* of matches to be made. As fairies, we're bearers of magic, but as students of match, it's our job to be wielders of love for anyone and *everyone*, anywhere and *everywhere*. Or, at least, we *should be*."

"Maurelle," Nissa whispered urgently at her side as Suzette's head snapped up and all the Elders gazed speculatively at Maurelle.

Maurelle just squared her shoulders and declared, "I don't make matches. I foster courage. I don't dispense love. I offer hope. I don't hope for contentment. I'm a servant to joy. And you can't have that without risk. I can put them in each other's paths, but they have to take each other's hands. And if a puppy is involved or not, it's *always* a risk. But the higher the risk, the greater the reward, which in turn means the greater the *joy*. If they work, she will be forever grateful that he saw her for the beauty she truly is, and he will be forever grateful that she trusted him with that honor."

"You can't really argue that," Orla said quietly.

Maurelle tossed her head and the loose curls around her face bounced. "No, you can't."

"Careful," Nissa whispered at her side. "I think they're listening to you. Don't push it."

She turned to Nissa. "He's going to make her happy."

"You really can't know that," Nissa replied gently.

"Yes, I can. Because even if *he* actually doesn't, he was the catalyst where *she* let herself *try*. She talked to him. She put herself out there. She gave it a shot. So maybe if it isn't him, and I still think it'll be him, it'll be someone because she'll know next time it's worth it to open yourself up and take a chance at happiness."

"And you can't really argue that," Orla repeated, her voice holding a smile.

"I find you very vexing," Aelfric stated irately.

Maurelle looked to him, thinking she'd made her point, but more, they'd caught it (finally), so she asked in horror, "Why?"

"Because you're right."

"Oh for goodness sake," Suzette muttered.

Aelfric looked to his right at Suzette. "You can't disagree."

"I don't. Maurelle *is* vexing." She blew out a breath before finishing, "Precisely because she's right," She then flung an arm before her. "But now what are we telling the other fairies?"

Aelfric peered out over the Gathering.

"I suppose," he started in a boom, "we're telling them to take a chance on love."

Nissa gave a little clap of her hands.

Suzette rolled her eyes.

Orla smiled.

Meeric nodded his head.

Aelfric continued to look severe, but his eyes were dancing.

Maurelle grinned and let out a fairy burst of twinkle dust for joy.

The End

PS: Maurelle had been right.

He made her happy.

And she returned that favor.

And both of them did the same for their children.

All four of them.

One of whom was named Ginger.

And another was named Billie Joe.

The End???

Rock Chick Renewal

A short story from the Rock Chick Series
featuring Tod, Stevie and their posse

DEDICATION

This short is dedicated to the memory of my beloved Rick Chew.
You are missed.
Extravagantly.
Yahtzee!

MR. AND MR.

"SO WHICH ONE OF YOU is it?" Tod asked as he strolled from the kitchen at the back where he'd entered the house, into Indy and Lee's living room to see the array of Rock Chicks lounging all over their furniture (and there were so many of them, some of the Chicklets were on the floor).

"Sit down, Tod," Indy bossed.

Considering the boss aimed his way, which was *not* acceptable, Tod put a hand on his hip, and for good measure, jutted it *and* his lip before he bossed right back, "You summoned me here so just lay it on me. Are we planning a kidnapping, a rescue, a robbery, a cover-up, a stealth mission, a makeover or other?"

"We're planning a wedding," Ally returned.

Tod's eyebrows shot up, as did his blood pressure.

"Excuse me?" he demanded and then glared at each unmarried Rock Chick in turn (these would be Stella, Sadie and Ally). "Which one of you didn't tell me first?"

"Honey bunch, just cool your jets and sit down." It was Daisy now doing the bossing.

She'd also come up behind him in order to shove him into one of Indy's armchairs, an armchair that Jet hastily exited so he could aim his ass at it.

This he did.

But he did it speaking.

Or, as was his way, *declaring*.

"I think it's been downright *ratified* that I'm the official Rock Chick Wedding Planner. And we've now had *four* nuptials, so not a single one of you is uninformed about the fact that every second of planning is *essential* to providing a matrimonial experience à la Tod that is all it can be." He waved a hand in the air. "Now, I'll allow that I might not be the *first* officially unofficial Rock Chick who's called when one of the Hot Bunch pops the question. And I'll put out there right now, if it's during hanky-panky, as Roxie got her proposal, I don't *want* to be the first to get the call post said hanky-panky. But I damn well better be the *second* one, post-coital notwithstanding," Tod informed the three Chicklets in question (those being Stella, Sadie and Ally).

"Uh . . . you're not the official wedding planner of this one," Jules told him.

Tod's eyes narrowed.

Okay, so the tangerine and chocolate wedding he suggested for Indy and Lee was perhaps a bit avant-garde for this group. You had to have a certain kind of *chutzpah* to pull off such a feat as tangerine and chocolate. And although these women had that in spades, it wasn't the right kind to pull off the sublime experience of the boldest *tangerine* and the richest *chocolate*.

But he hadn't missed a step in the planning and execution of Indy's, Jet's, Roxie's and Ava's weddings (Jules was up the duff when she and Vance got hitched so she went the Justice of the Peace route, to his eternal mortification, he could have *killed* a shotgun wedding—though he'd never tell her that).

"And tell me precisely how I've fallen from grace," Tod demanded.

"I think that's my cue."

This was said in a deep voice that Tod would never admit out loud to anyone, especially the Rock Chicks, *most* especially the Hot Bunch, and *most most* especially his loverman, Stevie (though he suspected Stevie knew, as Tod knew it did the same to Stevie), gave him a thrill down his spine every time he heard it.

Lee was walking down the stairs and it wasn't simply because the bannister was a half wall that hid his hands that Tod didn't notice he was carrying anything in them.

Yes, Tod's crazy, annoying, hilarious and beloved Rock Chicklet Indy had won herself a magnificent prize when she landed *that* man.

However, when his six-foot-two, broad-shouldered, loose-hipped, dark-headed, square-jawed frame rounded the bannister at the bottom of the stairs, Tod saw he was carrying a bottle of champagne in one hand, the stems of two upended flutes in his other.

This was highly unusual and the highly unusual part of it was that he'd need ten times that amount of bubbly and many more flutes for this crowd.

Lee came right to Tod.

"You'll need these where you're goin'," he stated, lifting both hands to indicate what was in them.

"Where am I going?" Tod breathed, staring up into chocolate-brown eyes, because, really, the Hot Bunch wasn't called the Hot Bunch for nothing.

And Liam Nightingale was the leader of the pack.

Lee stepped away and Tod jumped in his seat when he barked, *"Yo!"*

Tod tore his eyes away from Indy's hunk-'a-burnin' love as the front door opened and he saw Ava's hunk-'a-burnin' love, Luke Stark standing there.

Honestly, it was good these girls had caught these men. If they hadn't, such things as a car exploding in front of their house (Tod and Stevie lived in the opposite side of the duplex to Indy and Lee) ruining Stevie's carefully hewn legacy of a fabulous front lawn would be unforgiveable.

But if Tod and his Stevie got to partake of this kind of eye candy on a normal basis, there was a lot that was forgivable.

A *whole lot.*

Luckily they did get to partake on a more than normal basis.

For instance, right now.

Stevie and Tod had had many conversations trying to rate them from hottest to not-as-hottest. These conversations were debated passionately. Hell, just two nights ago they'd settled on Lee, Luke, Hank, Mace, Eddie, Vance, Ren and Hector.

But when Hector's head could suddenly be seen around the jamb of the front door, Tod instantly shot him to the top spot.

"Get up, Tod. It's time to get this show on the road," Lee ordered, and Tod looked back to him (and settled him back on the top spot the instant he did).

"What's happening?" Tod asked.

"Get up, honey," Indy coaxed, her voice soft, and at this unusual tone, Tod twisted his neck to look behind him where she was standing.

Her beautiful face was soft too and her eyes were moist.

Tod's heart started racing.

His Indy girl never cried.

Never.

"What's happening?" he repeated in a whisper.

"Up, sugar," Daisy said, now grabbing his hand and pulling him out of the chair she'd pushed him into.

The Rock Chicks surrounded him, all with varying but similar expressions to Indy's, all with eyes pinned on Tod.

"Will someone—?" he started.

"Just go," Roxie stated, her hands on him, as were others, pushing him toward the front door.

Hector had disappeared. Luke got out of the way. Lee handed him the champagne and flutes before he was shoved into the small foyer and toward the open doorway.

He saw Vance holding open the security door.

As he walked onto the front porch, he saw Hank and Eddie standing together in the yard, Hector approaching them.

He also saw Ren and Mace standing at the wrought-iron gate at the front of the yard that led to the sidewalk.

And then he stopped seeing Hot Bunch boys.

Instead, he saw *the* Hot Bunch boy.

His Stevie.

His Stevie standing, facing Tod, in the back of a horse-drawn carriage that had twinkling fairy lights all around its edges.

It was then Tod needed the Rock Chicks in order to stay upright and moving as they guided him to the carriage.

And his Stevie.

They stopped him at the side and Tod gazed up at his partner, his lover, his best friend, his everything-and-had-been-since-time-began-because-they'd-been-destined-for-each-other-since-the-earth-started-rotating-around-the-sun.

"What's happening?" he whispered to Stevie.

Stevie smiled down at Tod, his beautiful brown eyes sparkling.

Then he answered, "Thought we'd take a carriage ride and drink some champagne after you agree to marry me."

Tod sucked in a breath.

Stevie wasn't finished.

"That'll give us the opportunity to have some time alone together before the Rock Chicks' engagement party which starts in . . ." he looked at his watch then back at Tod, "forty-five minutes."

Tod was stuck back in time.

When Stevie said no more, he forced out, "Married?"

"We made our vows, we had our commitment ceremony," Stevie replied gently. "Now we're just making it official."

"Married," Tod whispered reverently, not tearing his eyes from his man.

"Married," Stevie whispered in return.

Tod kept whispering. "I love you."

He thought he heard a couple of sniffles and a quiet whimper from around him, and he felt someone come close and take the champagne bottle from him, but all he really heard was Stevie replying, "I love you too, baby. Now get in the carriage so we can get liquored up in preparation for a Rock Chick party."

Stevie held his hand out to Tod.

Without hesitation, like always, like it would be forever, Tod took it.

Stevie helped his Tod into the carriage.

By the time he sat next to Stevie, the Rock Chicks and Hot Bunch were surrounding the carriage on three sides.

Stevie took the champagne from Indy and started unwrapping the foil from the cork.

Tod leaned into his lover and said under his breath, "I can't believe you told the Rock Chicks and Hot Bunch you were proposing to me *before you proposed to me.*"

Stevie looked his fiancé in the eye. "Don't pretend you didn't want it this exact way."

Tod harrumphed, mostly because Stevie was right, but Tod's lips were never going to form those words (ever, about anything).

Stevie looked to the driver and called, "We can go now."

The driver clicked his teeth. The carriage jolted. Tod held on to Stevie. Stevie popped the cork. And suddenly all around them bits of orange and brown paper started floating.

Tangerine and chocolate confetti.

Tod turned to skewer Indy with his gaze.

But he didn't mean it and she knew it, which was probably why she was smiling so damn big.

Silly, sweet, crazy, loving bimbo.

"You don't throw confetti at an *engagement*," he educated her haughtily.

"Every time you walk into a room from now until the day you get married, we're throwing confetti at you," she returned, pulling more out of her jeans pocket and tossing it as she and the others started trailing the carriage when the horses began to move. "Get used to it."

"Fire and ice for wedding colors!" Sadie cried.

"Violet, fuchsia and charcoal!" Ava yelled, throwing more confetti that drifted around Tod and Stevie.

The Hot Bunch were hanging back, standing in the street wearing various smiles from full-on, glamorous white (Eddie and Hector), to half-smirk (Luke), to twitches (Hank and Lee), to shit-eating (Vance), to head shaking (Mace), to reining-in-laughter (Ren).

But the women were following them on the trot, throwing the dregs of confetti they had left and shouting out colors.

"Peacock!" Stella called.

"Salmon and baby pink!" Jet shouted.

"Straw and plum," Jules yelled.

"Coral and sangria!" Indy bellowed as the horses started to trot and the carriage pulled away from the trailing women.

"*Sparkle!*" Daisy shrieked, falling well behind the others seeing as she was trying to keep up in clear plastic platform go-aheads that Tod couldn't tell from his distance, but it looked like they had butterflies embedded in the soles. "Don't matter what colors, just as long as there's *lotsa sparkle*!"

Ally just stopped in the middle of the street, threw up both her hands in devil's horns and bellowed, *"Righteous!"*

Suddenly, alighting from an El Camino that had parked on the street, a huge man with a wild russet beard and a wilder head of graying blond hair, roared, *"Jesus Jones! What'd I miss?"*

The Rock Chicks faded back.

The carriage moved forward.

And Stevie took a flute from Tod.

He filled Tod's first.

Then he filled his own.

Tod gave him a look and inquired, "Did you buy me bling?"

Stevie caught his eyes. "Am I marrying the only man I've ever loved, that man being the same one I've lived with for decades?"

"Yes."

"Then yes."

Tod smiled.

Stevie smiled back.

Then he leaned in and kissed his fiancé, hard and wet, but sweet.

When Stevie pulled an inch away, he whispered, "It's just a renewal. You've been my husband for a long time, honey."

Tod lifted his hand to Stevie's cheek and whispered back, "Same."

Stevie raised his glass. "Toast. To Mr. and Mr."

Tod raised his own glass. "To Mr. and Mr. Forever and for always."

They clinked.

They sipped.

They sat back.

And after Stevie set the champagne bottle into the silver ice bucket affixed to the side of the carriage, he pulled the bling out of his trouser pocket and slid the platinum engagement band set with diamonds on Tod's left ring finger where it nestled with the marvelous-in-its-simplicity platinum band he'd given Tod at their commitment ceremony.

They then held hands, drank champagne, and trotted through the dusk shrouding Baker Historical District in Denver.

TEN MONTHS LATER, AFTER THE Rock Chicks did indeed shower

Tod with varying shades of confetti nearly every time they saw him, in a ceremony that was pure class (with the colors of a peacock feather, because seriously, how fabulous was *that*?), Tod and Stevie were married.

The End

Connect with Kristen Online:

Official Website: *www.kristeashley.net*

Kristen's Facebook Page: *www.facebook.com/kristenashleybooks*

Follow Kristen on Twitter: @KristenAshley68

Discover Kristen's Pins on Pinterest: *www.pinterest.com/kashley0155*

Follow Kristen on Instagram: KristenAshleyBooks

Need support for your Kit Crack Addiction?

Join the *Kristen Ashley Addict's Support Group on Goodreads*

CPSIA information can be obtained
at www.ICGtesting.com
Printed in the USA
FSHW012231171218
54537FS